Pandora's Razor

Hope's War–Book 2

By Ray Strong

if
Impulse Fiction

Pandora's Razor
Hope's War–Book 2

Ray Strong

Copyright © 2021 Benjamin R. Strong Jr.
All rights reserved
Published by Impulse Fiction, Pleasanton, CA

Cover Design: Ricardo Castro

ISBN 978-0-9863599-6-5

Library of Congress Control Number: 2021948093
LCCN Imprint Name: Impulse Fiction, Pleasanton, CA

Pandora's Razor

Dedicated to:
Marina, Yuri, Veronica, and Elizabeth

My brightest stars are you.

Pandora's Razor

Contents

Chapter 1 Haven, Jira-1 System, ET 2188 1
Chapter 2 Free space 44
Chapter 3 Haven, Jira-1 System 48
Chapter 4 Mars-6, Sol System 51
Chapter 5 Etna Station, Etna 320 System 56
Chapter 6 Calliope, Tau Ceti System 58
Chapter 7 Enterprise Station, Procyon A System 72
Chapter 8 Jira-1 System 94
Chapter 9 Echoes, ET 2177................................... 121
Chapter 10 Jira-1 System, ET 2188 128
Chapter 11 Mars 6, Sol System 161
Chapter 12 LeHavre Station, Jira-1 System 163
Chapter 13 Free Space... 165
Chapter 14 Enterprise Station, Procyon A System .. 172
Chapter 15 Mars-6, Sol System 217
Chapter 16 Calliope, Tau Ceti System 220
Chapter 17 Enterprise Station, Procyon A System .. 225
Chapter 18 Enterprise Station, Procyon A System .. 261
Chapter 19 Free Space... 315
Chapter 20 Etna Station, Etna 320 System 323
Chapter 21 Echoes ET 2142................................... 390
Chapter 22 Etna 320 System, ET 2188................... 400
Chapter 23 Asteroid NEM-Sx, Etna 320 System 437
Chapter 24 Free Space.. 448
Chapter 25 Jira-1 System 452
Appendix: 456

Chapter 1
Haven, Jira-1 System, ET 2188

When our gods go to war, it is we mortals who suffer.

From *the Diary of Neuchar de Merlner,* Europa, ET 2112

Johnston Rift

The grey cloud stretched to both horizons, racing Meriel Hope's caravan to the refugee camp. Behind them, the cloud dwarfed the thousand-foot-tall dome of Stewardville and flashed with arcs of static lightning.

A lurch of the armored personnel carrier woke Meriel with a bang of her head on the barred window, and she slapped her thigh for the sidearm that wasn't there.

"You're jumpy," her sister Elizabeth said from the driver's seat.

"He's coming back, Liz. I can feel it," Meriel said. With a tight grip on the grab handle, the wiry twenty-two-year-old gazed to the right and the Johnston Rift. There, just months before, they had repelled the invasion of BioLuna's mercenaries and General Khanag's corsairs.

"Not today." With a thumb, Elizabeth pointed behind them. "And not through that."

Meriel glanced back as the dust cloud approached the evaporation towers that helped to humidify the arid desert. "The evaporators will trip off soon."

Elizabeth nodded and tapped the dashboard console. Above it on the windshield, a distorted image appeared of the weather officer from the orbiting space station, LeHavre.

"Can you see through this crap, Rick?"

"It started on the other side of the moon, Ms. Hope," the station reported. "And you won't outrun it. You have ten minutes from your current position to find shelter or—"

Above them, lightning arced, and the image quivered.

"Will we beat it?" Meriel asked.

"Sure," Elizabeth said, turned off the road, and lofted the APC over the berm. The hard landing slammed them against their restraints but did not slow them or the caravan that followed.

At the edge of the camp, Elizabeth slowed at a dense crowd and honked.

"Move it or nobody eats!" she shouted through the window.

The mob grumbled and slapped the doors, but made way as the APC crawled forward into the barnyard. There, volunteers distributed ration packets and water from the back of a wagon. On the wagon bed, a tall man with a farmer's build and a t-shirt tan led them: Meriel's partner, John Smith.

Elizabeth stopped at the barn, where volunteers scrambled from the caravan and hurried inside with sacks and boxes. When the claxons honked a warning of the coming storm, Meriel gave them the "hurry" arm signal.

On the way to the wagon, dust devils collided and vanished in tiny clouds, and through them ambled a boy of four years with a rope dangling from his belt. Before he wandered into the crowd of angry men, Meriel kneeled in front of him.

"And who do you belong to?"

He pointed to an elderly refugee who reached up to accept rations from John. With a smile, the boy handed his rope to her, and she led him to the old man.

"Find shelter," she said, and pointed up to the wall of dust rushing toward them. "You only have a minute."

He hugged her and offered her a ration packet, but she shook her head and gave the child a rare piece of hard candy. As they walked away, John called from the bed of the wagon.

"You're late," he said, and pulled on the mask and goggles that hung from his neck.

She put her hand on his. "Where are Sandy and Becky?"

"Inside the barn with—"

The claxons interrupted with the "Find Shelter" tone, and Meriel turned as the mile-high cloud swallowed the Stewardville dome and the huge evaporation towers. But at the edges of the yard, the crowd of men still lingered.

"So, why are they hanging about?" Meriel asked.

More men joined the crowd, angrier men less cowed by hunger. In their hands, they held scraps of bucky-sheet and plastaglass that could cut steel.

Meriel waved to her sister at the door of the barn and engaged her link with a tap on her visor. "Tell the farmers to keep the kids inside and close the dust seals. Then bring the APC around front."

While Elizabeth rallied the volunteers, the crowd closed in, and a thick man elbowed his way to the front.

"Stop right there," Meriel said.

With one hand, he mopped the muddy sweat from his neck and with the other pointed to the barn. "That food is ours."

"Not yet," John said and stood at Meriel's side. "It still belongs to the neighboring farmers. We're protecting it."

"It's meant for us, and we can protect it ourselves. Isn't that right?" The mob behind him grumbled assent and flashed their weapons.

"It's meant for everyone," she said. "And we aim to get it to them, not just you." Without moving her head, she glanced at the approaching storm and pulled on her goggles.

The big man sneered. "Open your stores, and we'll let the kids go."

"What happens to the kids isn't up to you."

"Yes, it is," he said, and those behind him rushed forward.

Meriel ducked the first attacker's fist and pacified him with a quick punch to the crotch. At the same time, another attacked with a sharpened pole, but John grabbed it and used his momentum to run the thug into the barn wall.

From around the corner lumbered the APC with Elizabeth at the wheel. Stopping at the edge of the barn, she jumped from the driver's seat and grabbed the triggers of the sonic cannon. The front row of attackers fell with a mild pulse, but rioters stepped over their fallen comrades and climbed aboard. She fought them off with a stunner and a boot and swung the weapon toward the crowd.

Before Elizabeth could fire again, the tempest slammed into them with stinging grit and dust that damped the canon's aural field. With the weapon weakened, the rioters swarmed over the APC, and Elizabeth scrambled to the barn.

Near the wagon, the big man charged Meriel with a makeshift blade, but a gust of grit forced him to close his eyes. She dodged his arm, but the edge of the weapon slashed her thigh. Before he could turn to attack again, she kicked him in the kidney and sent him sprawling headfirst into the wagon wheel.

Meriel retreated to the barn defended by pitchforks and baling hooks. Before she reached it, a dirt-gray truck roared into the yard and helmeted soldiers with dust gear jumped from the vehicle to surround the yard.

"This is the Haven Marines," blared a loudspeaker. "Disperse or face arrest!"

A fit man with captain's bars, Jake Abrams, climbed from the cab and signaled the Marines to round up the stragglers. While his men loaded the rioters into vans, Abrams turned to John, pointed to the barn, and tapped his ear.

John nodded and took Meriel's arm to shelter in the barn, but Elizabeth flagged Meriel over to a body.

When Meriel reached her sister, she put a finger to her eye to mirror the red mark growing at the edge of Elizabeth's goggles. "You OK?"

"Will be," Elizabeth shouted over the roar of the storm. "Look." With her boot, she brushed the dust from the arm and raised his sleeve to expose the tail of a tattoo at his forearm: a snake coiled around a blade.

Meriel jumped back as if it was alive and pulled Elizabeth close.

"I'll meet you inside," she said and waved toward the barn.

With the dust obscuring everything under a gray haze, Meriel searched outside the barn, focusing on the footings that supported the walls and the structural joints. Finding nothing, she returned to the barn door. But next to the door, taped to the shutters of the window, was a small cylinder.

With a tap on her visor, she sent a vid to Abrams. "Captain, can you identify this?" His voice disappeared in the storm's roar, but not his panicked expression.

She ran inside the barn and gave John the "Imminent Danger" signal of crossed arms.

"Everyone to the cellar!" he shouted and opened the cellar doors. "Storm's getting worse."

Together, they hustled the farmers' kids down the stairs while the adults, including refugees who sought safety from the riot, followed with the supplies.

At the top of the stairs stood John's older daughter Sandy, fidgeting with the plaid patch covering her left eye. Her younger sister, Becky, with unkempt hair the color of the lamb in her arms, stopped and pulled at her sleeve. But Sandy did not move as others bumped her on the way past.

Meriel removed her goggles and joined them. "Becky, hon. Get your papa. We'll be a second," she said and took Sandy's hand. "Hon, we need to get to the cellar right away."

"Not again," Sandy said, with deep furrows in her brow.

"Don't worry, hon, it's not the—"

"I'll take her," John said, picked her up, and carried her down the steps.

As the last of the stragglers filed past Meriel, a flash blinded her, and a blast knocked her off her feet. She gulped to stop the ringing, and when her ears cleared, the wind screeched through a rip in the barn wall.

On her knees, she scanned the barn. Dust swirled inside as the plastisteel wall fluttered in the wind, tearing its way to the corner of the roof. Behind a string of hay bales stood the boy with the rope, staring wide-eyed at the old man at his feet. He lay still, bleeding from a fresh wound above his ear, his shirt opened to expose an abdominal scar. She checked the pulse at his neck: dead.

The ragged groans of shearing plastisteel brought her attention to the roof where a corner separated from the column. She turned to the boy who held out his rope to her again. But she picked him up instead and ran for the cellar.

As the last corner anchor tore, the roof lifted free. The storm took the walls next and tossed hay bales that knocked Meriel against the cellar door, unconscious.

Pack Out

Meriel opened her eyes and blinked to find Becky and Sandy holding her hands and John kneeling next to her on the cellar's dirt floor. Above them, the storm roared, and dust seeped through the door seals.

"Welcome back," John said, frowning at the cut on her thigh. "That'll need stitches."

Meriel nodded and sat up, wincing at the headache.

"That wasn't the storm," Sandy said and hugged her.

"No, it wasn't. Where's the boy?"

John pointed to the corner of the cellar where the boy sat with a neighboring farmer. "What about the old man?"

She shook her head and rose.

"Hey, we need to treat that," John said to her back.

She limped to the corner, where the farmer wiped the boy's nose. "Is he OK?" Meriel asked.

"Bloody nose is all."

"What's your name, hon?" Meriel asked, and the boy replied with gibberish that ended with "Misha."

"That's Cetian," a man said and joined them. "From a mining colony in the Tau Ceti system. Says his name is Misha."

"Ask him if he has any other relatives here."

After an exchange, the boy shook his head.

"Can you stay with him?" Meriel asked.

"I've got my folks to take care of."

"Just for now?"

The Cetian nodded, and Meriel turned to leave. But the boy held up his rope, and she kneeled to hug him.

Becky joined them with the lamb in her arms and a six-legged armored beaver, her indigenous pet *lermel*, Dumpy, skittering around her feet.

"You think he'd like to pet the lamb?" Becky said.

"That would be nice, sweetie, and thank you. Can you keep him company?"

"Sure," Becky said, and sat next to the boy.

After a kiss on their foreheads, Meriel returned to sit by John, and Sandy wiggled in between them. Across from them, Elizabeth sat with a flechette pistol in her lap and her eyes on the storm door.

"Anyone else hurt?" Meriel said and accepted a canteen from her sister. John shook his head and took a can of suture seal from the med kit.

From her slashed pants pocket, Meriel removed the slim volume of de Merlner's *Meditations*. The blade had cut deep into the cover, and blood stained the edges, but the book had protected her. She put the book on the bale and lowered the waist of her pants to expose the bleeding wound, an inch from the femoral artery.

Sandy cringed. "Ouch."

"I'll be fine," Meriel said, took a drink to rinse the grit from her teeth and spat blood on the dirt floor.

John kneeled to spray the antiseptic bandage on the cut, and she brushed a lock of hair from his forehead, grayed with dust that covered everything on Haven. With a smile, he took her hand.

The lights flickered, and she scanned the faces in the cellar, sweating and frowning, hovering near the dirt walls. "Everyone is afraid."

He nodded. "I talked to the farmers before. They won't feed the refugees if they're threatened with harm and another riot. And they won't be bringing their families to help again."

"Did they save the supplies?"

"Most everything."

"Then get them busy, John. If they aren't coming back, let's pack out extra ration kits before they leave."

He kissed her and stood. "Assembly lines!" he called, and a score of farm kids and a dozen parents hurried to set up tables.

"Go help your papa," Meriel said. After a hug, Sandy left to help John, and Meriel pointed to the pistol in Elizabeth's lap.

"That's new."

Elizabeth held the weapon up and offered it to Meriel to admire. "It's a gift from Abrams."

"This can make a mess."

Elizabeth grinned and returned the pistol to her lap. "It surely can," she said and pointed to Meriel's wound. "Another inch and that thug could have killed you," she said, and patted the pistol. "Next time wear a sidearm."

"Kids could get caught in the crossfire, Liz."

"That won't stop the bad guys. So, outside when you saw the tattoo, why'd you jump?"

"It looked familiar. We need to find out where it's from."

"It's just a tat, M," Elizabeth said and pulled up a search on her link. "You can't be sure it's them."

"I think Khanag will sneak fighters in with the refugees if he can."

"You're paranoid."

"Maybe I'm not paranoid enough. Khanag is the Archtrope's executioner. If the Archtrope and his fanatics get a foothold here, we have no place to run to. There won't be a safe place for us in the entire sector."

Elizabeth's bracelet flashed. "It's Abrams," she said, and tapped it.

"Parts of the barn tore through the camp," Abrams said over the link. "We have two dead up here. Anyone hurt there?"

"One casualty from the bomb. Others are minor injuries. We made it to the storm cellar. Did you learn who planted the explosive?"

"Negative. We're questioning the rioters now."

"Found the leader?"

"Not yet. I'll stop by after the storm. Out."

"They're coming," Meriel said and left her sister to guard the door.

At pack-out tables, the farmers arranged boxes of raw food to subdivide into meal rations. And there Meriel took her place in the assembly line next to Sandy.

Reaching for a filled packet to weigh, her visor flashed, and she blinked to engage her link.

"Penny's up on LeHavre and says to call after you see this," Elizabeth said, referring to Penny Hubbard, another of the orphans from their home starship, Light Speed Merchant *Princess*.

A GRL flashed across Meriel's visor. She blinked twice, and a holovid focused on the entrance to a Carbon-14 mine.

```
"IGB news exclusive ET/2187:231:18
"This is Aaron Kreft of IGB News em-
bedded with Station Troopers. Today,
Troopers raided a mining colony on La-
lande-C6 after grand jury testimony
identified it as one of four sites us-
ing slave labor. Reports that the UN-
SEC named BioLuna Corporation as a si-
lent investor rocked the stock market
and drove the industrials index to its
lowest point in a year . . ."
```

In front of uniformed Troopers, a line of men kneeled in ankle and wrist restraints. Behind them, one by one, shackled men with hollow eyes filed out of the mine, gray men frail as sticks whose filthy overalls draped their bones like silk on coffins. Boys in their own chain gang followed as if life had already left them. And behind them came girls with painted faces and gaudy clothing. When asked by the reporter, they raised their shirts to expose abdominal scars, and Meriel's hand went to the scar crossing her own body.

Behind those in line appeared the ghosts of her mother and father and the two score adults who died aboard the *Princess*.

```
   "No colonies have offered to accept
them, so the fate of these poor vic-
tims remains unclear. The Biadez Foun-
dation has offered interim aid,
but . . ."
```

The rumble from the storm outside morphed into the hiss of ventilators in the mines. Her breath quickened in the stale air and sweat beaded at her temples as if she stood beside them at the mine entrance. With a blink, her family vanished from the image, and with another blink, the vid ended. But she could not erase their hollow eyes.

A hand gripped Meriel's. The line of ration packets had backed up, and the children stared.

"Merry, are you all right?" Sandy said.

Meriel took a deep breath and nodded. "Hon, I need to call Aunt Penny. Can you take my place?"

"Sure," Sandy said, and smiled at her promotion.

Meriel returned to the hay bale near Elizabeth and tapped her visor. Penny's face appeared.

"Hey, Penny. Liz said you have something on the tattoo."

"Did you see the vid?" Penny replied after the time delay.

"It's horrible, but other than giving us another reason to hate BioLuna, why show me?"

"You saw the abdominal scars?"

"Yes. An old man who died here had a similar scar."

"I don't think their organ donations were voluntary."

"Penny, we just had a riot and bombing here, and I need to know who's behind it. Liz said you found something on the snake and blade tattoo."

"Oh, yeah. You don't remember?"

"Remember what?"

"A corsair who committed suicide after the *Tiger* hijack had the same tattoo."

Meriel sat hard. *An Archer goon here?*

"M?"

"The *Tiger* firefight is blurry now. Are you sure?"

"Yes. The bodies are here in the med school morgue."

"So, just one corsair has the tattoo. Then it doesn't directly connect the corsairs to the Archers and Khanag."

"You have the photo of the Archtrope and Khanag with the corsair captain who died on the *Tiger*."

"It's not enough, Penny. They can spin it as coincidence. We need something that will embarrass him and take his focus away from Haven. Something that shows he's not who he says he is."

"Well, the Archtrope may be connected to the organ thefts. I'm building a dossier with the organ consent discrepancies."

"That'd be a big help, hon. Send me a GRL, and I'll take a look."

When Penny signed off, Meriel paced and glanced at the farmers and their families in the cellar.

Archers. Haveners don't know what's coming. Will they be ready? She waved to her sister.

"What is it?" Elizabeth asked.

"Penny told me the tattoo you found on the rioter is the same as on one of Khanag's corsairs. That means Archers are already here."

"Maybe he's just some loser who washed out of thug school," Elizabeth said and sat next to her. "Or he didn't bow and kiss the Archtrope's ass often enough." Between her fingers, she twirled a flechette from the pistol at her side. "So, what's bugging you?"

"Liz, they're coming for us again. They're smart and will kill us . . ." She stopped as pain gripped her gut, as it did any time the idea of life without her sister and the *Princess* orphans crossed her mind. She sighed as the ache subsided. "It's not just us anymore. Sandy and Becky are already targets. And so are our neighbors and Stewardville and LeHavre Station. The Archtrope and BioLuna will put us all in chains."

"How can we stop them?" Elizabeth said.

"We don't need to stop them," Meriel said over the rumble of the storm. "We only need to keep them busy somewhere else, somewhere a long way from here."

"If they find out you're trying, M, they'll come for you again."

As she walked back to the pack-out line, Meriel turned back to her sister. "They're coming anyway, Liz, and I can't just sit here and wait for them."

Ebeneuer Wasteland

The overcrowded hold of the tramp shuttle reeked of fear and sweat from the scores of men, women, and children huddled together. On the gallery above them, twelve rough men stood watch, their bandoliers bristling with blasters and pulse rifles. With each gust from the storm outside, the floor lurched, and a new waft of vomit swirled.

In one corner, Lars Yuan sat with his family, still disoriented from the hyperspace jumps. But his stained and wrinkled suit had endured the trip in better shape than his family had.

He smiled. "Almost there, kids. This is what we dreamed of."

His wife, Marta, bit her lip, and his two children frowned.

This wasn't their dream. Not at all. But Haven would be a fresh start and keep them off a low-g asteroid. The colony meant opportunity, and a refuge from Marta's petty embezzlement charge that had revoked their citizenship on Dexter Station.

It took all their savings, a life insurance withdrawal, and loans from friends, but they made the cash fare. And the inter-station credits Lars had hidden in his bags would help them get a fresh start.

"What's the temperature like, Mom?" asked Julia, a frail teen they hoped would thrive in the Haven air.

"Tropical."

The ship lurched again as the storm howled through the hull.

"Doesn't sound like it," his eldest son, Yuri, said as he shook his link in his chunky hand. "I'm outta juice, Pop. And there's no compute resources to sync with."

"When we land, son. They're sure to have a visitor center."

"I read Haven doesn't have an industrial infrastructure yet, or—"

The shaking ended with a bang, and the guards hustled to the passenger deck and stood by a wall with batons drawn. The wall lowered into a ramp, and the dust roared in, replacing the foul air with fresh but obscuring everything in a gray haze.

"Welcome to Hell," Corporal Greiber said over the whir of gears. "Last stop!"

A dozen of the guards took packs and weapons and filed out into the storm, but the refugees did not leave.

"There's a storm outside," Lars said. "Where's the dome? What's—"

Greiber's scowl wrinkled the scar on his chin. "That's Nature. Get used to it," he said as he threw bags out the door. "Out! And take your crap with you."

Hydraulics pushed bales of supplies onto the cracked dirt while the remaining guards herded the passengers off with cattle prods. Some passengers with masks grabbed their belongings and disappeared into the storm. But most clustered together near the ship in the choking dust and cowered at the chirps and growls of alien beasts that sounded much more dangerous than the briefings suggested.

"Which way to the welcome center?" Marta said. When no one replied, she led the children through the swirls of gray, searching for the bale with their name on it. After rifling through it and finding no goggles or masks, she wrapped the tent around her children.

As the tent snapped in the wind, Sven dug through the bale.

"Two days' water. Three days of dehydrated soy paste," he said and ran back to the ramp.

"Hey, there's no extra water to make the food," Sven shouted above the roar of the storm.

"Back off!" Greiber said and warned him away with the spark of a cattle prod.

"Our water will only last a day. And there's no compass or link. This isn't what we paid for!"

Greiber tossed him a link and pushed a button on the bulkhead. "Call customer service."

Sven caught the link as the ramp began to close. "Hey! What about our personal bags?" he asked, worried about the credits he had hidden there.

"Opps," Greiber said through the last sliver of opening before the ramp clanged shut.

The link was dead. And when Sven flipped it over, the device fell to pieces in his hand and blew away in the wind.

The ship disappeared into the storm, and Sven rejoined his family, holding them close in the suffocating dust as the growls circled closer.

Johnston Rift

After the storm subsided, Meriel and Elizabeth viewed the rubble of the barn from the cellar stairs under a tarp, shielding them from the muddy rain. Outside in the battered camp, Marines stood in rain gear, guarding the medics who removed the dead and treated the injured.

When the rain fell clear, the youngest of the refugee children ran past to play in the puddles for the first time in their lives. Nearby, Sandy and Becky sat with Misha, learning his dialect, while Misha petted the lamb.

"How's Tommy?" Meriel asked to distract herself from the boy. Tommy Spurell was another orphan from the *Princess* and Abrams' competition for Elizabeth's attention.

Elizabeth shrugged. "OK, I guess. I don't see him much with the militia deployments. He's trying to arrange an interview with IGB for us." She sighed. "M, I need a favor.

"So, ask."

"The *Thompson* hasn't committed to the routes through LeHavre, and I'm stuck here dirtside."

Mariel raised an eyebrow. "You sure you want to go back with them?"

"No, but they hold my contract. I'm getting antsy here on the dirt. Will you ask Molly if there's an empty berth on the *Tiger*?"

"Sure. And I'll check if the route includes Etna. Did they ever file charges?"

Elizabeth glanced at the sky. "Not that I've heard. And they're not coming way out here."

Meriel gazed at the horizon and bit her lip.

Elizabeth took her hand. "You still thinking about the riot?"

Meriel nodded.

"It's just one guy with a tat, M."

"Maybe. But maybe there are more." *Lots more.*

A jeep sloshed through the mud and from it jumped Captain Abrams. Without a hello, he joined them under the tarp and tapped his helmet.

"Abrams recording. Lieutenant John Smith here with Elizabeth and Meriel Hope. What set off the riot?"

"Not hunger," John said. "It looked planned, aiming to control the food."

"And that means control of the camp."

"The riot gave someone the opportunity to plant the bomb."

Abrams nodded. "If they can't control it, they'll take it from everyone."

Meriel raised her hand. "The bomb wouldn't have taken the roof off without the storm."

"Meaning they knew the storm was coming?" he said with a raised eyebrow, and she nodded. "I wouldn't go implying there's a traitor on LeHavre. But I'll mention that in my report."

"The food here won't last without the farmers supplying more," John said. "And they won't deliver to angry thugs."

"Any evidence they're speaking for the rest of the refugees? Do they have the camp behind them?"

"Not that we've seen," John said. "The others are frightened."

Abrams nodded to the Marines. "My men will stand watch until we can get something permanent."

"We can ask the refugees to help."

"Civilian engagement will produce theft and a black market."

"That's cynical."

"Perhaps, John. But I've seen food shortages before on 61-Cygni-4. Desperate and frightened people are capable of lots of mayhem. I'll inform Stewardville. That's it?"

Meriel raised her hand again. "Sir, the refugee casualty here left an unaccompanied minor. Where can we take him?"

Abrams shook his head. "This is all new, Meriel, and nothing's set up for them."

"Any camp leaders?"

"Seems you fought them today," he said as he walked back through the rain. "I'll escalate to Colonel Lee."

Abrams's jeep splashed away, and Meriel turned to John.

He smiled. "Sure. Let's take Misha home with us."

"I know Khanag's behind this," Meriel said as they sat again.

"It doesn't have to be Khanag," her sister said.

"Yeah? How many other ruthless bastards do you know who target children?"

Elizabeth narrowed her eyes. "The UNE uses atrocities as an excuse to step in."

"Abrams said 'desperate and frightened people are capable of lots of mayhem.' So, who is so desperate to bring the UNE here?"

As Jira-1 neared the horizon, Sandy and Becky dried off the younger kids, and John and Meriel hitched the horses to the wagon for the ride home.

"XO says you signed up for the next tour," he said.

Meriel blushed and nodded. "I've got to pay for the repairs on the *Princess*. It's mine now, or will be, and she needs lots of work."

"Didn't the Pacific League offer to help?"

"The bigger the loan, the bigger their piece. I want this to stay our ship."

"It's just a ship, M."

"It's more than that," she said and turned away, unable to explain how wrong he was in a way he'd understand.

But John wouldn't let it go. "Why can't—"

Elizabeth returned with a wrench in her pocket and grease-stained hands. "Hey, kids. I'm gonna need another favor."

"How can we help?"

"I busted the ATV on the way here and can't fix it. I need a tow to the Bantu Marine Base."

"Sure, it's on our way," he said, and coupled the APV's tow bar to the wagon.

During the first hour along the dirt road to Bantu, Elizabeth entertained Sandy and Becky with tales of space adventures, while Misha fed handfuls of native scrub to Dumpy. When the children drifted off to sleep, Meriel rolled Becky over to Elizabeth's lap and climbed up to the driver's seat next to John. After being silent the whole trip, he opened up.

"What you worked so hard for is right here, M."

"It's what I hoped for, John. The orphans safe and together, with a future far away from the mining colonies." She took his arm and leaned her head on his shoulder. "Haven was a bonus. And I never dreamed of you and your girls."

"But you want to leave it and go back to space."

"Just for a while. Space was always part of my dream." She squeezed his hand. "The orphans and I are spacers, John, and the *Princess* is our home."

"You have a home here."

Maybe just a home base, not home, her mother had said. "You gave me a moon, John. But I want the stars, too. And after I fix the *Princess*, I'll have it all."

"But we'll be here."

Meriel's stomach ached. "I . . . I thought you'd be joining us, you and the girls. At least for a few circuits."

"It's safer here."

"We've been over this, John. We're fixed targets here, and—"

"And so is the route of a merchant spaceship."

"But we can move our route, we can't move the farm or Haven."

"We're safer at the farm, M."

"You mean the farm we rebuilt after Khanag blew it up, right? They'd be safer on LeHavre."

"Their home is here, M. And so is yours. Just like your mother wanted."

"I'm not my mother, John," she said and gazed at the stars. "Sandy thinks my journey through space is my songline, and my songline is my home. I promised her I'd make part of it here with you."

She leaned on his shoulder again, but John tightened his jaw and returned to silence.

A single light rose over the horizon to identify the guard shack at Bantu Boot Camp. Behind the shack, a wide ramp sloped down and blended into the soft shadows from Thor's crescent. John stopped at the shack, and Elizabeth set the girls to rest and left the wagon to hail the sentry.

John tapped his link. "M, if you're leaving again, you need to know what you're facing out there."

A holo appeared with a priest of the Holy Vision, one of the Archtrope of Calliope's fanatic sects, and a reporter's voiceover.

> "Lance Freiden here for GNN with breaking news. Meriel Hope, the troubled survivor of the *Princess* disaster, has released a new vid admitting the so-called Treaty of Haven was a hoax.
>
> "Her wild charges stained the reputations of the most influential leaders, corporations, and NGOs in the galaxy, charges that illustrate the growing animosity between merchant spacers and Earth, humanity's home.
>
> "Here's Ms. Hope just a few minutes ago."

"Jeez, more propaganda—" she said but then stopped and stared when the camera panned to her kneeling before the priest.

> "I'm sorry for the upset I caused everyone. The Treaty of Haven document was actually a prop for my virtual theater group. I meant it only as a hypothetical of what might happen. I have no animosity toward the Archtrope and his followers, who I admire for their charity work. BioLuna and President Biadez . . ."

"Crap." She tapped the link to pause the vid, turned away, and closed her eyes. John took her hand.

"That's the avatar of you Khanag created?" Elizabeth asked as she rejoined them.

Meriel nodded. "How will anyone know that's not me?"

"There's more," John said and tapped his link again to show the priest absolving Meriel with a hand on her bowed head.

```
"Ms. Hope's childhood, fraught with
abandonment—"
```

Elizabeth threw the flechette against the side of the wagon, where it stuck with a *thunk*. "'Abandonment?' Hell. They murdered our folks." From a hip pocket she retrieved a flask, took a swig, and handed it to her sister.

```
" . . . and drug abuse after the
Princess affair, can only be described
as difficult."
```

Meriel took a long pull from the flask. "Those records are sealed."

"They're ignoring the part where Khanag killed everyone," Elizabeth said.

"Which left me as the only suspect."

"Who believes a twelve-year-old could be that homicidal?" John asked.

Meriel took another sip from the flask and leaned against the seat. "People will believe anything if it's repeated enough. BioLuna and the Archtrope have deep enough pockets to replay that for centuries."

Elizabeth narrowed her eyes. "So why release this now? The Archtrope and Biadez have been quiet since we kicked their ass in the last invasion."

"I thought they backed off," John said.

Meriel shook her head. "It means our story is getting traction and they need to squash it. Our evidence from the

Tiger attack and the Treaty of Haven exposed their corruption." Dark shadows lined her forehead in the light from the guard shack. "If they can bury our story or discredit it, the public pressure comes off, and they'll invade again."

"You need to speak out, M," Elizabeth said. "You need to respond to this."

"All of us do—"

"Specifically, you. You're our public face."

Meriel nodded. "I can't face spacers thinking I'm an Archer sympathizer." She drummed her fingers on the flask. "Something smells. I think they're planning something."

Floodlights glared at the bottom of the ramp as Bantu's massive blast doors opened, and a guard waved from inside.

"John, help me with the APC," Elizabeth said.

He followed her around the back, and Elizabeth set the vehicle's brakes. After they chocked the wheels, he turned to her and shook his head.

"Damn, Liz. She has a home here," he said and unhitched the safety cables.

Elizabeth leaned against the fender. "The happiest times of her life are on the *Princess* with our folks and the kids. She wants to share that with you."

"I know. It was her dream to get you and the orphans back together. But she found a life for you here on Haven."

"It's more than that, John. The last time she felt this safe was right before Khanag killed our folks and split us kids apart. She doesn't trust it. Everyone she loves is here now, but Haven is still vulnerable. She has nightmares about having it torn away again, of you and the girls and us orphans dead or gone."

He lifted the tow hitch from the wagon, leaned on the tailgate, and crossed his arms. "She wants to go. What the hell do I do?"

From the open doors rolled a truck to tow the APC into the compound, and on John's signal, Meriel pulled the wagon away.

"She loves you, John," Elizabeth said and waved to the tow truck. "If you want her in your life, let her go. She'll come back."

Elizabeth guided the tow truck into place and the guard coupled the APC to it. When it lurched into motion, she returned to the wagon and handed the flask to Meriel.

"Keep it," Elizabeth said. "Oh, and Tommy got the interview with IGB. Eleven hundred day after tomorrow. IGB studios on LeHavre."

"Are you coming back to the farm with us?" Meriel said.

"Nah. I think I'll stay and help Abrams fix the APC."

"Later tonight?"

"Maybe tomorrow," Elizabeth said with a wink and followed the APC into Bantu.

"I feel it," Meriel said as John climbed onto the seat beside her and took the reins. "Biadez, the Archtrope and their friends." She took another swig from the flask. "They're planning something."

"Certainly," he said and pulled away toward the farm. "But not tonight."

His confidence did nothing to tranquilize her, and when a trail of light caught her eye, she glanced up to check it was just a shooting star and not a missile.

Back on the farm, Meriel sat in bed between the girls and Misha reading Becky's favorite nursery rhymes. Sandy lay next to her with a new eye patch that matched her pajamas and stared at the ceiling. When Misha began to snore, Becky propped her head on her elbow and paused Meriel's link.

"Merry L, why did Misha and his grandpa come to Haven?" Becky said. "We don't eat much better at home than at the refugee camp."

Meriel sighed. "As tough as it is here, Haven looks better to them than what they have."

"But why here? There's lots of exoplanets between here and Sol."

"Sure. And lots of them have colonies. Even the low-g asteroids. People have found ways to live almost anywhere."

"If people can live anywhere, why here?"

"Because Haven is special," Sandy said.

"Why?"

"For one, we can walk and breathe normal outside. For two, Papa can grow things 'cause we fixed the dirt, and we have water."

Meriel smiled and nodded. "Haven is priceless, hon. It's the only place other than Earth where people live on the surface. We can open doors without dying and walk without being crushed or floating off into space."

Above the bed, a night breeze carried scents of manure and grass to flutter the curtain.

"It's the only place you can open a window," Meriel said.

"The only one?"

"The only one."

"We only need to get used to the dust," Sandy said.

Meriel nodded. "Most exoplanets are like Ross 128 and have no air to breathe. Others are completely toxic or too hot for liquid water."

"What about the stations?" Becky asked.

"They're nice, but they won't allow most people to stay. Almost everyone lives on ships or in colonies, and many are horrible."

"Like Lalande-C6?" Sandy said.

Meriel sighed and bit her lip. "I hoped you hadn't seen that."

"Kids see everything, Merry," Sandy said.

"Did you understand it?"

Sandy frowned and nodded.

"For many out here, Haven is their last hope."

"But the Biadez folks will take care of them, right?"

Meriel frowned. "I hope so. But Biadez and BioLuna are on the same team."

Becky rolled over to sleep, but Sandy stared at the ceiling and bit her fingernails.

"What is it, hon?" Meriel said and took Sandy's hand from her mouth.

"I'm sorry I was afraid today."

Meriel hugged her close. "You remembered the attack here at the farm?"

Sandy nodded.

"It's OK, hon. You were brave to go into the cellar even though you were afraid."

"I can't forget, Merry. With papa and you hurt, Becky and I were alone in the dark. We heard the shooting and explosions, and I didn't know what to do."

"I have things I can't forget, too."

"What do you do?"

"I try to keep moving," Meriel said. "And keep doing what I need to do. The more I stay in action, the less it stops me. Some things I don't want to forget, like my mom's death."

"Does it make you mad?"

"A little. Sad mostly. And that can stop me, too."

"I was little when my mom died. I didn't know what to do then either, but I missed her so much."

"Your papa was there."

Sandy nodded. "All the time. But it's not the same."

"He loves you more than he can explain," Meriel said. "And so do I."

"I know," Sandy said and snuggled in.

After Sandy fell asleep, Meriel returned to her bedroom and lay in her clothing next to John. But the excessive alcohol did not silence the nagging pain of her thigh wound or John's snores. With thoughts of the tattooed rioter, she rose and went to the kitchen.

Over the gouged and laser-burned floor, Meriel dragged a chair to the table, and on it she put the little book that had saved her life. From a cupboard, she took a towel and a bottle of whiskey, and from a drawer grabbed a tube of skin glue. Sitting at the table, she poured herself a drink, dipped the towel into it, and dropped the waist of her pants. The wound bled when she peeled off the suture-seal, and she clenched her teeth as she cleaned it with the towel and whiskey. Pinching the wound closed, she applied the skin glue.

While the glue set, she downed the glass and sealed the slice in the book's cover with the glue.

Alone at the table, she poured another glass and sipped the whiskey as the cool breeze of the desert night chilled the sweat on her shoulders.

A buzz from her link startled her. It was Penny Hubbard.

"It's the middle of the night, Penny."

"My supervisor went home. Do you have a holo-projector away from the kids?"

"They're sleeping."

"Oh, right. Link me up. You'll see."

Meriel slid the kitchen door closed and engaged the projector with Penny's GRL. A set of consoles appeared with Penny sitting in front.

"What am I looking at, hon?"

"A live-link to the lab here. I have a deep-scan from a miner from Lalande C-6."

"Why do we care?" Meriel said and aligned her real chair to the virtual one next to Penny.

"I checked the autopsy data and found an anomaly. The body has a transplanted organ with a consent form problem. And that implicates the Archtrope in a crime."

"How so?"

"He's trafficking in *conflict organs*," Penny said. "Transplant organs taken from people without their consent."

"Murdered?"

"Or from slaves in the mining colonies."

"How can you tell?"

Penny waved her fingers and a hologram of the left kidney appeared. "See, the fusions. He has a transplanted kidney."

"That's not unusual."

"But this is." Penny zoomed the hologram to the microscopic tattoo identifying the donor and chain of custody. "There." After a glance at the door, she tapped a man's ID badge on the console.

"That's handy," Meriel said.

"My date last night. Watch this." Penny removed her hands from the autopsy robot and blinked to engage her console. "Data search, consent records for transplanted kidney."

```
"Kidney donated by Korthon Zhao;
Proxima Centuri B. Organ sourced from
the Society of Pious Sisters clinic on
Etna."
```

Meriel tipped her head. "Sloppy paperwork?"

"Nope. Wait," Penny said and tapped her console. "DNA verification, Zhao kidney."

```
"Kidney DNA match to Marge Ito-
Tsoget, Seiyei Station . . ."
```

"Hear that, M? The consent records don't match the DNA of the organ. That's evidence of fraud and organ laundering." She waved her fingers above the console. "See here, Marge's encrypted biotag ID does not match the digital signature for the donor of record."

"Can't be a mistake?"

"No way."

"How does that implicate the Archtrope?"

"His affiliate vetted it. Watch," Penny said. "Galactipedia search. Society of Pious Sisters."

> "The Society of Pious Sisters or SPS Group: a 5400-C9 non-profit focused on charitable humanitarian work."

"Affiliation with Archtrope, Alan Biadez, or BioLuna."

> "Includes legal counsel to Archtrope of Calliope on the board of directors. Interlocking directorships with Saviors Corporation."

"Hear that, M? SPS and the Saviors Corporation produce over seventy percent of the chain-of-custody problems with transplant organs."

"That's high."

"Way high. And the Archtrope's involved. I added the tampered records of the SPS and Saviors Corporation to the dossier and will—"

The door to the med school office slid open, and Penny waved a finger to erase Meriel's hologram from sight but left the transmit on. Through the door, a narrow young man with an over-groomed mustache approached and stood by Penny's console as if he owned it.

"Hey, Milo," Penny said without enthusiasm.

"Hey gorgeous." He tapped on her console.

> Kidney of UOD match to DNA of Marge Ito-Tsoget, Seiyei Station . . .

"That's another consent mismatch?" Milo asked. "Good catch, kid."

Penny glared. "There are too many mismatches to be a QC issue."

"Nobody cares where the body parts come from, Penny. Especially the recipients and their families."

"The donors care. Archers are laundering organs through the organ banks, and you know it."

"This is a med school, not a police station. And we're in Compliance, not Forensics." Milo moved to her side of the desk and picked up a stylus. "Say, you're part of the team now. The gang's getting together for happy hour after work. Wanna come?"

"Sam is meeting me here."

"He's a kid."

"I'm underage."

He winked. "They won't care in blue-zone."

"I know the docks," she said and glared at him. "And you're too old for me."

Milo dropped his charming smile but did not move.

She frowned. "And I'm busy."

He scowled. "I don't give a damn how smart you're supposed to be. Remember, you're an intern here and your job is reconciling the organ consent forms."

Penny shook her head. "But I—"

"No, no," Milo said and waved his hand. "I know all about your examination of the *Tiger* corsairs. Just don't let your little side projects get in the way, or I'll replace you."

"Yes, sir."

As soon as the door closed behind him, Penny switched the live-link back on. "Weasel."

"Do we need to do something about him?" Meriel said.

"Not yet. Search Galactipedia for Marge Tsoget."

```
"Marge Ito-Tsoget, Citizen Seiyei
Station. Professor of Paleolithic Ge-
netics, Seiyei University. Husband:
Isaak Tsoget, Professor of Anthropolo-
gy, Seiyei University. Genographics
expert. Three sons."
```

"Wow," Meriel said. "A citizen and professor yet. Not what I expected. Seiyei must have thought well of them to let them have three kids."

"Search publications," Penny commanded and speed-read the abstracts. "Here, M. Read this one. Isaak criticized the Archtrope."

"Search organ donations by DNA match, Isaak Tsoget," Meriel said, and a second later, Penny's console squawked.

```
Pancreas of UOD match to DNA of
Isaak Tsoget. Organ sourced from the
Saviors Corp. (a 5400-C9 non-profit)
with a clinic on Etna Station.
```

"Damn. Her husband donated his organs to the Saviors Corporation."

Meriel flipped back to the cover of the data file, which displayed a still vid of the Tsogets in formal dress. "Was he a victim too? So, what happened?"

Penny gave her a knowing grin and opened a page in the dossier. "See here? Most of the mismatched organs are from missing persons. Many were tagged for emigration."

"Healthy people who won't be missed. Refugees."

"And their organs were all handled by the Society of Pious Sisters or the Saviors Corporation and the Archtrope's affiliates."

"All of them?"

"Well, mostly. And get this. The Saviors Corporation paid for the Tsogets' trip to Etna."

"Let me guess. One way?"

"Yup," Penny said and smiled.

"So they're running a black-market in transplant organs?"

"Is this enough to hurt the Archtrope?"

"Yes," Meriel said. "It shows a pattern of corruption in a charity he controls. And with the corsairs from the *Tiger* attack . . ." She frowned.

"That's good, right? So why aren't you happy?"

"He's a dangerous guy, Penny. And I don't know what he'll do if he finds out what's in your dossier."

"The Troopers should know about this."

"They're eight light-years away."

Meriel's link buzzed and a face with a chiseled jaw appeared on her visor. "I've got incoming, Penny. Call me as soon as you find more on the corsair with the tattoo."

"Sure, M. I'll add all this to the dossier."

"See you," Meriel said and blinked to switch calls.

Colonel Lee's face popped up on her visor. "Hi, M. I need to talk to John."

"He's sleeping, Colonel," Meriel said as she returned to the bedroom.

"Then wake him."

Meriel shook John awake, and when he nodded, she tapped her visor to project a holo.

"I need you to meet me on LeHavre," Lee said. "There's a meeting to discuss the refugee problems and immigration. I want you there. Day after tomorrow is the soonest we can get a shuttle to you."

"Why me?" John said and rubbed his eyes.

"We need a native who's clocked hours on other stations."

"But I'm not a Tech."

"You're a pilot and Nav-4. That's tech enough for anyone on LeHavre."

John opened his mouth, but Meriel put a finger to his lips before he could speak.

"Can we bring the kids, Colonel?" she said. "Liz and I have an interview with IGB, and—"

Lee frowned. "Not about immigration, I hope."

"No. Something personal. But I'm worried about leaving the girls here."

"The bombing today?"

"Yeah. The refugee camp is only a few miles away."

"Promise me dinner after the meeting?" Lee said.

John laid back and closed his eyes. "Done."

"Oh, and Meriel. We found the leader of the riot today."

The guy who tried to kill me. "Did he give up his friends?"

"He's dead. Corpsman at the refugee camp infirmary says his neck was broken."

John's snores drowned out Lee, and Meriel went to the hall. "Was he an Archer?"

"Unknown, M."

"Unusual tattoos?" she asked and leaned against the doorway.

"What are you getting at?"

"Colonel, one rioter had a tattoo that matched a corsair who suicided after the *Tiger* hijack to avoid interrogation," she said and paced the hall. "I think these are Khanag's goons. And that means the Archtrope is still angling for control."

Lee nodded. "If it's the Draconian League, they'll need foot soldiers."

"Right, Archers. Can Stewardville investigate?"

"The public pressure is off, M, and they'd deny my request."

"Why?"

"They think the Archers are just another strange but harmless cult."

She stopped pacing and leaned against the wall. "Spacers see them as ghouls waiting at the end of a long slide down to Hell. What about the Treaty of Haven that divvied us up between the Archtrope, Biadez, and BioLuna?"

"Stewardville thinks the treaty is dead now. President Biadez is hiding out on Calliope with the Archtrope, and BioLuna has ended their embargo of LeHavre Station. With Khanag lying low, there's nothing more to investigate. The Troopers think they've given up on Haven after the last failed attack, and—"

"I don't."

"And the bad guys don't have the funds to mount another attack from eighteen light-years away."

"What about our lawsuits?"

"LeHavre is working the legal angles through the courts on Lander. Sorry, but we'll have to wait for proof the bad guys are still active before Stewardville wakes up."

"Proof? Like what? All of us dead?"

"M—"

Meriel sighed. "Understood, Colonel, and thank you." She ended the call and returned to bed, but the threats clattered in her head.

"John, they're not taking this seriously."

"Huh?" he said between snores.

"I need to find out if there are more Archers here," she said and rose from bed. And on the way past the kitchen, she grabbed her visor and a stunner.

A rooster tail of dust followed Meriel's truck back to the refugee camp. As she pulled in, the Marines guarding the barn waved to her.

The camp was quiet with only the chirps of native six-legged *culpas* hunting for scraps of leather or wood to eat. Across the yard, a cigarette twinkled in a distant shadow, and she flipped the safety off her stunner.

"Hey, soldier," she called to a Marine.

The young man approached and smiled.

"Corporal . . ." she asked.

"Dekard, Ms. Hope. Can I help you?"

"Maybe. Did your squad find any pins or medals with a symbol like this?" In the dirt, she drew a figure of a flower with four petals.

"No, ma'am."

"Can you help me look for something similar?"

"Sure."

With his heel and rifle butt, he broke through the thin crust of dried mud, and in the headlights of the truck, she sifted through the dirt. Small knives, pieces of metal, a mini-tase, and ceramic knuckles surfaced: weapons any spacer might carry into a blue-zone bar. But where the big man had attacked her earlier that day, something glimmered in the dirt. She winced as she bent over to pick up a scrap of plastaglass that could slice through steel, her blood on the blade now a brownish mud. Next to it, she found a small lapel pin etched with a four-leafed-poppy symbol, an ancient apothecary's mark for opium.

A chill breeze blew through the camp and the hair on the back of her neck stood on end.

"Archers," she whispered and stood. *A souvenir? Maybe.*

"Are you all right, Ms. Hope?" the Marine asked.

She raised a hand and nodded, and after taking a quick vid, she gave him the pin.

"Give this to Captain Abrams. He'll know what it means. Can you show me to the infirmary?"

The Marine led her through the grid of temporary shelters to a tent a hundred yards from the barn. Within it was a solid structure with a locked door.

"Is that the morgue?"

"Yes, but you'll need the corpsman to let you in."

"Get him, please," she said and paced outside the door, unable to quiet her fears. *Someone with a tattoo that matched Khanag's pirate. And an Archer pin. Even together, they proved nothing. But if. . . Are they targeting us, or are we just in the way again? And if Sandy and Becky are in danger, I don't care which.*

The corpsman did not arrive, and Meriel's patience ran out. She scanned the room and muscled the flimsy door with a hard twist and a shoulder.

Inside, a dim red glow lit the room, and she tapped her visor for the low-beam flashlight. A row of cabinets lined one wall with a matrix of coolers where six dim LEDs blinked slowly. One by one, she rolled out the slabs and lifted the sheets until the third slab.

It was him, the man who called her out earlier and slashed her. But he did not have the blade and snake tattoo or other marks on his arms or legs.

"How did you identify yourself to your friends but not to the Troopers?"

She manipulated the cold flesh for to inspect between the fingers and toes, but still found nothing, even on his ears or inside his lips.

She sighed and relaxed with her back against the coolers. With a blink, she began a call to her sister to tell her the good news. Then she stopped, furrowed her brow, and peered at the body.

"So why'd you come after me?"

She tapped her visor to switch to UV light and inspected the body again. Nothing. Then behind his ear, a poppy tattoo shone in the purple light.

She jerked upright. *They're here.*

With a blink, she called Elizabeth. "Wake up, Liz. Wake up."

Meriel's heart raced, and her vision clouded. *Damn! Not now*, she thought and held the cross on her necklace as the panic took over.

Elizabeth appeared on the visor; her eyes still closed. "This better be important."

But Meriel did not hear her.

They're here. Her breathing quickened as images from her childhood returned, minutes after her mother died in her arms. *No, not now. Not again.* She glanced at the dead man, and her father's bloody face appeared on the gurney in the *Princess'* infirmary.

"Papa," Meriel said.

Staggering backward, she fell over a chair. When she sat up again, her twelve-year-old self reflected from a cabinet, surrounded by forty bodies. *No!* She held her hands to her chest to ease the searing pain and groaned.

"What happened, M?" Elizabeth said from far away.

Without responding, Meriel rocked forward and back with her hands on her chest, staring at her father's bloody profile.

"It's not them," she mumbled and blinked rapidly to interrupt the flashback. "It's not him."

Papa. Papa. She squeezed her eyes closed tight and invoked the memory of her father's sleeping face to dispel the bloody images from that day. As she rocked, she slowed her breathing and tried every trick the shrinks taught her to control her delusions. Gradually, her vision cleared to a reflection of her twenty-two-year-old body in the camp morgue.

"M. Come back. We're on Haven. It's the memories."

"Give me a second, Liz," Meriel said and got to her feet, but leaned with her back to the cooler. "The leader of the riot was an Archer."

"You sure?"

"He has a black-light poppy tattoo behind—" Meriel caught her breath. "Oh, shit. John and the girls," she said and sprinted out the door past Dekard and the corpsman.

"End call. John Smith, urgent." But his link only beeped. "Message. John, call soonest, we've got trouble. Send."

Meriel gunned the truck on the return to the farm, drifting around turns in the dirt road. Along the way, enemies jumped from every shadow and muzzles flashed from every reflection of the headlights. Images came of John's kids spending the rest of their lives defending their home world from the Archtrope's thugs.

She tried to call John again without success, then blinked twice to begin another call.

"Smith farm. Security console," she said, and a head up display of the farm's electronic defenses projected from her visor. The threat board was clear and the peripheral motion detectors were live but still. Then a quick rotation through the cameras showed no threats, and an aerial surveillance found no droids. The tension in her shoulders eased, but she did not slow.

After sending a vid of the pin to Elizabeth, she called her again. But Abrams' face projected from Meriel's visor.

"Sorry to wake you, Captain. I sent a vid you should see."

"The pin? Dekard sent me a pic. I'll escalate to Colonel Lee and Stewardville."

"And the leader has a black-light tattoo of a poppy behind his ear," Meriel said. "He's likely not the only Archer in the camp."

"Got it. Liz is here and—"

"Wait. John's not answering, and I'm worried about them on the farm. Can you have a Marine come take a look?"

"I'll send a team," Abrams said.

His image jostled, and Elizabeth's face appeared, puffy with the welt on her cheek growing into a bruise.

"M, what hap—"

"They're here, Littlebit."

"Who?"

"Archers. They were at the riot today."

"The capital will handle this, M."

"I don't think so. Colonel Lee said Stewardville has convinced themselves the threat is over. I think the bad guys are ramping up again."

"What the hell are we going to do about it?

"What if we go after them?"

"Come on, M. We don't have a fleet like Khanag's or BioLuna's deep pockets. We're little people out here. So how do you plan to do that?"

"Throw a grenade in the middle of them."

Elizabeth tipped her head. "Which means what, specifically?"

"The Archtrope's authority comes from his image of being a saintly man. It's a façade. Penny's building a dossier of discrepancies in the organ trade implicating him in organ laundering."

"Those rumors have been circulating for years and haven't cracked his image yet."

"Penny's got hard evidence, not rumors, and might get more traction."

"The media will spin it before it takes hold."

"I don't want . . ." she said, but her truck slid around the next turn. The road disappeared, and she flew into a sea of stars. The truck landed hard, and she skidded back onto the road without slowing.

"You OK, M?"

"I don't want to send it to them yet."

"Then how?"

"I want to send the dossier to Khanag so he can read it first."

"Why contact him at all?"

"Maybe we can turn our enemies against each other," Meriel said and took another hard corner.

"And you think Khanag's the weak link? Jeez, M. He killed our folks."

"I talked to him during the invasion. He believes the Archtrope saved him."

"He's a butcher," Elizabeth said and poured herself a drink from the bottle on the nightstand.

"Sure, but I think he's sincere in his belief—"

"He's a psychopath, M. How can you tell?" Elizabeth took a drink. "And how do you know it was Khanag who sent the Archers to kill you today?"

A shooting star lit the night sky, and memories came of missile trails through the busted ceiling of the kitchen and the assassin aiming his flechette pistol at Sandy.

At the next turn, her lights flashed off the crests of buffalo-sized *orbanths* and she jammed on her brakes. The truck careened off the road into a pack of wolflike *hiranth* that growled and snapped at the lights and the tires of the beast that spoiled their hunt.

And then they came for her.

She closed the window as they snapped at her with fangs the length of her fingers and clawed at the windows with two of their six legs. They couldn't digest her, but she'd be dead before they remembered.

"M, are you OK?"

"Yeah," Meriel said and gripped the wheel as the *hiranths* prowled around the truck and gnawed on the fenders. "I . . . I just want them to leave us alone."

"You opened Pandora's box when you found out who killed our folks, M."

"Kinda. I—"

A *hiranth* jumped on the hood, drooling and clawing on the windshield, and Meriel jerked back in her seat.

"I need them gone, Liz."

"Right. Well, how can you reach Khanag? His contact information isn't public, and he's been off the grid since the invasion failed."

Meriel tapped her fingers on the wheel, and when the hiranth interrupted with a growl, she slammed a fist against the roof.

"M?"

"I still have the link that Khanag used to record me for the avatar. He left it at the farmhouse."

"Then he'll guess it's from you."

"I want him to know. Hell, I don't know if this will work, but I gotta do something. I figure he's hiding near the Archtrope on Calliope. That's twenty-five light-years, and—"

"So maybe two days for a message to get to him," Elizabeth said.

"And the same for him to come here if he wants to talk to me."

"Or kill you."

Meriel smiled. "He already knows where we live. When he comes for us at the farm, the Marines will be there waiting for him, and we'll be with Abrams in Bantu."

"I'll tell him."

"I heard," Abrams said from behind Elizabeth. "Later, M."

"See you."

She honked, and the *orbanths* grunted their danger warning. Still in the defensive circle that surrounded the young, they rose and ambled away, stalked by the *hiranths*.

"That's what we need, a defensive circle," she said as she maneuvered the truck back to the road. *But we're alone out here, nothing but the other stations, and they're light-years away.*

The stations?

When Meriel arrived at the farm, the Marines were not there, and she rushed to check on the sleeping girls, and then John. She smiled at his peaceful snoring, but then frowned at the memory of him bleeding out on the kitchen floor. With her jaw set, she grabbed a rifle from over the fireplace and went to the kitchen. From the breaker box, she turned the inside lights off and the outside floods on. Then she keyed her visor to the security system and headed outside.

As she patrolled the farmyard to the edge of the field, she tested the motion and infrared sensors. A motion sensor blinked on her visor, and she dropped to the dirt. Flipping the safety off, she aimed into the dark, waiting for a target.

Her visor flashed.

"Corporals Izakoff and Brown reporting, Ms. Hope. Captain Abrams sent us to patrol for hostiles.

She sighed. "Welcome, Corporals. Light up your positions."

"Yes, ma'am. We have air drones and are casting those IDs as well."

On her visor, red dots appeared at the border of the farm with callouts for the new IDs. "Are your drones armed? We have kids here."

"Surveillance and targeting only."

"You're welcome to come inside," she said and tapped her visor to accept the new IDs as friendlies.

"No thank you, ma'am. If there's a threat, better to meet it out here in the open."

"Thank you," she said, stood, and walked back to the kitchen.

Grabbing the bottle of whiskey from the table, she turned off the floods, and sat on the steps as the cool breeze of the desert night chilled the sweat on her shoulders.

She tapped her visor to pull up Penny's dossier linking the Archtrope with the Society of Pious Sisters and the fraudulent consent forms. At the same GRL was Penny's copy of the coroner's draft report with the autopsy files for the corsairs who died trying to hijack the *Tiger*. Within it, she stopped to view the morgue stills. The first was the black-suited captain who had led the assault, his face etched into her last memory before a pulse rifle broke her back.

Next to his still, Meriel pulled up a vid where the captain stood next to Khanag and the Archtrope. Determination and pride marked the young man's face while Khanag's was stern and unreadable, but the likeness was clear.

"Why'd you try to kill everyone on the *Tiger*? Just to get to me?" The muscles of her shoulders tightened again. *And what if you had another chance at us?*

You'd kill us all.

Meriel took a swig from the bottle and tapped her visor for a call up to LeHavre.

"Hey, M," Penny said.

"Penny, if the Archtrope knows the dossier will hurt him, he'll try to destroy your evidence."

"Ahh, M, how is he going to find out about the dossier?"

"Penny, I'm giving you a heads-up. I'm going to send it to a few people. Once I do, we'll need to watch our backs."

"Not the media?"

"Not now," Meriel said and took another swig. "I think they'll bury it. You said you have the corsair bodies from the *Tiger* there."

"Yes. Here in the med labs."

"I thought the medical examiner locked them up."

"He did. We share the morgue."

"How's your security?"

"So-so. Dead people don't go walking away here. We have the DNA samples. So, why the concern for the bodies?"

"Data can be faked," Meriel said. "So can an autopsy report and everything else. But we can't fake the bodies. We don't want to lose the corsairs, but the captain in particular."

"Because he's in the vid with the Archtrope?"

"Right."

"I'll check our security."

"I saw the corsairs' DNA profiles in the coroner's report. Did you match them to anyone?"

"Jeez, M, I've been at this all day. Gimme a break. As soon as I can."

"Sorry, Penny. Great work. Call me—"

"Wait, M. The Tsoget's had three children. If both parents went missing and donated their organs, what happened to their kids?"

And what would happen to Sandy and Becky if John disappeared? "I don't know, Penny. Maybe you can find out. Talk to you soon."

As she stared into the night with the rifle in her lap, memories came of Khanag's drones poised to kill Sandy and Becky.

On her visor, she flipped through stills of the farm kitchen following his attack. Only the frame remained after the missiles and lasers. Blood stained the floor, some hers, some the Archer commandos, but mostly John's. And the sanctuary for the girls, the storm cellar, shredded by flechettes.

And what if he was here now?

Chapter 2
Free space

Tai-Pan

Twelve light years away, General Subedei Khanag's fleet winked-in near a helpless merchant ship and surrounded it. With no other ships within ten AU, its position was precisely known, because he had set their course. Khanag had hacked their victim's nav and short-jumped them to where the sphere of uncertainty was small.

"Do we have nav control?" Khanag said.

"Yes sir."

"Fuse the gun and come alongside," he said and rose. "I'll lead the boarding party."

It wasn't a battle. Just a single laser blast to disable the merchant's only gun and an explosive charge to hole the bridge and space the command crew. To subdue the remaining crew, a chute pumped corsairs inside. The outcome was settled in seconds, but never in doubt.

A tall man with black hair and eyes, Khanag slapped a riding crop on his boot as he strode through the discolored plastisteel hull breach and over a deck slippery with blood. Through the passageways, the last vestige of resistance echoed with the sporadic blasts of pulse rifles.

To his left, corsairs stood at attention behind the crew and passengers on their knees. He had seen their like many times, some cowed, some defiant. To his right, the dead were being stacked for disposal.

Life was cheap in the black and hauling bodies not worth the effort. They would leave the dead and the uncooperative on board and aim the ship at the nearest gas giant or star to disappear forever.

Khanag sat at the command console and waved his hand to produce the ship's records. With a few more gestures, he transferred the log and cargo manifest to his flagship, the *Tai-Pan*.

A woman with the bars of a merchant captain jumped from her place and clung to his leg. "Please let them go, General."

"You know who I am?"

"Yes, General Khanag, your reputation for ... Please. We're on an emergency mission with transplant organs desperately needed on Sirius."

"You're smugglers destroying the good works of the Society of Pious Sisters, and—"

"What?"

Bored with pleading and argument, Khanag whipped the woman with the riding crop until she released him, and he kicked her away

"Invite them, Commander, and round up the children," he said and turned to leave.

"His Holiness, The Archtrope of Calliope, invites you—"

Jeers interrupted. "Invite, hell, that maggoty—" said one, but the wet crunch of a boot in the teeth halted the protests.

Khanag walked back to the man who held his hands over his bleeding mouth and shot him in the face, spattering blood on the crew and his shoes. Without bending over, he wiped them on the sleeve of the dead man's shirt.

"Pay attention," Khanag said as he surveyed the captives. "This offer will not be repeated. Continue, Commander."

"His Holiness invites you—"

The voice faded as Khanag returned to the *Tai-Pan*, but he knew every word. He had delivered the same speech hundreds of times. Some submitted to the brief invitation to join the Archtrope's believers in building a beautiful new world of peace and equality. Those who refused, died.

From his command chair, Khanag reviewed the manifest. One set of files listed organs and tissue types. There were a few discrepancies, always possible among the billions of transactions. But he did not bother to check the provenance of each, instead trusting the Archtrope's condemnation.

It saddened him. Countless deaths, so many at his hands, to cleanse the spaceways of miscreants. Once the Station Troopers had wiped the pirates from space, smugglers and black marketers had filled the vacuum, and these were only the latest.

To his left, a monitor displayed the line of men, women, and children who had submitted to the Archtrope's vision. In restraints, they filed into his fleet's troop carrier and received the pills that would drug them into passivity. But he paid no attention to the new supplicants and gazed out the window at the stars.

"Comm," he said. "Give me a message update by priority."

"We're running dark, General, and haven't synced with a beacon."

"Sync with the comm memory from the merchant and wipe it. They won't need it."

"Aye, General," the comm officer said, and a moment later, "Incoming."

"Put them through."

```
His Eminence has accepted your re-
quest for a private audience to dis-
cuss your petition. Please report
soonest and maintain EM silence.
   Renaldo Suzuki, Calliope.
```

"XO, plot a course for Calliope," Khanag said.

"Aye, sir," came a woman's voice over comm.

"Next message, sir," the comm officer said.

```
  Escort needed for settlers to Jira-
1. Stealth approach required.
Acknowledge.
  Tov Aljitnuud, Central Command, Cal-
liope.
```

Khanag narrowed his eyes and rubbed his chin. "Jira-1, that's Haven and an open border. Why do they need an escort?"

"Unknown, sir," the XO replied. "I'll tight-beam orders to Captain Dingane. When we arrive at Calliope, his squadron will escort settlers to Jira-1."

He sneered. "Is the Hope woman still there?"

"Yes, sir."

"Keep the fleet together. We all may be going to Jira-1."

Chapter 3
Haven, Jira-1 System

Johnston Rift

Thor's fading crescent ended the false dawn as Meriel sat on the steps with the rifle in her lap.

And what if he was here—

The clang of pipes on chains brought her to her feet with the rifle at ready. Past her raced a lermel a yard in front of two culpas twice its size. The lermel wiggled his way into a stack of irrigation pipes and squealed.

Meriel slammed the screen door, and the culpas stopped and turned to her, black except for the eyes that glowed blue in the light. She stomped her foot, and the native predators scurried away.

"Motion detectors activated, Ms. Hope," Izakoff said from her visor. "Your status?"

"Just native fauna, corporal, and thanks for your attention. Good night."

She sighed and raised her eyes to the night sky where the rains had cleared the air of dust. Thor had set to the west, exposing the Milky Way, and within that glow shone DX Cancri, Jira-1's reference star. To her left gleamed Wolf 359, where she went EVA for the first time, and to her right shone Lalande 21185 where she met John. *Home*, she thought with a smile. But a glance above showed Procyon where the *Princess* was attacked, and her parents killed.

It's starting again. Will it be now?

A small hand took hers, and she flinched again.

"Papa said the stars shine brightest on the darkest nights," Becky said.

Meriel kneeled to the girl by her side and Misha who held her other hand. Smiling, she kissed their foreheads. "You should be in bed."

"So should you. I heard Dumpy."

"He's hiding in the pipes, hon. Off you go. I'll be there in a minute."

"OK," Becky said and opened the screen door to let Dumpy scurry past them into the house.

After returning the rifle to the mantel, Meriel scanned the metadata in Penny's dossier to confirm the absence of digital tracks. Then she copied the files to the q-chip that hung with the cross on her necklace, her mother's gift before she died.

From the back corner on the top shelf of a cabinet, she retrieved the link Khanag left before trying to kill them. After another swig from the bottle, she held her finger over the reply icon.

Will this just make things worse?

Meriel went to the girls' bedroom and leaned against the door frame. On one side of the room, Sandy snored gently. On the other side, Misha and Becky lay side by side with Dumpy curled up at their feet, eyeing Meriel with suspicion.

What life will they have if Archers come to threaten them every day?

She stared at the link again.

And will this improve their chances?

She sighed and then hit reply to send the dossier to Khanag.

Back in their bedroom, she lay next to John.

He woke, put an arm around her, and kissed her. "Hey, sailor. You here for a sleepover?"

"John, can we leave for LeHavre tomorrow?"

"We can't afford it, and Colonel Lee is bringing us up in a few days for free. You worried about the girls?"

Meriel nodded. "Let's visit Bantu after your meeting."

"Sure. Why?"

"I'll tell you tomorrow," she said, wiggled closer, and returned the kiss.

One more day to safety. We just have to get up to LeHavre.

Chapter 4
Mars-6, Sol System

Ellen Biadez paced across her ivy-covered gazebo, scattering the carpet of peach petals on the wooden floor. Her pearlescent gown draped an exquisite figure maintained by surrogate childbirth and exhausting exercise. On her shoulder, a fragile petal lingered, and she crushed it between her fingers.

Music from the ballroom nearby floated past her security into the gazebo. This event marked her return to Sol society after a few deadly dull months on Calliope with her husband Alan, the former president of the United Nations of Earth. And a small part of the UNE security force granted to him patrolled outside.

She flicked the ash from her cigarette and appraised the luxurious gardens of the Septimus Hotel on Mars-6. Natural woods, marbles, and plants smuggled from Earth covered the concrete and steel from Martian sources. The largest share of it was hers, and BioLuna and the Archtrope of Calliope owned the rest.

Past the ivy trellis shimmered a reflecting pool that stretched to the rim of the city's dome. Beyond it lay the windswept expanse of the Amazonis Planitia and the sinuous erosions of the Medusae Fossae. In her mind's eye, the canyons became the pulsing arteries of her enemy's heart, and she reached out and placed one between her thumb and finger. With a pinch, she sneered, imagining the agonizing death of a thorn in her side: Meriel Hope.

The pendant on her necklace buzzed, and she tapped it. The image of a lean man with hungry eyes appeared: Cecil Rhodes, President of BioLuna, the galaxy's largest medical supply and pharmaceutical conglomerate.

"Where are you, Cecil?"

"At the party."

A glance to the ballroom entrance a hundred yards away confirmed Rhodes standing by the door.

"On my way," she said and dropped the smoldering butt of her cigarette on the pink blossoms where it burned through the petals to scar the priceless hardwood floor.

"You need to see this first. Are you secure?"

With a wave she dismissed security and pressed a tiny blue light on the door frame to activate the sound curtain. When the outside shimmered and the music died, she tapped the pendant.

"Speak freely."

Rhodes' image swapped to a holo of a conference room that filled the gazebo with her standing next to the table. Framed by a panoramic star field behind them, two men sat opposite her.

"Pause," Ellen said, and the scene froze. "That's Kerrick Tembo, Lander's Pilot-Master. And Station Master Urden Peg from Wolf next to him. And the nebula behind them is Orion. That's Wolf Station?"

"Yes."

"Have they ever been in the same room together?"

"No."

"Who's recording?"

"Our man from Enterprise."

"Hmm. Resume," Ellen said, and the holo continued.

"It's starting, Urden," said a tall man with graying temples. "Haven upset the balance."

Peg frowned. "What do you mean?"

Tembo tapped his ear, and a holo appeared on the table of the familiar blue planet Earth. "Earth has been the center of the universe for . . . well, forever." As he spoke, the image zoomed out to Sol system, and farther to the near stars, with Sol and the major colonies and stations highlighted, until Haven appeared at the far edge of the sphere.

"Colonies have spread out radially from Earth, first with the planets and then the near stars. It's not just the economic center but the spiritual center as well. Humanity is balanced with Earth at the center."

"That's now?"

"That's until last year," Tembo said and stood. "But the Hope sisters blew up BioLuna's news embargo and made Haven public." He went to the window and waved a hand to the stars outside. "The word is out now, and tens of billions of people smell opportunity out here. Sol won't be the heart of the universe anymore—"

A flat voice came from out of view. "We're expecting demic and transcultural diffusion sparked by the exposure of Haven as a livable moon."

Tembo nodded and leaned with his hands on the table. "And money and power will shift before the people do. The economic center will move away from Sol toward Haven, and that means towards Wolf, Lander, and other stations out here in our sector, but mostly Enterprise. Sol won't sit idle for the loss of power, and the UNE will react."

"The discovery of the Americas shocked Europe," the flat voice said. "Within four hundred years, power had shifted from there to North America."

"Exactly, Rivan," Tembo said. "The discovery of Haven has shocked Earth. But money and power travel faster than light now. This shift will only take a few decades."

"And you propose?" Peg asked.

Tembo paused and glanced at each of those in the room. "That we redirect our attention outward rather than inward toward Sol."

"Haven?"

He nodded. "And do it together. We either team up or we die separately."

Peg frowned and snapped his fingers. White noise filled the audio, and phantom images moved on the screen before Rhodes' face appeared again.

"Did Riven get more?" Ellen said.

"No. You understand what this means?"

"Yes. The far stations will form an alliance and squeeze us out unless we intervene. Who's leading this?"

"The Tech Masters on Enterprise Station," Rhodes said. "They suspect Earth will find a pretext to force the trade hubs into exclusive agreements with the UNE."

Ellen lit another cigarette and took a drag. "They're right. Do we have a leak?"

"My staff believes the techs are using game theory with minimax probabilistics to—"

"Spare me their bullshit," she said with a scowl. "Your staff has no appreciation for the subtleties of people and politics. You're the CEO, what do you think?"

"I think Tembo is expecting our initiatives," Rhodes said. "And we can't afford for them to shut us out. Eighty percent of Sol's new product prototypes and replicator programs come from the far stars. Hell, BioLuna's most profitable products came from LGen which is now on goddamn LeHavre. The UNE needs to call an emergency session and—"

"F'em, Cecil, *we're* the UNE. And if the stations expect a pretext, then we need to act before they put their guard up. Begin operation *Sarajevo*."

A high-priority message from LeHavre station interrupted, and Ellen scowled. "That bitch."

"What is it?"

"Well, apparently the Hope twit is in touch with Khanag."

"You think she's working with the Archtrope now?"

"Or teaming up against him. It's a reply, so we're not likely to decrypt it without Khanag's link." She paced the gazebo, smirked, and tossed her cigarette into the flowers. "Tell Yutousov to use the *Princess* as the trigger."

"That will cause lots of collateral damage, Ellen."

"So what?" she said and marched from the gazebo, surrounded by her security. "And it has the bonus of silencing the Hope sisters for good."

As Ellen walked through the massive ballroom door, the orchestra struck up the fanfare. At the top of the stairs, she stopped, smiled, and flung her arms wide. On the dance floor below her, the most influential media and political personalities in Sol system applauded. And from among them, Rhodes joined her.

When she took his arm, she said. "Let's see the Hope slag wiggle out of *Sarajevo*."

Chapter 5
Etna Station, Etna 320 System

Etna Station—On Station

Dean Julian Yutousov waved a hand to refresh the wall of data on the transplant organ markets. An elegant man in a proper business suit, his only flaws were the scar over his left eye and the twitch of his little finger.

Because of its importance to human health, the organ market was audited to be secure from manipulation. But Julian's firm had written the program decades ago with a silent partner, the Archtrope of Calliope, and Julian had written the security module. And with the most powerful quantum computer center in the quadrant, and the largest DNA database in the galaxy one floor below him, his stranglehold on the market was profound, but hidden.

Data flashed red on his screen, and he tapped his ear. "Can you explain the drop in organ prices, darling?"

On the veranda outside Yutousov's office, Christine Blanchette sunned herself with a view of the expansive public gardens of Etna's white-zone, a reward for brokering biologics and transplant organs to powerful people the Archtrope planned to corrupt.

"The Cephus League has taken over the route from Cho-sho to Alice Station," Blanchette said. "They're dropping the price to secure their markets."

"That's the Seiyei region. His Holiness will not be pleased."

Blanchette draped her body with a wrap complimenting her violet eyes and entered his office.

"Let's request General Khanag remind the Cephus League that the Society of Pious Sisters controls that territory."

He nodded. "The organs will disappear from the market causing the price to spike. Then we'll deliver our rebranded organs into the market at the higher price."

"Are you sure we can deliver? Khanag can be rather careless with contraband."

"I'll hedge with futures," he said and sneered. "And we have a backup. BioLuna has untapped 'human resources' in mining colonies the Troopers haven't discovered."

She yawned. "The public would swoon at your efficiency." An incoming message tickled her ear, and she raised an eyebrow. "Julian, here's an interesting mission." With a blink, she passed the message to her partner.

"Operation Sarajevo," he said and read the updated operational orders. "This will finally stop the shift of power to the stations and restore the UNE out here."

"We're retired, darling."

"But here's an interesting twist," he said and waved a finger to highlight a subsection for her.

She read it and raised an eyebrow. "His agents have tried to get her before."

"But we haven't. And Sarajevo will change everything."

"I'll book a jump to Enterprise," she said and tapped her link.

He scratched the scar on his forehead. With a few motions, he engaged the quantum computers to search the galaxy's largest genetics and social database, everything their crawlers and sniffers could glean, legally and illegally. "Everyone has a weakness," he said and examined the tissue specs of Meriel Hope. "And I know hers."

Chapter 6
Calliope, Tau Ceti System

The Immacula

Massive buildings surrounded the expansive plaza of the Immacula, Calliope's new religious and administrative center. With its hundred-foot-tall columns, no one had been bold enough to reproduce this architectural style since the EU Revolt of 2087 destroyed the Vatican. That is, no one until the Archtrope.

On a balcony overlooking the plaza, a slender woman with high cheekbones leaned with her back against the railing. Her long flower-print dress covered her from ankles to wrists and billowed gently in slow motion in the reduced artificial gravity.

Beside her stood a handsome man in a dark shirt covering his wrists, the only ornament on his clothing a pin engraved with a poppy fixed to his red collar. Behind them stood an expansive complex of housing, hospitals, and service buildings. Above them, "Calliope, World of Peace" glowed in a three-dimensional hologram above the plaza's central pillar, and the woman faced her holographer.

"Good day, people of the galaxy," she said. "This is Charlene Hunter Samuelson from the Interstellar News Wire to report history in the making. The United Nations of Earth has honored the Calliope Foundation with a seat as a voting member, a first for a nongovernmental organization. And here on Calliope, the Archtrope has built a large new refugee facility for victims of the immigration wars. I'm here with

Renaldo Suzuki, spokesperson for the Calliope Foundation. Renaldo, tell us about this impressive new complex."

"Thank you, Ms. Samuelson. The Archtrope commissioned these facilities to aid the victims of the immigration battles near Seiyei Station."

"That's very charitable of His Holiness."

"Yes, it is. The refugee center is yet another example of his Eminence's love for humanity. He has unselfishly offered to shelter all the pious who have professed their faith in him. For decades, his loving arms have encompassed refugees from the wars of immigration along with the addicted and abused. And because of the generous donations of so many in your audience, he will build many more facilities in places where the refugees are most needy."

Samuelson turned and gazed at the plaza below where men in red robes and tall hats walked toward a bonfire followed by priests with high red collars. Behind them men and women in cassocks shuffled in sandals to a solemn dirge, their heads bowed and covered. Each carried something in their hands, pulled a cart, or hauled a skid.

"Where are the children?" she asked.

"In school."

"And the babies?"

Suzuki's brow twitched. "Procreation is natural wherever adults gather. But we discourage intimacy while the refugees seek peace and redemption."

When the cassocked penitents passed the bonfire, they threw in what they carried.

"What are they burning?" Samuelson asked.

Suzuki folded his hands. "They are destroying reminders of their old life; memories they wish to discard. This will cleanse their spirits for a life of purity and piety in aid to their fellow man."

"Including books?"

"Perhaps. Some words tempt us away from the path. Burning them removes the temptation to return to a life of sin."

"But such priceless—"

Suzuki raised a hand. "And thus, a sincere demonstration of commitment to their new life."

After a struggle to stifle her disgust, she nodded. "This is a remarkable achievement," she said as the plaza continued to fill with supplicants. "An entire colony at peace with one another, working collectively for the good of humanity."

"Yes, and this is only one of the many charities and NGOs within the Calliope Foundation. The Soldiers of Providence, for instance, guarantee shipment of life-saving drugs and medicines throughout the galaxy. And the Society of Pious Sisters now partners with all the major health care providers in this sector. Together, they supply a quarter of the transplant organs at low cost with no overhead, free delivery, and surgical staff."

"And you train the people here to help?" she said.

"Of course. We will assist them in rebuilding their ruined lives and return them to society as productive citizens."

"On a more controversial subject, how do you respond to the recent allegations of General Khanag and the Archtrope's followers hijacking merchant spacers?"

Suzuki recoiled. "Absurdities. Those claims are preposterous slanders by infidels who wish to impugn the good works of our most revered leader." His eyes lost focus as if he were reciting a script. "If any of his followers are proven to be implicated in such atrocities, we would support the strongest of sanctions." He waved his arms over the throng in the plaza below. "We Archers respect all life and have committed ourselves to the peaceful teachings of our prophet. Since that Hope creature has just confessed to fabricating the slanderous Treaty of Haven, I am certain all charges will be dropped."

In the plaza below, the cassocked supplicants kneeled followed by the red-collars that dotted the crowd. Only the red-robes remained standing in formation, transforming the path to the bonfire into a mandala.

When a large man in white robes appeared at the top of the pillar, the music stopped, and the standing priests knelt.

Suzuki bowed and nodded to Samuelson who touched the sleeve of her dress to shift it from the colorful print to a neutral gray and she bowed.

"We must end our interview now," Suzuki said, stood between her and the plaza, and opened his arms. "His eminence will now hold a private ceremony for his worshippers."

At Samuelson's signal, the holographer stopped recording and followed her and Suzuki inside to the visitor center.

"That's a wrap Tim," she said to the holographer. "And send a copy to Seide. I'll meet you at the shuttle port for the ride to orbit."

"Where will you be?" Tim asked.

"I have some background to dig up." She tapped her bracelet and a holo with a schedule appeared. "Our ship home will leave in an hour, so make sure you're on it."

Suzuki led Samuelson to an estate with a view of the Archtrope's palace. As an acolyte waved a fan of ostrich feathers nearby, she accepted a sparkling water.

"I am curious, Renaldo," she said. "Why does the palace seem so familiar?"

"His Eminence modeled it after a decrepit mausoleum on Earth once referred to as the 'teardrop on the cheek of time.' He chose it to honor the recovered drug addicts he numbers in his flock."

"Yes, now I remember. The Historical Society criticized him for aesthetic appropriation. 'An offense against humanity,' they called it."

Suzuki frowned. "You disapprove?"

"I'm a journalist. It's not my place to judge." She tipped her head to the acolyte. "Is he a new refugee?"

"No. The newest members of the Archtrope's flock live and work in the barracks across the square. There."

He pointed to a row of concrete slabs conveniently out of view during the interview that at a glance might be mistaken for a prison.

How can I get a vid of those barracks off Calliope, and what will they do if I publish it?

"Is this part of the palace?" she said to distract him

"Of course not. This building is for the high priests to be nearer His Eminence."

"I thought everyone was equal here."

"You sound skeptical, Ms. Samuelson. We're all equal here, of course. But you can't expect those who have studied with his Eminence their entire lives to have the same accommodation as those who have just arrived."

"Does he live in quarters like this?"

"Oh, no. I've never been in the palace, but I hear it is much more beautiful."

"Is that where President Biadez is staying?"

"No, he's recovering in his own private compound across from his Eminence."

"If I may ask, Renaldo, the biographical materials say the Archtrope is descended from . . ." She paused and checked her link. "The Great Khan. Why is that important to him?"

"You don't believe?"

She raised her chin. "I'm a journalist, Renaldo, and what I believe is not important here."

"Well, his holiness teaches us that all the great things in our world, everything in existence, was created by the will and the vision of the Imperials."

"And who are they?"

"The prophet kings from the pharaohs to the Caesars to the Great Kahn. God blesses us with such men because we cannot rise above our passions and weaknesses."

"Like insects," Samuelson said and locked her eyes on him.

Suzuki straightened his back and raised his chin. "Now, that's a misquote. His holiness never said that. But you must admit it's often hard to tell. Today, after centuries of rudderless and chaotic growth, humanity needs a visionary leader. That leader is the Archtrope, the highest ideal of humankind, descended from Gilgamesh, Solomon, and the Khan."

As he spoke, Suzuki gazed past her and smiled as if he had glimpsed heaven.

Samuelson stiffened. "History may have a different interpretation of—"

"Not history, Ms. Samuelson. Destiny. And prophesy. All great religions tell of the redeemer to come. And the Archtrope is He."

"One of the Imperials?" Samuelson said, struggling to keep the tinge of fear from her voice.

"Yes. He has the birthright to rule and demonstrates his competence by consistently acting in the interests of others."

A priest approached, stood in front of Suzuki, and bowed.

"Excuse me, please," Suzuki said and stepped away to confer with the priest.

With Suzuki's attention elsewhere, an acolyte refilled Samuelson's glass and dropped a tiny q-chip in her lap. She put her hand over it, synced it with her implanted link, and blinked to play the audio.

```
"Please! We need your help. Most of
those who arrive on Calliope die here—
"
```

Run, her legs told her.

Suzuki turned back to her "Now, where were we, Ms. Samuelson?"

She jumped to her feet with a fist clenched around the q-chip.

Suzuki's eyes narrowed. "Is anything wrong?"

"I need to leave for the shuttle now," she said with her heart in her throat.

The Palace

From the Archtrope's palace, Edward Seide, Editor-in-Chief of the Galactic News Network studied the hijacked real-time feed from the holographer.

Nearby, the Archtrope studied him with eyes that lurked under a heavy brow. He leaned back on his couch as a concubine peeled him a grape, and another tied his graying hair into his iconic top knot. Years of self-indulgence had melted the muscle from his large frame, but his flowing robes helped hide his corpulence.

"Brilliant, Edward," The Archtrope said. "Rebranding Khanag's Draconian League as the Soldiers of Providence was a nice touch."

"After editing, I will distribute it to our affiliates," Seide said.

"And this will be your first in a series of daily broadcasts?"

"Yes. And we project a rebroadcast multiplier of," he waved a finger over his link. "Sixteen million through the wire services."

"Good," the big man said as he poured himself a peach liquor confiscated from a convert. "Samuelson's interview and the Hope woman's avatar should drown out the accusations about the Treaty of Haven."

"It would be better if Hope denied the treaty in person," Seide said.

"We're working on that."

Seide gave him a furtive glance. "I think it's time to drop the myth of the Imperials."

The Archtrope raised an eyebrow. "And why would I do that?"

"You've already established yourself as an influential humanitarian and interstellar leader."

"It's not enough. Descendance from the Imperials gives me the cloak of authority of the ages, of Caesar, of Alexander. Ordinary people cannot understand such power."

"A mystical ancestry is unnecessary," Seide said and checked his link. "Your reach by demographic—"

"I disagree. My followers need more than mortal flesh to worship. That mystery is why the popes crowned the kings of Europe, to ennoble the local thug with the authority of heaven."

"A lie, however pretty, keeps you vulnerable to exposure. It almost exposed you before."

"It's not a lie, Ed. It's a narrative you helped to create, if I remember correctly. Without it I am like you, powerful but a cypher to history, a brief placeholder like Alan Biadez who will only be remembered by UNE bureaucrats. But as an Imperial, I am the thread of the greats, and my people need to know it."

"A fiction," Seide said and poured himself a glass of the same liquor.

The Archtrope strode through the room like a prince. "And who's to say the stories of Gilgamesh and Solomon are not fiction as well? People like me make the future, Ed. My legions of Archers know me as the gleaming beacon for future generations to follow, and I will not disappoint them." He chugged his drink. "And it's a better story than 'street rat.' So, no more talk of removing my crown."

"Yes, your Eminence."

"Oh, and before Samuelson leaves, ask her to stop by for a visit."

Seide stiffened. "Why?"

The Archtrope waved his hands to open the curtains to his private gardens. "Why? She's a talented reporter with a media presence and a promising career. She has served us well." He licked his lips. "And should be rewarded. Yes?"

"She has a busy schedule, Your Eminence. And has more value in my organization as a reporter than another of your concubines."

The big man glared down at Seide. "I get to say what's more valuable." He popped a grape into his mouth. "What's one more ambitious climber to you?"

New lines appeared at the corners of Seide's eyes, and he dropped his gaze.

"And shouldn't you be more concerned about your daughter's precarious health, Edward?"

At the mention of his child, Seide's moral algebra shifted, and he bowed. "I'll see to it, Your Eminence."

From the balcony, the Archtrope admired his expansive private gardens and fountains. "That interview should quell the allegations. No one will assail our piety after this."

"There will be more speculations after Sarajevo."

"Not about us. Ellen Biadez will have her fingerprints on that."

"But she's your ally, Jim."

The Archtrope glared at him. "Associate. That homicidal witch is nobody's ally."

"She's smart and—"

"She's just another c . . . Another bitch driven by her lusts," he said and leered at a concubine across the room. "And the media is losing interest in the Treaty of Haven. Thank you again, Edward."

"Speaking of Haven, the news feeds are restarting after BioLuna lifted the embargo," Seide said and brushed his hand over his link. The holo of Samuelson's interview dissolved into a vid with men in lab coats and scrolling data.

"Ah, yes. You're my eyes and ears to the galaxy. Tell me what scurrilous gossip abounds." He waved his hand as if to dismiss the rumors. "And what's this?"

"LGen leaked details of a new immune reaction suppression drug that'll break down in the recyclers."

The Archtrope glared as he marched toward him and put a thick arm around Seide's narrow shoulders. "And?"

"If the Tech Masters allow its use on stations, the colonies will adopt it and kill your . . . your other businesses."

"Is that what you think? That our future depends on one drug?"

Seide's hands trembled, and he avoided the Archtrope's stare.

The Archtrope smirked and clapped him on the shoulder. "Anything else?"

"Our agents on LeHavre are warning about preparation of a dossier tracking DNA markers through the organ supply chain. It proves the Pious Sisters and the Saviors Corporation illegally accepted organs from missing persons."

The Archtrope sneered. "Echoes from long ago in my wicked, wicked past. Before Kelton perfected the DNA masking." He studied Seide. "Don't be concerned, Edward. It's too late to push that old story. We control too much of the market and the media to be impugned. The 'rich and powerful' depend on our organs and will not let us falter. The demand is too high from those who want to live a few more months or to save their loved ones. States and stations will fall before they shut my organ pipeline."

"The polls say your customers prefer cloned organs."

"Not if they have to wait a decade for them to mature. Kelton hasn't figured out that piece yet or how to deliver at the volumes we need."

"But using the conflict organs from Seiyei and—"

"Nonsense. Our customers don't care one bit where their precious body parts come from. They only care that the organs can't be traced and embarrass them in public." He frowned. "Do we know the source of this new dossier?"

"Not yet."

A young woman in a priest's robes entered and bowed. "Your Eminence, General Khanag is here to see you."

Seide raised his eyebrows. "He's not visited since his son's death?"

The Archtrope shook his head. "I advised him not to." He glanced at Seide. "Find the source and distribution for the dossier, Edward," he said and waved Seide from the room.

A moment later, General Khanag entered and, with bowed head, kneeled before the Archtrope.

"Thank you for coming, Subedei. We've missed you here. What brings you in person?"

"I've come to request last rites for my son," Khanag said. "His crew and Isolde have—"

"We've spoken of this before, Mouse. The Hope terrorists executed them on the *Tiger* without trial and made that impossible."

"I understand, Your Eminence," he said. "But perhaps an exception—"

"Until our enemies are vanquished, we must be content with our private rites." He placed his hand on Khanag's shoulder. "Come with me, Subedei."

The Archtrope led him to an adjoining room where a single flame hovered in midair. Along the alabaster walls, the light reflected off niches holding jasper urns and golden plaques.

"This room immortalizes those most favored in my eyes. It is where I meditate upon those who have given their utmost in our service, but whose heroism I cannot declare in public."

He led Khanag to an alcove with an urn. Inset beside it was a picture and an inscription: Captain Nurendra Khanag.

The general kneeled and lowered his head once more. "Thank you for this honor, Your Eminence."

The Archtrope handed him a golden box engraved with ornate filigree. "Within are psalms the choir sings every day in our private services to guide your son's heavenly journey." He narrowed his eyes over a sly smile. "I included the documentation on your mission to board the *Princess* a decade ago that saved Calliope from invasion. And your son's mission on the *Tiger* to end the Hope family's reign of terror. She's a bad seed and her kind needs to be extinguished from the galaxy or there can be no peace for the faithful."

Khanag's jaw tightened, and his lips narrowed.

"Rise," the Archtrope said and gripped Khanag's shoulder. "You must control your passions now. We need the Hope woman to speed up our plans for Haven. Then we will scatter their bodies through the universe to further our cause. When our enemies are vanquished, I will open this room to the righteous and they will praise your son the way we do. That time is near, Mouse. But be patient. Until then, other villains afflict us and must be dealt with."

Khanag bowed. "My fleet is eager to return to service."

"Smugglers and black marketers are plaguing the organ deliveries to Chosho from the Pious Sisters. Offer them eternal life and worship with them as brothers."

"And if they decline?"

"Their lives should be like those of all insects. Short."

"Your will be done," the general said and bowed again.

"You are one of my chosen, General. And you will not disappoint me."

"Yes, My Lord," he said, turned, and tapped his link. "Coming aboard, XO. And maintain silent running until our mission is over."

After Khanag left, the Archtrope signaled for Seide to return and raised a hand, into which a scantily clad concubine put a drink.

"Khanag's son's body still rests in the LeHavre morgue," Seide said.

"Yes, with the other corsairs from the *Tiger*."

"We need them gone before the coroner's report and other evidence is released. It will be more difficult to guide the narrative after that. You've arranged for their disposal?"

"Of course," the Archtrope said.

"That may challenge your relationship with him."

"Only one thing would, and your children's lives depend on that remaining our little secret."

"I thought the general would retire after the death of his son on the *Tiger*."

"Yes, it hit him hard. He blames himself for underestimating the Hope sisters." His sly grin reappeared. "I have harnessed his hatred for them, and he will not rest while Ms. Hope lives."

"She's a dangerous wild card."

"And I will play it to our advantage. But see that he doesn't touch her yet. I need her for a bit longer." He rubbed his hands together. "Now, for some fun."

He lounged on the couch to watch as his newest worshippers burned their most precious possessions, at least those his priests had not already confiscated. With a snap of his fingers, six more concubines entered with trays filled with bowls, platters, and decanters of Earth delicacies unavailable outside Sol system.

Seide cleared his throat. "Your Eminence, you've set Khanag on the hunt for ships of the Cephus League. They're the ones carrying those organs to Chosho, and they're all honest merchants."

"Those organs will go to the deserving, to the gifted who will now have the years they need to fulfill our plans."

"But the organs are going to the rich, not the gifted."

"God has gifted them their bounty." The Archtrope smirked. "And they are simply sharing it with us to help grow our flock."

"Many call that immoral."

"Bah. Morality changes with fashion. What is corrupt in most of the galaxy is now legal on Etna."

"And you had a hand in that," Seide said under his breath.

"Who are we to say something is immoral when it's legal? And my organ business will not be corrupt when the UNE legitimizes it."

"But—"

The Archtrope waved his hand. "No one cares, Edward. The donors won't be missed."

Seide stared at the floor. "Sarajevo will cause immense collateral damage. The sector may not recover."

"Which will be great for business, Ed," he said with a sneer and closed his fist. "And it will bring Haven within our grasp again."

Chapter 7
Enterprise Station, Procyon A System

Enterprise Station—Inbound

A jolt of stimulant woke Captain Stark when UNE Destroyer *Intrepid* winked into the Procyon System from hyperspace. Familiar with jump disorientation, he rose from his sleep net as consciousness slowly returned.

"Pilot, report."

"Sir. Inbound to Enterprise at 1.6g. Dock secure. ETA 1422 local time."

"Comm?"

"Sync complete, Sir. Status green-3, calm as a muffin. Ambassador Bakshi wants a word."

"Acknowledged," Stark said. "XO please join me in my ready room in ten."

The captain dressed quickly, and after a brush of his pragmatic crew cut, entered the adjoining cabin a step ahead of his executive officer.

He sat at the conference table where a blue dot blinked, but his XO remained standing. A compact woman with steel-blue eyes, his XO never sat on duty, aware her compact frame unconsciously diminished her authority, especially in a chair.

"Bakshi wants a chat," Stark said. "Speculations?"

"I think we still need an explanation for the sudden diversion to Enterprise, sir."

"Orders. We're ferrying a high-ranking diplomat to a UNE negotiation."

"This is a destroyer, sir. He could have taken a packet boat to get here sooner or a luxury yacht for comfort." She leaned over with her hands on the table. "Permission to speak freely, Captain."

"Granted."

"I think we're here to imply pressure during his negotiations."

"It's a peaceful mission."

"Yes, sir. But this is a heavily armed warship."

"Why would he need our muscle?"

"Perhaps he will propose a trade agreement the station doesn't want."

"I'm sure Ambassador Bakshi has many other assets with which to negotiate," Stark said.

"I disagree, sir. Not out here. And why did Bakshi bring his own UNE Security Force?"

Stark nodded. "The USF are the ambassador's honor guard. Did Major Glinnik double the sentries at the small arms locker?"

"Yes, sir."

"Please stay while I speak with the ambassador." Stark tapped the blinking blue dot. "Mister Ambassador, you called?"

The holo of an overweight white-haired man with narrow eyes appeared in the chair next to him. "About time, Captain. Any reason for not getting back to me sooner?"

"Ship's business, Mister Ambassador. I'm sure you understand."

"Yes, yes, of course. My staff and I thank you for a comfortable journey, Captain. We are well rested and have enjoyed traveling with you. Did we make good time?"

The captain glanced at the flight data summary on the active wall. "Excellent time, sir. We should dock in approximately seven hours."

"That's early, isn't it?"

"Yes, sir.

"Captain, I have arrangements on Enterprise I can't change." He raised his nose. "There are formalities and ceremonies we must observe. You understand, of course. They are not expecting me until 1500, and protocol demands—"

"I'll delay our arrival until 1500."

"Well, thank you, Captain. I'll put in a word—"

"Will that be all, Mister Ambassador?"

"Yes."

Stark tapped the desk to break the connection and the blue light dimmed.

"Why is he delaying our arrival?" the XO asked.

Enterprise Station—On Station

In his laboratory on station, surrounded by a sea of monitors, server racks, and cloning tanks, Nickolai Zanek listened to a holovid from Meriel.

"They still won't let me board the *Princess,*" Meriel said. "Jeremy mentioned there's another roadblock in Court-5. Once I have custody of the ship, I'm figuring to bring it here to LeHavre so I can supervise the repairs."

Nick spun on two wheels of his tricked-out wheelchair and checked his consoles. Jeremy Bell had a small practice with a private client list and had taken Meriel's case pro bono years ago.

"Insert," he said. Parsecs distant, they could not have a real-time conversation, but his apps made it seem that way. "It'll cost you a fortune to drag the *Princess* ten light-years. Besides, Enterprise has better dry docks, and they're cheaper. And I can find trustworthy contractors for you here. Continue."

"I'll be on the *Tiger's* next tour, so keep your calendar open," Meriel said and then leaned toward the camera. "Be careful. I think the bad guys are hatching something new."

"They're always hatching—"

A ping alerted Nick to two guests entering the corporate offices of Enterprise Cyber Security, the shell company that maintained his anonymity. At the desk on the deck above his lab, his android secretary switched itself on, straightened its tie, and squared its shoulders. Nick switched on the quantum tomography scanner and other sensors and then leaned back to observe the interaction.

"Good afternoon," the android said with a smile. "And welcome to ECS. You can refer to me as Mr. Stenopolis. How can we help you?"

"Good afternoon," the portly man said, squinted, and leaned forward. "Pardon me, are you an android?"

Stenopolis kept his smile. "I prefer to think of myself as an enhanced life form."

"No offense, but is your owner available?"

Nick furrowed his brow. *And why does he want to speak to me specifically? Business types expect pre-screening.*

"I'm sorry," Stenopolis said. "He's unavailable at the moment. I will handle the first phase of your inquiry, sir."

The man frowned.

Stenopolis raised an eyebrow. "I have other duties, Mister . . ."

"Ansone. And my associate here is Ms. Jenick."

At his side sat a woman with brown hair and glasses perched on an odd nose, and a link-bud that blinked behind her ear.

Nick's console beeped with the first reports from his surveillance monitors.

```
No biometric data available. Sub-
jects are actively scanning.
```

"Countermeasures?"

```
Countermeasure summary: conductive
body suits, EM filters, makeup
```

Body suits will mask the pulse and blood pressure. Business types don't need that.

"Sten," Nick said. "Amp the sensitivity until we defeat their countermeasures, or we can't work with them."

The console beeped as Nick's sensors scanned the eyes and voices of his guests and combined those with the blood pressure and pulse sensors built into their chairs.

```
Stress analysis indicates Ansone and
Jenick are aliases.
```

Hmm, slight blood pressure rise, but pulse even: phony names, but they're comfortable with them.

"My associates have recommended ECS highly," Ansone said. "We hope that—"

"Who, specifically?"

Nick checked the console for the QT scans that penetrated their disguises. A body suit added forty pounds to the male, and makeup covered a scar over his left eye. The woman wore colored contacts over violet eyes, and a prosthetic that hid a Greek nose.

"What?" Ansone asked.

"Which of your associates recommended us?" Stenopolis asked.

Nick's instruments focused on Ansone's hand to highlight a twitch in one of his little fingers. *Rejuve poisoning? How many years has the guy got before it fries his brain?*

"We aren't at liberty to say," Ansone said. "But we've performed our due diligence."

Nick's console blinked green. *He's telling the truth. But who recommended me?*

The sniffer in Ansone's chair finished its analysis of his exhalations:

```
Drugs below detection. Animal pro-
tein for lunch, not soy.
```

Rich folks, these.

"Your contact information is public domain," Ansone continued. "And you aren't hard to reach."

The android smiled. "Just hard to work with."

Ansone laughed. "They said that too. We wish to engage your expertise in encrypted monitoring systems."

Nick's console flashed green again.

"Yes, we pride ourselves in—"

"And we need the data to travel through existing infrastructure."

Where did they hear I can do that? "Pursue this question," he told the android.

"To monitor what specifically?" Stenopolis asked.

"You understand we can't disclose everything."

"We register all our work with an independent auditor," Stenopolis said. "If ECS suspects any ... questionable activity, we must alert the police."

"Yes, of course. Please have no concerns in that regard."

"I ask again, to monitor what?"

Well done, Sten. Nick smiled, proud Sten had them interacting as if he were an actual person.

"A ship in dock. We plan to renovate it as a gift to the owner. An anniversary surprise. Before we begin, we need to know if someone is monitoring us."

Nick's console flashed a second after Ansone finished speaking.

```
Speech analysis: Clandestine. Proba-
bility of illegal intent 85%.
```

Nick nodded. "Or maybe a security sting. Let's check, Sten. Delay for six weeks."

"Apologies, Mr. Ansone," the android said. "But our firm is booked for the next six weeks. Let's schedule a preliminary requirements meeting then."

"That won't work for us," Ansone replied. "We must start rather soon to assure our surprise isn't discovered."

The console beeped:

```
Time pressure. Negotiation Tactic 1.
Expect financial incentive. Counter-
ing.
```

"We're exceedingly sorry, but we cannot reschedule our current clients," Stenopolis said.

"We can make it worth your while to change your priorities. Our client is quite wealthy."

```
Implied threat. Expect intimidation.
Danger, Will Robinson.
```

Illegal and powerful. What will they threaten me with?

The android frowned. "Again, we're sorry, but ECS is contractually obliged to keep our scheduled commitments. You wouldn't want us to jeopardize a promise to you, now, would you?"

"Excuse me," Ms. Jenick said. "Our associates implied your business might not survive close legal scrutiny. Perhaps if we notified—"

The console blinked red.

```
Concrete threat. Possibility of
sting 10%.
Recommended response: Feign moral
outrage and defend against charges of
unethical behavior.
```

"Proceed," Nick said.

The android sat up straight and raised his eyebrows. "Ms. Jenick, I assure you our work will withstand legal review. You might ask the same of your client."

Pandora's Razor

```
Decision: Decline or Accept. Decline
recommended.
```

Ansone leaned forward. "My associate didn't mean to impugn—"

"Confirm decline," Nick said to the android. "And disengage."

Stenopolis put his palms flat on the desk. "Mr. Ansone, Ms. Jenick, with that I must conclude our business. Thank you for the opportunity, but we must decline your offer. Good day."

Stenopolis closed its eyes, but Nick continued to monitor his guests. They remained seated, banging the intercom on the desk for attention and waving in front of Stenopolis. After a few minutes without response, Ansone nodded to Jenick, and they left.

Nick's console chirped.

```
How'd I do?
```

"Well done, Sten," Nick said to encourage the android's self-learning AI. "Please run the scans of Ansone and Jenick through the facial recognition program and search the net for a match. We should know who these people are."

```
On it, Nick.
```

He closed the office and spun in his chair while doodling q-chip architectures in the air.

```
Do you know what they wanted?
```

"I think so. They want to tamper with a ship on the impound docks."

```
Why?
```

"I don't know. And why the hurry? I'll bet there's only one vessel whose legal status is scheduled to change within the next six weeks."

```
Yes. LSM Liu Yang GCN 14993:026
```

"That's Meriel's ship in disguise." He rocked back and balanced on two wheels. "What do criminals want with the *Princess*?"

***

Five hours later, Stenopolis interrupted Nick's upper body workout. "Nick, the recent clips of the *Princess* are complete."

"Results?" Nick said and grabbed a towel.

"The aft-lateral impound dock monitor had an anomaly."

"Show me."

On the wall, the android displayed a vid of the dock camera in which a shuttle without running lights drifted past. It did not land near the M22 dock or the *Princess*, hidden in plain sight as the *Liu Yang*. But a light flickered from the shuttle, and a few seconds later, a flash replied from a cargo bay porthole.

"Well now, that shouldn't happen. Rewind. Repeat frame by frame."

The review confirmed the flashes weren't reflections and nothing appeared on the hull or through the dark windows when he zoomed the vid.

"Sten, start recording. If a crime is in progress, I need to cover my ass."

"Creating record," Stenopolis said. "Title Decline of Ansone Contract. Subtitle Irregularities regarding *Liu Yang*. Entry. Time stamp. All channels. Audio."

"The *Princess* should be sleeping. Sweep all real-time EM emissions, Sten."

Monitors lit-up with waveforms of radiation spectrum, but only one was active.

"That's a surveillance spider, Nick."

"You little rascal," Nick mumbled. "You're illegal." *Are you the same one that almost caught Meriel during her visit?* "And why are you still there? Tap the video feed, Sten, and let's have a look."

Stenopolis projected the spider's camera on the wall and four views appeared.

"Cut the UV and IR. Visual and sound only."

Nick followed the droid through its rounds, past natural wood banisters and compartment doors even prettier than Meriel's stories. And on the walls, children's drawings and crafts hung, the remains of Meriel's childhood. *No wonder she loves it.*

Turning a corner, the droid passed an open door with a brownish blotch extending into the passageway. The spider's camera poked inside the room, exposing a stain that covered the deck and splashed on the walls.

"This must be the infirmary, where the passengers and crew were tortured and killed," Nick said. *But not Merial and the orphans.* "Note. Not paint but dried blood." *She must have relived the whole nightmare when she visited. But she never complained. Her hands shook and tears tracked her bloodless cheeks when she returned, but she was smiling at the success of her mission.*

At the hold, the droid passed two men wiring a small box to a line of translucent barrels. But it continued its rounds, and Nick lost his view.

The spider was his only means to find out what was going on. But hijacking it was unlikely: spiders were top secret, and their code was closely held proprietary data. But a long shot was better than none.

"Sorry, little buddy," Nick said. "Looks like I'm gonna need to yank your leash a tad."

"Are you referring to me, Nick?"

"No, Sten. But learn what I'm doing."

The spider jerked and resisted when he hacked the root control, fighting his remote input. As soon as he was in, Nick isolated its service request and alert system to make sure it could not call for help. The spider's intruder prevention was unhackable, so instead he sent it on a chase for errant code. In the struggle, the spider lost its magnetic grip on the deck, tucked its spindly legs near its body, and floated into the ship's passageway.

"Sten, decompile the command code and dump its memory before it completely flakes on us."

Searching for the motor controls, Nick picked through the code and found its primary function: self-defense. Beyond that, icons and acronyms scrolled: darts, tasers, bolas, nets, blades, and injectables from tranquilizers to neurotoxins. As menacing as their insectile shape appeared, the actuality was far more dangerous.

"Ah, here it is. Surveillance." Icons for probes appeared, and he isolated those for a camera and microphone within the visual and aural frequency range for humans.

"Now how do I move it?" he mumbled aloud and isolated the controls for the maglocks and legs. Fighting its programming, Nick forced the spider to walk, but controlled by a human with no experience with two legs much less eight, the spider twitched and turned in circles.

"Agh!" Nick said and banged the console.

"You appear to be struggling, Nick," Stenopolis said. "Can I help you?"

Nick gave the monitor a side-eye, leaned away from the console and cracked his knuckles. After connecting a second three-axis controller, he folded four of the spider's legs to its side. With the remaining four, the spider stumbled back to the cargo hold and snaked a camera probe around the bulkhead door into the cargo hold where the two men worked.

"So, what's in these?" the small nervous one asked.

"Organics," the stocky one said, his bald head shimmering with sweat. "Nothing fancy.

"What about the triggers?"

The bald man wiped his hands on his pants. "Dead for now. A failsafe. We have an hour to get off the ship before the remote activates." He stopped. "Where's the security spider?"

"On its rounds, I guess."

Nick withdrew the probe from their sight.

"You imbecile. I told you to bring it."

"I'm not touching a spider. It's got needles all over it."

"Leave it," the bald man said. "No one will recognize the pieces. C'mon, let's go."

Pieces?

Nick directed the camera probe back inside, but the droid's intruder defenses finally overcame Nick's hack. The spider twitched again, and the video blacked out.

"Crap," Nick said and scanned the diagnostics. "Oh no you don't, little buddy. You're not committing suicide while I've got you."

He boosted his signal to regain control, and when the video feed returned, the men were gone. With the droid alone now, Nick walked it to the barrels.

Each translucent barrel was divided into two sections, one an opalescent white and the other a dull orange. Outside each barrel at the division was a small box.

Detonators! he thought and tapped an encrypted text to Meriel.

```
They're trying to blow her up. No
time.
```

Nick locked the spider's legs and stared at the barrels. *An explosion on the* Princess *would be bad.*

"How stupid are these guys?" Nick mumbled. "If this goes off, they may not clear the area in time. Sten, if that's an explosive in the barrel, what could it be?"

"Insufficient information, Nick. But the volume is approximately one hundred gallons."

"The guy said 'organics.' Make a guess."

"ANFO powder."

"Simulate explosion on Liu Yang, dock M22," Nick said. "Execute."

A visualization showed the blast with debris peppering Enterprise like a shotgun.

"Damage estimate?"

"Thirty-thousand casualties from initial depressurizations. Station wobble will require evacuating another hundred thousand. Repairs completed in one year."

"Evacuate?" Nick said. "Where would we all go? Is Enterprise the actual target?"

"I can't answer that, but I could analyze it for you."

"Later maybe. Any mitigations?"

"Liu Yang is in the shadow of *Helmut's Inferno*. That will shield Enterprise from debris."

"Simulate."

The new visualization showed the bigger ship receiving much of the debris intended for the station.

"Damage estimate?" Nick asked again.

"Approximately one-thousand casualties from depressurization. Station stabilized within fifty minutes and will remain habitable. Repairs completed within one month."

The spider's video feed quit again.

"You little rascal," he said and boosted his signal but could not regain control. "I need to hijack a stronger transmitter."

"Based on Enterprise rotation, the closest transmitter is near the red-zone security wharf that services the impound docks and the *Princess*."

"I can't hack that from here."

"No, Nick. But there's an IT cabinet nearby."

He leaned back. "I'll have to get closer." And that was a problem. He'd been hiding for more than a decade and would not voluntarily reveal his location now. But he had no choice.

He frowned in a mirror and tamed his wild black hair with a thick gel. To attenuate his biotag signal, Nick slipped on a shirt of woven bucky tubes. Then he pressed the old scar on his wrist until it flashed blue to activate his phony tag: the same hack he used to get Meriel past security and onto *the Princess* a few months before.

He threw two six-axis controllers and a head-up IO console into his saddlebags and then wheeled to the garage and ECS's custom transit pod. After programming his destination, the pod merged into a stream of other pods and jostled for position. As his pod negotiated its place, he sent an anonymous message to station security.

```
Possible terrorist threat, dock M22.
```

In the event someone might question him, he logged a complaint from a retailer to give him an excuse for his mission.

Nick's pod parked itself near the red-zone wharf closest to the *Princess* and unlocked his chair. Freed, he wheeled himself to a tiny network cabinet outside the secure area and wedged his chair inside.

With a fiber tap, he piggybacked on a secure channel which would keep him hidden unless he energized a security function. Then he synced his console to record his actions.

Before contacting the spider, he checked the security feeds and found they had not initiated an alert. *Sure, they would investigate my call first. But not even a warning?*

Nick scanned for the spider's EM signal again and found it staggering back to its normal sweep. After a few taps on his console, he reasserted control, and returned it to the barrels. Connecting one of the spider's probes to the control module, he captured the outputs.

He could read only two pinouts: a two-state line with zero, one, and a timer that decoded to 38:43 and counting down. He connected another probe and dumped the code from the detonator module.

"Override, where are you," he mumbled as he scanned the decompiled code, which soon became obscured with the hash symbols of encryption.

The onboard AI expected something delicate. But it won't expect a crowbar.

Through the probes, he fed the control module a virus and then a root kit with his own AI. Lines of unencrypted code appeared, but no login or override. And the clock continued to count down. It was a game his AI would win, but not in time.

I need to go downstream.

Each of the barrels had a trigger module networked to the control module with optical fiber.

"Old school," he mumbled and tapped the signal. *Only fed a repeated binary zero and one. Presence: can't interrupt this or it might detonate.*

With the droid's probes, he opened the nearest trigger module. It was hard-wired to a chip and enclosed in a plastaglass slab he could not get into without equipment he had left in his lab. And without access to the chip, he could not recode the logic. But only two wires led into the barrel.

Wow, all that fancy triggering and only two leads. Have to do this the hard way. With the second controller, he maneuvered the spider's probe, gripped a lead, and tugged. *Careful now, careful . . .*

"Network problem?" came a woman's voice behind him.

Startled, Nick flinched, causing the spider to yank the lead free, and he cringed. Instead of the flash of an explosion, he caught the reflection of a policewoman in vest and cap standing behind him.

"Uh, network issue, yup." Nick turned his head to her. "Officer . . .?"

"Gentri," she said and scanned his phony biotag. "Show me."

"Yes, ma'am," he said and displayed the bogus work order on the wall of the cabinet. "The IT tunnel by B33. A glitch is causing the tram to skip a stop. Just annoying the hell outta the retailers."

Gentri tapped her wrist, and the visor of her helmet flashed green. "Interesting ride you got," she said absently as she read the work order.

I don't have time for this distraction. "You got something against people with enhancements?

"Jeez, no."

He returned to his work, but she did not move. "Something wrong?" he asked.

"The desk sergeant noticed you're working near red-zone."

"This is the closest hub."

"You ever eat in that neighborhood?" she asked with narrowed eyes.

Nick guessed the question was to verify the work order. "Only Rhee's. I like their kimchi."

On his head-up display, the timer continued to count down. *Gotta end this.* "Hey, it's just a job."

She smiled as if recognizing him as human for the first time.

"Say, you hear anything about a security alert?" he said and pulled another lead wire.

"You're not supposed to scan the secure feeds."

Nick moved the droid to another trigger module. "Come on. Competition is cutthroat. I need an edge."

"We haven't had an alert since the UNE Navy scheduled Fleet Week here," she said and checked her link. "No. Nothing got past dispatch."

They ignored my call. Why?

Should I tell her? No, they'll just arrest me. And the bomb will explode while I sit in restraints right over there in redzone.

When Nick did not continue the conversation, she nodded and backed away.

"Well, good luck," she said and returned to her security pod.

"Yup."

Twelve minutes left, the timer read.

Five barrels to defuse and twelve minutes left. That's two minutes to defuse each barrel, but I'm taking three. I won't make it.

If the triggers detonated as soon as the timer ran down to zero, he would not have enough time. He sent another anonymous alert, priority one this time:

```
Confirmed   security   breach.   M22
dock.
```

Moving the spider to the next barrel, he jerked the wire free.

"Nick," Sten said. "Sorry to disturb you. I recorded a macro and can run it on other pairs of the spider's limbs."

"Thanks, Sten. That will give me four minutes for the last barrel. Plenty of time."

But as Nick moved the droid to the last trigger, he lost all signal but the video feed. The droid was catatonic, and his controls would not wake it, even after boosting the signal.

It committed suicide. "Oh, crap." *What's security doing with my alerts? Gotta tell her now.*

"Officer Gentri!" he shouted over his shoulder, but she was out of sight.

"Damn, damn, damn." *No time.* He hacked into the security server and tripped the Red Alert. *I'm gonna leave fingerprints all over this.* He hit the button. *There goes my anonymity.*

The station lighting dimmed, and red emergency lights flashed.

"All personnel to their designated safe harbor," blared the annunciators. Groans and shudders pulsed through the bulkheads as the blast doors closed. In nearby red-zone, officers froze, unprepared for a real vacuum breach alarm, and then ran to the station-side of the doors.

Nick stared through the spider's frozen eyes as the membrane opened and colored organics mixed in iridescent swirls.

"Crap," he said and crossed his fingers as the signal reached zero.

Maybe it won't . . .

A brief flash outside the red-zone window lit up the IT cabinet.

"Damn," he said. "Hey, Sten. You still recording?"

"Yes, Nick. You almost saved your friend's ship."

"Almost. But at least Enterprise is safe. Log the time, Sten, 1425."

Nick sighed and turned to face the red-zone windows as Enterprise's rotation brought the impound docks into view, but the muzzle of Gentri's stunner blocked it.

"Hands on your head," she said.

A second, brighter flash forced them to cover their eyes. When his vision cleared, he glanced past the officer's weapon to the window as a large section of jump fan spun toward them.

"Better hold on to something," he said as the debris sliced through the docks and opened red zone to vacuum.

Enterprise Station—Inbound

On final approach to Enterprise, *Intrepid's* communications officer interrupted Captain Stark's update to the ship's log.

"Begging your pardon, sir, but we have a security alarm on Enterprise."

"Where?"

"The impound dock, sir."

Before the comm officer could say more, a flash lit the room for a microsecond before the window's EM filter attenuated the radiation.

"Confirming the alarm, sir. Apparent explosion on dock that—"

"Officer of the Deck," Stark said. "Call General Quarters."

The claxon announced Battle Stations and the watch officer responded. "Aye, sir."

"Contact Enterprise Station and get an—"

A larger explosion flashed near the first, and when the window cleared again, he viewed rubble from the explosion fly toward Enterprise and shear off a hundred-foot chord of the torus. From the hole drifted debris that included bodies caught on the wrong side of the blast doors.

The watch officer's voice shouted over the comm. "Pilot, full astern. Gunnery Officer!"

"Sir!"

"Vaporize any wreckage heading our way."

"Aye, sir."

"Comm," Stark said. "Alert Major Glinnik to scan for hostiles and send the XO to me. And wake Doc Orocho to scramble sick bay. Put him in touch with Enterprise Emergency Services and offer our help."

"Aye, sir."

"And get me a damage report on Enterprise," he said as debris targets sparkled outside the window.

"Aye, sir." The blue light blinked on Stark's console again. "Sir, Ambassador Bakshi is requesting a word."

Stark scowled and tapped the light. "Yes, Mister Ambassador?"

"Captain, you've heard the news?"

"Yes, sir."

"A cowardly act of terrorism has damaged Enterprise," Bakshi said. "She is one of Sol's few friends out here in the boonies and we must assist."

When the XO entered, the captain put a finger to his lips. "Humanitarian assistance will be—"

Bakshi interrupted. "Oh, no, Captain. The Assembly of Citizens on Enterprise has invoked the Aldebaran Accord. We're obliged by the Accord to serve and protect them as if they were in Sol System. You understand what this means, Captain? Military command is transferred to civilian authority."

Stark frowned. "I beg your pardon. This is a military vessel, and we report to UNE High Command."

Bakshi chuckled. "I will grant you a few minutes to review the Accord and your orders, Captain."

The blue light dimmed, and the captain cut the connection. On the wall, he pulled up his orders and next to him, the XO displayed a copy of the accord.

"Here," the XO said. "'Article 9. Invocation of this Accord places priority of security support and investigation immediately below security of Earth and Sol itself. Until direct orders from ComSec arrive, military resources in proximity to signatories are under command of the highest-ranking UNE diplomatic personnel above G-18.'" She flipped to the end. "The signatories include the UNE and Enterprise."

"And here," Stark said. "Mission Order 36. 'Ambassador on board will represent the UNE in all matters of galactic trade and mutual security.'"

"Bakshi is G-20."

"'Military resources.' We've been translated into bureaucratic double talk. Do the Marines report directly to Bakshi now?"

"No," the XO said. "The chain of command under you doesn't change. Except you now report to the ambassador."

"You know anyone on station?"

"Yes, sir. Admiral Morrell, the Security TechMaster."

"Find out who's running the investigation," Stark said. "Discretely. And keep the USF away from C&C."

"This is convenient. Ninety seconds after an attack on Enterprise, a ranking diplomat has commandeered a UNE destroyer."

"What does Bakshi plan to do with a warship?"

The XO narrowed her eyes. "We might thank him."

"And why's that?"

"If he'd not delayed our arrival, we could have been part of the debris."

Enterprise Station—On Station

The explosion removed a quarter of the *Princess,* from cargo-2 to the engines. *Helmut's Inferno,* docked alongside, shielded Enterprise from the blast.

But the shrapnel ripped into the larger vessel and lit up the ship's volatile organics tanks which stored biomaterials for the organ trade. The aft jump fans tore free and spun toward the station, slicing like saw blades through red-zone and opening it to space. Equipment spilled from the offices and corridors through the gaping hull followed by security personnel who would die within seconds.

The IT cabinet was too small for Nick and Gentri both, so the policewoman ran to her patrol pod and climbed inside. But the escaping air pulled the vehicle toward the gash in the hull and vacuum. The closing blast door stopped the plastisteel pod, but it wedged itself in before the door sealed airtight leaving a gap three feet tall and fifty feet wide.

Other debris and people now flowed from nearby blue-zone through the gap and out into open space. If the blast door did not close in a few seconds, the entire arc of the torus would depressurize along with everyone in it, including the policewoman and Nick.

"No, no," he mumbled, struggling to reach behind him and close the IT cabinet door. For more mobility, he unbuckled himself from his chair, twisted around, and slid it shut. But the air within now screeched past the door seals and out to vacuum.

Before he could buckle himself back in, the station wobbled, and the deck bucked as the missing mass altered Enterprise's angular momentum. Maglocks on his chair gripped the deck to protect him, but without the safety belt, he floated weightless. A few seconds later, the station's stabilizers compensated, bounced him against the wall like a rag doll, and slammed him back into his chair.

After righting himself and buckling his belt, he recovered his security hack, and increased the hydraulics on the blast doors. When the pod's frame finally buckled, the window popped free and Officer Gentri escaped as the doors closed to within a millimeter, and rubble filled the remaining gap.

Two of those pieces of rubble were the warped IT cabinet door and Nick's wheelchair.

Chapter 8
Jira-1 System

Haven—Stewardville Shuttle Port

At dawn, as Jira-1 peeked over the edge of Thor, Meriel walked through the shuttle port cafeteria line ahead of the *Tiger's* XO, Molly Vingel. They had just finished screening potential gunnery mates and stayed for breakfast before the ride up to LeHavre.

A slender brunette with a spacer's short hair, Molly glanced over her fork at Meriel. "What's your assessment of the interviewees?"

"I think they're twitchy and will shoot first, ma'am," Meriel said.

"Right. And that's the wrong response for a merchant ship." Molly raised an eyebrow after a bite of mashed potatoes. "Damn! What do they put in this stuff?"

"Nothing. It's fresh food from the farms nearby."

Meriel had the same reaction to her first meal on the surface. Station food was all made of a soy-mush blend grown in the hydroponic and aeroponics tanks. Nutrition Techs combined that with artificial flavors, colors, and indigestible fiber to simulate the diet on Earth.

But food on Haven was extraordinary: meat had an emotional punch; breads had a yeasty smell rather than injected air in zero-g ovens. But the taste of fruit and vegetables was unknown to spacers.

They moved to the next station where Molly stuck a fork in a red ball. She took a bite and raised her eyebrows. "It bites back. What's this?"

"That's a radish."

"So, this is what we've been missing?"

"Yes. Even in white-zone, they can't afford to eat like this often."

They found a table, and Molly dug into her meal.

"I'd recommend you lighten up on the sausage," Meriel said. "The fat can upset your stomach and you won't fit into your uniform tomorrow." She softened her voice. "Have you considered my offer?"

"Our contracts have two more years, M. Richard and I have plenty of time to think about jumping ship for the *Princess*. So do you. Have you asked anyone else?"

Meriel blushed. "I'd rather have you."

"So, they dismissed your offer?"

"They decline when I say I want to work crew."

Molly nodded. "Confuses the chain of command to have an owner on board, but that's what you've asked us to do."

"I trust you, XO. And you know I obey orders."

Molly paused mid-bite and eyed her.

"Well, mostly."

"Your family doesn't have the ratings to work the ship without outside help yet."

Meriel set her jaw. "I'm gonna do this. I just want you to be a part of it."

"If Richard and I leave the *Tiger*, Jerri and Socket might want to join your new venture too. You might make them an offer."

Their links beeped with the boarding alert, and they rose and slipped their trays into the recycler.

Waiting at the security checkpoint, Meriel brought up another subject. "Ma'am, permission to bring Sandy along on the next circuit?"

"The *Tiger* isn't a cruise ship, Chief. If you're gonna crew, you'll need a babysitter and pay her fare."

"I'm thinking she'll work," Meriel said.

"We don't need cabin boys."

"Cargo trainee."

"Get her a zero-cert and log some hours in null-g and we'll talk about it."

"Yes, ma'am. And Elizabeth wants to sit bridge. Her ship won't pick her up, and she's bored here dirtside. She has certs for Manager-3, Exec-2, and Nav-2."

"Communications?"

Meriel frowned. "Comm-1."

"She could shadow Socket. Or we could ferry Liz to one of the *Thompson's* stops." Molly tapped the link on her lapel and a holo of a packing list from GNI appeared on the table. "Say, you know anything about this?"

"Teddy sent it."

"Who?"

"Theodora Duncan."

"The 'Where's Teddy' Teddy? The 'Zen of Nav' Teddy?"

"Yup," Meriel said. "She designed the *Tiger's* new nav system they installed at LeHavre."

"She's Galactic Navigation?"

"Yeah, that's her."

"Damn. For someone so influential, we don't know much about her."

"She likes her privacy," Meriel said. "I'll bet that's a nav upgrade."

"It's solid, M. What's she gonna improve?"

Meriel smiled as they entered the shuttle airlock. "Wait and see. Maybe it has fire control for the *Tiger's* new laser cannon, and we won't need a gunnery mate."

LeHavre Station—On Station

The shuttle ride to LeHavre was short but bumpy and without windows to distract them from the noise and vibration.

Exiting the airlock, Meriel ran her fingers along passageways formed from aerogels stuffed into expanded glass welded to bucky-sheets, evidence the Techs cobbled the entire station from ships that carried them from Earth's L5 Lagrangian decades ago. Unlike Lander and Wolf, LeHavre's impoverished past did not embarrass them. This was how the Techs thought: maximize efficiency, minimize waste. It had to go somewhere, so why not use it?

Around her, information kiosks recited LeHavre's history for the entrepreneurs and ambitious who came for the opportunity, and the rare but rich tourists who could afford the trip.

Many of the residents who greeted the newcomers were the original cast-offs who had left Earth orbit for an unknown moon. And with them, they brought their biomedical genius and a century of innovation in sustainable living on the L5 space station.

They arrived twenty years ago, with fuel and resources exhausted. The most desperate left the safety of their ships to farm on the hostile surface of Haven and those who failed still huddled under the domes of Stewardville.

After saying goodbye to Molly on the shuttle dock, Meriel stopped at the large window.

"Liz can wait," she said and gazed outside with a clarity unavailable through Haven's thick and dusty atmosphere. Thor's massive blue-green arc was visible along with five of Haven's seven sister moons, but Haven's tiny submoons hid in shadow. And beyond them shone the stars.

On her eleventh birthday, Nick had snuck her onto Enterprise's white-zone agricultural deck. There, she touched a hundred-year-old redwood and soaked up the calming beauty of the grasslands and farms and forests found on Earth. But even that did not match her love of the stars.

As much as Meriel loved the farm, the stars would always be her home. LeHavre was space but not the stars. But before she could return, she needed to nail the interview to prove she was no Archer sympathizer.

***

Elizabeth nursed a beer in a quiet corner of the Iron Door, a spacer dive near the blue-zone docks known for its rough and anonymous patrons. Next to her was an open stool she'd reserved with another beer intended to loosen up Meriel before the interview with IGB.

Over the bar, Charlene Samuelson's tour of Calliope played, with Suzuki's response to her question.

```
Absurdities. Those claims are pre-
posterous slanders by infidels who
wish to impugn the good works of our
most revered leader. If any of his
followers are implicated in such
atrocities, we would support the
strongest of sanctions. We believers
are humanitarians and respect all
life . . .
```

Elizabeth considered throwing her drink at the display but yelled, "Turn that shit off," and curled her lip. As she turned away, her bracelet chimed with news about her cousins.

"Debrief, *Esperanza* crew. Status."

A tiny holo of a bust popped up on the bar with scrolled text.

```
Esperanza crew disbanded after bank-
ruptcy 2176—
```

"Skip to updates."

```
One update. Kaori Bhatt.
```

A station girl in a short skirt moved onto Meriel's empty seat and showed some extra leg to her prey. Without speaking, Elizabeth leaned her shoulder into the woman until she scowled and took her date to another corner.

Elizabeth rolled her eyes and took another swig of her drink. "Status. Kaori Bhatt."

```
Died of unknown cause. Seiyei clin-
ic.
```

Damn. Seiyei. Right in the middle of another immigration conflict. "Authority?"

```
Coroner. Biotag DNA profile match to
Pacific League crew records.
```

"Disposition?"

```
Cremation.
```

Right. Disposed of before anyone found out what killed her. "Who identified the body?"

```
No data.
```

No data. Another of their cousins had been sucked down the drain into the mining colonies or black-market enterprises and ended up fertilizer. It was a system where every bad choice left you with only worse choices, and the only difference was how fast you hit the bottom.

That could have happened to me and the orphans if Meriel had not found Haven.

A rough type pushed his way next to her and rested an elbow on the bar to plant his face a few inches from hers. A quick check of his insignia showed he was a cargo-2 from the LSM *Fitzgerald*.

"Hey gorgeous. You up for a sleepover?" He grinned, but his breath said he'd been here too long.

"You're smooth," she said without turning.

"I'm on temporary leave. Clock's ticking, babe."

She glanced at the adjoining seat he hogged and looked him square in the eye. "I'm saving that spot."

"For me, yeah, I know."

"You're new here? New route?"

"Uh, yeah."

"So, sailor. I'm saving that spot for someone *else,* and I'd like you to leave."

He didn't move, and when her link buzzed, she tapped her bracelet.

```
   Hey, Littlebit. Just out of customs.
 See you in three.
   M
```

The guy closed in. "Littlebit? What does that mean?"

Elizabeth took a sip. "A little bit of trouble."

He smiled. "Really? That's what I'm looking for," he said and leaned over.

When he grabbed her thigh, she put her drink down and dug her thumbnail into the base of his thumb until she found the pressure point. He relaxed his grip, and she twisted it, pulling him toward her and off balance. Grabbing his hair, she pulled his face down to meet her rising knee. His nose broke with a loud crack, and she pushed him away from the bar.

The hubbub silenced at the thud of his body on the deck and the patrons turned to her. When Elizabeth shrugged, they returned to their drinks and conversation.

***

Meriel entered the bar, stepped over the unconscious spacer, and took the empty seat. "You know him?"

"Nope." Elizabeth pointed a thumb to the full glass in front of Meriel. "That's yours," she said. "I heard Cousin Kaori died on Seiyei."

"From the *Esperanza*?" Meriel asked and Elizabeth nodded. "Cause?"

"Unknown."

"Any other kin surface?"

Elizabeth shook her head, and they toasted in silence.

"So, what did John think of you sending the dossier to Khanag?"

"I didn't tell him," Meriel said and stared at her drink.

Elizabeth raised an eyebrow. "Everything OK there?"

"I don't know, Liz. I feel like I'm just playing at family."

"You're still figuring it out. So, what's the issue?"

"Becky wants a mom, but Sandy doesn't. The only mom I know was ours, and she was there 24/7 on the *Princess*."

"While she could."

Meriel nodded and raised her glass. "I don't know any other life except space. They do."

"What does John say?"

"He wants me here, but I love it out there. I just want to get the *Princess* fixed as soon as I can."

"What's the hurry? You have a home here if you want it."

"I don't feel safe here, Liz. I want to bring them with me on the *Princess*. The girls want to come along, but John's settled in."

"M, that safe place you've been looking for since our folks were killed, it doesn't—"

"I know. It doesn't exist."

Elizabeth nodded. "The only safe space is the one we make."

Meriel stared at her drink. "Maybe if I leave, I'll take the danger with me, and they'll be safe and—"

"Afraid you'll infect them with your rotten karma?"

"Maybe. I don't know."

"Stop it. They love you and you love them. Or did you forget?"

"No."

Elizabeth clinked her glass on Meriel's. "Then get comfy. Bringing us here fulfilled your promise to mom."

"Mom said to never leave you."

"And me you, but we're not your reason to live anymore. You have John and the girls now. So, what do you want for you, just for you?"

Meriel blushed and dropped her gaze. "All of us on the *Princess* like it used to be."

"That's a sweet memory, M. But it may not be our future. We all get a choice now." She tipped her head to the display. "Say, did you see the puff piece on the Archtrope?"

"Samuelson's? Yeah, I caught it on the ride up." Meriel took a drink and shook her head. "How can we counter propaganda like that?"

Elizabeth downed her drink and stood. "Did you hear the Archtrope's mouthpiece commit to building more refugee facilities?"

"Yeah. I think he's planning one on Haven," Meriel said and joined her.

"He didn't mention Khanag or his Draconian League."

"I'll bet they just changed the name to the Soldiers of Providence, or whatever. You ready for the interview?"

"Are you?"

"I can't just sit around and let them get away with this. This is our home base, Liz. And I won't forget how Khanag went after John and the girls to hurt me."

At the exit of the bar, Elizabeth stopped. "Know where we're going?"

Meriel nodded and led her to the tram. As it exited the torus shell and spiraled to the opposite side of the station, Meriel gazed out the window, while Elizabeth bit her lip.

"You may be going EVA into a supernova," Elizabeth said. "And taking the rest of us with you."

"You scared?"

"Hell no. But maybe we should be."

At the IGB News studios, a nervous young man offered his hand.

"Meriel and Elizabeth Hope? I'm Tim. Come with me, please," he said and hustled them into a featureless green room with only a couch and a chair. As soon as they sat on the couch, stylists fussed with their hair and makeup.

"Now Frank . . . that's Frank Masure. He'll be your interviewer. You've seen his casts, no? He's quite famous in this sector."

Elizabeth frowned and brushed the stylists' hands away each time they tried to add a blush or eye shadow. Meriel did not stop their fussing, but as soon as they left, she returned her hair to her pragmatic ponytail.

"Well, Frank will be by in . . ." He checked the link on his clipboard. "In a minute for a word with you. After an introduction by the producer and a short biopic, we'll ask for your comments on the recent vids and summarize the issues. You're in front of a green screen so we can change the background post-production. The camera will love you both, so just relax! Sound good?"

They nodded but had no idea what he meant.

Tim left and Frank Masure entered with a charismatic smile and shook their hands. "Ms. Hope. Ms. Hope. Pleased to meet you both." He sat in a larger chair not quite facing them, his pleasant expression never leaving his face.

"Relax now. This will be fun. Don't mind the room. It'll be much more interesting when the effects people do their magic."

Three spheres the size of her fist floated into the room and positioned themselves to each side and in front of them.

"And don't worry about the cameras. We'll pick the angles that flatter you in post."

He smiled again, and they smiled in return.

"It'll be just the three of us in a quiet conversation between friends. We're aware your story is sensitive—we've done our homework here—and can touch some nerves. You'll have complete control of what appears in the final interview. Take as long as you want to answer my questions. We want to give you a chance to tell your side. Right?"

They glanced at each other and shrugged.

"Ready?" He raised a finger, the lights dimmed, and a diffuse glow from the opposite wall cast them in a soft light. His charismatic smile reappeared, and he faced one of the floating spheres.

"This is Frank Masure with IGB News. We're here on LeHavre for an exclusive interview with Meriel and Elizabeth Hope, survivors of the *Tiger* hijack attempt and the most recent invasion of Haven, the habitable moon of Thor, Jira-1's gas giant. People don't know much about Haven yet, Ms. Hope. Some skeptics think an Earth-like planet is a fantasy."

"Well, 'Earth-like' is a stretch," Meriel said, aware her role was not that of a travel agent for increased immigration to Haven. "Even compared to the Australian Outback. Then add a trillion alien wolves. And it's actually a moon. You're invited to come down and see for yourself."

"I'll take you up on that, Ms. Hope."

Elizabeth rolled her eyes.

"Now, you were the one who exposed the Treaty of Haven that tied UNE ex-President Biadez, BioLuna Corporation, and the Archtrope of Calliope in a conspiracy to takeover Haven."

"Yes," Meriel said.

"But a few days ago, the Calliope Ministry of Truth released a holo of you confessing you concocted that treaty."

"That was a deep fake."

"How so?"

"The Calliope vid used an avatar of me—"

"Avatar?"

"Ah, a reconstructed holo of me created without my permission during the invasion of Haven," Meriel said.

"And you say the purpose is to contradict your accusations against the Archtrope and BioLuna?"

"Yes. The fake is—"

"Which fake? The Treaty of Haven or your avatar?"

Meriel took a breath. "The avatar is a fake intended to subvert the evidence we submitted to the court on Lander. That evidence documents the conspiracy to invade Haven and hijack the *Tiger*," she said as she fidgeted with the cross and chip on her necklace.

"Those documents are unverified."

"There are tens of thousands of affidavits from witnesses on Haven and LeHavre. Two invasions are verified by court records and a ruling against BioLuna—"

Masure leaned back in his chair. "BioLuna. That's one of the so-called co-conspirators."

Elizabeth crossed her arms and tipped her head. "So-called?"

"Those judgements were uncontested, and the United Nations of Earth doesn't recognize them."

"This isn't Sol," Elizabeth said. "Those rulings are valid in other systems and stations."

"So, you still claim the Haven Treaty is evidence of a conspiracy between BioLuna, the Archtrope of Calliope, and UNE President Biadez. And their collusion resulted in the attacks on the *Tiger* and the *Princess*."

Meriel sat up straight. "Claim? Well, yes. People died on both ships. We didn't make that up. There are coroner's reports and ship records." She fiddled with her necklace again.

"I couldn't help but notice," he said, his eyes fixed on the pendant in her fingers. "Is that the cross of JCS?"

Elizabeth narrowed her eyes.

Meriel dropped her hands to her lap and blushed. "My mother gave it to me just before she died. It's been with me through many hard times."

"They say JCS started on Earth but didn't catch on there."

"Is there a purpose to this?" Elizabeth said.

"I think the audience will want to know more about Meriel. It'll help your case if they identify with her."

"Earthers have their own beliefs," Meriel said. "Spacers like to think God is out here with us and travels with us wherever we go."

"And so do our demons."

She smiled. "You've read de Merlner?"

He leaned over with a finger to his lips. "Don't tell my producer."

Meriel returned the smile. "Spacers don't think like Earthers, at least not yet. We're not afraid of open space or technology."

"Do you believe?"

"I'm beginning to."

"How can you believe in God after all you've been through?"

"Because I'm still here and those I love are safe, for now. 'After all we've been through.' Well, that's a miracle."

"Now, one issue brought up is to challenge your credibility using your documented history of drug use—"

"Stop," Elizabeth said. "We didn't agree to discuss that."

Meriel raised her hand. "It's bound to come up, Liz." She turned back to Masure. "They prescribed the meds to relieve symptoms from my . . . trauma on the *Princess*."

"The *Princess* tragedy, yes. Can you tell us—"

Elizabeth leaned forward. "What the... Did you say 'tragedy'?"

"Well yes, I—"

"Where the f... where do you get off," Elizabeth shouted. "That was more than a 'tragedy.' That was torture and mass murder by cold hearted thugs under the command of General Khanag."

"There was no evidence—"

"Are you blind *and* deaf? *We're* the evidence, you moron. Forty people died, and we kids survived only because those butchers didn't find us. We provided the testimony years ago."

"I understand the courts are still—"

She stood. "Give me a break. This was a mistake, M. Time to end this," she said and walked out.

A deep furrow etched Masure's brow as he faced Meriel. "I'm sorry if I upset your sister. I didn't mean to offend her or challenge your story. Can we continue?"

She nodded.

"The *Princess* . . . disaster. May I call it that?"

"I'd prefer massacre."

"You were only twelve then. It meant your childhood was cut short during your formative years."

"So what?" she said. "I skipped the 'finding yourself' teen BS." It was true, but she never found that part of herself. It was lost, stripped from her after years of PTSD. Until Haven.

"When you appeared on the Enterprise docks after the *Princess* . . ."

Meriel flinched as a holovid played of the Enterprise docks when the *Princess* reappeared. Blood covered her torn pajamas, and she stood wide-eyed and motionless.

"Turn that off, please," she said, turned away, and blinked repeatedly to suppress the flashbacks. *Not now!* "What are we doing here? Where are you going with this?"

He raised a hand, and the vid ended. "Ms. Hope, the images from that day struck a chord with—"

She shook her head. "This isn't what we agreed to. We came here to talk about the phony avatar and the Haven invasion."

"I'm sorry, Ms. Hope, but GNN is pushing the drug abuse angle hard. A little more understanding of the events will add to your credibility. And some goodwill from our audience may help your cause."

"And yours. No. I won't play the victim here to boost your ratings or be the tragic poster child with big eyes and a teardrop."

"That's not what I intend, Ms. Hope. A trauma like that would break most of us, and people—"

"I don't think about it."

"It must be hard to put that out of your head, to heal—"

"I mean it," she said. "I *can't* think about it. It happened. It's back there and I keep it back there."

"But you had therapists to help you cope with—"

"The therapists told me I was lying. They separated me from my sister until I parroted their bullshit. When I finally gave in, they drugged me to keep me quiet."

"You claim the Biadez Foundation did this to you?"

"There you go with that word 'claim' again. Yes, I damn well claim. Check their records. Alan Biadez is a rat, but the Foundation was the only group that helped us. They got us good ships and decent fosters."

"They came after you again."

"Nice people are naïve and easily used. The people on top are slime."

"So, your feelings about the Foundation are ambivalent."

Meriel cocked her head and narrowed her brow. "Of course I'm ambivalent. Why the hell—"

The producer interrupted with a blinking light and Masure excused himself.

Meriel closed her eyes. *You're trying to show them you're rational and not a squealing bitch. But I can't let them slander my folks . . .*

Her heartbeat drummed in her ears again, and she opened her fists to massage the scar on her palm. When she opened her eyes again, Masure was walking toward her.

"I'm sorry, Ms. Hope, but we're out of time today. Let's get together again to continue our conversation another time. Yes?"

"Well, OK." She said and stood.

Masure extended his hand. "It was a pleasure speaking with you."

After shaking his hand, Meriel joined her sister heading for the shuttle docks.

***

Masure joined the producer in the control room. "She's agreed to come back."

The producer switched off the monitors and waved his hand to dismiss the crew. "Frank, that's a date I don't want you to make."

"But the charges she makes—"

"You want to drag us into a he-said-she-said between Lander and Earth? You're not that naïve. Our Sol system advertisers would dump us in a heartbeat.

"We're way out here, Jack. There can't be that many."

"They make our profit." He poked a finger into Masure's chest. "And your bonus."

"But the *Princess* story. It bleeds. It should lead. Conspiracy, deaths, orphaned children, invasions . . ."

"It's old news, and it's a downer. Where's the light here? Where's the 'we survived on grit and pulled ourselves out and made a success of our lives'? How did these folks end up?"

"They're farmers and spacers," Masure said.

"Right. Who cares about farmers? And she throws luggage around—"

"She's a Logistics-5, a cargo chief—"

The producer rolled his eyes. "Like I said. This isn't inspiring, it's grueling . . ."

"She never gave up."

"Maybe she should've, long ago," the producer said and turned to leave.

Masure grabbed his arm. "This isn't a vid, Jack. These are real people who went through hell and back. They're talking about a group secretly trying to take over this entire sector by force."

Jack peered over his shoulder and scanned the control room. "And may come for us if we piss 'em off," he said in a hushed tone. "You have no idea how influential these people are."

Masure frowned. "Influential enough to spike an unflattering story?"

The producer narrowed his eyes. "Read the tea leaves, Frank. Cut it and do your career a favor."

***

"Ouch!" Becky said as the nurse injected the new biotag into her shoulder.

"Crybaby," Sandy teased. But Becky poked her in the patch covering her own new embedded ID.

Sandy winced. "Stop, you'll break it."

"Nothing will," John said. "These little things are pretty much invulnerable."

"Where's yours, papa?"

John pointed to a spot near his appendix. His was the same type of biological identity tag Meriel and every other spacer wore. Entrance to the station required one, so the girls' first stop on LeHavre was the blue-zone quarantine clinic for the procedure.

The nurse tapped a finger on a projected console. "Let's see now. Alessandra Smith?"

"Sandy."

"I'll add your nickname."

"It's not a . . ." she stopped and glared at her father.

"And Rebecca?" the nurse said. "Will that be Becky?"

Becky leaned forward and smiled. "How about Galatia?"

John shook his head.

"Yes, ma'am."

"That's it," the nurse said. "Your tests are clear, and your ration cards are synced." She turned to John and pointed to his knee. "Do you want me to schedule a tune-up?"

He rapped a knuckle on his prosthesis. "No thanks."

"Then you're all cleared to enter the station."

John waved goodbye as he led the girls outside the clinic where Meriel waited. His link beeped, and he tapped it.

"I need to take this, M. The LeHavre Assembly of Citizens is meeting to discuss the refugee crisis."

She nodded and took the girls hands. "How about lunch?" she asked, and the girls beamed.

When they entered green-zone and the station proper, Meriel turned to the girls.

"What do you think of your new biotag?"

"None of our friends at school have these," Sandy said with a timid smile.

"Right. We're gonna be spatial, huh," her sister said.

Sandy laughed.

"What?"

"Special, spatial. Get it?"

"Oh, yeah," Becky said and grinned at her accidental joke.

"Well, don't go bragging too much," Meriel said. "You need biotags on the stations, but lots of folks on Haven don't like the idea of any ID at all. Right, John?"

"What?" John said and lowered his link.

"Haven folks don't like IDs, right?"

"Sure. Hon, we may have to stay here another day or so."

"How come?"

"The Assembly is having trouble deciding what to do about the new settlers. Colonel Lee booked us a suite at the Commodore with a view of Thor."

"That could work," Meriel said. "Penny and Sam can take the girls to the sims after dinner and you, and I can spend the evening together."

"We're good with that," Sandy said.

Becky jumped as a small hemisphere whizzed past their feet. "What's that?"

"A delivery bot," Meriel said.

"What's the difference between bots and droids, M?" Sandy asked.

"Droids think, kinda. Bots don't," Meriel said.

"How do you tell?"

"Usually you can't tell by looking at them."

At an intersection, Sandy stopped. "I'm lost, Merry."

"It's a torus, hon. Everyone gets lost. C'mon."

She led them to the bulkhead intersection and a question mark icon. When she tapped it, a 3-D schematic appeared. "Every station has these at the intersections."

Becky smiled and used her hands to manipulate it, zooming in from a panoramic view until their image appeared at the kiosk. She waved, and her image waved back.

"How can it see us?"

Meriel pointed to the ceiling where a black ball had tucked itself into a corner. For a moment, eight spindly legs cycled through an assortment of needles and bladed weapons as if to warn them not to stare. When done, it curled up again, but two red dots stayed aimed at them.

Becky's eyes opened wide. "What's that?"

"A security spider. A droid," Meriel said.

"What are those pointy things on its legs?" Becky asked and slipped her hand into Meriel's.

"Most of them will make you go to sleep."

"What about the others?"

"Better we never find out."

A short tram ride delivered them to a café popular for its kid-friendly cuisine, and Sandy and Becky picked a table with a window over the promenade. Meriel showed the girls how to sync their dietary profiles to the kiosk, after which, the girls ordered one of everything on the menu. Each time they asked their father if they could order something, he nodded and continued to work. When the first plates arrived from the replicators, their eyes gleamed at the array of unusual dishes. And then the carnage began.

John's link blinked yellow. "You maxed out our rations, girls."

"Borrow some from dinner," Meriel said.

"That already includes our dinner and tomorrow's breakfast."

"Well, we're Colonel Lee's guests, so ask him to up our allotment."

John smiled, tapped his link again, and rejoined the meeting.

"I remember the first time Liz and I had station food." It was a treat, but her parents had not had the connections John had to fund a feast like this.

"Where?" Sandy mumbled through a stuffed mouth.

"Lander."

"M, why do they call it Lander Station and not Lalande? Etna and Cirrus Stations are named after the star system."

"It's a spacer nickname," John said.

Becky glanced at Meriel and raised her eyebrows.

Meriel chuckled and leaned over to whisper. "Lander is how spacers pronounce Lalande when they're drunk."

Sandy paused with her fork an inch from her mouth, and she frowned. "What's this, M?"

Scrolling through the menu holo, Meriel found a picture matching the slice of pinkish orange with yellow stripes lying on a white cube. "Sushi. That one's called *sake nigiri*."

"Wow, this is good," Sandy mumbled and took a bite. "What's it made of?"

"Rice with raw salmon."

Sandy paused. "Raw fish?"

"Don't worry, nothing is raw here, and the nearest seafood is fifteen light-years away."

She took another bite. "Hot!" she said and grabbed for the water glass.

Meriel checked the kiosk. "That's called w*asabi*, a kind of horseradish."

"Horse what?" Becky asked.

"It's a vegetable, but real spicy," Meriel said as Sandy swallowed. "You OK, hon?"

Becky scanned the menu and searched through the basket of utensils for a pair of chopsticks. "Says here you eat them with these." She tried to pick a sushi without success, then stabbed it and held it up in victory.

Sandy took another bite and squinted at the fresh jolt of wasabi.

"Ick," Becky said after her first taste, dropped the chopsticks, and grabbed a pastry with a red dollop on top. She bit into it but stuck her tongue out as if she had eaten dirt. "What's this, Merry."

"Strawberry shortcake."

Becky shook her head. "That's not strawberry," she said and attacked a slice of chocolate cake instead.

With both girls preoccupied with their desserts, Meriel smiled at John. But his eyes were glued to his link and did not budge at her frown.

Bored, she tapped the window to engage a news feed from the capital at Stewardville.

```
"Marines relocated another two hun-
dred squatters from the Ebeneuer
```

> wasteland to the Terni Refugee Camp.
> Interviews determined the squatters
> were not aligned with the recent inva-
> sion but were part of a coyote opera-
> tion. Without training in the hostile
> Haven environment, these immigrants
> face almost certain death. Local citi-
> zens are protesting the lack of re-
> sources needed to support the in-
> creased . . ."

Meriel waved her hand between John and his link, and he raised his eyes.

"You seeing this? Terni. That's the region allocated to the Archtrope in the Treaty of Haven."

With a few fingers, she zoomed the image. The Terni camp had grown from a few hundred to thousands in only a month and was already overwhelming the capital. With another tap on the window, she switched to an inter-station feed.

> "Lance Freiden at GNN reporting from
> Etna Station. We are receiving reports
> of freedom fighters on Haven resisting
> the fascist land holders . . ."

"Freedom fighters, my ass. We're losing the PR battle," she said, but John had already reengaged with his link. She changed to a less biased news feed.

> "IPB Galaxy Watch reports today that
> food rations at Terni refugee camp
> have become dangerously low. Refugees
> have overwhelmed local supplies and
> food theft is rampant as . . ."

"Damn!" Meriel said and put her hand on John's. "They're going right ahead with it. Like we didn't stop the invasion. Like this is f'ing Plan B! John, we need to find out how many Archers are at Terni."

Sandy and Becky frowned at her, but John kept his attention glued to his link. When Meriel's bracelet buzzed with an incoming call, Sandy tapped it, and a fuzzy picture of Penny appeared.

Haven—Ebeneuer Wasteland

Through clouds of dust, Abram's huge APC followed two ATVs to a small camp in the Ebeneuer Wasteland bordering Terni Province. Dismounting her ATV, Penny Hubbard adjusted her goggles and scarf and approached a collapsed tent that flapped in the wind.

Tooth and claw marks marred the tent, and Penny reached out for it, but Sam Spurell, her closest friend from the *Princess*, caught her arm. She jerked away from him and lifted the flap. Under it lay a family, dead from exposure. Bite marks from culpas and hiranths marred the bodies.

"They never learn they can't digest us," Sam said.

"It doesn't stop them from taking a taste," Penny replied.

Captain Abrams jumped from the APC to join them and tapped his helmet. "HQ, this is Abrams on patrol near the Terni camp. We have another group of dead refugees." He turned to Penny. "Thanks for helping the corpsmen at Bantu, Penny. So, what do you think happened here?"

"You say there are more like this?" she said and gently brushed the dust from the faces of the dead.

"Scattered around the area. Like they were waiting for something."

Another section of the tent whipped in the wind, exposing the body of a boy about twelve years old. Penny gasped, spun around, and sat in the dirt.

Sam kneeled by her side and put his arm around her.

"That could have been Harry," she said referring to Anita's brother, the youngest of the *Princess* orphans. Her goggles fogged, and when she removed them, tears traced muddy lines down her cheeks.

"We haven't seen him for months," Penny said. "And his ship won't include Haven in their circuit."

"But he's OK, Penny. The Troopers are looking after him."

She nodded, and after Sam took her hand, she stood, and they returned to examine the adults. All had similar abdominal scarring patterns like organ donors and tattoos on their palms.

"We need to call Meriel. Captain, please find a comm path through this muck."

Abrams nodded and led them to the satellite link in the APC. The sidewalls of the vehicle protected them from the storm, but Meriel's holo shimmered with distortion.

"John's here with me," Meriel said.

"Hi, Aunt Penny," Becky and Sandy said in unison.

"Hey, kids. I need to talk to your folks, is that OK?"

A moment later, John's image appeared next to Meriel's.

"I see your location on the monitor," Meriel said. "You're near Terni?"

"Yes. We found another group of ten. Evidence of organ donation. They may have been dumped here. Why, M? It's expensive to ship bodies."

"It's a cheap way to manufacture a crisis and force the UNE out here."

"Look at this." Penny played a vid of the palm tattoos.

Meriel frowned. "They look like old QR scan codes for inventory control."

"They're on the children too."

"Do any have snake and blade tattoos like the corsairs?"

"No."

"Sam, is your brother there with you?" John asked.

Sam leaned closer to the link. "Tommy's on the farm with the militia."

"Why the militia?"

"Gangs of refugees raided some farms this morning and kicked the families off their land."

"Armed gangs?" John asked.

"Yes."

"Where'd they get the weapons?" Meriel asked but got a shrug in reply. "What about the Marines?"

"They're redeploying near Stewardville," Sam said.

John shook his head. "That'll look bad, trained soldiers against civilians. Any evidence the gangs attacked your victims?"

"No."

"Thanks, Penny. I'll meet with Colonel Lee soon and will tell him. Anything else? Captain?"

"No, John. Out."

Penny grabbed Abrams's sleeve and pointed to the adult victims. "Send one to the LGen med school morgue for autopsy. Ping me when it's on the way," she said, mounted her ATV, and sped away in a cloud of dust.

LeHavre Station—On Station

When John ended the call, Meriel put her hand on his link.

"The coyote operation is a cover for infiltrating Archers, John."

"I heard. And now they're dumping organ donors to make us look bad."

"We can't support all the unprepared people."

"I know. It's out of control. They'll—"

"They'll need to make their own food, and they can't do that without knowledge of our environment, and . . ." She paused. "What are you smiling about?"

"You referred to Haven as *our* environment."

"Yeah, yeah," she said and rolled her eyes.

"What was that about visiting Bantu after the trip back?" he asked. "You mentioned it the other night."

Meriel blushed. *Opps.* "Yeah, well . . . Penny and I, mostly Penny, put together a dossier implicating the Archtrope in the illegal organ trade."

John stopped with his fork an inch from his mouth. "And?"

"I sent it to Khanag."

He put the food down uneaten. "And you're telling me about this now?"

"I'm trying to protect you," she said and blinked to suppress the memory of him dying on the kitchen floor during the last invasion.

He nodded. "Next time, tell me first."

"We'll be at Bantu when . . . if the shitstorm hits."

"And how long will we need to stay?"

She dropped her gaze to her lunch. "I didn't think about that."

"He may not act the way you expect, M."

An alarm for their upcoming zero-g training broke the tension. "Finish up, girls. We want the whole half-hour."

They turned to her with rings of chocolate frosting on their mouths and wide eyes as if she had caught them with their fingers on the candy button of the food replicator.

"I want to come here more often," Becky said.

"The shuttle is expensive, sweetie."

"Papa's got a diplomatic pass," Sandy said as she wiped her mouth. "He can sneak us here in his baggage."

Meriel smiled, licked the napkin, and cleaned the chocolate frosting from Becky's chin. "Smugglers already. Being spacers will be easier for you than I thought."

The girls beamed, but John frowned.

As she finished wiping Becky's chin, the news feed replayed the confession by her avatar. At the end came the image of a young girl, alone on the Enterprise docks, covered in blood.

With a gasp, her hand went to the scar along her body as images of the Enterprise docks swept over her with all the horror and pain. She blinked rapidly and slowed her breathing, but the flashback she had suppressed since the interview hit her again in a rush.

"No, not again."

Chapter 9
Echoes, ET 2177

Free Space, ET 2177

Eleven-year-old Elizabeth shook Meriel hard. "M. M, please. You've been here too long, and we're cold."

Meriel sat with her back to the closed infirmary door and ignored the murmur. She hugged herself with bloodless fists and rocked back and forth, lost in her pain.

"What's wrong?" Elizabeth said. When Meriel did not respond, she reached out to open the door.

Meriel grabbed Elizabeth's hand and gripped it hard. "No!"

"Ow!" Elizabeth backed away, rubbing her wrist. "Are you OK?"

"No," Meriel said and focused on a memory of her mother's arms and her last bedtime story.

> *"Soaring past her misty veil,*
> *Seven sisters near her sail . . ."*

She put a hand on Elizabeth's chest as she had done with each of the adults in the room behind her. At the beat of her sister's heart, she hugged her tight and sobbed. "You're alive."

"Don't be dumb. Of course I am. M, we can't sit here." She put her shoulder under Meriel's arm. "Here."

As she struggled to stand, Meriel winced, and the lower half of her PJ top slipped away to expose a long red wound.

Elizabeth's jaw dropped. "I'm sorry," she said and fumbled to hide the wound by lifting a button. A tear fell as she helped Meriel to her feet. "We gotta go."

Meriel nodded. "This way," she said, and the orphans came to her.

There were eight children left: her sister Elizabeth, Tommy and Sam Spurell, Penny Hubbard, Erik White, and baby Harry in the arms of his older sister, Anita. All were dirty from hiding in the cargo hold, and Anita's nightgown was stained with pee. They understood Meriel's directions, but she was only twelve and did not know how to save them.

We're already dead. But maybe . . .

"Tommy, Liz, don't let the kids open any doors."

She followed her mother's instructions and led the children to the alt-nav compartment, past burn marks on the bulkheads and over the grit of shattered plastaglass.

The pirate sounds of unloading freight and pings that rang the hull like a bell had gone quiet. Absent as well was the steady whoosh of life support, and only the hum of the engines broke the silence. And around them, the emergency lighting flickered: the *Princess* was dying.

She put a hand on the bulkhead. "Please. Stay with us. Just awhile longer."

With all of them secure in the tiny room, she booted up the nav console and gave each of them a tranq pill to ease the disorientation of jump. Then she took the q-chip from her necklace and held it.

Jump was unpredictable, and she hoped they would dissolve into the plasma of a star rather than reappear in the deep black without the fuel to return.

She closed her eyes.

A tug on her sleeve dragged Meriel back from the darkness.

"M. M. Can you hear me?" Tommy said.

She opened her eyes and found the kids staring at her.

"Are we going to see our folks?" Sam asked.

She winced at memories from the infirmary. "Maybe soon. Just be quiet and take your tranq."

After taking her own pill, Meriel held the medallion on her necklace with the cross of JCS and recited her mother's last words.

"Have faith and never leave them."

Elizabeth took her hand, and Meriel put the chip in the reader slot.

The console spoke.

```
"Destination: Enterprise. Initiating
jump prep. Begin proximity check."
```

Lights blinked, and the nav computer behind the smoked plastaglass wall lit up.

"Hold hands," she said.

```
"Proximity clear.
```

"Execute."

They stared at her: twelve-year-old kids didn't initiate hyperspace jumps.

```
"Jump in three, two, one . . ."
```

Procyon System—Enterprise Station, On Station, ET 2177

The Pilot-Master adjusted icons on his console within Enterprise Station Traffic Control. "Tug HJ-49, proceed to Quadrant sixteen and dock AH-45 . . ."

Tech Masters and apprentices crowded the facility. Each stood at separate consoles to guide vessels from the thousands of nearby mining colonies and scores of distant stars. Mid-room, a colossal holo tracked interstellar shipments as they winked into and out of hyperspace. Colored trajectories appeared of every moving body capable of interacting with them, manned and unmanned. Fingers touched the lights, and data appeared in pull-downs.

Commander Susan Morrell, the Security Master charged with protecting the station from terrorists and errant projectiles, stood at the main console. She was a professional, great-granddaughter of one of the Station Troopers who had cleared out the pirates a hundred years earlier and made space safe for shipping.

Next to her stood Adam Lightfeather, the Chief Pilot-Master and Traffic Director, second in line to the Station Master.

"All inbound merchant vessels expect delays. Repairs underway on D-5 through 86."

"LSM *Holden,* wait at Quadrant five for tug—"

"Hey, tell them Judy is waiting here for their Nav officer."

Judy reached over and switched off his mic. "Stow it."

A claxon blared and a red icon flashed at the outer beacon shown on the large display: an object had appeared where it should not. Lightfeather waved a finger at the new icon, and the room echoed with the blare of an EM screamer from an escape pod. A separate hologram displayed a close-up of the location along with trajectories and local traffic that might intersect.

"What's an ePod doing out there? Identify. And cut the audio, Chuck. Judy, plot the trajectory and clear the path."

Another red icon reappeared further from the station. Both had the same information on the pull-downs. The object was not coasting inertial, and they could not plot a course. A third icon now blinked further away, implying the vessel was faster than light.

"It's not a pod," Judy said. "It's a ship. And it may have jumped again."

The display margins flashed a danger signal.

Lightfeather leaned over the console. "If it's FTL, this is stale data. Yellow alert for traffic control. Chuck, plot a course based on those winks."

Console operators sat straighter as they charted trajectories.

Commander Morrell tapped her ear. "Alert, exec. I want you monitoring."

A red line emerged that would pass close to Enterprise, but not intersect its path. "Quadrant three, ma'am. Deceleration is logarithmic. A standard decel program from a Nav-RR9I device."

"That's a merchant nav," Lightfeather said. "Identity?"

"Not from the EM screamer. It's sucking up the bandwidth."

"Prove to me that's not a missile," Morrell said.

"Can't do that, ma'am," Chuck replied.

"Security alert for unidentified projectile heading for Quadrant three. If it gets within five hundred klicks, vaporize it."

When the lights changed to red, new consoles came alive and uniformed officers ran in to man them. One holo showed the station with status lights for pressure integrity. Others showed defensive ships and weapons that could affect an object with that mass.

"ID received sir. LSM *Princess* GCN 13442:88."

Lightfeather glowered. "That damn pilot will wind up in prison. Along with the captain."

"How close?" Morrell asked.

"It's inertial now and decelerating."

"Where will it end up?"

"A thousand klicks, ma'am."

Lightfeather raised an eyebrow. "Someone cares about us."

"Intercept and scan for ordnance," Morrell said. "Including nukes."

"If it's clean, send a tug to tow it in," Lightfeather said. "Chuck, you have the comm."

"Where are you going?" Chuck asked as the pilot and security masters headed for the door.

"To arrest the crew," Lightfeather said. "Nobody pulls shit like this near my station."

***

Meriel shivered in the dark as shadows rushed about outside the foggy airlock window. As soon as the docking clamps engaged, umbilicals connected to restore power and commodities. The lock's panel lit up, and life support replaced the stale, cold air with fresh.

A voice came through the PA. "LSM *Princess*. This is Enterprise Security. Open the door and debark, one at a time."

Meriel closed her eyes and smiled. The spirits of the dead who roamed the ship had made sure they arrived safely. But when she laid her hand on the bulkhead, it was cold. The spirits had left, and they were all alone.

Status lights blinked green, and Meriel twisted the recessed handle. As the door slid aside, a spotlight shone through the door, and she raised her hand to shield her eyes.

Through the glare, scores of uniformed men on their knees aimed pulse rifles at her. Behind them stood reporters with cameras and hundreds of onlookers. Laser sights flickered around the airlock and converged on her chest.

"Raise your hands and walk forward."

From the shadows, Meriel Hope stepped out barefoot in torn pajamas, covered in blood, and stopped. One soldier stood and approached, but an officer took her arm.

"Hold your position, Sergeant Oliver," the officer said.

This was as far as Meriel could go. Her feet would carry her no farther.

After scores of layovers, Enterprise was her second home. But this world was strange: a world without her parents, a world without people to take care of her and her sister, a world where they pointed deadly weapons at her.

"Hands on your head." The voice said, but Meriel could not respond. "Hands on your head. Now!"

The shouts faded away, the faces blended into one another, and the world blurred to gray, until a hand slipped into hers. She glanced to her right where Elizabeth gazed up at her. Tommy took her left hand, and the three stood together. Around her, the other children came and huddled together in the glare of the lights.

Oliver shook off her commanding officer's grip and rushed to Meriel. "Child, are you OK?"

"No," Meriel said and collapsed.

Chapter 10
Jira-1 System, ET 2188

LeHavre Station—On Station, ET 2188

"Are you OK?" Sandy said.

No, echoed in Meriel's head. Her hands shook and eyes glistened, and she blinked repeatedly to interrupt the visions. In front of her, the news vid was still frozen on the scene from the Enterprise docks.

"Merry L?"

She turned to Becky's voice and worried face.

"Something's wrong again, Merry," Sandy said.

Meriel hugged the girls. "Not anymore." *Damn, all these years and it's like yesterday.*

Finally ignoring his link, John reached over to put his hand on theirs. "You want to lie down?"

"No. Talk to me."

"They've gotten worse since the *Tiger?*"

She nodded.

"Did you talk to the clinic about—"

She pulled her hand away. "I'm done with meds, John. And that's all they've got."

"Boost can—"

"I don't care. I'm done."

"How about we take a break and go to our room?"

"No. I need to be moving." She checked her link and stood. "Saddle up, girls."

As they rose to leave, Sandy took her father's hand, and with her other hand slipped the remaining cookies into her pocket.

At the door to the gym, John's link buzzed again.

"Damn. They moved up the meeting with Colonel Lee."

"I can't train two at once," Meriel said.

"I'll bring Becky back at 1300." He held out his hand. "Come on, baby girl. Duty calls."

Becky put her fists on her hips. "I'm not a baby anymore."

He kneeled in front of her. "No, you're not. How about honey bunch?"

She screwed her mouth up and shook her head.

"Princess?"

"Like Merry L's ship? I like that. But I want to stay and watch, papa."

"Sorry. We'll be back in a few hours. Then it'll be your turn."

Meriel squeezed his hand. "Tell Lee we're losing the public relations battle. They need the influential stations to get ahead of the lies, a defensive circle like orbanths. And we need more hydroponics in the refugee camps, and—"

John interrupted her with a kiss and smiled. And with a nod, he left with Becky for his meeting.

"Just you and me, now," Meriel said to Sandy.

Compressed air packs, helmets, poles, and equipment for zero-g athletics lined the walls of the entrance to the multi-g gym. This was the station's main arena with low-g versions of most common sports.

Meriel signed them in and took her to the lockers, where Sandy pinched her nose at the stench of the sports teams and nervous Techs who qualified here.

"Leave everything in the locker, including the cookies," she told Sandy. "Use the jumpsuit and keep the pockets zipped. Do you have a hair tie?"

"Yup. Why?"

"You'll see. Now, come with me."

As they left the locker room, athletic men and women in colorful uniforms crowded in from the gym. And from the last of them, Meriel took a remote.

Sandy pulled her to the door and put her hand on the handle, but Meriel held her back.

"Lesson one: never open a door without a safety check."

"Why?"

"Space isn't like Haven or Earth. On a ship or a station, there may be high-dose radiation, a hard vacuum, or a low-oxygen confined area on the other side. Every bulkhead and blast door has status indicators. See the lights on the side of the door? They come in all shapes and sizes, but they mean the same thing—if you see anything but green, do *not* open the door."

"Got it."

Sandy stepped inside the cylindrical core of LeHavre's axis and appeared to be walking, but she did not go anywhere. She giggled and stretched until her tiptoes touched the deck. A second later, she spun head over heels.

"Lesson two: before you enter a room, always check for the handholds," Meriel said and pointed to the padded handles inset into the walls. "The entry lights don't include a gravity indicator, and you may be weightless on the other side." She used the remote to dial up the g's and Sandy drifted back down.

Across ten meters of padded deck, Meriel led Sandy to the middle of the gym. "First, orientation. We're at Haven's gravity. Feels normal, right?"

"Yeah, but strange. Like tingly."

"Uh-huh. Gravity is artificial here at the core. Ships will vary it depending on their acceleration."

Sandy furrowed her brow and stared at her. "What do you mean, *depending*?"

"Don't worry about it, just get used to the tingle. Now, the station rotates slowly but you can't tell if you're not paying attention." She pointed to the ceiling about thirty meters away. "See the stars there?"

"Yeah."

"That's how you can judge the rotational speed," Meriel said. "By watching the stars outside."

The girl frowned.

Slow down. This is her first time. "They don't teach the physics of space at school?"

"Papa said he'd teach our class next year."

"That's fine. Now, hold my hand and jump."

Sandy leaped a foot off the deck.

"That's Haven's normal gravity."

Meriel's body sagged as she dialed the remote up to 2.5g, and her back ached: her souvenir from a broken back.

"Bend your knees. Now jump."

Sandy tried but fell and could not lift herself off the mat.

"That's about at Jupiter's cloud tops." She reduced the gravity to 0.2g. "Try again."

"Whoa!" Sandy said as she jumped six feet up and spun.

Meriel reached up to grab her by the ankle and righted her as she drifted back to the mats. "That's about M2, Haven's big submoon."

She zeroed the artificial gravity, and completely weightless for the first time in her life, Sandy grinned. Her loose hair fluffed, and she spit out a mouthful.

"Use the hair tie," Meriel said.

The girl tied her hair up, but every move of her arms added some spin to her body.

"It'll be like that with everything in zero-g," Meriel said as she held her still. "Everything is a projectile and you'll run into it or inhale it unless it's secured. Now, try to get to the wall."

The child flailed her limbs, but nothing happened. "I can't move."

"Right. You only move when your muscles push or pull against something," she said and pointed to a wall where short bars slotted into the foam walls. "That's why those handholds are there. Not to stop you from falling, but to give you something to push against. So, what do you do now?"

Sandy shook her head.

From her pocket, Meriel took a small device. "This is compressed air. You have one in your suit. Take it out and point it in the direction opposite of where you want to go. Now pull the trigger."

The girl held the device to her chest and squeezed. It screeched, but instead of moving anywhere, she rotated in place again. "Whee!" she said and laughed.

Meriel tucked her toes under one of the handholds, grabbed Sandy, and stopped the spin. "Hold it near your tummy instead. That's your center of mass." She demonstrated and glided to the wall and the handholds. "Now you."

Sandy followed and grabbed a handle.

"That's Newton's first law of motion," Meriel said. "Without that push, we don't move. And once we're moving, we'll keep going until something stops us. That's Newton again."

"Do I need to remember the names of things?"

"No. Just remember what happens. Now I'm going to spin you. If you feel queasy, focus on a single spot that's not moving. OK? Now, arms out."

From the waist, Meriel spun the girl clockwise. "That's angular momentum. You'll keep spinning until another force stops you. Now fold your arms onto your chest."

Sandy's spin increased. "Whoa!" she said and opened her arms and legs to slow.

"Good," Meriel said, and returned her hands to Sandy's waist. "You've got it."

Sandy laughed as she slowed, but when she stopped, her eyes widened, and she held her stomach. Meriel took the throw-up bag from her jumpsuit. But before she could reach Sandy, the girl let out a loud burp, followed by a big smile.

"Now, to get anywhere, you need to jump, and if you don't want to bump your head a lot, you need to know how to land. You've learned the principles already."

After reducing the grav to a quarter of Haven's, she coached Sandy to tuck and untuck in a different direction. Then she zeroed the gravity.

"Now follow me," Meriel said, jumped, tucked, and flipped. On the opposite side, she looked up to Sandy. "When you land, keep your knees bent so you have spring left to push off again. Now jump. Try to flip the way I did and land on your feet."

Sandy flipped, but over-rotated and landed on her hands and face.

"That's close," Meriel said. "Everybody's mass is in different places, so you need to practice and find what works for you. Now, follow me," she said and jumped again.

Over the remaining quarter-hour, Meriel trained Sandy on the zero-g exercises, three-point landings, and flip-turns. She programmed an accuracy test made from holographic rings that alarmed when she broke the circle. Sandy kept breaking the beam, and it beeped each time to remind her.

"I suck," she said.

"You're lots better than me my first time."

"Really?" Sandy asked.

"Really." Meriel did not say she was four years old her first time through the rings. Born in space, Haven was her first experience with a steady gravity.

Meriel glanced down to reset the remote, and from the corner of her eye, spotted Sandy taking a cookie from her pocket.

"Put it away, hon. We don't want crumbs in our eyes or noses."

Sandy pursed her lips and returned the cookie.

Meriel studied her. "My rules aren't optional. In space the slightest mistake can kill you, and that would make me very sad. And if you forget the rules again, I won't take you along on my next tour. Understand me?"

Sandy nodded and dropped her gaze.

The lights blinked.

"Time's up," Meriel said and led Sandy back to the lockers as a group of athletes filed past them into the gym.

After changing clothes, Meriel took Sandy to the bleachers to wait for John and Becky. Sports fans viewed from cafés and their apartments with the multi-monitor set-ups that made it easier to follow the zero-g action, so they had the bleachers all to themselves.

The athletes warmed up in 1.15g, Haven normal, and then turned off the artificial gravity. They bounced and spun in every direction, pushing off each other and practicing turns and spins. To Sandy, it appeared like a ballet.

When an athlete pushed off from one side of the core to the other side, Sandy stopped munching her cookie.

"What is it?" Meriel asked.

"The woman who jumped across. She curved in... in mid-flight. I thought you said once we're moving, we travel in a straight line. How does she do that?"

The athlete pushed off again to return to her original position, and Meriel nodded. "She's not curving. We are."

"What?"

"Remember I told you the station is rotating?"

"Uh-huh."

"Well, she did move straight. But as she moved, the station rotated around her. We're rotating with the station, so, to us, it looks like she's turning. Got it?"

Sandy nodded.

"And the athlete knows the opposite side is moving, so she needs to aim for the spot that'll be there when she arrives. It's kind of like your slug-shooter back on Haven: if your target is moving, you need to lead it. But you're riding with the slug."

Sandy nodded. "Got it. You have to predict where it'll be depending on the speed."

"Right, and in this case, how fast we're rotating."

"And you have to guess how far away it is," Sandy said and bit the cookie. "Cool."

Meriel put an arm around her and pulled her close.

It wasn't cool: judging distance with just one eye was difficult. Sandy's eye patch separated her from her friends and kept her from of acrobatics and sports. It was why Becky always beat her at badminton even though she was younger. Sandy tried to act like it didn't matter, but it did. The boys she grew up with drifted away. And more than once, she had come from school in tears after the other kids mocked her from her blind side.

The buzz of Meriel's bracelet interrupted with a day-old message from Nick.

```
They're trying to blow her up. No
time.
```

"What the hell does that mean?" Meriel said.

"What did papa mean when he said they want to run Haven like the stations. Aren't they run the same already?"

"No, hon."

"Why not?"

"Well, mostly because people like freedom," Meriel said. "That's a big reason so many people want to come to Haven, to be free."

"Aren't the stations free?"

"Not as much. Ships even less."

"Why?"

"Limited resources," Meriel said.

"I don't understand."

"Well, we need lots of things to stay alive, like air, water, and food. Compared to Haven, Earth has pretty much unlimited supplies of these. But stations have only what they can create, recycle, or import, and ships have only what they're able to store."

"Haven doesn't have much water, so we're more like a station than Earth?" Sandy said.

"Right. We need to be careful, or it won't be there when we need it."

Sandy nodded and took another bite of cookie.

"Do you know the story of the ant and the grasshopper?"

"Yeah, they taught it in school after they explained what ants and grasshoppers are. And what winter is. It's the *gril* and the *kintil* here. You want the summary?"

"Sure," Meriel said as the players lined up in the core, and the whistle blew to begin the game.

Sandy sat back. "Well, the kintil and gril are friends. They both need water to live and have a hard time during the annual drought. The gril is only the size of my fingernail and works hard all summer to store moisture from the dew. But the kintil is as big as my thumb and drinks and plays and makes fun of his little friend. So, the drought comes, and the kintil dies because he didn't store any water. Is that it?"

Meriel nodded. "And what's the moral?"

"It teaches us playing all the time is stupid. We have to work and save something extra in case of hard times."

"That's right."

"But we're just kids, M. Adults are the ones who need that lesson. We don't know how to do those things yet."

"Hmm. Well, knowledge is one of those things you can store for when you need it later. And that's what school is for. So, that's the story, but there's a longer version."

Sandy raised her eyebrows. "What is it?"

"Well, the gril loves the kintil and doesn't want it to die, so it gives the kintil a share of the communal water supply."

"Sounds like a nice gril," Sandy said.

"It is. But the kintil is thirsty. And the drought lasts a few days longer than expected. So, most of the colony dies of thirst, including the kintil they sacrificed to save. The few survivors have to beg from other colonies. But the others had rationed their water better and had just enough for themselves but no extra to share."

"Harsh. The whole colony dies."

"You understand why they don't tell the long version."

"Sure. It's a terrible story.

Cheers interrupted as one team scored in the game outside.

"So, what's the lesson?" Sandy asked.

"Well, when you have limited resources, you need to be tough sometimes when you make choices."

"And the Station Masters are tough?"

"Yes. They have to be, or stations die."

"LeHavre doesn't seem so bad," Sandy said.

"The Tech Masters limit their authority to things we need to survive and leave most decisions to the Assembly of Citizens."

"So, what are the survival things?"

"Security, engineering, life support, basic food supply, sanitation, recycling, trade, raw materials . . ."

Sandy pointed to the teams clumped into a scrum in the core. "Gravity?"

"Right."

"That's pretty much everything."

Meriel smiled. "It's usually the things you never notice, so it's less intrusive than you'd think. They just limit our choices in most areas."

"Then I've got a question."

"Shoot."

"Grils only live for a few years, right?"

"Right."

"But stations live forever."

"That's the plan."

Sandy spoke slowly. "So, it's like drought all the time here. And if you don't have enough air, or food, or some vital thing, there's no place else to go and you die. If someone talks you into giving up something essential, you die. And it's over. Forever."

"Yup. That's what happened in the first hundred years in space. Some leaders sacrificed a little too much for short-term gains, and some stations died, and thousands of people died with them. That almost happened to L5."

"Where papa was born."

"That's right."

"And Earth and Haven have fewer of these requirements."

"Uh-huh," Meriel said. "Lots fewer."

"So, Tech Masters have ways for stations to survive with limited resources, right?"

Meriel nodded.

"And that's what they're proposing for Haven?"

She nodded again.

"Got it," Sandy said and smiled.

"Did the Techs pick our lunch today?"

"No. But they made sure it wouldn't kill you."

She reached into her pocket. "Good. Then how about another cookie?" she asked, as if the story was nothing more than common sense and did not touch every moral nerve in humanity.

After a bite, Sandy asked, "If the Tech Masters limit the citizen's behavior, who limits the Tech Masters?"

"Good question, sprite."

Techs

John and Becky rode the lift to white-zone for his meeting and debarked at a tree-lined promenade. Past cafés and boutiques in the shopping district, they walked until statues of civic heroes marked the entrance to Freedom Park.

"Do you recognize this, hon?"

"Freedom Square, Papa. This is where they have the parades."

"Right. Those buildings at the edges are the Assembly of Citizens for LeHavre Station."

"They make the laws?"

"Right. For LeHavre, but not for Haven. Do you know why I brought you here?"

Becky shook her head.

"Come," he said and led her through the park past plaques commemorating important events and monuments marking their victory in three invasions by the mightiest forces in the galaxy.

At the second of the three invasion memorials, he stopped and kneeled. Across one name, he brushed his hand, as he had many times before.

Becky followed her father's hand and traced the name with a finger. "Annie Smith. That's mama's name."

"And Pastor Lee's wife is next to her. Do you remember why they honor them?"

"They told us in school they broke that 'Hydra' thingy at Kilgore."

"And stopped an invasion," John said. "You know what the hydra is?"

"It steals comm signals. I used to play with the controller."

"That's right. You were young then. Do you have any memories of your mom?"

She nodded once, but then shook her head. "Sandy tells me stories about when we were kids, so we don't forget. And sometimes we pretend we're militia soldiers defending the farm and mama is our commander. I kinda think I remember her smell when I sit in Merry L's lap, but Mama was softer."

John's eyes softened, and she hugged him. But she was antsy and bit her lip.

"What is it, Princess?"

"Papa, I want Merry L to stay with us."

"She lives with us now."

"I mean all the time."

"I'm not sure she feels at home here, Princess."

"Well, that's our job now, isn't it?"

"She wants to return to space."

Becky dropped her gaze. "And I can't go. Sandy will go with her soon, and I'll be alone."

"I'll be with you."

She turned away. "You're busy."

John took her cheeks and faced her. With his thumb, he wiped the tears from her eyes. "I'm sorry, Princess," he said and held her tight. "I'll make more time for you."

His link buzzed again, but he ignored it, stood, and lifted her onto his shoulders.

John carried Becky past the administrative offices to the Technicians' Quarter and the Council of Masters. Unlike the Assembly buildings, those here were devoid of decoration: not austere, but respectful, suitable for an organization that held the public's trust but not their affection.

When they reached the lower ceilings of the Tech Administration District, John let Becky down and held her hand for the rest of the journey. To the left, they passed the Council Chamber where Tech Masters made policy and discussed the driest and most important data on LeHavre. Opposite, profiles in relief of men and women filled a dark gray wall, and below each was a range of years.

John stopped and led Becky to the profiles. "This wall was taken from L5."

"That's where you were born? Near Earth?"

He nodded.

"Who are they?" she asked.

"These are the Station Masters who kept us alive through the hard times. Good people. They once called them Ship Masters when they thought of stations as vessels. These people figured out how to keep a station working for hundreds of years despite wear and tear and limited resources. But they also developed a system that allows us to live free."

He brought her to the entrance and the oldest of the reliefs: Cynestar Donovan, the first Ship Master of L5. Only the Techs bothered to remember her name: not because she was unimportant to space colonization, but because she was the first to put the lives of the residents above the return on investment, and only the Techs cared.

A thick man met them and extended his hand, exposing military tattoos at the shirt cuff. "Mr. Smith? I'm Sven Tervain, secretary to Master Jerrett."

John shook the offered hand. *Security*. "I'm actually here to meet Colonel Lee."

"Yes, sir. He told us to expect the two of you. And this must be Miss Rebecca?"

She curtsied. "Princess, if you please."

"Yes, ma'am. May I get you something to drink?"

"Water for me," John said and turned to Becky. "Your Highness?"

"Grape juice, please."

The door opened, and a man with pursed lips and a red face walked out. Behind him, a thin man in a business suit shook hands with Colonel Lee and ran after the red-faced man.

"This way, Mr. Smith." Tervain said. "Princess Rebecca can stay here with me if you wish."

Becky aimed a suspicious glare at Tervain and took John's hand. John shrugged and led her into the room. But before the door closed behind them, she glanced over her shoulder and graced the secretary with a conspiratorial wink and regal wave.

Inside, Colonel Lee greeted John with a handshake. He was their neighbor, and on Sundays, Pastor Lee at the local church. But today in his tightly creased uniform, he was Colonel Warrin Lee, Representative from the Parliament of Haven and John's Militia commander.

"Hey Missy," he said to Becky who replied with a shy smile.

"You understand this is an informal discussion, John. And confidential."

"Of course."

Lee turned to two others in the room. "John and Rebecca Smith, I'd like you to meet Station Master Harold Jerrett and Chairwoman Svetla Lukas."

Their names were legends on Haven. Jerrett was the ultimate authority of the LeHavre Tech Masters. Lukas chaired the Council of Masters, the deliberating body of the Techs. They ran the Techs, and the Techs ran the station: at least everything not subject to popular will and opinion.

He shook their hands. "Just a moment, please," he said and leaned over to Becky. "If you stay you need to be quiet. Or you can go back outside with Mr. Tervain."

She eyed the door and frowned. When she held out her hand, palm up, John tapped his link to shift to her profile. After he gave it to her, she found a corner of the conference table and played quietly. In front of her, a hologram popped up with kittens climbing on play structures and tumbling with each other.

Lukas smiled at the girl and twisted a ring on her finger to darken the window overlooking the Council Chamber and brighten the holo.

"Thank you, Sven," Jerrett said as the burly secretary set drinks in front of them. "Sit, please, John."

"I'm honored to meet you both, but why am I here?"

"We want your insights. You've spent more time out near the other stations than the rest of us, John. To almost everyone out there, Haven and LeHavre are myths."

"You've seen the news about the immigration riots?" Lee asked.

John nodded.

Lee leaned over the table. "We need to head this off. It's getting out of control. Some Haveners are threatening to shoot the squatters."

"'Squatters'? Isn't that harsh, Colonel?" Lukas said.

"Semantics, ma'am. Squatters, refugees, or settlers. It doesn't matter what you call them. They're here and they're starving. Farmers like John are feeding them, but they fear the harvest won't be enough to feed their own kids and the . . . newcomers alike. More are coming, and—"

A loud roar stopped the discussion, and the adults turned. Becky's hologram kittens had grown into lions and two males now fought each other for dominance. She quickly tapped the link but too late. John put a finger to his lips, and the girl scowled but quit the game and sunk back into the chair with her arms folded across her chest.

"Colonel, we heard Haven is talking about reorganizing the government more like the Tech Masters here," Jerrett said.

Lee nodded.

"How is that going to work?" John asked.

Lukas replied, "The same way it does here, but with—"

"Haven isn't a station."

Jerrett raised his hands, palms up. "What's the difference? You have finite resources and infrastructure and can't support an unlimited population."

"Stations can limit their birthrate and stop new people from landing. Haven can't."

"Techs don't have our moral limitations either," Lee said.

Behind them, Becky stood by the live-action window running a popular world-building game and manipulating life-forms in the food chain. Her current project was an underwater obstacle course, and she was a *gorpa*, the Haven equivalent of a squid, as a *tark* hunted it.

Jerrett leaned back. "Well, I rather think we have a higher priority: survival first."

John nodded. "The lifeboat problem."

"We don't have enough data to make decent estimates about Haven's environment," Lee said. "Or how long it will take to terraform it. We won't put the indigenous life in zoos and make this into another Earth."

"Eek!" Becky said from the window with a hand over her mouth as the *tark* munched on her *gorpa* avatar. "Sorry."

John put a finger to his lips again.

Lukas's ring blinked, and she went to the window. "Continue please," she said and tapped the ring.

"Haven doesn't need more control," Lee said. "We need more resources."

"Or less demand," John said. "Fewer immigrants. Colonel, you may be right about running Haven like a station. We can't have majority rule. When the refugees become the majority, they'll exploit the farmers, and everyone will starve.

"We're the gorpa," Becky said.

Lukas turned to her. "What?"

"Becky, please," John said with a frown.

Lukas raised her hand. "What is it, dear?"

"The tarks will eat the gorpa."

Lee smiled. "And we're the gorpa."

"She's right," Jerrett said. "The tragedy of the commons."

"Too many want to come," John said. "We can't stop them, but we can't feed them either. Haven needs your help."

"LeHavre won't shoot civilians out of the sky for you," Lukas said.

John leaned over the table. "It's not just families, ma'am. Smugglers use the storms to drop off Archer combatants along with the refugees."

Lukas glanced at Lee. "How can you tell the difference?"

"We have a few clues," Lee said. "But I think you can only tell by their behavior." He frowned and shook his head. "If the farmers think the refugee ships are ferrying thugs who plan to steal the land that feeds their kids, you won't need to shoot the coyotes out of the sky. The farmers will do it themselves."

John raised his hand. "What if we work with the nearby stations to limit—"

Applause interrupted, and Lukas waved her fingers to mute the sounds from the chamber below. "We don't want to get tied into alliances right now."

"We're the poor cousin out here," Jerrett said. "If we let the big stations on board, they'll trample us. Look how Sol uses the UNE to bully the near stars." A document appeared above the desk, and he dismissed it with a flick of a finger.

Lee shook his head. "I disagree, Sir. We don't want LeHavre to be independent. We need the stations."

"Colonel, we're too weak to negotiate," Jerrett said. "They're even demanding a fuel subsidy for those traveling through."

John smiled. "Laugh at them. Change the conversation."

"Slow down," Lee said. "What do you mean?"

John took a breath. "None of you are spacers, so you—"

"We all live in space, John," Master Lukas said. "You don't think of us as spacers?"

"Not really. It's a point of view, ma'am. People here orient themselves like the station was the center of the universe and try to make it just like Earth."

"The agricultural decks?"

John nodded and opened his hand over the table. A holo of a console appeared, and with a tap of a finger, the ceiling transformed from a neutral beige to an ocean of stars marred only by the structural ribs of the torus.

"You see the stars as 'outside,'" John said. "The same way they do on Earth, and Mars, and the large colonies. But spacers sail the sea of stars, and they see stations as ships. They know that Haven dwarfs even Enterprise."

"How is that relevant?" Jerrett asked.

"You don't get it yet. Haven has what everyone wants. Land. And they *must* deal with us."

Jerrett furrowed his brows. "They haven't mentioned—"

"Just because Enterprise didn't put it on the table doesn't mean they don't want it. And we need their help to limit immigration to sustainable limits."

"What's in it for them?"

"They don't have any good options except to work with you. Look. The transports can't get here unless they refuel at the nearby stations. If we decline to accept the immigrants, the ship will return there. Those stations don't have the resources to support them. That puts them in a bind. So, move the choke point back upstream to the stations."

Lukas gave a thumbs up in front at the window for the Council below and returned to the table. "Yes, but we can't refuse them. Like Harold said, we won't open fire on them."

"Then bluff. We're a mystery to them. They don't know us or what we're willing to do."

"How are we gonna deal with the coyotes?" Lee said. "They're small and many."

John stood and paced. "Maybe cut their profit margins."

"What do you mean?"

He stopped and put his hands on a chair-back. "Smuggling is expensive across fifteen light-years."

"You've been spacing for a while, John," Lee said. "You speak from experience?"

"Smugglers are in business. Steal their business."

"How?" Lukas asked.

"Make it *our* business. Take it from them. Provide the transport ourselves."

"You can't be serious," Jerrett said.

"Cut the ticket price but require training in a trade needed here."

"Teach them to find gorpa," Becky said.

Lukas smiled. "What do you mean, dear?"

Becky turned to Colonel Lee.

"It's from last Sunday's lesson," Lee said. "Give a person a gorpa and they eat for a day. Teach them to fish for gorpa, and they eat for their entire lives. Is that it, Becky?"

She nodded and disappeared under the table.

"That's right, Princess," John said. "We train them in farming or aeroponics or soil processing. That'll help us better match the food supply to population."

Lukas raised an eyebrow, and Lee tipped his head to John. "I told you."

"Give us a moment." Jerrett said and began a quiet conversation with Lukas.

An airplane made from a drink napkin glided to a stop on the desk near Lukas. At the other end of the room, Becky bit her lip and ducked below the table. The chairwoman glanced at the toy, picked it up, and placed it on the chair beside her. A moment later, it disappeared.

John leaned toward Lee. "Meriel has been scanning the news outlets allied to the UNE. She said Sol is pushing propaganda we're terrorizing the squatters. We have to counter the story, or they'll apply legal pressure through Lander."

Lee nodded. "Got it."

Jerrett turned back to them. "Who's going to tell Enterprise we're ready to bargain?"

"And when," John said. "We need to do this before the Archers get a foothold."

Recoil

As they left the gym, Meriel's link buzzed with a message from Jerri Vonegon, the *Tiger*'s pilot and nav chief.

"Chief Hope, the captain requests all bridge ratings report to the D0-6 simulator."

"I'm on my way to meet John," Meriel said. "Is it mandatory?"

Molly's voice came on. "Only if you want to sit nav. It has a new sphere calculation based on John's insights."

"Thanks, ma'am."

"Acknowledged. Out."

"Merry L, what's the big deal about this 'sphere' thing you and papa talk about?"

"It's jump math, hon. When we're FTL, we're like quanta, a probability with a series of possible destinations . . ."

Sandy's eyes glazed over.

"The farther you go, the bigger the uncertainty in your final position."

"Like shooting my rifle on the farm? The farther away my target, the harder it is to hit."

"A little," Meriel said as she led Sandy into the lift. "Every star and planet can pull a spaceship off course."

"Like Haven's gravity pulling my bullet down."

"That's right. But space has lots of different gravities. They're all moving, and we don't always know exactly where every mass is. So, the course gets less certain the farther you travel. That's the error, and we call it the 'sphere' because it's three-dimensional. When the sphere is too big, you need to stop and recalibrate.

"That's what papa does?"

Meriel nodded. "And he's good at it. A smaller sphere means a longer jump, and that means fewer jumps and shorter transit times."

"Money," Sandy said.

"Right. And it's less likely you'll jump into a star or somewhere you can't return from."

"Got it. So, the new nav system Aunt Jerri mentioned has papa's improvements?"

"That's right," Meriel said, and a broad smiled crossed Sandy's face.

Leaving the elevator, Meriel's bracelet buzzed again with a message from Elizabeth at the shuttle port on Haven.

```
Just landed back on Haven. Check
IGB. Now. And sit down first.
```

"IGB feed," Meriel said and leaned against the wall to listen.

```
"Terrorists attacked Enterprise Sta-
tion today and left two thousand sta-
tioners dead or missing. Quick action
by security limited the destruction to
the red-zone docks. Investigation on-
going . . . Speculation is an explo-
sion near the impound dock . . ."
```

Is Enterprise OK?

```
"Gravity instabilities have left
many with nausea . . . Techs say they
will restore stability within the hour
and tethers will no longer be need-
ed . . ."
```

Meriel called her sister back. "Liz, did you hear more about this?"

"No, but the news updates are continuous," Elizabeth said. "I'll call if I find out more."

Meriel jotted a text for John.

```
Call when you can.
M.
```

Meriel took the girl's hand. "Let's go find your father."

"Will this delay our trip?" Sandy asked as Meriel pulled her towards the elevator.

"Maybe. Enterprise was our first stop."

"Is it safe?" Sandy asked, but Meriel did not answer.

***

In a blue-zone bar on LeHavre, Penny sat with Sam and sampled brews.

"I miss The Gear Case on Enterprise," he said.

Penny sipped a stout. "Weren't you underage then? Who snuck you in?"

"Nobody. I walked in with the crew of the *Edwards*," Sam said.

A handsome young officer leaned over the bar to block Sam and smiled at her. Ignoring her glare, he put a hand on her arm. She took a finger, bent it backward until he released her, and pushed him away.

"Buzz off," she said, but as she turned back to Sam, she leaned an elbow on the bar and hid her face with her hand.

"What?"

"By the bar. That's Milo, my supervisor." She glanced up again to see him staring at her. "Crap," she mumbled and raised her drink to him.

Milo sneered and returned to chatting up a beautiful woman.

"She's too pretty for him," Sam said.

"And too expensive," Penny replied. The link on her collar buzzed, and she tapped it. "The body's here. Drink up."

In the morgue, Penny stood over a grav sled holding the corpse from Terni. From a tray of instruments, she poked a small needle into his finger and inserted the needle into a machine.

"What are you doing?" Sam asked.

"The first tests are for pathogens and a DNA screen." She snapped a switch, and a translucent red curtain swept across the length of the body. "Then a tissue scan."

She took a vid of the scarring on his abdomen and another of the palm tattoo. "How about finding out where this tat is from."

"Wide search," Sam said. "Body art, civil and criminal."

```
"Closest match four percent."
```

A range of tattoos appeared, all abstract or highly geometric.

"What did Meriel say about inventory?" Penny asked as she pushed the grav sled to the refrigerator.

Sam nodded. "Wide search parts, logistics, inventory."

```
"Closest match seventy-six percent."
```

Crates and parts assembly codes scrolled by on the display.

"Decode," he said. "Stop. Item one. Penny, what's this? 'HLA-C, Chrome 15: HERC2.' Eye color? Phenotype?"

Penny studied the vid. "Phenotype. A genetics characterization." She frowned. "Why would they do that? Sam, check the dossier and see if any of the corsairs have tattoos on their palms like this."

"None," Sam said.

Penny shook her head and opened the refrigerator door to return the refugee's body.

Instead of an empty slab, she found the med school's IT tech, her date from earlier that week.

"God!" she said, jumped back, and put her hand to her heart.

"What?"

"Sam, this is the IT guy I stole the badge from—"

Before Penny could finish, the lab went dark, and she froze in the navigation lights that beamed through the lab windows.

"I'll go check the utilities cabinet," he said and left for the corridor.

"Hurry."

She turned at the sound of a scuff behind her but stopped after a pinch on her shoulder. Stunned, she could not resist as unseen hands dragged her to a chair.

"Argh," she grunted and found her voice. "Who are you?"

A small lamp blazed from the sled and hid a man's face in the shadow.

"Let's discuss the Tsogets," he said while removing grey bricks from a bag and setting timers on them.

"Who's that?"

"Come now, you recently viewed profiles for Marge and Isaak Tsoget, and we need to know why such obscure academics interest you."

"Like I said, who's that?"

He gave her a side eye and placed a brick in the adjacent lab nearest the torus shell. When he returned, he leaned over her and slapped her in the face.

"You're not paying attention," he said and opened a small case with delicate instruments. "This can go easy or hard. I like hard. Who else are you working with? Your friend on the slab said you dated."

"You didn't have to kill him."

He set another gray brick near the IT hub. "No, but it was more fun that way."

"If you hurt me, I won't tell you anything."

"You won't have a choice. Where do you keep the corsair bodies?"

The woman Penny had seen in the bar with her supervisor entered the morgue. "Any progress yet?"

"We're just getting serious. What did you do with her boss?"

"They'll find him in a week or so. Where's her friend from the bar?"

"Down the hall."

The woman went after Sam while the man set a fuse in another slab, the timer counting down.

He took a pick from his case. "Last chance."

The lights came back on, and a few seconds later, Sam barged in. "Oh sorry, Penny."

"Look out!" she shouted, but too late, as the woman poked a blaster into his back.

Sam raised his hands. "You're not supposed to have that on station."

"Over by the girl," the woman said and pushed him.

He faced the woman with an innocent smile and backpedaled. "Hey, I'm a friend from the surface, and—" He tripped on a stool and dropped his arms to catch himself, which incidentally knocked the blaster from the woman's hands. Undeterred, she rocked Sam with two quick jabs. But her right cross crashed into a lab tray of sharp instruments Sam had grabbed to defend himself.

The man turned toward the noise and drew his own weapon. But before he could fire, Penny kicked him in the stomach and the head, shoving him face first into the grav sled. From the sled, the corpse fell and pinned the attacker under the dead weight.

Sam's opponent wound up for a kick, but he tapped the collar-link he had keyed to the morgue's gravity controls to zero the g's. The slow rotation of the torus was not enough for the woman to keep her footing, and her angular momentum spun her into a cabinet.

Sam was a spacer and accustomed to weightlessness, and before she could regain her balance, he pushed off the wall and kicked her into the passageway. As she clawed her way back to the morgue and the gun that still hovered there, the console spoke.

> "Priority search complete. Two DNA matches found for Tiger Corsair-8, Le-Havre Station Medical School—"

Freed from the dead weight of the body, Penny's attacker grabbed the gun and pointed it at her. But without a stable footing, his aim was off, and the slug shot past her into the lab next door.

The slug nicked a grey brick and a blinding white-orange fire sprayed onto the methane and oxy tanks which exploded, blowing a hole in the hull, and opening it to space. The explosion cut the utility cables and rammed the assailant into the bulkhead.

Pressure doors slammed closed before they were sucked into space. But the doors trapped the female attacker outside where she followed the air and equipment out the breach. As she drifted away, she struggled for a few seconds and became still.

Sam found his footing on the mass of the grav sled and pushed. His heel landed on the man's jaw, and when Penny held a bone saw to his throat, Sam took the gun.

"You OK?" Sam asked Penny as he tied the man to a gurney with surgical tape.

"A little stiff from his drug still," she said and rubbed her hands together. "You zeroed the gravity?"

"I saw the woman coming and thought we'd need help before security got here. She didn't move like a spacer."

"How are you still moving?" the attacker asked Penny. "The catatonic shoulda lasted longer."

She smirked. "You didn't do your homework. My metabolism and dopamine levels are abnormally high." She pointed to the countdown timers now approaching sixty seconds and turned to Sam. "How soon did you say security will get here?"

"Is there another way out?" Sam said.

She shook her head.

"Airlocks? Maintenance hatches?"

"The first explosion would have sealed them. It's tight as a drum."

"Except for that big hole." Sam said and faced the attacker. "If you don't disarm them, you'll die too."

"I go to a better world His Eminence has built for us."

"Crap, another Archer," Penny said.

Sam examined the bricks of incendiaries and timers and prepared to pull the detonator out.

Penny stopped him and poked their attacker. "Are there more?"

He grinned.

Security in hard-suits approached through the breach, and Service Techs appeared across the passageway. Only thirty seconds left.

"Just these will take out the entire lab and our rescuers," Sam said.

Penny nodded. "And the morgue."

The lab groaned and lurched as the lab separated from the torus, restrained only by a few intact cables.

"It might be better if we break loose," Sam said as the morgue and lab floated toward a tram tube.

Penny patted the man down. "Not yet."

From his shirt pocket, she retrieved a link displaying the same numbers as the countdown timers. She tapped a button and all the timers stopped.

"How could you know?" the man said.

She shook her head. "I guess they don't recruit for brains. Quiet now," she said and pricked him with the pin he'd used to paralyze her.

Comfortable in zero-g, Penny and Sam floated until the centripetal acceleration from the slowly rotating station settled them and everything loose onto the wall farthest from the tethering cables.

Sam pointed a thumb to the last message on the console as it drifted past. "The DNA search. That was about the corsair captain from the *Tiger*?"

Penny nodded. "He was just entered into the database."

"Who was the match with?"

"I think I know," she said. "We need to call Meriel. If I'm right, the dossier is a bomb and could blow up in her face."

Sam pushed himself to a window. Outside, maintenance workers in warm-suits and hard-suits jetted to the lab to reconnect restraining cables and life support.

"We may be here awhile, Penny—"

A billboard flashed as a tram raced by.

```
Station Security Alert:
  Meriel Hope, please maintain your
 current position.
```

"And she may have her own problems."

***

In a green-zone corridor on the way to John, Meriel stopped as a claxon blared her name over the PA with the same message Sam and Penny had read.

What's this about? Is John OK? Becky? She pinged John but raised an eyebrow at the response.

```
This link responds only to Security.
```

Can they do that? "Call your dad, Sandy."

When John did not answer his daughter either, she texted.

Meriel scanned the area, but escape would be trouble with Sandy along. LeHavre was home and they should have nothing to fear. She sighed and dropped her shoulders. "Nothing to be afraid of, hon."

The LeHavre police arrived and behind them, the helmeted blue uniforms of the UNE. Meriel stiffened and took Sandy's hand. *The UNE.* That's *to be afraid of.*

"What is—" Meriel began.

The police sergeant interrupted. "Please Ms. Hope, these men want a word with you and ask that you go with them."

"Who are they?"

"They're UNE Security Forces from the *Intrepid*."

"Is this a police order?"

"No, not by any means," the sergeant said. "They say it's a request for an interview."

"What's the UNE doing here?" she said to an opaque visor. When the USF officer did not answer, she turned to the sergeant. "Will you stay with me?"

"Yes, if you wish."

"And please call John Smith. This is his daughter, and I will only release her to his custody."

"Of course, and there should be no worries. This is simply a courtesy visit. Is that OK?"

Meriel nodded, and two USF uniforms confronted her.

"Meriel Hope, are you the legal owner of the *Princess*?"

"Yes, but I don't—"

The USF officers took each of her arms and a third officer put restraints on her wrists while Sandy still held her hand.

"Wait!" the police sergeant said. "You told me this was simply an interview."

A USF officer shouldered him aside. "The interview is over. Meriel Hope, you are under arrest for acts of terrorism on Enterprise Station, mass murder, and attempted murder of all residents."

"What? I just heard about that. How—"

"Your ship caused the damage."

"No way—"

"It exploded and took part of Enterprise with it."

Her legs shook. "Blew up? The *Princess*?" The future she had worked so hard for, risked so much for, to help the orphans was gone.

The police sergeant's jaw dropped. "You can't for a moment think—"

A USF officer pried Sandy's hand away from Meriel's.

The risk to Sandy overcame Meriel's shock. "No! Let her go!" she shouted, butted her head against a blue uniform, and pushed another into the wall. Behind her, the third lifted her bound wrists, but she lifted her heel and kicked him in the groin. But another squad of USF officers approached.

She leaned over to the LeHavre police officer. "Don't let them take her."

A blue uniform put a baton around Meriel's neck and hoisted her off her feet as another sedated her. A third officer elbowed the sergeant away and grabbed Sandy, kicking and screaming. With the targets restrained, the USF surrounded them and dragged them down the corridor.

The police sergeant stood in front of them and held his arms out. "You can't do this!"

"We're the UNE," a blue uniform said, aiming a blaster at his face and shouldering him out of the way.

The USF rushed them through the green-zone corridors, bypassing immigration and customs. But news travels fast on a small station.

When they opened the doors to the blue-zone docks, hundreds of jeering civilians waited for them. Workers yelled from the gantry cranes and threw debris. One officer stopped and spoke into his headset.

A few moments later, fifty more armed blue uniforms in riot gear filed out of a huge warship and formed a double line. Between them marched the arresting officers with Meriel and Sandy.

Captain Stark stood at the airlock and surveyed the confrontation. Next to him stood Ambassador Bakshi with a sneer on his face.

Sven Tervain elbowed his way through the crowd with Master Lukas in his wake, followed closely by John and

Becky. Stark nodded, and his Marines let the chairwoman approach but held John back.

"Sir, there must be a mistake," Lukas said. "We're a sovereign station and your officers have no authority to—"

"My authority is not an issue here," Stark said. "My orders are to arrest a terrorist, and I won't release her."

"The child isn't involved in this. You must free her. Please, sir."

The ambassador gazed at her with contempt. "She was apprehended with the fugitive and may be part of this heinous act."

"She's only twelve years old. I beg you, leave her with us."

Bakshi waved his arms. "What do we care? Pick her up at Enterprise."

Stark turned to Lukas and frowned. "Ma'am, I cannot break the cordon for a mob and still guarantee her safety. I promise to keep the child safe from the terrorist."

"That's not what I—" Lukas began.

"No!" John shouted as the USF hustled Meriel and Sandy toward them. He waved to Sandy and pushed forward, but Tervain stopped him.

Lukas grabbed his arm. "No, John, we can't fight them here. The Marines are on Haven."

"We'll be able to do even less on Enterprise."

"Please, they'll destroy us."

John pulled free. "Let me go with them!"

Becky tugged on his hands. "No, papa!"

"Please, John," Lukas said. "We'll do our best to free them."

Lukas waved to the ambassador. "By what authority do you—"

Bakshi sneered from behind the blue uniforms. "By the Aldebaran Accord, stations may request UNE aid to respond to acts of piracy or terrorism."

"We're not a party to that treaty," Lukas said.

"Enterprise is."

"But LeHavre is a sovereign—"

Bakshi snorted. "You're nothing out here. Recognized by no one."

"We have standing on Lander."

"Lander isn't here, and you don't speak for them."

"Papa!" Sandy called as the USF pulled her past toward the *Intrepid*'s airlock.

"Sandy!" John shouted and waved and then put Becky's hand in Tervain's. "Watch Becky."

"You can't do this!" John shouted as he clawed his way to the cordon. But a USF officer slammed the butt of a pulse rifle into his forehead, knocked him down, and pointed the rifle at him. Before the officer could shoot, Tervain blocked his aim.

"Who the hell do you think you are to infringe on the rights of our citizens?" Lukas yelled.

The ambassador sneered and pointed out the window where the *Intrepid* lay docked, its missile bay doors open, and laser cannons aimed at them.

"We're the UNE," Bakshi said. "Who the hell do you think *you* are."

As Sandy and Meriel disappeared into the airlock, John stood, and Becky jumped into his arms. Lukas glared and pressed against the USF security chief who restrained her. The citizens booed and cursed, but otherwise remained peaceful as the USF backed into the airlock.

When the warship undocked, Lukas took John's arm. "You're going to get her?"

With Becky's arms wrapped tight around his neck, John said, "If I can raise money for a ticket."

"We'll take care of that. We have a mission for you."

Chapter 11
Mars 6, Sol System

The window overlooking the Amazonis Planitia on Mars clouded, and a newsfeed appeared.

> "Damage to Enterprise is severe but has been contained to the red-zone security docks. One suspect is in custody while the hunt is on for others. Hundreds of lives lost in the breach . . ."

In a close-up of the red-zone docks, a spray of debris and sparks from drifting cables emphasized the damage to the missing slice of the torus. But as the vid zoomed farther out from the huge station, the damage appeared minimal.

Ellen backed up until she ran into the arm of an overstuffed chair and threw her glass to shatter against the wall.

"What the hell happened! Why wasn't that worse?"

"Someone intervened," the voice said.

She closed her eyes, clenched her teeth, and took a deep breath.

"Ms. Biadez? Ms. Biadez?"

"*Who* intervened?" Ellen asked.

"Unknown. Enterprise security isn't talking."

"Find out," she said. "And Ambassador Bakshi?"

"Untouched. Inbound during the explosion."

She frowned and shook her head. "Damn, a dead ambassador would have brought the whole fleet out there." She lit a cigarette and paced the room.

"Ms. Biadez?"

"Wait," she said and kicked a droid that scurried from her path.

"We may salvage this. Has the Enterprise Assembly of Citizens invoked the Aldebaran Accord?"

"Yes, the contingency was executed."

"Then we need the Assembly to sign the new treaty before the Tech Masters declare Enterprise safe and operational. That will move our timetable in."

"That'll look like extortion."

She scoffed. "Who gives a shit? We own the media and control what it *looks* like. We only care they sign. Is our man in place?"

"Yes."

She kicked the little droid that swept up bits of her broken glass. "And learn to make a f'ing martini," she said and kicked it again.

"And if the Techs intervene in the negotiations?" she said.

"We have a plan in place for that."

"Nothing subtle, I hope. Chaos is to our advantage. And what about . . . the Hope girl?"

"The UNE will have her soon."

Ellen stalked the little robot again as it tried to skitter out of her way. "Wiggle, wiggle," she said with a sneer and kicked the droid again, this time fatally.

"What?"

She smiled as the little robot stopped moving and went dark. "And make sure they never let her go."

Chapter 12
LeHavre Station, Jira-1 System

LeHavre Station—Outbound

On a bunk in a small, padded cell, Meriel recovered from the sedative. Cold metal brought her eyes down to the cuffs circling her wrists and the bar separating them.

"Where are we?" she said, rose, and went to the door.

"Outbound from LeHavre," said a voice over the PA system.

"Let me see Sandy!"

"Quiet now, that'll do you no good."

"I want the girl," she said again in a calmer tone.

"She's a few meters down the hall. Go see for yourself. You push the door, and it'll open right up."

Meriel kicked it and the door cracked open, but she hesitated. "Why would you help me?"

"Really. You can walk right out. Better hurry, though."

With a curled lip, Meriel held out her hands with the restraints. "What are these?"

"Ah, won't take the bait, huh? Those are amputation cuffs. The boys and I have a pool on how far you're going to get before the blood loss drops you."

"Why are you doing this?"

"My sister's kid was caught in the blast on Enterprise. He's on a ventilator, but his brain is gone. You can't imagine what a few seconds at near-vacuum does."

A memory came of the *Tiger* attack and bodies floating outside the ship. "Yes, I can."

"I'm betting you're a psycho bitch who thinks she can brass it out without her hands. Take a step outside the door and you'll bleed out during jump. Here, let me help."

After a click and whir, the door opened further, and a small baggie with a tranq pill slipped inside.

"Please, put us together," she said. "Sandy's never been to space."

"We're one-g continuous. She can't tell.

"She's alone. Please."

"She's with someone who'll care for her."

"I know how you people take care of kids. I want to see Sandy!"

"Not possible."

She banged her head on the door until blood flowed down her forehead and she collapsed, dizzy.

"What was that about?" the voice said.

"I'm gonna say you tortured me in custody."

He laughed. "Go ahead. You're a terrorist, remember? They'll love that." He chuckled. "Tell them it was First Mate Silvik who beat you up: no, no, viciously molested you. Yeah, I like that. I'll get a medal for—"

The claxon interrupted.

"Oh, I forgot to mention. Our jump alert is shorter on Navy boats."

"Crap!" She reached for the tranq, but the destroyer jumped before the pill found her mouth and nightmares overwhelmed her.

Chapter 13
Free Space

UNE Intrepid

Meriel woke clammy from the familiar dream of the pirate attack on the *Princess*, her hands gritty from the crushed tranq pill.
She stood to continue banging on the door, but the white pain from the headache brought her back to her knees.

"Who the hell put those things on her," came a woman's voice from the passageway. "I don't give a damn about your protocols. They're banned. Take them off."

The cuffs clicked and fell away, and Meriel rubbed her wrists. "Who are—?"

"Ms. Hope," the woman said, "I'm bringing Alessandra to you. Please back away from the door."

After Meriel backed up to the opposite end of the cell, the door opened, and Sandy rushed in and hugged her.

"You OK, sprite?"

The girl nodded but did not let go.

A thirty-something woman in a tailored business suit with well-manicured nails and a hairstyle suited for a steady gravity leaned against the wall just inside the door. "You're welcome."

Meriel studied her open face and unthreatening stance. "You're not afraid to be in here with me?"

"Should I be?"

Absolutely, Meriel thought. *Is she naïve or just manipulative?*

The woman approached and stood flatfooted with her feet parallel and reached out her hand.

Incautious or not trained to fight.

"I'm Jennifer Churchill, your advocate."

Meriel returned the firm grip and steady gaze. *Naïve.* "You're my what?"

Jennifer handed them juice packs. "Your lawyer. Special Counsel appointed for you by the UNE."

And the UNE ex-president wants me dead. Meriel sat on the bunk with Sandy and eyed Jennifer with suspicion. "I have a lawyer."

"What's the name and I'll contact them. They may be able to assist."

"Jeremy Bell. On Lander."

The lawyer took a seat on the bunk and tapped her bracelet. "Oh, my. He's civil, not criminal, and not licensed by the UNE. He might not be of much use, but I'll invite him to consult."

"Yes, please. And please contact John Smith on LeHavre. He's her father. She needs to be with him."

"Already done, Ms. Hope. I advised him to bring his custody papers."

"And please accept any calls from Theodora Duncan."

"Do you have her number?"

"No. But she may find you."

"Might she possess any exculpatory evidence?"

Meriel turned away and shook her head.

"Now, we'll need to craft your guilty plea before we dock to anticipate the—"

"But I didn't do anything."

"Too late, Ms. Hope. There's more than enough evidence to convict you."

"I'll let a jury decide."

Jennifer smiled. "Oh my, how quaint. There will be no jury. An administrative judge will hear your case."

"The investigation will prove me innocent."

"The investigation is over, Ms. Hope."

"But it's only been a few hours!"

"They have the evidence, and it's enough."

"Can I see it?"

"When we get to Enterprise, we can review it together."

"Have you seen it?"

"Some, and it's enough to convince a judge."

What in hell could tie me to blowing up my own ship? "Like what?"

"They have a vid of you on the *Princess* within the last year."

"That's not possible."

Jennifer tapped her link again to display a holovid of Meriel in a warm-suit at the *Princess's* airlock.

Meriel shut her mouth. *Damn. The surveillance spider.*

The lawyer nodded and smiled. "Ah, yes. I understand now. No, don't tell me anything. Now, let's prepare your guilty plea. However, I need to warn you your accomplice is being detained."

Meriel jumped to her feet and raised her arms. "I didn't do anything. How can I have an accomplice?" Sandy tugged on Meriel's hand, and she sat again.

"Nick Zanek? Security has evidence of his involvement."

'They're trying to blow her up,' Nick's message had said. "He said 'they.'"

"Who?"

"Nick."

"Then you know him?"

"Yeah, yeah," Meriel said.

Jennifer stood and paced. "You'd be a terrible witness under cross-examination."

"Nick knew what they were doing. He caught them and warned me."

"He contacted you before the event?"

"Just before, I guess. My link will show that. Can you get it?"

"It's being held for evidence. And I'm not sure it helps you."

"But he must know what happened. Can you let me see him?"

"I'm sorry. The courts would never allow it."

"Can you talk to him?"

"No. He has his own problems, Ms. Hope." Jennifer stopped pacing and sat again. "Now, if the judge accepts your guilty plea, and you say you acted alone, that will spare your friends from being investigated."

"What do you mean?"

"Well, the *Tiger* was docked at Enterprise at the same time as your visit to the *Princess*." Jennifer checked her link. "I believe your crew-mates, Sergeant Cook, Ms. Soquette, and Ms. Vonegon took leave at that time. A Mr. Smith as well. I'm guessing he's Sandy's father?"

"They didn't know what I was doing."

The lawyer shook her head. "Terrible witness, just terrible," she mumbled. "Well, if the court finds any of them in any way culpable, even for transporting you on or off station, they could spend the rest of their lives in the mines."

"So, if I admit to something I didn't do, my friends, who also did nothing wrong, will avoid prison?"

Jennifer nodded and stood as if the discussion was closed. "Now, about your plea—"

"Not until I talk to Jeremy."

"Ms. Hope, I don't think—"

"Jeremy first."

"As you wish." Jennifer turned to Sandy and nodded. "Miss Smith. Come with me, please."

"Let her stay," Meriel said.

Jennifer nodded. "I'll stop by again before we jump," she said and closed the door behind her.

Meriel scooted back on the bunk until her back rested against the wall and pulled her knees in. When Sandy nestled close, Meriel put her arm around her.

"Well, kid," Meriel said. "I sure didn't expect your first trip to space would go like this."

"I've got a headache."

Meriel tapped the juice pack in the girl's hands and opened her own. "Drink up. The jump field sucks the electrolytes from your body. It'll go away in a few minutes with a little juice."

When Sandy opened her pack, Meriel found the girl's fingernails bitten to the quick. Meriel frowned, and from her neck, took the necklace with the cross and q-chip and held it out.

"This was my mom's," Meriel said. "It'll protect you."

"Sounds like magic."

"Faith, hon. Show me your ankle."

Sandy complied, and Meriel wound the necklace around her ankle, clipped it, and tucked it into the girl's sock.

"It helped me when I was having a rough time. It's not about the object. Think about your dad and your sister and me and how much we love you."

"Who are these people?" the girl asked as Meriel held her tight.

"The UNE, hon."

"You used to swear at them a lot."

Meriel nodded.

"I saw papa on the dock. Why couldn't he help us?"

"The UNE had blasters and could have hurt lots of people."

"What's gonna happen now?"

Meriel put a finger under Sandy's chin and lifted it to peer into her eyes. A furrow marred the girl's brow, and Meriel rubbed it away with her thumb.

"Well, your papa will come and pick you up, that's what's gonna happen."

"I mean what'll happen to *you*?"

"I'll be OK, hon. Jeremy and Aunt Teddy will help," Meriel said, and Sandy's shoulders relaxed under her arm.

"There's no tingle. Are we on the surface?"

"No. We're accelerating at one-g to a jump point."

"It feels like gravity."

"Same thing, pretty much," Meriel said, stopping short of a lecture on general relativity.

Sandy rose from the bunk and walked the three paces to the door, running her fingers along the padded bulkhead. "This is like my room. But I have a dresser and a mirror."

"It's a warship, hon."

"Where are they taking us?"

"Jennifer said Enterprise. You'll like it there. The sims are terrific, and I have a friend who knows them really well."

"Tell me."

"Well, before my parents . . . died, Liz and I would go to the sims on Enterprise with Tommy, especially the dino-sims. I think they call it *Raptor City* now. LeHavre doesn't have anything so sophisticated yet."

Sandy touched the sink and turned the faucet. "And I have hot water. Go on."

"Well, Tommy and I were always stopping to help Liz, so the dinos usually ate us a few minutes into the game. Or we'd die of infection or starvation. One time a holo appeared of an explorer dressed in hunting clothes. He had an old slug-shooter rifle and a beat-up hat and said his name was Nick."

Sandy returned to the bunk and laid her head on Meriel's lap. "Is that the guy Jennifer mentioned?"

"Yup."

"What happened?"

"He froze the game just before a raptor pod was going to attack, and he told us what to do."

"Told you what?"

"It was simple. He said to listen for squeaks. That meant they were hunting us, and we needed to hide. Later we got trapped in a cave by an allosaurus, and he used rocks on the walls to tell us where to go."

"Is that fair?"

"Here, it looks like this." Meriel drew on her palm. "A triangle of four dots to show direction and a tail of dots for distance. It was so clear to us, we didn't need to think about what it meant."

"Sounds like cheating."

"Between visits, he taught us other stuff, so we didn't need so much help."

"For instance?" Sandy asked.

"Well, first aid using primitive roots. Entry pre-checks to prepare for what's on a new level. How to analyze the territory of predators and avoid what attracts them."

Meriel looked away. "After my folks died, and Elizabeth and I were isolated in social services, he snuck messages to us. He knew all the ins and outs of the station and could always reach us. And when they split all us orphans apart on different ships and wouldn't let us talk to each other, he gave us a secret way to communicate."

"He loves you a lot."

Meriel nodded. "We love him too."

"I guess Nick could help now."

"Yeah. But it looks like he's mixed up in it too." She squeezed Sandy again. "Don't worry, it'll work out. Now, close your eyes and remember the zero-g lessons we practiced today."

Sandy closed her eyes. And as she rotated her arms and hands the way Meriel had taught her, Meriel frowned and studied the door for weaknesses. *Patience. There will be a time . . .*

Chapter 14
Enterprise Station, Procyon A System

Enterprise Station—On Station

Station Master Kofi Sikibo kept his white-zone office devoid of personal effects and any other sign a human held his position. He hid the clutter associated with his many responsibilities in the rooms next door. There, his adjutant, IT Domain Master Rivan Tellar, organized the data feeds for Sikibo with robotic efficiency.

Sikibo's desk floated four feet above the deck, so he could stand as he worked. A back injury he'd sustained as a young maintenance tech had left him with two postures: erect and prone. The latter was inappropriate for meetings, and thanks to his tall and narrow frame, the second was intimidating for anyone in his presence.

"Get them the hell off my station!" Sikibo shouted. "They don't have jurisdiction here."

Jergen Belson, President of the Assembly of Citizens, tapped his fingers on the chair. "The Aldebaran Accord gives them jurisdiction in matters of terrorism, Kofi."

"They don't have authority over our security teams."

After Belson blinked twice, his link projected an image of a UNE destroyer. "That's their authority."

"This is an internal matter, Jergen. Who invoked the Accord?"

"I did. The Assembly demanded it. There's no way your techs would wrap this up this century, and we need to tranquilize the populace."

"But all your evidence is from anonymous sources," the Station Master said. "And circumstantial."

"It's fascinating though, isn't it? Madness. Drugs. Terrorism. Motive. Such a fun story, eh?" He waved his hands. "You're being unreasonable, Kofi. Sol has always been a profitable trade partner and they're only concerned about maintaining ties."

"Earth is afraid of Haven. They're hardly a dot on the charts and you're ready to cut them out. Starve them. Haven't they been through enough at the UNE's hands?"

Belson shook his head. "My, my. You buy those rumors from the drugged-addled terrorist they have in custody?"

"Lander has a judgment against BioLuna for the Haven invasion, Jergen. That's not a rumor."

"Kofi, we've been friends for a long time, no? Believe me, the UNE has no fear of Haven. They only want to help us."

Sikibo considered his old rival's lie. "How does occupying our station and removing our ability to adjudicate our own criminal cases help?"

"This is only one case, Kofi. They'll leave as soon as we're safe."

"Without a trade deal?"

Belson's eyes darted away for a moment. "Kofi, they're—"

"You can't force a deal down our throats, Jergen. No other station will comply unless the Council of Masters agrees."

"Of course. No one is thinking of any such thing."

"No one? Ambassador Bakshi is here throwing favors around and teasing businesses with—"

"The populace isn't pleased with the Techs, Kofi," Belson said, and his upper lip twitched. "They think you slipped up."

"That's what you're telling them, and you know it's not true."

Belson rose and stood behind his chair. "Kofi, the citizens are spooked. There hasn't been a serious depressurization for decades, and the wobble hit white-zone this time."

"They should be happy we've done our job so well."

Belson scoffed. "As an engineer who spent his entire career saying 'no' to people, you shouldn't expect gratitude. Safety needs to be perfect or the lack of it someone's fault. You should realize that by now."

"And the Techs are the ones at fault?"

"Come, come, Kofi. Don't be shy. This is your responsibility. The citizens will blame you unless you find someone else they hate more than you. Be grateful we have the perfect scape . . . suspects to pin this on."

"No one can protect this station better than the Tech Masters."

"That might be true. But they'll blame you anyway." Belson paced the office. "No one wants to be reminded they're zooming through space a few inches from vacuum. Kofi, come now, you know you're not liked. You don't let anyone have any fun."

"You don't believe that Jergen."

"It doesn't matter what I believe. The people are afraid, and when they lose confidence in the Techs, they leave. Emigration is already increasing."

"They lose confidence only when the Assembly tries to compromise our safety and survival for the interests of profit and power."

"That old argument? Come now. This is today, and today the citizens are unhappy with the Techs, not the Assembly. If I call for a plebiscite, they'll vote to keep the UNE here until they feel secure again."

"And what of our Station Troopers who've kept us safe for a hundred years?"

"Not safe enough or we'd not be having this conversation. Yes, my old friend? You will consider the UNE's trade pact?"

"Not until I see a just trial fairly conducted, Jergen. If they want us to trust them, let them prove they are worthy of it."

Belson inspected his fingernails. "Of course, Kofi. We want the same thing and expect no less from the judge."

"Judge? No jury?"

"No, the UNE has put aside those relics and relies on seasoned judges now rather than a flighty and emotional jury. Don't worry. She'll get a fair trial." He glanced at the Station Master. "So, what will make you happy until then?"

Sikibo crossed his arms. "I want the UNE forces to have a lower profile. The citizens you represent are afraid of them. It looks like an armed takeover."

"They're allies, Kofi."

"They're an armed force answering to a foreign government. What if we substitute Troopers and make the UNE less visible?"

"I will suggest it to them. But it's out of my hands until they declare the terrorism threat over and the station safe. You can help make that happen."

Sikibo blinked and waved his fingers to pull up the repair schedule. "Thirty-six hours and the infrastructure repairs will be complete."

"The UNE will be more amenable when the Techs confirm the convictions."

"Convictions?"

"Sorry, my clumsy use of words again. When the Tech Masters conclude your review of the verdicts. You fix the station and I'll whisk the UNE away. Then we'll put this matter behind us. Agreed?"

"Agreed."

"Dinner with Hanna? She misses you, Kofi."

"After we're secure, Jergen. Until then, we're both busy. Give her my regards."

"Goodbye, my friend."

Belson left the Tech offices and took a lift to an overlook of the agricultural deck, the most exclusive region of whitezone, and leaned with his hands on the railing.

As President of the Assembly, this was his domain, given to him by the citizens of the station. Or rather, everything the Tech Masters left for him, which seemed to shrink every year.

He blinked to engage his link. "You heard?"

"Yes. He won't cooperate," the vice president said. "Can't the engineers understand how beneficial a stronger trade agreement with Earth will be? How lucrative?"

"What does it matter that the little outpost at Haven misses a few meals?" Belson said. "And when they're hungry enough, they'll be open to offers more favorable to us. They have an entire moon; they'll recover."

"The future of the sector is there."

"Eventually, but not yet."

Belson cut the connection and gazed over the arboretum fearing for his old friend's life, and his own.

Enterprise Station—Inbound

"The *Intrepid* winked-in ahead of us," Jerri Vonegon said to the *Tiger* bridge crew, inbound to Enterprise, tired and disoriented from the long jumps.

The *Tiger* ran on thin margins, and a rush trip with one paying passenger could break them. In an age when photons were free and fuel was expensive, mass cost too much to push between stars, and everything possible was reduced to data for local replication. People were the rarest cargo: few could afford it, and fewer were worth it.

But this was different: Meriel was crew, and Sandy was family.

In the center of the bridge, Captain Richard Vingel, Molly's husband, sat tall in the command chair. John worked the nav-b station next to Jerri, the chief-pilot. To her side, Suzanne Soquette sat the comm station and nodded with a smile that always seemed a flirt.

An icon blinked on Socket's console, and she touched it. "What is it, Liz?"

"Don't ping. Don't sync," Elizabeth said.

Socket glanced at Captain Vingel who nodded. "Take a bio-break and come forward."

A minute later, Elizabeth stood at the bulkhead door, and Captain Vingel waved her inside.

"What emergency justifies violating security protocols, Ms. Hope?" he asked.

"Sir, I got this from Teddy on the outbound beacon from Jira-1," she said and transferred the message to the overhead displays.

```
Liz: I learned they plan to arrest
M. The UNE may name the Tiger crew as
accessories. I'll go in and bring a
friend of yours. If you go, don't an-
nounce, don't sync. Ping on anonymous
22b4f. I'll meet you.
```

"Teddy. That's Theodora Duncan?" the captain said.

"Yes."

A big man with short blond hair, Sergeant of Marines Cook, squeezed sideways through the bulkhead door and entered the bridge.

Molly followed Cookie and sat the second chair. "So, we're all at risk."

"Comm," the captain said, "Can we go in dark and download to find out if we're suspects first?"

John raised his hand. "Sir, I have to go on station to get Sandy."

"Noted."

Molly glanced up from the new nav instructions. "I suggest masking our ship ID. Ms. Duncan included that capability in the nav update."

The captain smiled and shook his head. "Was she ever a pirate?"

Elizabeth leaned against the bulkhead and studied the ceiling. "Not that she mentioned."

Socket nodded. "I'll spoof the sender as a proxy to mask our ID. Then download from the comm beacon without uploading."

"That's illegal." The captain turned to Molly. "XO?"

Molly nodded. "I'm in."

"I masked our ID, Captain," Socket said.

"And we're dark?"

"Yes, sir. I downloaded from the beacon and pinged Ms. Duncan's URL. The UNE indicted Meriel for mass murder and terrorism."

"Where's Teddy?" Elizabeth asked, but the crew stared at her silently. "Not the game, silly. Really, where is Theodora Duncan?"

A light flashed on Jerri's scopes followed by a faint line as the ship's EM caught up when it winked back in from hyperspace.

"There she is. I think she knew our course."

"Lucky guess?" Captain Vingel said and crossed his arms. "How much more does her nav system do that she didn't tell us about?"

Thirty minutes later, a yacht approached the *Tiger,* and a tight-beam flashed. Socket tapped virtual buttons, and a hologram of a small woman in a business suit appeared on the Tiger's bridge.

Elizabeth waved. "Hi, Teddy."

"Hi, dear," Theodora Duncan replied. With a blink, her glasses shimmered, and the view swapped to an outside camera. "Meet *Amelia.*"

"That's a lot of 'go' for such a little mass," Molly said with an eye to the yacht's enormous jump fans.

"Yup," Teddy said with a grin as a man leaned into the holo beside her. "This is Jeremy Bell, Meriel's attorney from Lander."

Elizabeth waved. "Hey, Jer."

"Pilot, bring us about," the captain said.

The ships maneuvered to dock, and Elizabeth introduced the *Tiger* bridge crew. When she reached Jeremy, John interrupted.

"Mr. Bell, what will happen to Sandy?"

"Call me Jeremy, please. You should be able to pick her up as soon as we dock, Mr. Smith."

Elizabeth frowned at them. "What about Meriel?"

"Nothing new. She's still in UNE custody on—"

"They're light-years from Sol, for God's sake," John said. "How can they pin this on her? She's been nowhere near the *Princess.*"

Elizabeth blushed.

Cookie caught her expression. "What, Liz. What's going on?"

"Well, technically—"

"What do you mean?"

"You remember a few months ago when Meriel found the manifest? On the *Tiger's* last stop here before Khanag's pirates attacked you?"

"Yeah. So?"

"Well, she got it off the *Princess.*"

Socket put her hand to her mouth. "Holy sh—"

"She's dead—" Jerri said at the same time. "Oops, sorry."

Jeremy cleared his throat for attention. "Ahem. You are my clients now, and this conversation is privileged. Understand? No one talks to anyone outside this group. You tell them to talk to me, right?"

"We have representation from the Pacific League," the captain said.

"Not for terrorism or conspiracy. Are we clear? Just respond to my text, and I'll record the paperwork. Continue."

"Why couldn't she visit the *Princess?*" John said. "It's her ship."

Jeremy shook his head. "Not at the time. It was pending sale for non-payment of dock fees. And she still doesn't have legal access."

"What about the rest of us?" the captain asked. "Are we at risk?"

"Hard to say. They might use you to extort a confession from her. If you want your freedom, don't acknowledge your presence."

"Any word from Nick, Teddy?" Elizabeth said. "He doesn't answer my pings."

Teddy shook her head. "I haven't been able to reach him either."

"Was he . . ."

"He's not on the list of casualties, dear."

A document overlaid on Jeremy's holo as he scrolled through it. "He may be involved. The indictments mention an accomplice and some crafty hacks."

Elizabeth bit her lip. "How much time do we have?"

"If the trial is fair and above board, it should take awhile. Administrative trials are like military tribunals."

Cookie waved a dead cigar. "They incarcerate early and rule late to round up all the combatants."

Jeremy nodded.

"Then that's our tip," Elizabeth said. "If everything moves at a slow pace, we should expect a fairer trial."

"And if it's rushed, it'll be bad," Cookie said. "How'll we know?"

Captain Vingel interrupted. "I thought 'the wheels of justice turn slowly but grind exceedingly fine'"

Elizabeth sat. "This isn't about justice, or the damage to Enterprise. This is payback for exposing the damn Treaty of Haven."

Jeremy raised his hand. "Put that aside. First, we need to deal with the charges against Meriel."

Teddy waved her fingers over her console. "The *Tiger* can't dock at the station until your legal status is clear. Meanwhile, John, come aboard and we'll drop you on Enterprise to get your daughter."

"XO. Prepare to dock with *Amelia*."

"Aye, Captain," Molly said, and she and Jerri returned to their consoles.

"I need to see Meriel, Jeremy," Elizabeth said.

"Not until you're cleared."

"Don't you have an assault charge pending on Etna?" Captain Vingel asked.

Elizabeth closed her eyes and nodded. "Damn. I'll figure out something."

A few minutes later, John and Elizabeth transferred to the *Amelia,* and the ships parted.

The *Amelia* was a private yacht, small by spacer standards. But what was small for an interstellar merchant was big for a yacht, and most of the *Amelia* was outfitted for luxury suites and jump engines. At the airlock, Teddy and Jeremy met Elizabeth and John.

"Hey Punk," Teddy said and hugged Elizabeth. "Welcome aboard, Mr. Smith."

He shook her hand. "John, please. I'm honored to meet you." He turned to Jeremy and shook his hand as well. "Mr. Bell, can you show me what you know about Sandy's whereabouts?"

"Sit, John," Jeremy said and swapped the *Amelia's* status dashboard on the active wall to display a vid of Enterprise Social Services.

"How long before we dock?" Elizabeth asked.

"Two hours twenty inertial," Teddy said and led her to the bridge. "Say, Meriel pinged me she sent the dossier to Khanag. Do you think that had anything to do with these troubles?"

"Hard to say. She just sent it day before yesterday. The Enterprise incident was soon after."

Teddy nodded. "They could have had this in the works already."

"And we didn't know . . ." Elizabeth stopped and raised an eyebrow as a droid, tubular with gangly protuberances, floated past them toward the galley. It drifted without legs and rotated its lid a full cycle like a radar dish.

"What do you call the hot dog?" Elizabeth asked.

"Eddie. He came with the ship. Gratis, from the naval architect.

"Eddie?"

"EDy. Eidetic Deputy. He can man nav and comm if I want to single-sail, but that's no fun."

"You don't use droids in Heinhold's," Elizabeth said, referring to Teddy's bar on Lander. "Why here?"

"Well, I like 'em smart, and when they're this smart, it feels like slavery."

"You called it 'he,' not 'it.'"

Teddy blushed, "He came with a male body—"

"Fully functional? Cute: Teddy and Eddie. So, what did your beau think?"

"Torsten got jealous and swapped his . . . its body with his maintenance bot's. But I kept the name."

"Batteries?"

"No. H-Ox fuel cells."

"Damn. Can he talk?"

Teddy shook her head. "But he's a good listener." She called to the lounge. "John, Jeremy, join us."

On reaching the bridge, Teddy pointed to the empty stations. "Take seats, all of you."

Elizabeth took the comm chair, Jeremy sat XO, and John at nav.

Teddy glanced up at the overhead display from *Amelia's* nav console. "You missed the upgrade briefing on LeHavre." She pushed a virtual switch to play an instructional program. "Start here."

Elizabeth interrupted them all with a wave. "Listen," she said, and wagged her fingers to transfer the news feed to the head-up display.

```
This is Taryn Ldong of the Steward-
ville News in Johnston City, Haven.
Unidentified armed fighters have land-
ed near Terni. They say their purpose
is to defend refugee immigrants from
local farmers . . .
```

John shook his head. "Wrong. That's an incursion. I know those farmers, and they would never attack refugees. Hell, they've been building shelters and training centers for them. Sorry, Teddy. I can't just sit here," he said and left the bridge for the lounge.

Teddy followed and settled onto a couch. "If not refugees, who do you think is behind the incursion?"

"LeHavre thinks smugglers are bringing in mercenaries to protect their turf. Meriel says they're Archers."

"They both may be right," she said and turned to the droid. "Juice, Eddie."

"Do you have something stronger, Eddie?" John asked.

The droid tipped its lid in a nod.

"Then bourbon neat."

"Two." Teddy put a hand on his. "Meriel speaks well of you, John."

He smiled. "I learned nav from your vids. That's how I met her."

Teddy returned the smile. "Did they tell you I added your EM calibration trick to the nav upgrade to shrink the sphere?"

"I'm flattered."

"No one will know the option's there unless they're looking for it. You and the *Tiger* will still have an edge." She held his hand. "Meriel loves you and your girls, John. I know she feels terrible Sandy got tied up in this."

He nodded. "I just want them both home with Becky and me."

"I'm curious, John. Did the Vingels mention route jumping? New routes?"

"Not to me. The Pacific League limits our franchise to the nearby stations, like Lander. What are you getting at?"

When Eddie distributed the drinks, Teddy sipped hers, but John gulped his and returned the glass. "Another, please."

"Torsten, my beau, works the inner stars," she said. "He mentioned changing shipping patterns. Leagues are dropping routes and ships."

"That's a long way from here."

Elizabeth joined them from the bridge and accepted a drink from Eddie.

"Did you finish the briefing?" Teddy asked her.

Elizabeth downed her drink and picked up a delicate figurine from an alcove. "Pretty much."

Teddy turned back to John. "Trade is shifting, John, and it's shifting in our direction. Haven changed everything."

"That's what BioLuna understood decades ago," Elizabeth said, emphasizing her point with a wave of the figurine. "They kept a news blackout because they knew when humanity found out about Haven, half would want to go there. And BioLuna wanted to control it first."

Teddy rose, removed her treasure from Elizabeth's hands, and returned it to its place. "The people who hear the whole story will turn their back on the UNE for good."

"They may never hear it," John said. And when the *Amelia* lurched with final docking maneuvers, he left for the airlock. "Let's go get Sandy."

Enterprise Station—On Station

A sterile reception room greeted John and Teddy at Social Services. Here, mothers waited in fear for the status of their missing toddlers. Others awaited a brief visitation under controlled conditions. And from this room, officers of the court took minors injured in domestic disturbances to the clinic. It was almost as secure as red-zone, since children were often the most at risk when adults fought with each other.

John leaned against the ballistic ceramic window and glared. "And why can't you release her?"

"Please, Mr. Smith," the clerk said, leaning back. "Her interests are our primary concern, and we can't just turn her over to someone from . . . from, well, nowhere."

"She has a biotag. She's my daughter."

"I'm sorry for the difficulty, but her biotag identifies her as a citizen of somewhere called LeHavre. Yours says you're an employee of L5 Corporation on Lander and not a resident there."

"L5. That *is* LeHavre," John said.

"Where's that?" the clerk asked.

"Jeez, where have you been for the last year? LeHavre Station. Jira-1 system. Just ask them."

She narrowed her eyes. "It's not our job to ask, sir. It's your responsibility to provide the proper documents and we'll—"

"I'm her father. Take a DNA sample."

"Paternity checks aren't our job, either. And paternity has nothing to do with legal custody. Just produce the proper—"

"What bureaucratic bull—"

The ceramic window fogged, and a policewoman took a step toward them, but Teddy waved her away. She pulled John from the window and returned alone.

"Excuse me, Miss . . ." she said to the clerk.

The window cleared.

"Mrs. Stropchik, ma'am."

"Mrs. Stropchik, I'm Theodora Duncan and a friend of the family."

The clerk checked a display. "Yes, yes, here you are in the records. You're a citizen here on Enterprise . . . and Lander and . . ." Her eyebrows rose. "I've never seen—"

"Yes, yes. If Alessandra's biotag identified this man as her father, would that be enough?"

"But it doesn't, and—"

John pushed against Teddy's stiff-arm. "She just got it a few hours ago on LeHavre."

Teddy dragged him away again. "You're not helping. Now stay," she said and returned to the counter. "The documents you requested of Mr. Smith, show me what you need."

The clerk waved a finger, and a list appeared on Teddy's link.

"These are all new policies," Teddy said.

"Yes. The Council of Citizens mandated them to combat child trafficking."

"So, if we had made this request yesterday, there would not be an issue."

"Well, that really doesn't matter now. He's from Lander, and we don't know where the girl is from."

"You don't recognize Haven or LeHavre?"

She checked another display. "No ma'am."

John leaned over to the window again. "At least let me see her."

"I'm sorry sir," Stropchik said.

"Thank you," Teddy said and took his arm to leave.

She dragged John out the door, and neither paid any heed when he bumped into a female maintenance worker with violet eyes.

***

The doorframe blinked green as Jeremy Bell entered the waiting area of the new detention center. Inside, he worked his way through construction techs and past armed USF officers to the end of a line that snaked along the deck to one of four ballistic ceramic windows.

At a door in the corner of the room between two USF uniforms, a young woman in a business suit waved. Jeremy cut the line to the grumbles of others and elbowed his way past rows of plastic benches below one-way windows and surveillance cameras.

"Ms. Churchill?" Jeremy said. "Pleased to meet you. Is our appointment with Ms. Hope arranged?"

Jennifer handed him a blank red badge. "Yes," she said and led him through the door. At the end of a long hall, she stopped at a window and held her badge against it. The window defrosted, and a USF officer gazed down at them with a nod to Jennifer. Jeremy pressed his badge to the window, and a list of security clearances appeared. The officer nodded, tapped his console, and Jeremy's likeness appeared on the window and blank ID. The thick door buzzed and cracked open.

"Follow the yellow line," the officer said, and the window frosted again.

"I understand why Ms. Hope insisted on you," she said as they walked down the narrow passageway. "Magna cum laude at Cygnus Law. Youngest partner ever at Ankelov and Jurich."

"Those records are sealed, Ms. Churchill."

"Top Secret access is authorized under—"

"Let me guess. Under the Aldebaran Accord. And I presume our other rights as station citizens are abrogated as well?"

She blushed. "Why did you resign the Ankelov partnership?"

"Let's say I had a better offer."

"The most prestigious law firm in the quadrant and you found a better offer?"

"I left with my soul," he said.

She opened her mouth, but he raised a hand before she could speak. "Long story."

They stopped at the body scanners where Jeremy emptied his pockets into a tray and raised his arms. The scanner flashed green, and he stepped out into an empty room with a single windowed door where Jennifer joined him.

No one came to meet them, and Jeremy pointed to a bench. "Seems we have a minute," he said, and they sat. "We don't get many Sol System lawyers way out here."

She smiled. "My firm assigned me to get a deposition from the Pacific League here on Enterprise."

He nodded and scanned the room for surveillance cameras. "How was the ride?"

"Long. I'm not used to jump disorientation, Jeremy . . . ah, Mr. Bell."

"Jeremy is fine. Were you here during the attack?"

"Luckily, no. My transport was late and docked just after the explosions."

Furrows appeared between Jeremy's eyes. "Jennifer, is there a reason someone would want to intimidate you?"

Jennifer raised her eyebrows. "No."

"How about someone you care for?"

"What are you getting at, Jeremy?"

"That you might have been a victim as well. Who assigned you to Ms. Hope's case?"

"The judge knows my firm and requested me."

"Quite an honor," he said. "And you rode along on the *Intrepid* to arrest Ms. Hope?"

"The judge wanted her to have representation all the way. Quite caring, I thought."

Jeremy nodded and paused. When she did not explain further, he took a breath. "Enough about us. Let's discuss the case," he said, touched his wrist band, and a checklist appeared in front of them.

"Have you been to visit Social Services?" she asked. "Alessandra Smith?"

"Only remotely. Her father is there now to retrieve her."

"She's a wonderful girl."

"Yes, she is," he said and opened his fingers to enlarge an item on the checklist. "Who added the kidnapping and child endangerment complaints against Ms. Hope? She lives with the family. She and Sandy's father are a couple."

Jennifer frowned. "There's no legal relationship between them in the records. Any related charges will be dropped if Sandy's father doesn't press them. OK?"

"They might have left her at LeHavre."

"I wasn't consulted."

"Right," he said and scrolled to another item. "Who's your team?"

"What do you mean?"

"The legal team. You and who else?"

"Well, I'm her counsel and the bench behind me is deep."

Jeremy's eyes bored into her as if interrogating a suspect. "How deep? Who specifically?

"Hansen and Brimmek."

He nodded. "Who's the partner in charge?

"Tavo Goryeo," she said.

"He's white-collar crime. Extortion. IT fraud."

A crease appeared between her brows. "You've examined my firm?"

"Old habit. You volunteered?"

"Rather, I accepted the assignment from the court."

"Who's the prosecuting investigator?"

"Kamal Kostanza."

"What do you know about him?"

"He's a Senior Prosecuting Investigator for the UNE. Courts martial and high-level political charges."

Without turning his head, he scanned for surveillance, and turned his back to a camera in the corner. "A fixer?"

"Not sure."

"Who's the presiding judge?"

"Marshal Sobrietz."

Jeremy put his hands together, tapped his link, and the list disappeared. "Yes. The nature of the case is clear to me now, Ms. Churchill."

"Jennifer, please." She straightened her back. "I'm not sure what you mean. I assure you I am competent to—"

"Jennifer, I am sure you're an excellent attorney and advocate. Given the right materials you're more than qualified to handle Ms. Hope's case or any like it."

She blushed.

"Now, what evidence did the investigators present?" he asked.

"They showed me a vid of Ms. Hope on the *Princess* taken a few months ago. And—"

"Did they tell you where it came from? Who made it? How they made it?"

"A surveillance spider," she said.

"That shouldn't have been there?"

"Right."

"What else?"

"A list of forensic evidence the prosecution presented to the judge," she said and transferred the information to Jeremy's link with a swipe of her fingers.

"Did you see it? Or verify the chain of custody?"

She shook her head. "I'll appeal admission."

"Did you advise Ms. Hope of her limited options?"

She nodded.

A guard finally came to the door and waved them forward. "You have twenty minutes."

She stood, but Jeremy frowned, and she sat again.

"You're new to this, Ms. Churchill," he said.

"Jeremy, I'm—"

He shook his head and spoke quietly with his head lowered. "You're new to this. Review the case files for L5 v. BioLuna and the *Tiger* investigation report. Both are filed on Lander and readable on the Galaxis legal library. Then read the *Princess* files here on Enterprise. Don't just skim the summaries. Read the full reports. Yes?"

"Yes."

He nodded and stood. "Let's talk to our client."

After a final body scan, two guards led them through the door into a conference area and a table outside Meriel's cell. Her hologram appeared, standing in a red jumpsuit with her arms crossed.

"Him first," Meriel said, and Jennifer returned to the annex.

Meriel laced her fingers together. "Where—"

"Wait, M." He placed a tiny red pyramid on the table and pushed the tip. When it flashed green, he replied. "Sandy's in Social Services."

"What's the green thing?"

"A privacy curtain. We can speak freely now."

"How is she?"

"Status says she's fine. Healthy, but lonely."

Meriel bit her lip and twisted her hands into fists. "They'll kill her spirit in there, Jeremy. You have to get her out."

"John's there now with Teddy filling out the paperwork. I'll meet them after this. Now, how are you?"

"I'm fine. Just worried about Sandy."

"John will take care of her. You need to worry about yourself now. OK?"

Meriel nodded.

"First, you don't trust Ms. Churchill?"

"She's a UNE plant. How can I?"

He tipped his head. "She's brilliant."

"She's naïve."

"We need her," Jeremy said. "Be candid with her unless I advise otherwise."

The room shimmered and her image wavered.

"What's that?" Meriel asked.

He tapped the pyramid. "Security is trying to penetrate the curtain. Continue."

Meriel nodded and massaged her thumb. "I didn't do this, Jeremy."

"Of course not. But somebody did, and they framed you."

"Who would put so many people at risk?"

"We may never know. But our job now is to prove it wasn't you in the short time we have."

"Nick may know what happened. He sent me a message—"

"You were in contact with him within the last seventy-two hours?" he asked

She nodded slowly.

"Keep that between us."

"Why?"

"Ms. Churchill does not represent you both."

Meriel dropped her gaze. "I think she knows."

He frowned. "How?"

"I, ahh, kinda let it slip." She leaned forward with her hand to her neck where her cross once hung. "Do you know where Nick is?"

"We can't find him. They might have him under wraps."

"How do we get to him?"

"Sergeant Cook will work on that."

"Jennifer said you're civil."

Jeremy nodded. "I gave up criminal cases awhile ago."

"Why?"

"Teddy may tell you sometime."

She sighed. "So, what have they got on me other than the spider vid?"

"I've got an angle there. Someone put the spider there illegally, which taints the vid and the source."

"Who provided it?"

He tapped his link and scanned Jennifer's case files. "Anonymous. Posted to the net."

"It could have been fabricated."

"Unlikely. It has an origin tab in the packet header."

She rubbed the scar on her thumb again. "I don't want to deny I was on the *Princess*, Jeremy. That's where I got the cargo manifest implicating the Archtrope and Biadez in the murder of my parents."

He nodded. "We want them to throw out the spider vid as evidence. So, we don't want you to admit you were there unless it'll save your life."

She glanced away and bit her cheek. "But why blow up the *Princess?*"

"There could be something personal in that. One of your enemies wants to kill two birds with one stone."

"What do you mean?"

"Perhaps there was evidence left by . . . your parents' killers."

"*I'm* the evidence. But they didn't believe me."

"You were a kid with an inconvenient story, M. But let's return to our review." He projected Jennifer's list of evidence on the table. "They have texts between you and Nick discussing the *Princess*."

She scrolled through the list. "These aren't our messages. No one could crack Nick's encryption."

"Sure. The witness is an unnamed third party and the prosecution will have to produce him. Also, they claim to have DNA from a warm-suit you were wearing."

She rubbed the scar on her wrist where Nick's temporary biotag had once been. "Nope. I wiped it."

He nodded. "A plant, perhaps. We'll dispute it. Any biological material would be corrupted, but the tested sample was clean." He scanned the list and stopped at a lab report. "They've got a drop of your blood from the security shuttle."

She didn't respond.

"You didn't tell me about that."

"It's bogus, Jeremy. They'd never sweep every inch of the red-zone docks and shuttles."

"Sure, but they got it somewhere."

"I've left blood in lots of places in the last six months," she said with a crooked smile.

"We'll challenge that too."

"Is that it?"

He shook his head and played a holovid of 12-year-old Meriel in Social Services.

In the vid, she screamed at the therapists that the *Princess* attack was piracy, asking why no one would listen to her. She called them liars for insisting her parents were drug dealers. When she threw a lamp against the wall, the audio ended, and the attendants left the room. Meriel took a chair and banged it on the door until it broke in pieces. As the vid ended, she stood with her head against the door.

In her cell, Meriel pulled her knees to her chest and turned away, her shoulders trembling.

"M?"

Meriel held her hand up and took a deep breath. Moments later, she faced him with tears in her eyes and one hand covering the other to stop it from shaking.

"Get the rest of the audio," she said.

"Why?"

"Rewind. There, when I banged the chair against the door, I yelled 'bring my sister back.' And when I stopped and stood there, I begged them. I told them I'd take the pills without a fuss if they brought her back." She paused.

"'All you needed to do was ask,' they told me." Her eyes glistened. "They gave me the meds, but they still wouldn't bring Liz back. They never did. And once I was medicated, I didn't care anymore." She turned her head away again.

Jeremy laid his hand on the holo of Meriel's hand. "And they kept you all apart so you couldn't put the puzzle back together."

She nodded.

"Sorry, M. We'll subpoena the audio."

After a deep breath, she smiled as the vid looped. "I sure look crazy, huh?"

"That's the idea," he said and ended the vid.

"Everything we told them was true. All of it. We just didn't know why."

"They're using this as evidence of underlying psychosis."

She raised her hands. "Jeez, aren't my files confidential?"

"Enterprise was your legal guardian back when the Biadez Foundation took custody. They released your documents on a subpoena."

"I was twelve, Jeremy. No one told me anything." She shook her head. "How can they do this? What do they gain?"

"I suspect they want to exploit the diagnoses of PTSD and drug use and tie it to your assault arrests."

"Oh, crap. Yeah, those."

"They say that's your motive and, with your history and training, the means. You created the opportunity."

"A drug-addled evil genius? You sure?"

"No. We're peering through a fog here. But it's too convenient. They started the drug publicity right after you sent a copy of the Treaty of Haven to the media."

The room shimmered again, and Jeremy tapped the pyramid. This time only the two of them and the table were visible.

"Can Enterprise do anything? You said they were my guardians."

"Still are."

"Can you appeal to them?"

Jeremy leaned back. "I already have. But you're in UNE custody."

"The Techs still run the station."

"But the UNE has the guns." Jeremy sat back. "Are we ready for Ms. Churchill?"

"Wait. Tell Cookie and Liz not to . . . do something stupid."

He smiled. "Can you be more specific?"

"Tell them not to break me out."

He lost his smile and opened his mouth, but she waved him to silence.

"I'm serious. That'll give the UNE an excuse to move against Haven and all of you. They got me, Jer. They don't have to get the rest of you."

"I'll forward your message. You think the dossier you sent to Khanag is why they're framing you?

"Only he can read it."

"You two are on opposite sides," Jeremy said. "Just being in touch could scare people."

"If Khanag reads the dossier and turns on his boss, I'll be OK with this. The people I care about will be safe for a while longer. That'll make me happy, and maybe I'll get to hear he ripped the Archtrope's throat out."

"You used to be a nice person."

"Maybe once. Maybe before they came after the kids."

"Don't give up, M."

"I'm not," she said and leaned over the table. "And if Liz is interested in my boring life in here, tell her my cell has a single corner mounted camera to the left of the door and the walls are plastisteel. The cell door operates remotely. You can give her a description of the conference room here and the security protocols you encountered on the way in. Only if she asks of course."

"Ahhh . . ."

Her image touched Jeremy's hand. "And lie low until Sandy is safe with John. But if they move on her, they're coming for all of you. If I say anything with fire in it, run like hell and burn the bridges on your way out."

"I'll tell her, but . . ."

"Why us, Jeremy? We're small fish. How do they even know our names?"

"You keep getting in their way."

"I can't help it! They keep trying to kill us!"

He nodded. "Ready now?"

Meriel nodded but pursed her lips as he waved to the monitor.

"What about Nick?" she asked before Jennifer entered.

"He's a citizen and can petition the Techs."

Meriel turned away. "If he can reach them."

Neither of them said what they both thought: *And if he's still alive.*

Occlusion

Facing the door in a dark wig and four-inch heels, Elizabeth chatted up two Station Troopers in a crowded blue-zone bar. When Jeremy appeared with Jennifer, Elizabeth waved to them and shooed the Troopers from her table.

"Jennifer Churchill meet Elizabeth Hope," Jeremy said. "Excuse me, please. I have another appointment and can't stay." He hugged Elizabeth, shook Jennifer's hand, and left.

Elizabeth tapped the kiosk and ordered two drinks. "How is she?"

"Desperate for Sandy," Jennifer said. "And rather stoic to be facing the death penalty. Her own situation doesn't seem to bother her."

Elizabeth scoffed and rolled her eyes. "What the hell would you be like if your dreams got blown up? She's in shock for Chrissake. Her entire life's work for the last ten years has been to fix the *Princess* and get us together to work it. That's all gone now. Her only motivator now is Sandy. Take that away, and . . ." Elizabeth gazed off into the corner.

"What would she do?"

"You don't want to know." Elizabeth frowned. "So, how's the case?"

"We've challenged most of the evidence. If this were a jury, I'd have no doubt of acquittal."

A crease formed between Elizabeth's brows. "Uh huh. What about you?"

"I'm her advocate and will zealously represent her regardless of her guilt or innocence. I—"

"Blah blah blah. That's what you have to say. What do you *think*?" A drink popped up from the middle of the table shimmering with a fog that crawled over the edge of the glass like a demon trying to escape.

Jennifer dropped her gaze. "I . . ."

"You think she did it. Then you think she's a drugged-out crazy who'd destroy a station with hundreds of thousands of people on board?"

"The remaining evidence is circumstantial, but it's damning, Ms. Hope. Means, motive, opportunity."

Elizabeth shook her head. "Motive? She'd never damage the *Princess*. She loves that ship."

"I understand it was your home."

"A lot more than that. It was our hope. Our future. It was how we saw ourselves getting back together, some semblance of family where we could help each other."

"Your opinion isn't—" Jennifer said.

"Not just my opinion. Check her financials. Every cent she had went to saving our ship. Where are you from?"

"I grew up on Europa."

"Then you don't get it," Elizabeth said. "Keeping us together meant safety."

"How do you mean?"

"Ask for a jury trial. They'll understand."

"Why would that matter? I have confidence—"

"Ask a spacer parent where they want their children to grow up. They'll say on Earth or a station, maybe the Moon or Europa. But unless you're born there, that's impossible."

"I heard the family ships are overcrowded."

Elizabeth frowned and nodded. "They know some of their children won't make it," she said and brushed the fog from her drink with a finger. "Our cousins on the *Esperanza* lost their ship. The families broke up, and the kids disappeared into the mining colony cesspools. We haven't been able to find—"

Station security passed the window and Elizabeth turned her head to scout the rear exit. "Jennifer, if you see station security or UNE folk, let me know, ok?"

"Sure. I don't see how overcrowding—"

"We haven't been able to find any of them . . . alive," Elizabeth said. "Jennifer, spacers don't have citizenship anywhere. Every vessel is an island out in the black and a law unto itself. No one is looking out for us. No one. If we lose our ride, no place will take us except the mines and the shitholes."

"Surely, stations would . . ."

"Surely nothing," Elizabeth said. "Every station is living on the razor's edge of resources. Any new station kids come from the rich folks in white-zone or the Techs."

"I heard it was tough. They say your sister blamed Enterprise for, well, everything."

"No, she didn't. This was our second home. That's why Mom jumped us here. But even if Meriel were totally pissed at Enterprise, she'd never hurt innocent people."

"What about the drug history?" Jennifer asked.

"You know they forced the meds on her?"

"Jeremy told me. It was terrible—"

"She did it to be with me. And for us, to keep them from pushing the meds on the rest of us kids."

"Your sister was brave to sacrifice herself."

"When you're thirteen years old, you shouldn't have to think like that, Jen." She took a drink and leaned over the table. "For months, the shrinks browbeat her into believing her memories were fantasies to protect her from the horrors she witnessed. They said our story of piracy was a delusion. She was all alone and gave up fighting. And the meds took everything she cared about with them. Including us."

"The records show she was on them until the *Tiger* hijack attempt. That means she could have been rebounding from withdrawal."

"She wasn't on them that long."

"The documentation is extensive."

"They're phony, Jenn," Elizabeth said and leaned back. "After we got her clean, she pretended to take the pills so they wouldn't force the rest of us to take them. She had to fool the doctors because the meds were a condition to keep her job. And without that, she'd join our cousins in the mines."

"A relapse may—"

"No, she'd never have gone back."

"I understand you—"

Elizabeth raised her hand. "No, wait. Hear me out. When they split M and I onto different ships, I lost touch with her. Months later, Aunt Teddy and I found her and . . . she barely recognized me, Jen, they had her dose so high. She was just a kid, for God's sake." Tears glimmered in the corner of her eyes. "I was so afraid of losing her. She was all I had then: the only person who loved me for me, not what I did for them. Just me. You ever feel that?"

Jennifer nodded slowly. "A long time ago. So, what happened?"

"We put her in rehab. But it was like she didn't want to get clean."

"Why?"

Elizabeth blinked and ran her fingers around the rim of her glass. "When she was off the meds, she had to face the horror of all the death she saw on the *Princess*. And the emptiness. No one was there to love her and care for her anymore. She was too young for all that. When she was clean, she knew her nightmares were real."

"But still you say she stayed clean. For you?"

Elizabeth nodded. "And the orphans. For her, the price to feel the good things is to feel the pain. She'd never relapse."

"Do you have a record of her treatment?"

"It's a clinic on Lander," Elizabeth said and tapped her link. "Teddy, Theodora Duncan, will send you a copy."

"Ok, But her pharma records—"

"They're bullshit, Jen. Check her record... eighteen ratings in ten years and a Logistics-5. Nobody does that on drugs." She bit her lip. "After they killed our folks—"

"The prosecution's psychologists contend she's suppressed those memories and they're resurfacing as hatred."

"They're lying. She can't suppress it. She sees a real scar every day and grapples with PTSD that never leaves her."

"But the scar is superficial."

"It cut to the heart. Everything she loved died that day." Elizabeth turned away. "Everything but me and the kids and the *Princess*. She'll never let go. She can't."

Jennifer opened her mouth, but Elizabeth raised a hand to stop her.

"Every single day after we escaped, we kids had a sword over our heads ready to fall. Meriel made it visible; made it something to fight against so we didn't just... die out there in the black. Then she removed the threat. She did that for us. Then she did the same thing for Haven and made a home for us there. She's ours, Jen. We need her."

Jennifer shook her head. "Still? After all the trouble she's gotten you into?"

"And gotten us out of. Ask the survivors from the *Tiger* attack what they think about Meriel." She raised her glass and blew off the head of fog before taking a drink. "Even with all this crap, we may still get justice for our parents. She saved our lives, Jen. She never stopped fighting for us, and we can't stop fighting for her."

"That's an overwhelming obligation, to owe your life to someone."

"Yeah. We can't repay a debt like that."

"What do they do about it?"

Elizabeth shook her head. "What *can* you do? Just appreciate what she did for us and don't forget it." She took another drink. "And come when she needs help, 'cause she's not acting for herself."

"She didn't ask for help."

"She never does. That's why it's so important for us to be there for her."

"Where are they now?"

"We're all working spacers, Jen, and under contract. Some of us are taking leave on Haven right now, but we'll return to space. I told them to lie low, out of harm's way. But most are adults and have their own mind."

Elizabeth glanced toward the window. "She can't see the stars, Jen. I don't know how long she can hold out in there."

"It wasn't fair, the drugs—"

"Meriel had a chance on Haven to build something new, something for herself." She took Jennifer's hand and squeezed it. "We can't let them take that from her."

"What's happening isn't her fault."

"But she'll blame herself, anyway."

"The courts will be sympathetic to—"

Elizabeth slammed her drink on the table. "I don't want their f'ing sympathy, Jen, or yours. I want your promise to save her."

"I'll do everything I can," Jennifer said, and then tipped her head toward the door as station security entered.

Elizabeth stood and leaned over the table. "Help her, Jen. Please," she said and slipped out the back entrance.

Jennifer frowned as Elizabeth left the bar. Meriel's actions and her sister's testimonial did not jibe with the evidence she'd been given. *Sure, people lie, but* . . .

She tapped her link. "Jeremy, I have a few ideas for our defense," she said and rose to leave.

As she passed through the bar, a shadow with a scar on his forehead followed her out the door.

***

Jeremy took a public shuttle to white-zone followed by a utility passageway sans security cameras to a bar in green-zone's best neighborhood. When he entered, day passed into night as the torus rotated away from Procyon's yellowish light.

Inside, a few nondescript patrons listened to a retro-synth trio playing a C minor blues in a far corner. And along the entire wall stretched a window with an unobstructed view of the stars that would unsettle many citizens. It reminded him of Heinhold's, Teddy's place on Lander, meant for people with taste who shunned the crowds.

He sat at the bar and waited for the bartender, a humorless young woman with iridescent hair and a spacer tattoo of the constellation Orion on her wrist.

"Guy says he knows you," she said and nodded to a dark corner.

Jeremy turned, but Procyon's shadow hid the man's face.

She poured three fingers of whiskey into two glasses. "Bring these."

He took them, stood, and took a step toward the stranger, but the bartender grabbed his arm. In her other hand, she held an astronomical bill for twenty-year-old Scotch.

"He didn't pay for them."

Jeremy tapped the bill, and the register chimed. With drinks in hand, he walked to the stranger's table, and put the drinks between them.

"Business first," the stranger said from the shadows. As he reached out with a link, his suit strained over a muscular build that implied a past life as a brawler.

Pressing his thumb for a DNA scan, Jeremy transferred the funds.

"Got a name?" the man asked.

"Bell. And yours?"

"Mahn. But you know that, or you wouldn't be here. So why come to me?"

"You've got the longest history on this issue," Jeremy said.

"And you know that how?"

"You broke the Jeannine Aldersen murder case on Europa. You proved she was murdered to keep the existence of Haven a secret."

Mahn nodded.

"Then they burned you for it and ended your career . . ."

Mahn's face flashed a scowl of pain.

"And they stuffed you so far down a hole no one can find you."

"By choice. How'd you find me?"

"We have mutual friends. What do you have for me?"

"The invoice that says your clients bought the explosive materials is a forgery." He tapped his link to transfer the document. "This is the affidavit."

Jeremy read the document. "That's the only link between Ms. Hope and the organics."

Mahn leaned forward. "I don't know if your girl did this or not. But people wanted this to happen."

"Who?"

"Big people," Mahn said. "Bigger than anybody you know. They paid her or framed her. Doesn't matter. Word is the plan was for a lot more destruction, and I don't want to be here if they try again."

"Why the hell would they damage a station?" Jeremy asked.

"You're thinking small, pal. These folks don't give a shit about Enterprise. They want an alliance between the stations in this sector and Earth."

"The UNE?"

"That's one of 'em. But Enterprise is resisting."

"They don't trust the UNE."

Mahn nodded. "Your girl scared the hell outta the Enterprise Techs. The Haven treaty and the BioLuna embargo happened in Enterprise's shadow, and the Techs didn't know. The bad guys kept a habitable moon out of sight from the smartest people in the sector. That's power, man. Scary power. The same folks forced a UNE destroyer up Enterprise's skirt, and the Techs don't like it one bit."

"Why involve Ms. Hope?"

A sly grin appeared. "They can pin everything on her."

"The Enterprise damage?"

"There ya go, thinking small again. No. *Everything*."

"What do you—"

A stranger approached, and Mahn took his drink and leaned back into the shadows. When the stranger passed, Mahn leaned forward but lowered his voice.

"The public grants Ms. Hope some credibility because she's the pathetic little guy in the story, the sympathetic nobody. But if they tie her drug and assault history to a crime, it blows her image as the innocent little girl and makes her a great fit for the stereotypical drug addled terrorist of everyone's nightmares. That discredits her and flips the trust issue. It throws shade on her biggest charge, the Treaty of Haven conspiracy."

"Through an Enterprise conviction?"

Mahn nodded. "Or their concurrence with a UNE guilty verdict. The publicity will drag all the other charges down with it. Then they'll use that to flip public opinion on the *Tiger* incident."

"Wait. That was an attack by Khanag's corsairs."

He scoffed. "There you go again getting stupid. You can't connect the corsairs to Calliope or the Treaty."

"The bodies are proof. *Corpus Delicti*."

"Corpses won't help you. They're ciphers. Corsairs are outside the genetics databases, and you can't trace them to anything or anyone." Mahn signaled for another round.

"You know that's real Scotch."

"You can afford it."

"The media have vids of the corsair captain with Khanag and the Archtrope."

Mahn smirked. "Circumstantial."

"But there are eyewitnesses."

"Who are friends of your girl."

"And physical evidence of a hull breach."

"Doesn't matter. You're still thinking small, boyo."

"How does—"

The bartender delivered the next round of drinks, and Jeremy nodded.

"I thought you were smart," Mahn said. "They get her entire crew for murder and that'll intimidate the merchant leagues into compliance."

"But they're the victims."

"You're looking in the wrong place for justice. And get this, I've seen the start of a file on Hope's parents. They'll frame them as terrorists and blame them for the Hydra on Haven. If they do, the lawsuits on Lander against BioLuna will get overturned."

Jeremy sat back, deep creases in his brow, and sipped his Scotch. "And the whole sector falls into Sol's hands."

"Clever, huh?" Mahn said and took a drink.

"Who thinks like that?"

Mahn grinned and poked a finger into Jeremy's shoulder. "Suits like you. The big boys own the media, and once they discredit Ms. Hope, her friends will have convenient 'accidents,' and no one will care." He studied Jeremy. "I'll bet they tried before, didn't they?"

Elizabeth's assault on Etna. The attacks on Meriel. Jeremy nodded and stared out the window at the stars.

Mahn shook his head. "Your people had no idea what shit they stepped in when they pissed these folks off."

"And their next step is getting Ms. Hope's assault and drug history on the record in a conviction."

"Right. And for Enterprise to buy it."

Jeremy took a long drink and stared at the stars outside.

Mahn leaned over and softened his voice. "Maybe you didn't want this life and wish you'd kept a lower profile."

"I've been here before. A story for another time."

"Wrong. There won't be another time. And this meeting never happened. If these folks put you and me together, nothing you care about is safe. Got it?"

Jeremy nodded.

"And have the sense to not follow me out."

Mahn rose and left, and Jeremy turned to the window. As the stars passed outside, he nursed his Scotch and ignored the buzz of Jennifer's call. It was happening again, the intrigues that ended his former life.

The bartender dropped off another Scotch. "You gonna be OK here?" she asked with soft eyes.

"Yes, thanks. Just another day at the office."

She put a gentle hand on his. "This one's on the house."

He nodded and returned to the view out the window. The stars had always calmed him with their permanence and predictability. So simple and constant, their physics comprehensible, unlike the humans who kept making a mess of his life. But the stars did not help him today.

You can't hide if you care, Teddy had said to him back when their troubles first began. And no matter how hard he tried, he couldn't stop caring.

His link buzzed again, and he tapped it. "What is it, Teddy?"

"They won't release Sandy. We're stuck."

"I'll meet you back aboard the *Amelia*," he said. He downed his drink, paid his tab, and left.

***

On the walk from the shuttle to the *Amelia's* berth, Teddy and John struggled with how to cut the red tape at Social Services.

"What about birth records on Haven?" Teddy asked.

"They're kinda sloppy in Stewardville. I don't have documents like that for the girls. Or me."

"What about LeHavre?"

"They're better, but Sandy was born on the surface. She's only registered for a day pass on LeHavre, but the biotag identity should be recorded."

John waved to Jeremy at the *Amelia's* airlock. "They won't give me Sandy. It's like I'm an axe murderer or something."

"Open up, Eddie," Teddy said. "And bring us a round of Scotch."

"Is Sandy safe?" Jeremy asked.

"I think so," John replied. "But they won't let me see her. How's Meriel?"

"Concerned for Sandy." Jeremy shook his head. "I've seen trauma victims before. She seems resigned to this."

John frowned. "That's not like her."

"And the trial?" Teddy asked as she led them to the *Amelia's* lounge.

Jeremy accepted his fourth top-shelf Scotch of the day from Eddie. "If it's a fair trial, we'll be in good shape. If it were a jury, I'd not worry at all. But the venue and appeals process are troublesome."

"Venue?"

"The trial judge. John, I got your message and the list of documents Social Services wants. I understand their concern. They need to be careful with children to avoid human trafficking. Doesn't Sandy have a biotag?"

"She just got it," John said.

"How long ago?"

"A few hours before they took her."

"Then Enterprise should have Sandy's records from the comm sync with LeHavre," Jeremy said. "Why didn't they accept them?"

"The clerk told us Sandy's ID is on LeHavre, and they didn't even know where that was. Like we're some secret slave colony or something."

"Where did you get your biotag?"

"On LeHavre, before I shipped out for the first time."

Jeremy rose and paced with his hands behind his back. "I don't get it. If you're a citizen there—"

"No. They said my biotag identifies me as an L5 employee on Lander."

The lawyer frowned and nodded slowly. He sat, pulled up the custody documents, and examined them. Then he jumped to his feet. "I understand now. LeHavre doesn't legally exist to Enterprise. You're literally non-people. Your only legal identity is through L5 on Earth and Lander."

"But Haven has standing on Lander," John said.

"Only as the L5 corporation. Lander has no power to compel others without treaties, and LeHavre isn't a party to those treaties."

"How long will it take to retrieve records from Lander?" John asked again.

Teddy waved her hand. "Eddie, estimate route data transit, LeHavre to Enterprise via Lander. Expected arrival Enterprise."

His answer appeared on the active wall.

```
10:40 elapsed.
Data only.
```

Teddy reviewed the local ship traffic and nodded. "Eleven hours from now."

John paced the lounge. "And I can't even see her. Where the hell am I, Jeremy? Enterprise is supposed to be civilization."

"There's something else we need to discuss," Jeremy said. "Teddy, can we get the *Tiger* on a secure tight-beam?"

A minute later, Socket's image appeared on the wall. "*Tiger* here. Hi y'all."

"Ms. Soquette, is the captain there?"

"Present, Mr. Bell," Captain Vingel said.

"Richard, I have some clarity on your situation. I've the *Amelia* folks here. If you would alert the *Tiger* crew, please. I spoke with a detective . . .," Jeremy said and detailed his conversation with Mahn.

John shook his head. "Son of a b . . ."

"They're trying to turn us into murderers," Captain Vingel said. "Like they're doing to Meriel."

"Affirmative," Jeremy said. "Don't dock or announce your presence. And definitely don't get caught on station."

"They're going to rewrite history," Teddy said.

"Winners write the history."

John tapped his link. "Then we have to win." He rose and strode to the airlock.

"Where are you going?" Teddy asked.

"To the top."

***

On the bulkhead of the *Intrepid's* ready room, an underground vid played of USF soldiers dragging Meriel and little Sandy through a cordon of armed men to the *Intrepid's* airlock. From the crowd came roars of anger:

```
"This is an outrage! They can't just
come in here and take our people."

"I don't care what they done! We got
rights."

"There's no sovereignty when the UNE
has the guns!"
```

> "They're treating a little girl like a murderer! They can't do that!"

"It's a composite of lots of amateurs from different angles," *Intrepid's* XO said. "We look like shit, sir."

Captain Stark nodded. "Nothing on the major networks?"

"No, sir. The UNE is suppressing it from the news feeds, but it's leaking out through the net. There are hundreds of versions out there."

"Has the crew seen them?"

"Yes, sir."

"What does the chief of the boat think?"

"She's . . . open minded."

Stark nodded. "Don't discourage them."

The voice of his admin-bot interrupted. "Incoming, sir. Ambassador Bakshi to speak with you."

The XO stepped back until she was outside the camera's field and nodded.

"Go," the captain said and rose from his desk. A holo appeared with Bakshi. "Greetings, Mister Ambassador. All is well?"

"I've been in meetings, Captain," Bakshi said and another holo popped up. "I have Mr. Kostanza, the prosecuting investigator, on the line and I'd like you two to brief me. You first, Captain."

"Ms. Hope is in USF custody on station, sir," Stark said. "Without incident."

"Did you plan to attend her trial?" Bakshi asked.

"No, sir. The court is closed."

"Inspector Kostanza, if you please. Where are we regarding the trial?"

The holo panned to a dark-haired man with a weasel's smile. "Our investigation is complete, and the Hope woman's trial will start tomorrow. The accomplice will be tried after that."

Bakshi narrowed his eyes. "Who's the accomplice?"

"Enterprise is keeping the name sealed. Rumors say he's a kidnap victim turned by radicals years ago."

"Any idea who kidnapped him?" Bakshi said.

"No. But the Holy Star cult and JCS fanatics are common out here."

"What made him important enough to kidnap?" Stark asked.

"It was a long time ago, Captain," the inspector said.

Stark frowned. "That's not an answer."

The inspector raised his chin, but Bakshi intervened. "Where's the Hope woman now?"

Kostanza waved a finger over his desk and a vid of the USF security checkpoints alternated with a view of Meriel pacing in her cell.

"In custody," Kostanza said. "High-security. Well, as secure as is achievable here. The facility is new after the damage to red-zone."

"Secured by us, right? Not the station?" Bakshi asked.

"Of course, sir. The USF has her well-guarded."

Stark crossed his arms. "Why wasn't she kept aboard the *Intrepid*? There would be no security concerns if you'd detained her here."

"Optics," Kostanza said. "We need this to appear like a joint operation with Enterprise governance."

"Appear?"

The ambassador frowned. "An idle word, Captain. We are coordinating closely with the Assembly. What about the crew of her ship?"

"Intelligence says the *Tiger* debarked LeHavre but hasn't turned up near Enterprise."

"And the child, the Smith girl," Bakshi asked. "Where is she now?"

"Ms. Churchill delivered her to Social Services, where she's detained until her father brings the right papers."

"He's here on station already," Kostanza said.

"How'd he get here?" Stark asked.

"He disembarked from a private yacht that left from Lander. Ship named *Amelia*."

Kostanza waved his fingers again and the sleek silhouette of Teddy's yacht appeared on the dock with a close-up of her and John debarking.

Stark furrowed his brow. "And you're sure he's the father?"

Kostanza glared and his lip twitched. "Yes. Our intelligence confirms he's the parent."

Leaning with both hands on his desk, Stark said, "If he's the father, why isn't she with him by now?"

"That's an Enterprise matter, Captain," the ambassador said with an edge of impatience. "And what of the alliance with Enterprise?"

The prosecutor's voice projected pride. "We'll begin negotiation as soon as the Council concurs with the convi—"

Bakshi cleared his throat. "Ahem. Both of you, these are candid discussions, and I am sure you both appreciate the need for discretion."

Stark stopped pacing and leaned over his desk. "Have you made up your minds before the trial has begun?"

"Merely speculating, Captain. Judge Sobrietz will decide the matter." Bakshi opened his arms and smiled. "Your responsibility was to capture the terrorist—"

"The suspect," Stark said.

"Yes, of course. To capture the *suspected* terrorist and to support our negotiations. You've done an excellent job. The rest is beyond the scope of your mission, correct?"

Stark paused. "Affirmative, sir."

"Good, that's settled. You have both performed your duty admirably and Earth appreciates your efforts. I'll be observing the proceedings to assure Earth's interests—"

"For justice," Stark added.

"Yes, certainly, Captain. Now, on to other matters. The Earth Spring celebration is tomorrow night, and Beatrice has made reservations at *La Mère Catherine* for the Ostara party. She insists you both join us."

"I would enjoy that. Until then, sir. *Intrepid* out."

The XO returned to stand at the table as Stark checked his console for the reservation.

"Tomorrow night," she said. "Rather fast to complete a trial."

Stark leaned back in his chair and drummed his fingers on the desk. "New orders from HQ?"

"Negative. You're hoping for an excuse to decline the Ostara party?"

"If possible. Advise the crew, there will be no celebrations on board. They can celebrate as they choose on shore leave. And notify the Master at Arms to deploy Shore Patrol to the docks."

His XO smiled. "Spring on Earth? Are you going to wear a robe like your ancestors?"

"No. Full dress," Stark said and checked the location of *La Mère Catherine*. An advertising holo of the restaurant hovered above the desk with scenes of partiers in costumes of historic leaders and personalities, and he frowned.

"Not a fan of Gaia?"

"It's the snobbery of it all. Earth depends upon space for everything but food. Yet they treat us like primitives, even on Europa."

"So, you won't be returning to the ship tonight, Captain?"

"Orgies bore me. If you're off, meet me at the Blue Note."

He opened a file and rubbed his chin.

"Thinking of the party?"

He shook his head. "Curious. According to the investigator, the sole threats are in custody. And the Troopers and USF are present, so Enterprise doesn't need additional protection. Why are we still here?"

"Permission to speak freely, sir?"

"Granted."

"If we remain here under Bakshi's command, our mission is no longer protection but intimidation. And if Bakshi makes a mistake—"

Stark nodded. "Our fingers are on the trigger."

"And if we refuse, it's mutiny."

"Thank you for your candor, Exec. Dismissed."

Stark stood and paced. "Security app. Search."

```
"Engaged."
```

"Search registration for ship *Amelia*. Docked on Enterprise within the last twenty-four hours."

A second later, a record appeared naming Teddy as the owner.

"Search. Intelligence records. Associates of Theodora Duncan, to four degrees of separation. Sort by frequency of contact."

```
"T. Duncan is principal of Galactic
Navigation. Intelligence data requires
directive from ComSec."
```

He paced his ready room and frowned. "Duncan is a Designated Strategic Supplier?"

```
"Affirmative."
```

"Abort. Find connections between Ambassador Evan Bakshi and parties named in the Treaty of Haven."

```
"Access to communication content re-
quires UNE-SolSec approval."
```

"Addresses are sufficient. Begin."

```
"Degrees of separation?"
```

"Within three," Stark said and leaned back. "Chart contact frequency and density." He put his fingers together and rubbed his chin.

A holo of a bubble map appeared above his desk. One line connected Judge Sobrietz and former UNE President Alan Biadez. Stark walked around the holo with his hands behind his back until he spotted a thick line dominating the chart. He waved a finger over the terminal bubbles to expose the names of Ellen Biadez and Ambassador Bakshi.

"Captain's log. New file. Title: Irregularities regarding Enterprise mission and M. Hope. Time stamp. Begin entry . . . ."

Chapter 15
Mars-6, Sol System

Ellen Biadez sat up in bed, disturbing the vortices of cigarette smoke that drifted to the ceiling. Outside the window, a storm blew red dust that found its way past the tightest seals on Mars.

With a wave of her finger, a few decibels of the wind's roar filled the room, and she smiled at its chaotic power, until her lover's snores interrupted.

From the nightstand, she took an injection pen and loaded it with a catatonic. The sting of the shot in the side of his neck woke him, and he rubbed his stiffening shoulder.

"Ah, there you are, Stegy dear," she said. "I'm afraid our little tryst is at an end."

He kissed her hard. "When will I see you again?"

"Never," she giggled. "Well, at least not in your current form."

"But . . ." he said, raising his hand to his throat. He croaked, but no more words left his lips. His hands shook, and he struggled to rise, but his legs would not move.

"Don't fight it, dear. You'll only hurt yourself. And don't worry. Your wife and children will never know you spent so many nights with me. You've done nothing memorable in the last decade, so no one else will miss you."

His wide eyes searched the room as she tapped her link. From a hidden doorway, a team in white smocks pushed a grav sled into the room and threw the immobile man onto it.

Without turning, she waved as they whisked him from the room.

"Visitor request," the fluid voice of her security system announced. "Cecil Rhodes."

"Enter," she said, kicking her new droid. "Martinis for two, stupid."

Rhodes entered and accepted his drink from the droid. "I've been buzzing for a quarter-hour."

"I've been busy. And I've misplaced my link."

"Get an implant. You're living in the Stone Age."

"Implants are for drones," she said. "No one is f'ing with this body."

He glared at her and blinked to deactivate his implant while she lounged on the sofa facing the storm.

"No offense," she said to his frown. "Oh, don't be so sensitive." She patted the cushion next to her. "Come and sit, darling."

He joined her on the couch, and she lay her bare legs on his lap. "Any word on the trial?"

"It's proceeding as planned. That Hope twit still thinks this is about her."

"You can't blame her. You made it personal."

"She was in the way."

"So were Tours and Vienna," he said.

"What the hell are you talking about?"

He shook his head. "Never mind. What of your discussions with Stegman Tamari? He's your wedge in the Subcommittee to Interstellar Relations."

Ellen smiled. "I've taken a different tack, dear. Tamari is reluctant to adapt to our plans for Enterprise, and we need someone more tractable to keep the pressure on Asurini." *And someone less boring for my entertainment.*

Rhodes downed the rest of his cocktail in one gulp. "Do it fast. LeHavre is preparing to release an anti-rejection drug the stations can recycle."

"That'll be fun," she said. "The population will explode when their elders refuse to die, and white-zone will kick the little folk off if they have to."

"Sorry, but I want to stop it. The demand will kill six percent of my black-market business. We need this treaty with Enterprise signed quickly."

"Don't worry, darling. Once the treaty is signed, LeHavre will be too busy trying to feed themselves to bring their new drug to market."

"Then hurry, before the marketing buzz gets traction."

"I'll see to it," she said and rose. "Enough business, dear. I'm feeling snacky." Her robe fell open as she leaned over to kiss him. "Why don't you get ready, and I'll join you in a moment."

As Rhodes walked to the bedroom, she kicked the droid again. Its wheels spun before it righted itself and hurried from the room.

With her back to the window, she sent a message to UNE warship *Intrepid*.

Chapter 16
Calliope, Tau Ceti System

On the balcony of the Archtrope's palace, Edward Seide faced the gardens and fountains below as he read a message from Yutousov.

"A favorable verdict in the Hope trial is imminent," Seide said.

With his index finger, the Archtrope placed a black stone the size of his thumbnail on a display of the ancient Japanese game of Go.

"Yes. One stone among many," the Archtrope said. Icons near the board flashed standard responses, alternative moves, and the success probabilities of each. "However, she remains obdurate."

"You imagine her to be more important than she is."

"Perhaps, Edward. She is a small fish but useful." He put a hand on Seide's shoulder. "I can use her to leverage larger gains in this sector."

Seide frowned.

"You don't comprehend the game. You think like our partners who play chess and think the fall of a king shifts the power structure." He replaced one white stone with another white stone. "Nothing changes except the face of the ruler."

"Biadez?"

The Archtrope scoffed. "Yes. There was not even a tremor in our areas of influence when he fell from power. We live in an interconnected world where there is no 'king' to checkmate and end the game. Go is a better metaphor for our interconnected world, where we vie for influence in a domain or a region, each with its own princes," he said and grinned at Seide.

Seide nodded. "Such as the media."

"Yes, like your control of what the people know." He added another stone, and the board lit up with changing risks and opportunities. "And the game never ends."

"But the UNE is a partner, yes? And BioLuna."

"For now. Only because I am strong—"

Drugs, vice, and the organ trade, Seide thought.

"—and because they fear that strength."

And because you hold their children in the camps outside this window. Like my own.

"My strength is in the territory I control, not in a crown." He said with a hungry smile. "That is where the future lies."

He pointed to a corner of the virtual board with many of the tiny white Go stones. "See, here is Enterprise, locked in its sector, concerned with its survival, and well positioned for defense."

He pointed to two empty spots surrounded by stones, protected. "A double eye, Edward. That means they can't be captured or killed. That's called 'life' in the game of Go. Without 'life,' a single stone can flip who controls the region." His finger followed a trail of stones which connected to other regional stations. "Each intersection is an alliance. But all promises are conditional, temporary, and fragile." He tapped a finger on the board and the stones shifted before the device returned them to their positions.

"Where is Sol in your scheme?"

In the other corner, he placed a black stone. "Sol System is here, with life in its bubble and connections to allied space. But removal of a single stone, a single alliance will cause Sol System to suffer economically. The Moon and Mars don't want this."

"Sol? What of Earth."

"Earth has turned their backs, Edward. They are a spent force that cowers in fear of the stars, lost in their worship of the past. Gaia gives them purpose when they have no future."

"You can't blame them. Losing Brazil and the Atlantic cities to an asteroid was an existential shock."

"Rubbish. Brazil was just a convenient excuse for the totalitarians to seize control. If Earthers had not already colonized Mars, we never would have."

The Archtrope moved his fingers and a hologram of the game appeared in three dimensions. Labels popped up near the regions of power: Sol, Procyon, Sirius, Calliope, and others. Some had configurations of life, and many more were connected to those with life.

Seide pointed to a black stone in the shadow of Enterprise. "And what is this one?"

"Those are my people near Haven. I have the force to take the station, but the ground is what we want. We need a few thousand more pilgrims there before we move."

"What about your alliances with Sol and BioLuna?"

"I don't need them, and they have proven incompetent."

"But if the UNE allies with Enterprise, they can starve you—"

"That's the UNE's game, Edward, not mine. My followers can survive for thousands of years on Haven without a station. The citizens will yap their complaints as I grind them under my heel, like Seiyei."

"And Mrs. Biadez?"

The Archtrope put his arm around Seide's narrow shoulders. "Ah, Edward, how observant. Yes, of them all, that bitch plays the same game. But she wastes her passion on lust and revenge."

"This is a risky game."

The Archtrope grinned. "We play for the galaxy. Exciting, no?"

Seide removed a black stone, and half of the board flickered with the changing options and probabilities. And Haven shifted from black to white.

"Yes, Ed. Sometimes the entire game depends on the slightest move, or the weakest linkage."

A priest entered and handed a note to Seide. His eyes widened as he read it, and he quickly slipped it into his pocket.

The Archtrope glanced at him and frowned. "What are you hiding from me?"

Seide's voice tightened. "We found the point of origin of the dossier that incriminates you in organ smuggling."

"And?"

"Haven, sir."

"Care to explain your reluctance, Edward?"

"That's where the corsair bodies lie."

He laughed. "If you're worried about our little secret, it's too late. The bodies are ash by now and we can deny it all."

"And where is Khanag in this game?"

The Archtrope dismissed the question with a wave of his hand. "The general is a selfless and pious believer, a warrior for the cause."

"He doesn't want a bigger share of your . . . endeavors?"

"The business side of our enterprise was irrelevant after I pulled him from the drug dens. It changed him, what he went through."

"What *you* put him through."

A feral sneer crossed the Archtrope's face, and the editor flinched. "You think I'm a fool? Only one thing might disturb him, and our trustworthy agents have kept that secret for decades." He grinned. "Because your children's lives depend upon it."

"If Khanag changes his mind, he'll be dangerous."

"He understands we must erase our pasts to become soldiers of the future. And the need for adversity to mold the righteous into a sword for the Imperials." He looked into the distance. "Like me, he is descended from them, the conquerors, the prophets, and the intellectual giants destined to rule the galaxy."

"That fiction will be difficult to maintain if—"

"It's not a fiction, Edward."

"But you can't prove—"

He scoffed. "I don't have to *prove* anything. My statements are declarations of reality. Whatever I say, tens of millions of people believe, and the rest will have to adjust. Just like your news feeds. You create a reality with just enough truth to be believed, and others must organize within it." He pinched Seide's cheek. "That's why you're so valuable to me."

He turned to gaze out the window to the stars. "Prove it? I know it in the core of my being. At dawn I feel the thunder as my chariots race across Persia. During the day I hear my cannoneers bombard Vienna. At night I see the laser trails and nuclear flares as the UNE unites Sol under Earth rule. It's in my blood. My bones. And Haven is where we will begin the future of mankind."

The Archtrope lowered his eyes to the worshippers kneeling in the courtyard below. "They once worshipped the gods, awed by their power, driven by fear and guilt. Who's to say I'm not a god, Ed? I have the same power over their lives and their psyches." He pointed outside the window. "Ask the grovelers what they think. They cannot tell the difference. Biadez felt that godlike power and an election affirmed it."

"A corrupt plebiscite," Seide said, and hid his shaking hand behind his back.

The Archtrope moved another stone on the board. "It worked. And the destination of the dossier?"

In an unsteady voice, Seide replied. "Unknown, Your Eminence."

"Find out where that dagger is aimed," the Archtrope said and glared at Seide. "And get some additional leverage on the Hope woman, or her usefulness may be over."

Chapter 17
Enterprise Station, Procyon A System

Enterprise Station—On Station

On the crowded tram to the white-zone Tech Center, John scrolled through the advertising popping into view wherever his eyes turned. The citizens, still spooked from the recent attack and gravity failure, clung to straps while John, accustomed to an unsteady gravity, leaned with his back against the window.

At the Tech Center exit, he followed four Techs to the security checkpoint above which two security spiders lurked. Beyond the portal stood a well-dressed man and a common shuttle cart. As the Techs passed through the checkpoint, the wall identified each and their jobs as they took seats on the cart.

When John passed through the portal, the wall announced him.

```
The Honorable J. Smith, Envoy Ex-
traordinary, LeHavre Station.
```

The well-dressed man approached John and bowed slightly from the waist.

"Mr. Smith, I'm Rivan Tellar," he said in a lifeless monotone. "Master Sikibo has time for you. Come with me, please."

"You're aware of my situation here and of my daughter?"

"Yes, sir. The UNE delivered her to Social Services."

"What can—"

"Excuse me, Mr. Smith, but you will need to speak with the Station Master regarding inter-station matters. This way, please."

The Tech section of Enterprise's white-zone, across the torus from the Assembly of Citizens, was five times larger than on LeHavre. This region did not view the beautiful arboretums and farms like the political or financial centers did. Instead, the Tech Masters had located their offices beneath the agricultural decks to maximize the cultivated acreage. Asked by a reporter why they denied themselves the pleasure of the open fields, they smiled and changed the subject as if addressing a child.

This was the world of the Techs. The aesthetic here welded form to function without the chaotic color and bustle of the docks or the shopping areas. Rather than sterile, it conveyed a sense of calm and order.

The cart delivered them to an open space two levels high, and long enough that the deck curved with the arc of the torus. Across the mid-level, Tellar led John over a clear plastaglass walkway.

On the deck below, men and women in green fatigues with silver trim scurried between active panels that stretched from floor to ceiling displaying real-time views of the station. Interacting with each panel, teams checked station status through callouts and color-coded graphs.

A series of panels focused on crop and livestock yields against the backdrop of the sunrise terminator crossing the agricultural deck. One panel displayed the sea of vessels that formed a corona around the station. Another panel cycled through the pressure boundaries with integrity status and maintenance history.

Here in the realm of the Techs, it was clear the station flew through the vacuum of space a few degrees above absolute-zero, facts the citizens found distressing. The panels reminded the Techs how close they were to death so the people within could forget it.

At the far end of the walkway, Tellar stopped. "One moment, please, Mr. Smith," Tellar said and tapped on a link.

While he waited, John scanned the displays on the walls of bots repairing the recent damage to the red-zone impound docks and security. One panel detailed the sequence of replicators building the on-site material production and fabrication systems. In others, droids worked on the breach itself. It might have been fascinating, but John tapped his foot and frowned.

"This way, please," Tellar said and led John through a laboratory to a conference table near a group of technicians. From them, a tall gray-haired man in a lab coat parted ways and walked toward them.

"Mr. Smith, Station Master Sikibo," Tellar said and touched a tiny icon hovering over the table. From the overhead speaker came a high-pitched whistle.

"Welcome aboard Mr. Smith," Sikibo said. "Enterprise Station recognizes and welcomes LeHavre Station." He shook John's hand. "There now, formalities over. Rivan, excuse us, please."

The adjutant frowned but nodded. As he stepped away, Sikibo tapped the table. The surroundings glistened as if Tellar had passed through a waterfall, and the hubbub of the busy lab became muted.

John ran his hand through the field to make it shimmer. "A sound curtain?"

Sikibo nodded. "And visual. A little privacy to put you at ease. Excuse me if I don't sit. An old injury. Refreshments?"

"Water, please."

Glasses of water rose from the middle of the table and the men each took one.

"I received your letter of introduction from Master Jerrett on LeHavre," Sikibo said. "The scope he outlined for discussion was rather far reaching."

"Yes, sir," John said. "But at the moment, I want to talk to you about other matters."

Sikibo nodded. "Diplomacy can wait. I understand your daughter is under Enterprise supervision now, brought here from LeHavre—"

John narrowed his eyes. "By the UNE. Under duress."

"And in complicated circumstances."

"I'm her father . . ."

"Patience, Mr. Smith. Social Services needs to be careful, and I mustn't put my thumb on the scale, or I may become part of the problem. The child trafficking business is exploding in the far stars, and we must not let it take hold here. While it is in my power, we will protect her."

"What can you do?"

Sikibo blinked and waved his fingers over a virtual console. "Betty Oliver provides security for my grandchildren and has experience with Social Services. I've assigned her to your daughter."

"Thank you."

"Now, I understand Ms. Hope is your partner?"

"Yes. That shouldn't affect—"

"There's no guilt by association here, Mr. Smith. For you or your daughter. However, there's little I can do for Ms. Hope without more information. The evidence gleaned so far is rather damning."

"But circumstantial."

"Yes. And our station courts are reviewing her case. The Tech Masters here have an interest in rooting out the cause of . . . the events. More so than the UNE. But the Treaty of Aldebaran limits our options."

"She would never!" John jumped to his feet. His chair rolled from under him and crashed into a table of laboratory equipment, raising the heads of the nearby technicians.

"Sorry. But Meriel couldn't have done what they've accused her of. She loved her ship and would never harm Enterprise."

"I understand, Mr. Smith. We're conducting our own investigation and are under no obligation to confirm the UNE's verdict. But our hands are tied as long as she is in UNE custody."

John found another chair and sat, laying his hands flat on the table to stop them from shaking.

"Mr. Smith, you have pressing personal issues that need to be addressed. If you wish, we can discuss your role as the LeHavre Envoy at some other time."

John nodded, but there was nothing he could do right now but worry. "I'm only here to begin discussions, not to negotiate. I'm a farmer, and—"

Sikibo smiled and raised his hand. "It's fine, Mr. Smith. I'm a plumber by trade. Life calls us, and we answer. Now, I'm curious. You had the opportunity to petition the Enterprise Assembly of Citizens. Why contact the Techs first?"

John gritted his teeth. "When the UNE's thugs came for Meriel and my daughter, the Assembly on LeHavre was absent and silent. They still have said nothing and lodged no protest. But Master Lukas stood at my side at the docks and faced the UNE Ambassador and the USF's guns. I figured your Assembly of Citizens would be a spineless as LeHavre's, so I'm betting on the Enterprise Techs."

Sikibo nodded. "Proceed."

"Well, LeHavre would like a better relationship with Enterprise and the nearby stations. A first step would be to normalize citizenship and extradition between LeHavre and Enterprise."

"Yes. That would solve many issues, including your daughter's. But please advise your Station Master that our Assembly is pressing for closer ties with Sol System."

"I will advise Master Jerrett. LeHavre Station also wishes to discuss immigration to Haven."

"Immigration isn't a problem for us here," Sikibo said without expression.

"It will be. Transports and smugglers stop at Enterprise to refuel before heading to Haven. But our environment is fragile and hostile, and we don't have the resources to feed the immigrants. They'll die unless we send them back here."

Sikibo's eyes bored into him. "You're refusing to let them debark?"

"If necessary," John said. "We have the Marines and fuel to do that.

"I see. Many are refugees, John, without a home to return to. We can't support them here. What do you suggest?"

John leaned forward at the table. "The immigrants have a chance of surviving if they have the proper training and equipment. We want you to make refueling for the jump to Jira-1 and Haven contingent upon that training and equipment. Without that, we would be forced to turn them back."

"By 'equipment,' you mean for Enterprise to supply the food production and waste processing?"

John tapped his link and sheets of mechanical specs displayed on the table.

Sikibo scrolled through the list. "Aeroponics?"

"Ideally prototypes of those you have here on station. We don't have the replicator infrastructure you have in-system."

"Why?" Sikibo asked. "Earth proved there's no better place to grow things than in dirt, and Haven has lots of it."

"Our dirt has selenium and copper we need to remove before we can grow anything in it.

"Have you tried to bioengineer the seed?"

John nodded. "It takes many generations to bioengineer the uptake out of the root systems. But Haven doesn't have the water for large-scale surface farming: It evaporates too fast."

"I see. And if we don't provide these to you, Enterprise risks revolution when Haven sends the refugees back here."

John tapped his link again, and Penny's vid of the dead refugees on Haven appeared. "That's a possibility. And if you continue to send people to their deaths on Haven, the negative publicity will reflect badly on Enterprise."

Sikibo narrowed his eyes. "I'm not an imbecile, John. And threats are unnecessary. If the UNE declares a humanitarian crisis, they'll intervene here with enough moral authority to negate any treaties."

"Sorry, sir. I'm new to this. To avoid migrants backing up here at Enterprise, Master Jerrett has also offered to provide transport to Haven if you provide training. That will control the flow of immigrants and avoid a UNE intervention."

Sikibo raised an eyebrow. "You will transport them from here to Haven?"

John nodded.

Sikibo folded his arms across his chest. "This isn't just about refugees, is it? Earlier, you mentioned smugglers."

John nodded. "Some are Archer combatants."

"And their goal?"

"They're behaving as if the Treaty of Haven is still in force."

"Because you aren't strong enough to stop them," Sikibo said.

John frowned but nodded.

"So, while they're held up here for training, you can weed out the guerillas." Sikibo rubbed his chin as he paced. "Yes, that's interesting."

John's eyes hardened. "Haven and LeHavre Station can be an important part of your future, Master Sikibo." He leaned over the table. "With fewer strings."

Sikibo stopped pacing and stared at John. "Time for candor, Mr. Smith."

John was exceeding his mandate from Master Jerrett, but he could not let the UNE's bullying stand. "Alignments are changing because of Haven. You may need ... enhanced defenses."

"Other than the Troopers?"

"Yes."

"Enterprise is a friend to all. We have no enemies out here."

"You might rethink that," John said. "They have been coming for Haven for years. They may come for you now."

Sikibo resumed pacing. "You're speaking of the recent damage here?"

"The flexing of Sol's muscles in your neighborhood so soon after exposure of the Haven Affair must be . . . unsettling."

The Station Master stopped and fixed his eyes on John. "Please, I'm a simple man. Speak freely."

"Earth has interests out here and Enterprise is a pawn rather than the goal."

"Is this Master Jerrett's assessment?"

"No sir. Mine."

Sikibo's studied him. "I understand you've spent a few years in space as a bridge officer, mister farmer." John opened his mouth, but Sikibo raised his hand again. "Continue."

"Did they tell you a UNE destroyer threatened LeHavre with missiles?" John said and displayed a security vid from the LeHavre docks. With a few fingers he zoomed in to the *Intrepid's* open missile bays.

The Master's eyes narrowed, and his jaw tightened. "No."

"Haven has seasoned Marines experienced in ground and orbital combat, but no fleet. Enterprise has a fleet of Troopers, but no Marines. There may be a force-sharing accommodation."

"Our Troopers helped you during the last invasion," Sikibo said. "And without being asked, if I recall."

"Yes, and we're grateful. But there is no agreement in place, and we can't count on that again, especially with a UNE destroyer parked here."

"The Troopers are defensive, police really."

"So are the Haven Marines."

"Also, the Troopers are chartered by inter-station treaty, not a single station."

"Those treaties might be amended to include Haven and our Marines."

Sikibo nodded. "This has been constructive, and we have much to consider." He extended his hand and put his other on John's shoulder. "I will invite Masters Jerrett and Lukas here. You're invited to those discussions, Mr. Smith. And when this trouble is over, bring your daughter so we can introduce her to Enterprise properly."

With a wave, the Station Master disabled the sound curtain. "Rivan will escort you back to your ship. The *Tiger,* is it?"

John avoided Sikibo's trap with a shake of his head. "The *Amelia*, sir. And thank you."

***

Hanna Belson frowned and finished her wine. It was their usual dinner at home, with three place settings, but only two meals.

"How's Nickolai?" she asked and poured herself another glass of wine.

"Nick?" Jergen Belson replied. "He's fine, dear. Sedated and unconscious."

She sighed. "I'd like to see my son, Jergen," she said and poured wine into the glass at the empty setting. "I haven't seen him for over ten years."

Belson stilled like a mouse that smelled a cat. "You know that's impossible, dear. He's in a secure detention facility."

"Maybe just a vid?"

"I'm sorry. No."

She shook her head and blinked back tears. "Papa started all this trouble. It's his fault Nick's biological parents . . . died."

"But then we wouldn't have adopted him. And I enjoyed every moment of our time with him."

"He hated you for covering it up," she said and took a drink.

Belson scowled. "Only after he found out your father framed his parents for murder."

Hanna opened her mouth to speak, but Belson raised his hand. "That ship has jumped, dear."

"Ellen Biadez recommended the retreat on Calliope for Nick. Her kids liked it, but Alan was bored."

"Can Calliope restrict contact with the outside?"

She nodded. "Ellen confirmed they maintain a communications blackout."

"And technology? I think by now he could convert a replicator into a jump drive."

"I'll ask," Hanna said as she took another drink.

Jergen's link buzzed again.

"An envoy from Haven, you say. Smith? He's no friend of . . ." He took his whiskey and turned to Hanna. "Excuse me, dear," he said and left the table.

As Belson walked away, Hanna sighed, finished her wine, and poured another.

Inside his office, Belson waved a finger above his desk and a holo of Rivan Tellar appeared.

"Smith is no friend, Rivan. But we have leverage in Social Services."

"He and Sikibo discussed a trade deal and—"

"You overheard?"

"No, but his mandate was to propose trade deals with LeHavre."

"Thank you, Riven. We'll be in touch."

Hanna called from the dining room. "Jergen, are you coming back to dinner?"

"Give me a moment, dear." He swirled his whiskey as he reassessed which way the winds of interstellar politics blew.

A minute later, he waved a finger above the desk to make another call on a secure line to Ambassador Bakshi.

"Yes, Jergen?"

"It's as you feared, sir. The Station Master has opened a diplomatic channel to LeHavre. For the life of me, I can't comprehend why the Enterprise Techs don't grasp the opportunity of stronger ties with Sol."

"You know him best. Is this only a bargaining ploy?"

"No. Sikibo balks at your presence."

"You understand how vital it is to bolster relations with Earth, Jergen?"

"Yes, sir, and—"

"It might mean a wonderful future for you in interstellar diplomacy. If Haven makes a deal with anyone, we want it to be on our terms. Understood?"

"Yes, sir."

"Is the Station Master the roadblock to an alliance with the UNE?"

Belson was aware of how important his next words were to both Enterprise and himself, but betrayal did not come easy, even for a man with fluid ethics.

"Yes, sir. But he's not the only resistance to your overtures."

"Tell our friends to prepare for an opening on the Council of Masters soon."

"Yes, Mister Ambassador," he said and ended the call.

Belson pinged Sikibo without response.

```
Kofi. Vital that we meet. Call soon-
est.
J.B.
```

After sending messages to his travel agent and relatives, he returned to dinner with Hanna.

"Dear, I think it's time for you to visit your cousins on Lander," he said and stared out the window with its view of the arboretum, hoping his warning to Sikibo would not be too late.

"Wonderful, dear. Next week is—"

"Your ship leaves tonight."

The Tempest

Within the high ceilings and ornate woodwork of the Enterprise courtroom, Jennifer Churchill waited at a long table for the evidentiary hearing to resume. In front of her lay a slim portfolio. With a tap, an arc of holos and evidence vids fanned out, including one of Jeremy that was out of focus to those nearby.

At another table to her right, Kostanza fussed with documents projected from his link. In view of both tables, was the dock for the defendant. Instead of Meriel, a holo played of her aboard the *Intrepid*, hysterically demanding to see Sandy.

Opposite Jennifer looped a slow motion holovid of the explosion on the *Princess* and the damage to Enterprise. Anyone viewing the proceedings would have the horror burned into their consciousness.

A banister separated the two lawyers from the dais and the administrative judge, Marshal Sobrietz. Surrounding them were display screens and holo reconstruction areas.

Jennifer had just returned from recess after the prosecution laid out the case against Meriel. During the break, Jennifer and Jeremy reviewed the evidence, and she was confident of her ability to refute everything.

"Did you review the files I recommended?" Jeremy asked.

"I reviewed L5 v. BioLuna and the Treaty of Haven. Sure, BioLuna tried to screw Haven, and then invaded. But all that's tangential. We need to focus on the evidence presented here."

"And Ms. Hope's files?"

"I just got them, Jeremy. I'll look at—"

"All rise," interrupted a holo of a UNE officer to the left of the bench. "Judge Marshal Sobrietz presiding in the case of the United Nations of Earth, Enterprise Station, and aggrieved parties versus Meriel Hope. Court is now in session."

A holo of Sobrietz in dark blue robes with black stripes covering a portly frame materialized behind the bench and peered down at them through slim glasses.

"Ms. Churchill, the prosecution has presented a rather compelling litany of evidence," Sobrietz said. "Would Ms. Hope consider changing her plea to guilty?"

Jennifer stood. "No, Your Honor."

"Well then, proceed. Remember, this is a hearing, not a trial. Simply introduce the evidence you will submit in defense."

"Yes, your honor. Ms. Hope has a distinguished career as Chief Petty Officer with many citations. She is a peaceful and productive member of society without—"

"Not counting the assault arrests?" Kostanza said.

"Those charges were dropped, sir and should not prejudice—"

Sobrietz banged the gavel. "Let me remind you both this is an evidentiary hearing. And please contain your zeal, Mr. Kostanza. Continue, Ms. Churchill."

"Thank you, Your Honor," she said and walked to the rail. "The defense will present testimony the defendant had no motive for the acts she is charged with."

"Motive isn't a requirement for a guilty verdict, Ms. Churchill."

"No, sir. But it speaks to intent. Also, we will present evidence the DNA results entered by the prosecution are from corrupted sources."

"All DNA sources?" the judge asked.

The prosecutor leaned back in his chair and smirked.

"Yes, Your Honor," Jennifer said. "Further, the vid putting Ms. Hope at the scene does not confirm the explosives there at the same time and is tainted by the use of an illegal surveillance spider."

Kostanza rose and waved his arms. "So, someone simply superposed your client on a hologram." He pointed to the vid of the Enterprise damage. "And this was all just a terrible misunderstanding where thousands of citizens died horrible—"

"My courtroom is not the place for sarcasm, Mr. Kostanza."

"Apologies, Your Honor. But the families of those lost demand justice, the children with missing mothers and fathers cry out for—"

The judge rapped his gavel. "Another outburst and I will have you gagged, sir. Proceed Ms. Churchill."

Jennifer suppressed a smile. "Since the defendant's presence on the *Princess* is based on tainted evidence, we ask the court to dismiss all charges against her."

Sobrietz leaned back and squinted. "This is a terrorism case, Ms. Churchill. Whether or not the surveillance spider was there illegally, its footage still places your client on the *Princess* at an opportune time."

She frowned. "Then investigate who put the spider there. They had the same opportunity as the defendant."

"That is a concern for the investigators and not at issue today," Sobrietz said.

The judge's rejection stunned her. Before she could compose her thoughts, the prosecutor seized the floor.

Kostanza stood. "Surely, the rest of the spider vid will show the explosives at the scene."

"Then enter that segment into evidence," Jennifer said.

Sobrietz leaned forward with his elbows on the bench and deep furrows in his brow. "Ms. Churchill, you've just asked me to dismiss evidence from that spider."

"Sir, if you allow one part of the spider's memory, you must also allow the other. Otherwise, the court cannot presume the vid shows the defendant there at the same time as the explosives."

Kostanza's jaw fell open. "Objection. Argumentative. The spider committed suicide before we could retrieve the rest of its memory."

"Bullshit. You told us the spider was destroyed during the explosion. How can—"

Sobrietz rapped his gavel. "Objections are premature, Mr. Kostanza. And change your tone, Ms. Churchill, or I will hold you in contempt. Are we clear?"

"Yes, Your Honor," Jennifer and Kostanza said simultaneously.

Kostanza waved a hand dismissively. "The explosive materials could have been there since the *Princess* was impounded."

"Which would in no way implicate the defendant," Jennifer said. "Your honor, the security team on Enterprise scrubbed the holds during the original investigation of the *Princess* attack. Their investigation documented no such explosives."

The prosecutor stood. "Perhaps—"

"Further, the defense challenges the prosecution's assertion the defendant purchased and shipped the explosives."

Kostanza tapped his link, and a document appeared on the screen. "Exhibit forty-three is the receipt for the organics with her signa—"

Jennifer swiped an image above her portfolio, and an affidavit joined Kostanza's. "A confirmed forgery."

His smirk vanished. "She's a cargo chief. Someone with such knowledge could smuggle—"

With her hands on the banister, Jennifer leaned in toward the judge. "Speculation, Your Honor. Again, the prosecution has not produced any valid evidence connecting Ms. Hope to the explosives used. Especially into a high-security area under constant surveillance."

Sobrietz glared at the prosecutor through eyes narrowed to slits. "Yes, I see. Proceed."

Kostanza jerked erect and banged on his link.

Jennifer did not relent. "And regarding the purported drug history, we offer into evidence *Intrepid's* on-boarding report. Their med lab proves Ms. Hope has been free of—"

"Your Honor," the prosecutor said, "I request a recess to consult with my investigative team."

"Objection," she said. "Your Honor, the defense only needs a few minutes to present exonerating—"

Sobrietz pounded the gavel. "Granted, Mr. Kostanza. This hearing is recessed," he said and his holo blinked out. The prosecutor rushed out, the courtroom hologram faded away, and the space reverted to its featureless gray walls and ceiling.

Jennifer was alone now except for the holo of hysterical Meriel. She returned to the desk and tapped her bracelet.

"Jeremy, what happened?"

"The hearing may be over, Ms. Churchill."

Jennifer drummed her fingers on the desk, waiting for the hearing to be called back to order, and then stood to circle the desk with her hands behind her back.

No one had responded at the local numbers her firm had provided to assist her. And the admin service at the address she was given told her the office was vacant.

She sat again and pulled up the Hope files from Enterprise Social Services. With each document, the furrow in her brow deepened.

An hour later, Jennifer leaned back and stared at the documents. The stink of corruption was all over the *Princess* investigation: blaming the victims for the attack that killed them, labeling them as drug dealers as the only plausible alternative to piracy, and the stations rushing to quell the rumors and keep the tens of thousands of merchant spacers delivering goods. And Meriel's caretakers, the Biadez

Foundation, extorting a false story from a child, overmedicating her, and separating her from her only relatives.

But Jennifer could not believe it.

She called Jeremy, and when he did not respond, she left a message.

"Jeremy, I read Meriel's files, and I can understand how bad this looks for the Enterprise police and the Biadez Foundation. But why infer a conspiracy when stupidity and bureaucratic incompetence are everywhere. I'm sure if your fears were correct, the media would have been all over this."

She was about to end the message when her intuition kicked in. *They kept Haven a secret for decades. If they could do that, could they not spin the* Princess *affair?*

"And what did you mean you thought the hearing might be over? We've just begun. Call when you can."

As she tapped her link to end the call, the marquee on the dais lit up.

```
By order of Judge M. Sobrietz, the
evidentiary hearing in the trial of
UNE v. M. Hope is adjourned for the
rest of the day. We will contact you
when court reconvenes.
```

Then her link buzzed with a text.

```
The documents you submitted for con-
sideration in the case of UNE et al.
v. M. Hope are inadmissible.
  VSign: Clerk - UNE Security Court
```

"No way," Jennifer said, and hurried to meet Judge Sobrietz in white-zone.

"Wait here, please," a clerk said and entered the adjoining office.

As Jennifer paced, impatient to plead her case, she rested a palm on the wall paneling with a wood grain. *Natural woods?*

On the wall between the opposing doors was a window with a view of a forest of tall trees. *Is this the agricultural deck?* Her home on Europa had similar views, but outside Sol system, this would be some of the most exclusive real estate in the galaxy. This office was a loan, of course—even a UNE judge could not afford such rich appointments.

The clerk returned and held the door open. "You may come in now." She followed him, and he closed the door behind her.

Like the anteroom, wood paneling covered the office walls, but only in the few places not filled by books and exquisite artifacts from a hundred colonies. From behind a desk, Judge Sobrietz studied a link and did not raise his head.

"Sorry to—"

"Just a moment, please," Judge Sobrietz said and continued to read. "Sit."

Jennifer sat and scanned the titles on a nearby shelf: Dante, Machiavelli, Nietzsche, Ashevek . . . *Heady reading, but meant for a man of rhetoric, not of science.*

"Yes, Ms. Churchill. What is it now?"

"Sorry to bother you, Your Honor. The clerk has refused to allow entry of exculpatory evidence that—"

"I'm sure you understand why."

"No, sir. I don't. The defense can refute every document the prosecution has presented. It is ludicrous not to allow—"

His eyes narrowed, and he raised his hand. "Before you embarrass yourself further, the clerk declined your request on my order."

She paused. "Apologies, Your Honor, I meant no disrespect. But the additional evidence is more than sufficient to reopen the investigation. Article 46 of the Administrative Code says—"

"There can be no appeal in terrorism convictions."

"Wait, sir. There's no need to appeal. She hasn't been convicted yet."

He rotated his link to her. "I have the verdict here. I just haven't announced it."

"But Your Honor, the hearing began before discovery was complete. I hadn't finished presenting the evidence when—"

He raised his hand and sighed. "As you are aware, Ms. Churchill, this is an administrative procedure. The hearing is over when I say it is."

"Sir. Article 4 guarantees review of challenged evidence before—"

"These are exceptional times. Enterprise has invoked the Aldebaran Accord. And swift justice is in order."

"I'm sorry I don't understand. Section 34 of the Accord allows appeals when—"

He narrowed his eyes. "Your client is damaged goods, Ms. Churchill, addled by trauma and years of drugs."

"Excuse me sir, but if you believe that, then declare her incompetent to stand trial."

He glared at her. "Conditions will not allow that."

"Justice should be dispensed without regard to conditions. We need time to—"

"Justice delayed is justice denied," he said.

"Justice for whom? Certainly not Ms. Hope."

"For the people of this station. The citizens need closure and an end to their fear. That is what the people demand and what the UNE offers."

She leaned over in her chair. "But if Hope didn't do this, the perpetrators roam free to repeat their terror attacks."

"You say 'if' as if this question remains open."

"But Your Honor—"

He stopped her with a raised hand and sighed again. Coming to her side of the desk, he leaned against it, and folded his arms. The overstuffed chair she sat in allowed no posture except a submissive slouch.

"There now, Jennifer. May I call you Jennifer?"

"Yes, of course, sir."

"Jennifer, your rise in the ranks at Hansen and Brimmek has been swift and well deserved. I am sure that is partly because of your gifts at reading the currents in highly charged situations such as this. Did Tavo offer you the partnership you've been working so hard for?"

"No, sir, I—"

He peered over the rim of his glasses. "I'm sure if you keep on your current path that will happen sooner than you expected."

"You know Tavo?"

His eyes pressed on her, and she felt dirty. "It's a small galaxy where we find ourselves," he said and put his hand on her shoulder.

She subdued a shudder and avoided glancing to the exits, but when her shoulders tensed, he lost his smile. His expression turned to that of a judge rebuking a junior counsel at the bench.

"I need you to sense the forces at play here, Ms. Churchill, the undercurrents. Conflicts burn between the Assembly of Citizens and the Council of Masters here. We must conclude this affair rapidly or be accused of fanning the flames."

"But justice—"

He leaned over her. "Your father uses the shuttle to commute from Altona to court in Silvana, no?"

She cocked her head at the question. "On Europa. Why, yes sir. Every week." *Why would he tell me he knows my father's schedule?* "Why does that con—"

"Like I said, it's a small galaxy."

Her back stiffened. *It's a threat.*

As she sat pinned to her chair, Bakshi stood and returned to work.

"Give him my regards and tell him how highly we all think of you." He peered at her over his glasses again. "And please review your petition and return it directly to me. Good day."

The clerk entered to escort her outside the office without a word. And on shaky legs, Jennifer hurried to the public bathroom.

The woman in the mirror was a stranger, sweating and ashen with fear. Unable to control her trembling, she leaned over the sink and threw up.

***

When the door shut behind Jennifer, Sobrietz latched it from the inside and tapped his link. "Secure-A."

"Engaged," the link replied.

"Message to Tavo Goryeo at Hansen and Brimmek. Tavo, regarding your special advocate in the Hope terrorism case, I recommend reassignment. Permanent reassignment. I regret Ms. Churchill's ethics are not aligned to her ambitions. Or ours. Send."

From an adjoining room stepped Ambassador Bakshi. "That's unfortunate," he said and tapped his ear. "Rivan. Limit the communications of Jennifer Churchill and keep her from mischief. End." He glanced at Sobrietz as he strode to the door. "Make sure she never returns with an appeal."

***

Jennifer splashed water on her face, but her hands shook. All her life she had trusted the fairness of the system in which she played a small part. But now, the foundation of her reality lay in pieces.

How do I face my father after ignoring his warnings?

She leaned against the sink and tapped her link to replay a vid she had made on Europa a decade and a half ago.

"Come, sweetie," Micah Churchill called to his daughter.

Fourteen-year-old Jennifer took his hand, and they jumped on the cable car heading from the courthouse on Europa-4. It would be a brief ride from the Silvana City Center to Consolidation Square and Maiden Lane.

Today was a rare treat. Her father had prevailed in a tough case and saved his client from the death penalty. He had picked her up from school to play hooky, and of all the important people he knew, he chose to celebrate with her. Upon her, he showered all his love but never enough time.

They left the tram and walked down the row of small storefronts, and in front of her favorite sweet shop, he found a table overlooking the park. She ordered her usual Strawberry Ice Volcano, and he a vanilla milk shake.

In the park, water fountains shot high above in the reduced gravity, their drops falling back into a lake surrounded by trees grown impossibly tall. Her left brain knew it was part of the humidity control and water purification systems, but her right brain didn't care.

Across the tiny café table, her father waxed on about the evolution of jurisprudence from Natural Rights and Law.

"The law provides a framework within which humans can live free and cooperate by choice," he said. "Without it we would be ruled by the swords and the passions of the powerful as we have through most of human existence . . ."

She dug through the layers of flavored ice as he spoke of his recent case.

"The law protects the good from the bad," he continued, "and institutionalizes the sense of justice needed to sustain a civilization. It's not perfect, perfection isn't possible with humans; corruption always lurks unless we are diligent. But it is the best we have found yet. The more people who know the facts, the better justice is served.

"But beware the State. 'The best lack all conviction, while the worst are full of passionate intensity.'"

"Yeats?" she asked.

"My prodigy," he said and kissed her on the forehead. "Evil always hides in the dark corners, and an over-regulated society like the UNE has many such corners. Where regulations overlap or need interpretation, where the watchdogs are inattentive or delegate to committees and impenetrable algorithms, that's where corruption thrives."

Enthralled by his passion, she beamed at him.

He took her hand. "And sometimes only people like you and me stand between the state and injustice."

"You love the law."

He stopped speaking and gazed back with soft eyes. Then he hugged her tight.

"And without you," he said, "it means nothing. Nothing at all."

She tapped the link to end the vid and starred in the mirror.

How can I face him after this? How do I face Meriel now? Jennifer thought as the vid ended.

She checked her messages. Again, she found no response from her absent 'support team.' Her link buzzed.

"Yes, Jeremy."

"I got your message. Did the clerk log the evidence?"

"Something else has come up. It's about my father."

"What is it? Are you all right?"

Life returned to the face in the mirror as she considered her options.

"Jennifer, what's going on?"

"I'll call soon."

Slipping the portfolio under her arm, she hurried to meet Meriel.

The detention center appeared shabby only hours after her last visit. The USF soldiers who once gave her comfort now threatened within their opaque visors and body armor. "UNE

Go Home" graffiti and political flyers littered the walls. Past the windows in the corridor, holovids looped of Meriel's arrest on LeHavre by the same soldiers who stood guard inside.

This was not the smooth functioning of a professional bureaucracy. It was an animal feeding on the spirits of those who worked here, who in turn fed on the patrons they vowed to serve.

It struck her that her father's warnings that day in the sweet shop came not from the idle reflections of an accomplished professional. Instead, they came from his personal confrontations with evil, from his own battles with corruption. *In his decades in the justice system, papa must have seen both the best and the worst of it. How had he survived?*

The officer waved her forward, but she sensed his contempt behind the crystal window. Outside Meriel's cell, Jennifer sat at the bench struggling to dispel the nightmare she found herself mired in.

What would papa say?

Meriel's holographic image appeared across the table, a woman soon to be sentenced to death because her counselor had failed.

***

Richard Vingel frowned. "Exec, did you note the new ship ID Ms. Duncan gave us? We're a garbage scow now."

"And the best damn garbage scow in the galaxy, Sir," Molly said.

From the *Tiger's* comm console, Socket interrupted. "Incoming, Captain. The *Amelia* is coming alongside for a chat."

After the ships docked, John, Elizabeth, and Jeremy followed Teddy to the *Tiger's* mess hall. There Richard, Cookie, and Socket waited for them. "I suspect the trial has concluded," Jeremy said.

"That's quick. Isn't that the signal we've been waiting for?" Elizabeth said. "Don't we need to go get them?"

Jeremy raised his hand. "I think Teddy and I should contact Jennifer and not hear your plans. Please excuse us," he said, took Teddy's arm and left for the bridge.

Cookie spoke first. "We'll need the extractions to be simultaneous." He pointed his link to the active wall and in front of it appeared a holo of the station schematics. Then he expanded the region near Social Services. "Child Protective Services is here in Green 44r2."

"I know where it is," John said. "Is that just a schematic?"

Cookie shook his head and zoomed in through the grid of structure and tapped an icon. A vid popped up of the reception office with Ms. Stropchik on duty.

Socket raised an eyebrow. "I'm sure you shouldn't have that, Sergeant Cook."

"My buddies in the UNE Marines train for lots of contingencies."

"I'll bet the Tech Masters would like to know," Elizabeth said.

"And Meriel?" John said.

Cookie panned the schematic to a darkened patch in green-zone on the other side of the torus. "Jeremy confirmed they're holding her in these new high-security facilities."

"It's too far from Sandy."

Cookie nodded. "We'll need two teams."

"So, how are we going to get to Meriel?" Socket asked.

"On-station security has defense-in-depth for dangers from people, things, and processes," Cookie said and pressed an orange icon. On the schematic, vast regions of the common areas glowed orange. "Biotag readers, cameras, and roving security spiders cover the populated areas. Security is checking biotags continuously at the readers, and drones and spiders verify the bio markers. But they're tracking hundreds of thousands of people, so unless they're looking for us, we're lost in the crowd and invisible."

Elizabeth shook her head. "Even if they don't have warrants for us, we're friends of Meriel's and likely high on their list to track."

"What about the mechanical systems?" John asked. "Access ways?"

Cookie tapped a red icon, and other regions lit up in red. "These are the critical systems regions, food, energy, and pressure integrity, and the highest security. Access controls, cameras, motion detectors, and security patrols protect these areas. And security IDs are needed to pass the access control points."

"Which we don't have," Socket said. "So, we can't get in or out or muck around without getting caught."

"Right," Cookie said. "So that's a no."

"What about the process equipment?" John asked.

Cookie pressed a blue icon. "The Techs monitor the equipment continuously, but only alarm when the control limits are exceeded. You're invisible unless you break something. But—"

"But it's access controlled."

"Right. By security."

John leaned back and raised his hands. "Then we've got no way to get her."

Cookie smiled. "Infrastructure," he said. After touching the three icons at the same time, a labyrinth of interconnected paths appeared in green. "These are the unmonitored crawlspaces and passages where no one goes." He traced a path through the green regions from Meriel's cell in red to the docks in yellow. "Once you're in, you're invisible."

"How do we get from the ship to the infrastructure without alerting security?" John asked. "That's a surveilled high-traffic area."

Cookie turned to Elizabeth. "Liz, you met Jeremy on the docks. How did you do it?"

"The readers are glitchy," Elizabeth said, "and the smugglers keep them that way. You only need to know what to look for."

"Then we have a route to Meriel," John said. "How do we get her out of her cell?"

Cookie frowned again and ran his fingers over the schematic as he spoke. "I haven't figured that out yet. The mechanicals and electricals don't show any crawl spaces or ducting large enough for any of us to traverse. The wiring and security feeds are hardened. We'll never be able to intercept the signals. Jeremy said the walls are plastisteel. We'll never punch through that."

Elizabeth grinned. "Plastisteel. Recent?"

"Yes. These are new facilities after red-zone was spaced."

"I have an idea." She tapped her link. "Teddy, I need your droid."

"Sure," came Teddy's reply.

"Have him report to me immediately, please," Elizabeth said. "Cookie, transfer a copy of your schematics to Eddie. And don't forget Nick."

"Why do we need Nick?" Socket asked.

Elizabeth smiled. "You know the guy who designed the untraceable messaging system? The fellow who made your comm systems unhackable?"

"That Nick?" Cookie said.

Elizabeth nodded. "He's a wizard with anything connected. Where is he?"

"We have the John Doe that Jerri found in station security."

"That's the Troopers and Enterprise security," Cookie said. "These people are our friends."

John sneered. "Not anymore."

"Hold on, cowboy," Socket said. "The UNE are the bad guys here." She keyed her link to bring up Jerri's notes and swiped to display them on the wall. "The John Doe's chart says he's alive but unconscious."

"How can we confirm the John Doe is this Nick fella?" Cookie asked.

"Did they check him in with a wheelchair?" Elizabeth asked.

Socket scrolled through a chart. "No. But it says here his legs aren't functional."

Eddie appeared at the bulkhead door and Elizabeth stood. "That could be him," she said as she led the droid to the bridge.

Socket flipped through Jerri's notes and displayed the infirmary schedule on the wall.

"There's an appointment here for President Belson to visit him." Socket leaned back. "Why the hell would the President of the Assembly visit a suspected terrorist?"

"How are you doing this, doll?" Cookie asked.

"Shush."

"Let's call this 'Operation Barbarossa,'" he said with a gleam in his eye.

Socket turned to him. "I think you're liking this too much, soldier boy." She blocked his holo with her hand. "These are contingency plans only? Right? Just if the verdict is bad."

He gently pushed her hand away. "Right."

"And we need this to be surgical. Nothing lethal."

"Hey, I can be surgical."

"Sure." Socket's link buzzed. "Listen to this."

```
"News from Tech Center. Just in.
Station Master Kofi Sikibo was hospi-
talized . . ."
```

***

"I'm sorry," Jennifer said to Meriel's image.

"What's the problem? How did the hearing go today?"

"I was wrong about the UNE and the judge."

Uh oh, Meriel thought and sat on her bunk with her hands in her lap. "How so?"

"I went to the court with the exonerating evidence Jeremy and I put together. We had counter-arguments to every aspect of the investigation."

"That's good, right?"

"The judge . . ." Jennifer dropped her gaze. "The judge told me it didn't matter. He . . . he looked me right in the eye and said he wouldn't allow their admission. He had a decision in his hand waiting to release."

Meriel took a deep breath. "Guilty?"

"Yes," Jennifer said.

Meriel's hand shook, and she gripped it with the other. "They'll kill me like they killed my folks," she said as if reading a tech manual. "Just because we got in the way." She blinked rapidly and dug her thumb into the scar on her palm to dispel visions of her dying mother on the *Princess*.

"You expected this?"

Meriel nodded. "It feels different now that it's real."

And now they'll come after John and the girls, and my sister, and the orphans. And I won't be there to fight back.

"When you see Jeremy, tell him to remember the fire on Haven," Meriel said.

"What fire?"

"He'll know."

"I tried my best, Ms. Hope. I didn't know how bad . . ." She turned away.

This is my fault, Meriel thought. *If I'd kept my mouth shut, if I hadn't fought for the* Princess, *none of this would have happened.* Her inner voice would not stop and drowned out everything else. But she could not argue because it was true. *Haven will be shut out and starved. And it's my fault.*

"Maybe if I had submitted the evidence sooner," Jennifer said. "That's my fault."

The echo of Jennifer's despair interrupted Meriel's inner voice, and she jumped to her feet.

"No, Jen. It's *not* your fault. Look at me."

Jennifer raised her head.

"It was *never* your fault," Meriel said. "None of it. If you believe that, they win, they stop us from defending ourselves and fighting back, and they'll do it all again. You're not the cause of the evil that others do. Never believe that. Ever. Do you hear me?"

Jennifer nodded.

"You can't give up when you're still free to fight." She sat again. "You have a stake in this now. So, what do we do?"

"I'll need to talk with Jeremy and get back to you. I've never seen this . . ."

"Yeah, the reality of it takes getting used to. How deep it shakes you. You smell it now, the corruption. Like a stink you never noticed. You'll smell it everywhere now."

Jennifer nodded. "Now I know what your sister meant."

"Liz? What did she say?"

"Nothing," Jennifer said and glanced at her, but all Meriel could offer was a gentle smile. "I need to get moving before the judge files the verdict."

"Wait, Jen. I had a book when they arrested me that might help. Pick it up from the desk officer."

"A book. Really?"

"Not the whole thing. Just a part."

"How will I know what part?"

"You'll know. The pages are pretty beat up. My family reads it a lot."

After Jennifer left, Meriel examined her cell again. *I told Jen not to give up, but what can I do?*

No visible weakness was apparent. The vents were too small. The toilet and bed were built in. No hinges or locks were exposed on her side of the door.

With her hand, she brushed the soothing warmth of curing plastisteel. It was weaker than it would be in a few days, but even now was strong enough to keep her in and an army out.

Maybe when they transfer me? Maybe the next time they open my cell?

She paced like a lion in a cage, struggling to come up with a workable escape plan. But each new idea became more desperate and fanciful, but she could not stop, or the madness would devour her.

Patience. An opportunity will come . . .

***

In the waiting area of the detention center, Jennifer sat on a bench with her hands in her lap, staring at nothing. She scanned the room where everyone wore the same expression of confusion and desperation: staring into the distance, not knowing what to do next to save themselves or their loved ones; the same expression as hers.

Navigating a course through complex legal precedent and combating gifted adversaries delighted her. But not today. Today the life-shattering events happening to those here punched her in the gut.

If I do nothing, Dad will be safe from Sobrietz's threats. The partnership at my firm will be waiting for me. Life will go on. Meriel will be executed, and no one will blame me.

She sighed and a chunk of her soul left with each breath.

This isn't justice. This is evil. But what can I do?

No answers came.

She rose and went to the clerk to retrieve Meriel's book. It was small. "Meditations," the embossed title read. The cover had been repaired, and some pages were stained a reddish brown.

Blood?

As she walked out the door with it, she flipped to the most dog-eared page.

> *And once in an age, the arc of history bends around the wheel of one committed person who, acting from his or her own virtuous interests, changes the course of humanity: the child who raises the flag above the barricades . . . the girl who refuses to deny her love for God even while her flesh burns at the stake—individuals who grip a shred of civilization with both hands and will not give it up.*

Just outside the door to the detention area, Jennifer stopped at a bench and sat.

> *And through the fidelity of that individual, the complex interrelationships carefully constructed by the powerful to order society to fit their personal ideologies and selfish interests collapse under the weight of justice and moral right.*

Papa. That's what he taught me in words meant for a child.

She flipped back to the cover. *De Merlner. A book banned decades ago by the UNE. And father had read it.*

He'd said, "Evil always hides in the dark corners, and the UNE has many such corners."

"Hiding in the dark corners," she mumbled. *What was hidden? What can't I see?*

Her rational mind sliced through the darkness and the pretty life she had built for herself within it.

And it hurt.

Jennifer tapped her bracelet. "Bell, Jeremy." There was no answer, so she left a message.

"Jeremy, the judge has drafted a guilty verdict and won't admit our exonerating evidence." She bit her lip. "I advised

Ms. Hope. She's taking it rather well under the circumstances. Her only request was to remind you of the fire on Haven."

Unable to face the judgement of those in the room, she stood and turned to the wall.

"My firm chose me because . . . because I am naïve and trusted the UNE. The judge implied I'd be offered a partnership if I backed off. And he threatened my father if I appealed the verdict."

"If my ship had docked a few hours earlier, the explosion might have killed me too. I was brought here to put me in danger to intimidate my father."

She crossed her arms and stared at the floor where the shattered pieces of her self-image lay. In a hushed voice, she continued.

"It's clear the case against Meriel and the rush to convict her is to hide who actually did it. The only people who can shine a light into this dark corner are the UNE, but they . . ."

Jennifer stomped her foot and heads turned to her. "The UNE are unreliable and have given us no path to appeal. I am seeking the only alternative I can think of. And if I succeed, I will get in touch with you. I have given you access to all the evidence in case something happens to me."

Gazing down the corridor, past the citizens blind to the corruption around them, she put her plans in motion. She sent a message to her father, straightened her back, and walked to the tram with a draft of her appeal, unaware that all her messages had been blocked.

***

Socket tapped her link to display the feeds on the *Tiger's* bulkhead.

```
"News from the Tech Center. Just in.
Station Master Kofi Sikibo has been
hospitalized after a sudden stroke.
```

```
Jergen Belson, President of the Assem-
bly of Citizens, will hold the posi-
tion until the Masters can ap-
point . . ."
```

"The game has changed," Jeremy said as he rejoined them in the mess. "Time's up."

"I think we should stage our strike teams on Enterprise," Cookie said. "Teddy, can you drop us off?"

"Of course," she said.

About to finish yet another Scotch, John froze with his drink in midair. "Sikibo assigned his personal security to Sandy."

***

The door to Meriel's cell clicked and slid open. At the table outside the door sat Prosecutor Kostanza.

Meriel leaned against the portal but remained inside. "Where is Ms. Churchill?"

"Your advocate is unaware of this meeting, and there will be no record of it."

"Isn't this irregular?"

Kostanza smiled. "Highly. But that's the nature of my visit."

She left the cell and paced near the door, inspecting the conference room for escape routes. "If you could get what you want by any other means, you'd not be here. So, what do you want other than my scalp?"

"You understand a UNE conviction is imminent, yes?"

She nodded.

"And a guilty verdict means execution."

She nodded again.

"I am here to offer a reduced sentence for your cooperation."

"Meaning what?"

"If you admit to causing the explosion that damaged Enterprise—"

"If I lie for you, you mean."

"Semantics, Ms. Hope."

"Why in hell would I do that?"

"To save your life. Does that mean nothing to you?"

"If I go along with this, the killers go free, and many more innocent people will die."

"And if you don't, those closest to you may—"

Meriel lunged over the table but grabbed only air. His image was a hologram, a good one, that blinked out when she smashed the holo projector on the floor. But Kostanza popped up in another chair.

"Is that all you got?" Meriel said. "You've been threatening to kill us for ten years and never needed my help."

"Your cooperation could speed the release of the Smith girl."

Hope flashed across her face before her expression hardened to a glare. "If you had her, I'd swear I was the queen of the f'ing universe to free her. But if you had her, you'd not be talking nice to me." She smiled. "You're bluffing and I don't trust you or any part of your stinking deal."

"We can—"

"You can what?" Meriel put her fists on her hips. "You already have your conviction and the excuse to kill me."

"Believe us, Ms.—"

"Wait," she said and stopped pacing. "If you have a conviction, why do you need my confession? Son of a . . . You want Enterprise to go along with this crap. And you want me to make it easy for you."

"It would simplify matters and speed the—"

She grinned and folded her arms. "It's because I exposed the Treaty of Haven that Enterprise doesn't trust the UNE. They're afraid to partner with you. And even with your guy Belson on the Council, you can't get them to kneel."

"I didn't say that. I—"

Meriel glared at him. "You need to discredit me and the only thing keeping the spotlight on your corruption."

She stopped still, and all the events, coincidences, and speculations collided in her head and reassembled. *It's not me, or just Haven. It's . . .*

"You're aiming to take over the entire sector," she said with disbelief. "Including Haven."

Kostanza's ears reddened.

"Did you kill him?"

"Who?"

"Sikibo, the Station Master. What's one more after thousands."

He set his jaw and avoided her eyes.

Meriel stood straight, shocked. "You S.O.B. You nearly killed half a million people here for an effing trade deal."

He glared at her. "Not my call."

"Wait until I tell everyone what you're up to."

Kostanza sneered. "Your rantings will never leave this room."

She waved to the security cameras. "Did you hear him? He just admitted to conspiracy and murder. Hey, wake up—"

"There's no one there, Ms. Hope. Now, back to my offer. A reduced sentence and the girl released for—"

She picked up the nearest chair and threw it through his image. "You're bluffing. Sandy is safe in Social Services. You have nothing else I want, and I would never trade Haven for my life."

Meriel grabbed the second holo cube from the chair and pitched it against the wall. After grinding the shattered pieces into dust under her heel, she returned to her cell and banged the door closed repeatedly until the lock clicked.

Over the PA came Kostanza's voice. "We'll be in touch, Ms. Hope."

"What are you going to do?" Meriel called. "What are you gonna do!"

Sandy!

"Guard! Guard!" she shouted, but no one answered.

Chapter 18
Enterprise Station, Procyon A System

Ostara

The traditional shower of cherry blossoms met Captain Stark as he approached the dining room of La Mère Catherine.

Inside the door, the hostess waved him forward and wedged him through the crowd of celebrants, each in traditional pagan clothing. In the middle of the room stood a maypole around which children danced. Along the way, he averted the flirty glances and intimate touches of those selecting their partners for the evening's pleasures.

At a panoramic window, Captain Stark paused at the view. Outside, the aeration falls fell hundreds of feet from the height of the inner torus to the white-zone agricultural deck. And even though protected by a clear cylindrical canopy, it dominated the scene. Below them lay the green and tan expanse of the farms, and near the edge of the torus, the luxury homes. But he most enjoyed the irrigation river flowing through it to follow the torus's arc to the terminal lake.

At a table near the middle of the window sat Ambassador Bakshi, his wife Beatrice, and Kostanza.

"Welcome, Captain," Bakshi said and lifted his glass. "Merry Ostara."

Bakshi wore the silks of a raja and the prosecutor the cassock of a Wiccan priest. But both were practically invisible next to Beatrice.

Her dress befitted a Nubian princess in low-cut and high-hemmed animal furs with a modern crown of the Ethiopian nobility. She was beautiful as only a fortune in biologics and microsurgery could produce, but her wrinkled hands gave her away.

Stark nodded to each and sat between Beatrice and Kostanza.

"Welcome spring," Beatrice said, leaned his way to expose some extra cleavage, and kissed him on the cheek.

Next to Stark, Kostanza wavered in his chair, having begun celebrations early.

"Apologies for the paltry turnout," Beatrice said. "Ostara celebrations at home are huge."

From a priceless pearl clutch, she removed a small bag and a sculpture of a woman's torso with large breasts and placed them in the middle of the table. From the bag, she took a pinch of dirt and sprinkled it at the base of the figurine.

On each place setting, servers set bowls of red liquid that Stark hoped was wine, or at least juice.

"Let's begin," she said, closing her eyes and opening her arms.

"Oh, Mother Gaia, accept our sacrifice on this Ostara Day, and let us enjoy today and this coming year to the fullest. We thank you for the cycle of life that renews each spring, and for evolving us beyond the temporal to embrace your timeless love. Amen."

She drank from her bowl and Stark followed, grateful for the bitter tang of a cold beet soup. After the ceremony, servers filled their wine glasses and brought the first dinner course.

Beatrice startled Stark with a hand between his legs. "Will you join me later as my Ostara partner?"

Stark turned to her engaging smile.

"I have a private suite," she said.

Her invitation was an honor, especially from a noblewoman, and a ticket to Sol's high society, but he caught the ambassador's scowl.

"I would be honored, milady," he said and tapped his ear. "But I am on duty."

Bakshi cleared his throat and raised his glass. "To justice served and verdict advantageous."

They toasted and sipped.

Kostanza emptied his glass, beaming with victory. "The verdict is filed?"

"Yes, and on its way to Earth and Lander. And with Belson leading the Council of Masters now, we expect a quick confirmation of the guilty verdict."

Outside, below the window, citizens shook their fists and grumbled at a holo that looped a vid of Meriel being dragged onto a UNE ship while the USF kept the LeHavre residents away at gunpoint. Above the holo, a banner rotated with the message:

```
Enterprise's freedom is only guaran-
teed by strength! Resist UNE tyranny!
```

Bakshi sneered. "I have bigger guns."

They're not yours, Stark thought.

Beatrice frowned at the demonstrators outside. "It's appalling they have forgotten Gaia out here. The parades at home are glorious, with the best of each ancient culture in the fore." She shook her head. "And look at these heathens with their body art and drugs. They would be arrested at home for sacrilege against Gaia and reeducated."

"I think you mean stoned to death, dear," Bakshi said and took a drink.

"I can understand the stations desire for freedom," Stark said.

Beatrice raised her eyebrows. "You sympathize with them?"

"Ma'am, my job is compliance, not sympathy."

She laid a flower petal in front of the sculpture. "Gaia, damn the heathens who reject you."

"You're damning most of those who live out here," Stark said.

"So be it. The Goddess should strike them for their sacrilege."

Kostanza smirked. "What can Gaia do way out here?"

Beatrice scowled. "The same as she's done in the past: pestilence, famine, disease, and—"

"And war?" Kostanza said.

Bakshi glared at him. "Now, now. Let's return the conversa—"

Stark ignored Bakshi and turned to Kostanza. "The gods threaten war with the stations?"

"Not a threat, my dear captain," Beatrice said. "A fact. Earth sees the Enterprise deaths at the hands of that spacer terrorist, Hope, as Gaia's punishment for their blasphemy. And—"

In the promenade below the window, the protest grew to the edge of the Ostara celebrants where a shoving match devolved into fist fights.

"Congratulations, Mister Ambassador," Stark said. "You may have accomplished what the stations never could by themselves."

"And what is that, Captain?"

"Unity, sir. And unity means resistance."

***

In blue maintenance overalls, Cookie and Socket waited near the Tiger's airlock for the glitch to appear in dock surveillance—two blinks on the biotag reader followed by a ten-second freeze of the cameras. Their target was the bar across the docks: Robotomi.

Along the docks, merchant ships filled every visible berth until they disappeared in the mist past the upward curve of the torus. Squads of cargo loaders lumbered in and out of the holds, dumping freight into support vehicles queued up at each ship.

A drop of oil fell on Cookie's shoulder, and he raised his eyes as a jump engine rolled past on a gantry crane. In that moment of distraction, Socket yanked him from the path of a massive grav sled.

"How long are we supposed to wait?" Socket asked.

"Dunno."

Uniformed men with red bands on blue helmets appeared and Cookie pulled Socket behind a stack of bucky-sheets. "UNE Shore Patrol."

"I recognize them," she said as she picked up a few of the feather-light sheets and dragged them nearer to a ship. After two trips, the danger had passed.

"Those don't belong there," a cargo mate said. "Hey, you're not—"

The lights on the biotag reader blinked twice, and Cookie waved. "Sorry, chief." He took Socket's arm, and led her across the docks, keeping his face out of sight of the Shore Patrol and the security cameras.

Robotomi served the dock workers and anonymous spacers of blue-zone. Sprinkled among the regular crowd were the occasional professionals who didn't mind getting dirty and stationers who planned to.

This cycle, garlands of pine boughs hung above the bar and wreaths of spring flowers marked the Ostara celebrations. UNE Marines and Station Troopers alike crowded the bar but kept to opposite corners.

Socket maneuvered her way to a table and chairs in a corner with a view of the window. Outside, the Shore Patrol peered in and moved on.

Once inside, Cookie ordered drinks: two each. "We may be here awhile." He scanned the room and tipped his head toward a woman in a business suit chatting up two spacers with officer bars. "She's a buyer."

"She's a cruiser," Socket said, using spacer slang for a whore.

"No way."

"She's smiling. Buyers never smile."

A tipsy woman bumped her tush against the back of Socket's chair, so she pushed her chair back: hard. Standing behind the business suit, a UNE Marine grinned at her.

She turned away. "Jeez, save me."

"From what?" Cookie said.

The Marine walked to Socket and leaned over the table. "Hey doll. Dump the stiff and let's party."

"The lady is with me," Cookie said.

"You still here, stiff?" the Marine asked and gave Cookie a sneer. Then his eyes opened wide. "Well, I'll be damned." He snapped to attention and saluted.

Cookie grabbed him by the sleeve and sat him in a chair at their table. "At ease, Henry."

"Sargent Cook. I haven't heard of you since . . ."

"Mimosa-3."

"Yeah. What a cluster f—"

Not accustomed to being ignored, Socket leaned back but kicked Cookie unseen. "You gonna introduce me?"

"Suzanne Soquette, let me introduce Staff Sergeant—"

"Master Sergeant, now," the Marine said.

"Master Sergeant Patrick Henry."

"Honored, ma'am. And apologies for my rudeness."

Socket pushed a drink in front of him. "You two know each other?"

"Sergeant of Marines Cook here was our battalion non-com. Always found a way to fight beside us."

"You come in on the *Intrepid*?" she asked.

Henry nodded. "Captain Stark flew us in."

Cookie raised an eyebrow. "Captain? He should be an admiral by now."

"Except for—"

"Mimosa-3," they said at the same time.

Henry nodded. "He'd a made rank if he'd followed orders and blown us all to hell."

"So, what about Mimosa-3?" she said.

Henry glanced at Cookie, who nodded.

"Total FUBAR. We put down a rebellion on a mining colony near Alpha Centauri B. Thugs took it over and made slaves of the miners."

"A humanitarian mission?"

"Oh, *hell* no. The UNE didn't care who ran the place or how, only that they kept paying taxes. Thugs got greedy, and the UNE sent us in to 'pacify' them. Bloody."

"Collateral damage?" she asked.

"Lots. Sergeant Cook here negotiated a truce to stop the slaughter. Brass was totally pissed 'cause they wanted a bloodbath to set an example." He turned to Cookie. "They cashier you?"

Cookie shook his head. "Gave me a medal. Offered me a commission."

"Did you take it?"

"Took my thirty and resigned."

Henry smiled. "With a blonde, I heard."

Socket caught the faraway look in Cookie's eyes and took his hand under the table.

A civilian staggered into their table and Cookie brushed him off like an empty juice pack.

"What brings you so far from the core stars?" Henry said.

"Vessel security chief."

"Sounds dull."

"Not so much. I'm riding with six Marine certs aboard. Suzanne here is Marine-3."

"Pleased to meet you for a second time," Henry said. "You're on a patrol boat?"

"Merchant."

"Why so much fire power for a merchant?"

Socket laughed from her gut. "You hear of the Johnston Rift?"

"Haven? You were there?"

Cookie nodded.

"You in the Haven Marines too?"

"Reserve," Socket said and crossed her arms. "So, why are you guys here?"

Henry gulped his drink. "Scuttlebutt is we're to get used to a post out here. It's sure better than the asteroid bivouacs."

"Permanent?"

The Marine put his elbows on the table. "Some Marines and crew believe our future is out here. And there're bonuses to re-up."

She raised an eyebrow. "Why not re-up for Sol System?"

"No one on my ship has ever been to Sol, much less Earth. They don't let us soldiers near their precious planet or their ladies. Even for a pilgrimage—"

The UNE Marines interrupted with toasts to Gaia and a bawdy invitation to the Ostara celebration. But Henry did not raise his glass.

"You're not toasting Gaia, Henry?"

"Those guys are just trying to get laid." He shook his head and took a swig. "Faith in Gaia kinda drifts away when you're never gonna get there. Hell, half my company are JCS second."

Socket furrowed her brow. "Second?"

Cookie smiled. "Cause they're all Marines first."

"Oorah!" Henry shouted, and behind him a squad of his friends echoed the cheer.

Socket frowned and pulled Cookie toward her as the Shore Patrol passed the window again. "We're keeping a low profile, right? Then keep your buddy quiet."

From the bar, a Trooper in dark green fatigues raised a hand to his ear. "Are those more UNE babysitters?"

Henry stood. "And what's it to you."

The Trooper turned and leaned an elbow on the bar. "I hear you're ferrying some Earth pukes to harass us. You don't belong out here."

"We're here 'cause you're too pansy-assed to protect yourselves," Henry said.

"You're real brave fighting civilians again."

"You haven't been in a fight since your mama broke you of her teat."

The Marines rose to defend Henry, but twice as many Troopers rose behind their man who walked over and stood toe-to-toe with Henry.

Socket grabbed Cookie again. "The Troopers are our friends, Cookie. You have to stop—"

The Trooper glanced at Socket without dropping his chin. "Shut up, cruiser. Or maybe you want to be with a real man?"

Socket faced him with narrowed eyes. "Who you talking to?"

"You, bitch."

Henry's fellow Marines held him back as Cookie glared and stood. But Socket grabbed Cookie's arm and pulled him back down.

The Trooper inspected Cookie. "What you gonna do, big guy?"

"He's not gonna do anything," Socket said and kicked him in the crotch. The Trooper doubled over, and she grabbed him by the ears to pull his face to hers. "Now I can hear you better. Nothing to say?" She head-butted him in the nose with an audible crack. When he raised his head, she punched him in the face and kicked him back into his buddies.

"That's certainly not helping," Cookie said.

The Troopers marched toward them and faced off against Henry and his shipmates.

Cookie raised his hands with palms forward. "Just a misunderstanding, fellas. We—"

A fist flew, aimed for his face and another for his gut. He grabbed and twisted them and drove their owners to the ground. "We don't want any trouble."

Another attacker wound up to punch Socket, but Henry's fist stopped him. Four men down was enough to start a brawl that brought the Shore Patrol and the gray uniforms of station security.

Cookie took Henry aside. "Great catching up with you, Sergeant. But we were never here."

"Aye, sir," Henry said before rejoining the fight.

Socket and Cookie edged to the back by the bar, and when the bouncers retreated to protect the liquor, they slipped out the unguarded rear door.

In the service corridor, Cookie leaned back against the door until the latch clicked. From a dark corner at the end of the hall a thick man with no neck and a scar for an ear approached with a foldable wheelchair slung over his shoulder.

"The girl sent me," Cookie said.

The rough man faced him and handed him the wheelchair. "These things are hard to find,"

"You were well paid for it," Socket replied.

He eyed her and smirked. "Follow me," he said and led them around the corner, past broken surveillance cameras to a grated vent in the floor. From a pocket, he removed a device and tapped it, and the vent popped open.

"This is as far as I go," the man said and lifted the vent.

Cookie lowered Socket into the passage, handed her the wheelchair, and lowered himself down.

She pressed the sleeve of her blue coveralls, and the fabric changed to colors that blended with the bulkheads. Then she pressed Cookie's sleeve as he studied his map of the station infrastructure on a burner link. From her kit, she took black and white makeup and added streaks to their faces to fool the facial recognition systems.

Cookie scanned both ways along the passage and checked the schematic. Above him, the rough man locked the vent with a click.

"There's no way back now," Cookie said and headed toward the axis of the torus. "This way to our staging point."

***

In the playroom of Enterprise Social Services, Sandy sat with her eyes glued to the small window in the door, waiting for her father. But the only adults who came to visit were the attendants who escorted her to and from her sterile bedroom and the nurses who checked her health. These visitors surrendered their links before they entered and left with nothing from inside the room.

Cheerful pastels covered walls decorated with cartoons of cuddly animals unknown except in zoos on Earth. Next to them, fixed displays cycled through children's art.

These were not like the art from her school on Haven: the sunflowers, sunsets, and galaxy rises that were, for a brief moment, the most wondrous things in their world. Here were the images of things unknown to Haven kids: a robot cat, the curved perspective of a green-zone playground, the complex sims, and the green trees and grasses of a white-zone park.

In the drawers were old drawings. One was of a drooping sunflower with the name Anita written with a backward *n*. In another, a spaceman and dragon sat side-by-side studying a spaceship cracked open like an egg.

Sandy searched the shelves and mesh drawers for electronic devices she might use to communicate but found only digital art pads and plush toys without a network connection. She frowned: even Haven's toys had built-in connectivity.

She disassembled a pad and a display searching for comm chips or RF modules, even ancient UARTs, but found nothing. With no link or electronics, she went to a drawer filled with paper and colored pencils and drew her schoolhouse on Haven lit by Thor's glow.

The door clicked. Sandy stood and rushed to it with a broad smile, but a matron entered wearing a light green frock.

"Did papa come, Ms. Oliver?"

"I'm sorry, dear," Betty said. "No one has come yet with the proper documents."

What happened to Papa? Why didn't he come? "What about Elizabeth Hope? Did she come?"

"No. I'm sorry. Someone will be here for you soon." She reached into her pocket and handed a small package to Sandy. "These are for you."

Sandy opened the gift to find a few new eye patches and chose a fabric with a pattern of brown checks that matched her hair. "Thank you."

"What's that you're drawing?"

Sandy held up the picture. "It's the school my father rebuilt after Archers destroyed the first one."

"What's the blue-green circle?"

"That's a planet. Thor."

Betty raised her eyebrows. "So huge? What a rich imagination you have, dear."

"When will I be going home?"

"As soon as your father comes with the right papers," Betty said. "Do you have an appointment?"

Sandy frowned at her sarcasm but then brightened. "My birthday is coming, and I have a party planned."

"Well, I'm sure you'll be home in a day or so. Who did you invite?"

"Well, my family and friends."

"And someone special?"

She smiled with a nod and a blush at the thought of the new boy in class. Then she spotted a slight wrinkle in the matron's pocket that might be an electronic device she could use. "Can you help me? I can't find the blue pencil."

"Sure."

Betty reached up to open the drawer, and Sandy reached a hand into her pocket, but the woman turned, pulling the frock just out of reach.

Mission failure. "How about Merry L? Did she come for me?"

"Mary who?"

"Merry L Hope."

Betty winced as if troubled by an old memory. "Meriel Hope is in a lot of trouble. They're saying she hurt people."

Sandy stood and clenched her fists. "No, she wouldn't. She loves me and takes care of me and my sister, and her sister, and—"

"Maybe she was nice once. But children died in the hull breach because of what they say she did. Children like you."

"She had nothing to do with that."

"How could you know?"

"Because I was with her on LeHavre."

Betty raised an eyebrow. "It's much too dangerous for you to be with her."

"How can a hug from someone who loves me be dangerous?"

The woman blushed and sat facing her. "I'm sorry you're alone here, dear. I'm sure your father or someone will come for you soon. We just need to make sure you're safe while you stay with us."

Sandy backed away and balled her fists. "I want my papa!"

"When someone comes with the right papers, we'll come get you." A buzz came from her pocket. "Excuse me. I'll be back to help you finish your drawing."

"Let me see Merry L!"

The matron turned to open the door, and in that instant, Sandy reached into the woman's pocket and slipped the object into her own. When the door closed, she kicked and beat on it until her fists ached.

As Betty's footsteps faded, Sandy sat with her back wedged against the door, out of sight from the window above. She examined her prize—an old, flexible, and indestructible government issue link like the one her father had given her at home, and she had disassembled so many times before. She tapped the link, but it did not respond to her biotag.

With a fingernail, she split the device in two and peeled the layers apart. After snapping off the corner of the bioidentity circuitry, she pressed the layers back together. With the gadget unlocked, she attempted to connect to the station's network, but there was no handshake.

"Faraday cage," she mumbled. *A solid mesh must enclose the room, and no EM signal can escape. Just like kidnappers.*

When it's outside the cage, it'll send. So, how far does that go? She tapped the address to her father and Meriel's friends on the *Tiger* but stopped and leaned back. *I'm sure Papa knows I'm here and is coming for me. I'm not in danger... as far as I know. If I send 'Help,' he'll get scared.*

The door rattled and someone tried to enter but she had her back against it and resisted.

"Sandy, please let me in."

Sandy dug her heels into the carpet, still composing a message.

```
I'm here and . . .
```

The woman was strong and pushed the door open before Sandy finished.

"I'm sorry. I fell asleep," Sandy said and faked a yawn.

The woman narrowed her eyes, but Sandy reached out her hand with the link in it.

"Did you drop this? I found it by the drawers."

Betty took the link and inspected it.

"It's polite to say thank you," the girl said.

The woman lost the expression of a friendly grandmother and replaced it with the adamantine glare of a Trooper Commando.

An hour later, a knock on the playroom door woke Sandy from a nap on the couch.

"Happy day," Betty said. "Your father is here for you."

Sandy smiled and ran to the door.

"He's right outside."

"Did you see him?"

"Yes, dear. And you're the spitting image."

Sandy scanned the room again. "Is Elizabeth here? Cookie?"

"Only your father."

"I think I should wait for him here."

The matron glanced at her and the door. "It should be fine. Don't worry."

The girl did not move.

Betty kneeled. "Sandy, I understand you aren't comfortable. This is a new place with many strangers. If anything happens, I won't let them take you. Understand? You just tell me." She stood and held out her hand.

Something in the woman's eyes told Sandy she could trust her. A moment later, she took the offered hand and walked with her down the corridor.

Inside a small office sat a woman with a pretty nose and violet eyes dressed in a dark business suit. Beside her, a man with a scar on his forehead leaned over the table. He appeared much like Sandy with brown eyes and high cheekbones, except his work clothes were new. Two burly men in dark suits flanked them.

The matron approached with Sandy and signaled to the burly men.

"You two, outside," she said. When the men left, she waved a hand and the transfer documents popped up on the active wall.

The man with the scar held out his arms. "Sandy, honey, I'm so glad to see you."

"Who are you?" Sandy said.

"Don't be silly, girl."

She pushed her chair back and sidled next to the matron. "He's not my father."

"Hush girl," the woman in the dark suit said. "His papers are in order."

"Call Merry L. Or Elizabeth. Or Cookie! Please, this isn't my father. Please."

Betty tensed and narrowed her eyes. "Let's take a timeout and reexamine your papers, Mr. Smith."

"The clerk has already reviewed them and approved the transfer, ma'am," the businesswoman said with a sneer as she edged around the table. "Another review is unnecessary."

Betty's jaw tightened. "I'll decide that."

"You know children," he said. "Too much time alone on the farm. She's always been difficult. Come here, girl."

Sandy dug herself in behind Betty, keeping the imposter in view with her good eye. Beside her cheek, the link bulged in the matron's pocket.

"She's been hoping for an adventure like this," he said and grabbed for Sandy's arm from her blind side.

Betty intercepted his hand and bent his wrist back forcing him to lean forward. She released her grip and pushed the man away. "We're taking a break here, Mr. Smith. She's afraid . . ."

"Sandy come with me, now," the man said, rubbing his wrist, "or your mother will be very disappointed."

"My mother's dead!"

"See what I mean?" he said and reached for her again.

With the girl behind her, Betty edged toward the door. "We're done here, Mr. Smith, or whatever your—" She raised her hand to cancel the transfer, but the PA system blared.

> "Security alert: Master Sikibo hospitalized after a massive stroke. Personnel team SS6 report to the Tech Center."

"Oh my god!" Betty said and put a hand to her mouth.

In that split second of distraction, the windows of the small office frosted, and the imposter thrust a syringe at Betty's arm. She grabbed his wrist with her free hand, drew him toward her, and elbowed him in the face.

The woman with the pretty nose pointed a mini-tase at her, but Betty slapped it away and punched her in the face, knocking her into the imposter.

The men in dark suits slipped into the room and came for Betty who dropped one with a kick to his knee. But the other parried her leg, and his partner reached from the deck and seized an arm.

Trapped in the corner, Sandy struggled to escape, but could not maneuver around the melee. She dipped her hand into the matron's pocket to retrieve the link and hurried a message. But the imposter posing as her father seized her wrist, took the device, and smashed it on the floor.

"Oh no you don't."

From under the edge of the table, Betty retrieved a stunner, discharged it on one of the suits, and reached for the alarm button. "Secur—"

But the businesswoman touched Betty's arm, and she froze.

"What did you do to her?" Sandy said, but the suited woman scratched the girl's neck and paralyzed her too.

The remaining suit placed Betty into a chair with her back to the door and closed her half-open mouth. The imposter took her hand and waved it near the document display and the "Transfer Approved" box.

Violet-eyes squinted as her swollen eye closed, and she scowled at Betty. "You bitch, that hurt."

Betty fought the paralytic to reach the alarm, but violet eyes kicked her hand away and punched the helpless matron in the face until her knuckles bled.

"Enough," the imposter said, and draped Sandy over his shoulder. With the scene now appearing as peaceful as before, they unfrosted the window.

"See?" the businesswoman said as they left the office and waved to Ms. Stropchik. "She's tuckered out from all the excitement. Thank you so much for your help."

Outside the Social Services offices, the imposter's team carried Sandy into a private transit pod with the logo of the Biadez Foundation.

***

As John and Jeremy rushed through customs on the way to Social Services, Jeremy's link buzzed with a message from Teddy.

"We've got it, John," Teddy said from *Amelia's* bridge. "Lander logged Sandy's ID with yours."

"Is it all there?" John asked.

Jeremy tapped his wrist band and the custody documents appeared on the wall. He wiggled his fingers to flip through the pages and nodded.

"Forward a copy to Social Services," he said as they entered a tram and their links beeped again.

"Sandy," they said at the same time.

Ten minutes later, John and Jeremy leaned over the counter, staring at a confused clerk.

"There must be a mistake, sir," Mrs. Stropchik said.

"There can't be a 'mistake,'" John said. "She's my daughter!"

The clerk turned the display around. "I don't know who you are, but Alessandra Smith's father just picked her up."

"*I'm* her father. She must still be here."

"That's not possible, sir. We're very careful about such things. Mrs. Oliver is our security chief and oversaw the transfer herself. She's right there in the discharge office." Stropchik pointed to the glass enclosed office, stood, and waved. "Betty. Betty," she called and sat again. After typing on the console, she glanced back at Betty and frowned. "June, can you get Mrs. Oliver for us? Over in the transfer office. Thank you."

"She *must* be here," John said. "We sent the documents earlier."

The clerk raised her chin. "Excuse me, sir. Mr. Smith presented his papers earlier to the Foundation. They verified them."

"Who verified them?" Jeremy asked over John's shoulder.

"The Biadez Foundation. They partner with us here to—"

John slammed his hand on the counter. "How could you? Don't you watch the casts?"

"Those slanders? We've always found the Biadez people to be trustworthy and reliable. They provide valuable services for children here."

"Yes, we're well aware of their services—" Jeremy replied.

A shriek drew their attention to June retreating from the transfer office and Betty lying face down on the table.

John elbowed his way back to the counter. "You imbeciles! How—"

"Where did they go?" Jeremy asked.

She rose. "If there's been a mix-up, I'll file a complaint at once."

"Too f'ing late," John said. "We need to find her now!"

Jeremy tapped the back of his ear. "Teddy, they kidnapped Sandy. Can we get a location—"

Ms. Stropchik frowned. "Kidnapped is a bit strong, Mr. Bell."

Jeremy glared at her. "You don't get a vote," he said and grabbed John's arm. "Teddy says they're gone."

"How could they?" John said. "This is Enterprise." With a narrowed gaze at the lawyer, he raised his link.

"Barbarossa."

Security

Police Officer Rosalita Gentri stood at ease with her hands behind her back in front of the Security Review Board.

"Regarding the depressurization event, anything more to add Officer Gentri?" Admiral Morrell said.

"Yes, ma'am," Gentri replied. "This is my fourth interview. Am I under suspicion?"

"In no way, officer. And we commend your tenacity in such extreme circumstances."

"One thing more, ma'am. During my ID check, the accused asked if we'd received a security alert."

"There wasn't one."

"Yes, ma'am. But why would he ask?"

"Thank you, officer," Morrell said. "We'll append the record. But before your speculations affect your judgement, are you aware he had two biotags?"

"No, ma'am."

"You understand a conviction for a security violation of that severity is enough to get him spaced."

"Yes, ma'am."

"Dismissed. Enjoy your vacation, officer."

"Thank you, ma'am."

Gentri came to attention, saluted, and about-faced.

She shook her head. *If he was involved in the explosion, why did he ask about the alerts? But they said he was monitoring the ship that exploded.*

Outside the door, a balding man with a bar fighter's ear met her: her shift sergeant. Other than her partner, he was the only man she trusted to have her back.

"You here to babysit?" she asked.

He smirked. "No. I'm here to shoot you if you said something wrong."

He did not smile, and she was unsure if he meant it.

"How's Ricky?" she asked, as they walked back to their station.

"Your partner won't be in for a while."

"And his kids?"

The sergeant shook his head. "Oxygen deprivation. They're gonna let 'em both go."

She bit her lip. "He loves those kids." *They could have been our kids if he hadn't been such a shit.* "Were they serious about my vacation?"

"Yeah, Lieutenant Gunderson recommended it. Starts after your shift. Until then, you'll ride the desk and screen calls."

The police station had calmed down once they detained the terrorists and closed the investigations. Now it was back to routine, and she sat the most boring duty they had: screening calls for the desk sergeant. Between calls, Gentri's thoughts drifted to the nagging puzzle of the missing security alert.

She keyed her console to the message database.

"Search security incoming, within twelve hours of depressurization event."

```
Two-hundred-forty. Query?
```

"Is that alert still bugging you?" her sergeant asked.

She nodded. "Why would Zanek even tip me off about the issue? If he tapped the security feeds, he'd know we received it—"

"And that we didn't act on it. Was there a message?"

"Query messages for threat warnings," she said.

```
One message.
```

"Display."

```
Possible terrorist threat, dock M22.
```

"That's where the ships exploded," her sergeant said.

She confirmed with a nod and turned back to the display. "Time relative to enterprise damage?"

```
Event minus sixty-six minutes.
```

"Source?"

```
Anonymous. Cannot trace.
```

"Any other communications from the same GRL?"

```
Four.
```

"Display next, sequential."

```
Confirmed security breach. M22 dock.
```

"Disposition of incoming message."

```
Messages C/H, Classified Hoax.
```

The sergeant leaned over her console. "So, someone judged the calls to be cranks."

"Display other messages," she said, and the screen scrolled with illegible code. "Translate."

```
Override. Activate red alert.
Override. Close pressure doors, all.
Override. Double closure torque, im-
pound dock wharf pressure doors.
```

"What a moron," the sergeant said. "He f'd up and left his return address when he overrode security."

"Is that what the Security Masters found out?"

"If Zanek sent the alerts, either he's a complete hack, or he didn't give a shit about getting caught."

She shook her head. "He's smart enough to override security. And I'm alive because of it."

"Now, don't go wobbly on me, Gentri. He's the perp, remember?"

"So, who is this guy? The phony tag said 'Nick Zanek.' What did his real biotag say?"

She checked, but her console returned only.

```
Records sealed by order of Security.
```

Dead end.
Could Zanek be innocent?

She was not sure but packed up her research and addressed it to her precinct commander and Admiral Morrell. But she paused before hitting send.

"Who decided the messages to security were cranks?" she asked and queried the message disposition.

The sergeant shook his head. "That rookie is gonna get his ass whooped."

```
Lt. G. Gunderson.
```

"Shit," he said. "That's not his duty."

He's our precinct commander. And he wants me on vacation.

***

"Nick."

He ran from the voice, but Nick's feet were stuck in curing plastisteel, and he turned to the man's blood drenched hands.

"Nick."

He opened his eyes, blinked at the bright overhead light, and then scanned the room with the cabinets and equipment of a medical office. But he stopped at the sight of the man in his dream standing next to his bed, the face of his adoptive father he had not seen in person in thirteen years.

"How do you feel?" Jergen Belson asked.

"Like crap. Where am I?"

"In the Security Infirmary. You're under arrest for mass murder and terrorism."

"Enterprise is intact?"

"Of course."

Nick sighed. "Then why are you here? Oh, I got it. A sensitive matter your son is mixed up in that might embarrass you."

His father shook his head. "No, no. Didn't you read the news feeds after you disappeared? Radicals kidnapped you and kept you off the grid. Your mother and I paid a fortune to the kidnappers, but they took the money and didn't return you. You've been presumed dead all this time."

"I ran away—"

"I prefer our version," his father said and pushed a button on the bed to elevate Nick's head.

"—to hide from you."

"So, what new story will we create for you? Ah, yes, I've got it. Kidnapped. Abused. Stockholm syndrome. Whatever. And now a terrorist who's irrefutably guilty. It'll make a great vid."

"I was trying to save the station," Nick said.

"You likely did, and I am grateful. Unfortunately for you, some people didn't want it saved."

"You knew about the attack beforehand?"

"No, you idiot. I'm not suicidal. But I was aware my associates wanted a dramatic demonstration of the incompetence of the Tech Masters."

"Your friends intended to destroy Enterprise and—"

"Creative destruction," Belson said. "A little scare to give the UNE an opportunity to flex their atrophied humanitarian muscles."

Nick shook his head. "They meant to *destroy* it, not damage it. Hundreds of thousands of people could have died. Millions more in the sector would have suffered."

Belson paused and frowned. "And how do you know this?"

"They meant the *Princess* to be the detonator for the explosive organics in the neighboring ship. That was the actual bomb."

His father stared past the walls. "They're playing for the galaxy. One station is nothing to them. Even Enterprise."

Nick was not sure who his father was talking to. "This is your game?"

"God no! This game is at an entirely different level than I can play. I'm just trying to make sure we survive."

"I have proof the explosion was sabotage and who did it."

Belson eyed Nick like a warm steak placed on his table. "Where is this evidence?"

"You'll never know. But if anything happens to me or Meriel Hope, it'll be published."

"Ah, Nickolai, spare me the melodrama," Belson said and paced the room with his hands behind his back. "Whatever you think you have will be discredited and relegated to the fringe blogs. Ms. Hope had 'proof' of a galaxy-wide conspiracy at the highest levels, and now she faces legal execution."

Nick's jaw dropped.

"That's right. You haven't heard about your co-conspirator."

"What happened to her?"

"The UNE has filed her conviction. And the punishment is death."

Nick furrowed his brow and glanced at Belson. "Can . . . can you help her?"

"The UNE is pulling the strings on this one and has wrapped her up tight with circumstantial evidence."

"I'm not kidding about my proof. It'll show she wasn't involved."

Belson stopped pacing and narrowed his eyes. "I may have to reassess my alignments." He put a hand on Nick's shoulder. "Your mother misses you."

"She was never my mother."

Belson shrugged. "A political necessity. Hanna does care for you."

"Guilt. And pity."

"Yes, somewhat," he said and resumed pacing. "She's too gentle for the big game. I thought you were up to it. Once. But you chose to be one of the little people."

"Your friends always saw me as little people thanks to my chair. They saw that first and judged me by it."

"Your legs have never slowed you down, son," Belson said and softened his smile. "And they are the least of you, of who you are. Your disability never entered my mind, not for an instant. I saw who you were inside, what you might become and never considered your limitations."

Belson sat on the edge of Nick's bed. "I had such dreams for you. You could have been the avenue between the Masters and the Assembly. The reasonable voice."

"Your tool."

"An open ear. That wouldn't have been bad for you or me. Or Enterprise. It seems a fantasy now." He sighed.

"Now, what's to become of you? I can't have you trolling around, running your big mouth."

"You can't just get rid of me."

"Says who? You've been 'missing' for over a decade."

"Security knows I'm here."

"You still don't understand," Belson said. "We can do whatever we want."

"The Masters run Security."

Belson leaned over and grinned. "I run the Council of Masters now."

"What happened to Sikibo?"

"A stroke, I'm told. But I expect my inquiries will expose irregularities."

"You had him killed?"

"Lord, no! He's a friend."

"It's dangerous to be your friend."

"Where *I* live? Where *we* live? Very. You just didn't know how dangerous until you made friends with the Hope girls."

"You're not going to—"

"No, no, don't be silly. Hanna would never forgive me if they spaced you. Your Tech heroes think they have everything figured out, the options, the safety factors, the margins of error, their seven-sigma nonsense. But they always forget what motivates people and the extremes they're willing to go to."

He took Nick's hand. "Your guilty plea is on the record. Your mother has picked out a colony for you. It's comfortable. Without a single net connection. No one will ever hear from you again."

"Let me guess. Calliope."

Belson grinned again.

Nick raised himself on an elbow and cringed as his head throbbed. "But I have rights. I want a lawyer."

"This is a UNE matter, Son. Enterprise got outvoted." He rose and patted Nick's shoulder. "Good to see you again, Nickolai."

"You're not afraid I'll escape?"

Belson laughed. "Where you gonna go? You're in a secure red-zone infirmary without your wheelchair. I'll give your warmest regards to your mother," he said and tapped a device on Nick's neck. "Good night, Son."

After the door clicked shut, the room spun. Nick reached for the cold spot on his neck and tore off a patch holding a small artery tap.

"Ow!" he said, and with a finger, stopped the blood trickling down his neck.

When the room stopped spinning, he scanned it for communication devices that might help him escape. The only electronic interface was the light switch, and he imagined how he might put it to use. But his legs were immobile, which put the switch out of reach, and the wheelchair with his portable electronics was gone.

He leaned over to check the bed for wheels, and the room spun again, forcing him to lay back on the pillow to wait out the residual drugs.

A hiss brought Nick's eyes to the wall where a red line etched a ragged circle. The circle became a ring of sparks, the wall fell backwards, and through the cloud of dust stepped an angel.

A stunning woman in tight braids and coveralls that blended with the walls stood in front of the hole. In her hand she held a cutting torch, which she swapped for a stunner to match the one in her other hand.

Behind her, a giant of a man in similar garb flipped a small EM jammer onto the counter and unfolded a portable wheelchair. When they were both inside, they tapped their sleeves and their clothing switched to security jumpsuits.

"Target acquired," she said and came to Nick.

Pandora's Razor

The man took a deep breath. "I love the smell of ozone in the morning."

She leaned over Nick to wipe his neck and sprayed a coagulant on the wound. "Well, you're a sight."

"Ah, who are you?" he asked with his eyes focused on her unzipped neckline.

"Cool your jets, sailor," she said and zipped up her suit. "We're friends of Meriel. He's Cookie. I'm Socket."

"She mentioned you. Do you have a link?"

Socket peeked out the window. "We're on the clock, kid, no time." She peered out again. "Clear."

Cookie nodded and lifted Nick into the wheelchair.

"No, no, wait," Nick said. "I need a link."

"No," Socket replied. "On my mark."

"I'm not going."

They both stared at him as if he were delusional.

"Five, four—"

"I can save Meriel."

Cookie raised his fist. "Abort. How?"

Nick took the chip he'd been hiding in his mouth and held it out. "I have to send this to the Tech Masters."

"Really. That's it?"

"It's proof that'll exonerate Meriel. I need a link."

"So, what's on it?" she asked.

"A memory dump from the surveillance spider on the *Princess*."

"And what's so important about that?" she said but raised her hand. "Short version."

"It recorded the guys who planted the explosives. It'll clear her."

"How long do you need?"

"Thirty seconds."

Cookie dug the link from his jumpsuit and gave it to Nick.

"They're coming," Socket said and glanced out the door. "You have ten."

***

The police station's lights flashed red, and Gentri checked her wrist-link.

```
SECCON One. All security personnel
report.
```

"What the hell is it now?" her sergeant asked.

She tapped the link to acknowledge, and orders popped up.

```
Report to surveillance RZ-42 squad
room for briefing.
```

Her sergeant nodded. "After you."

In the squad room, they took seats in the back behind a score of uniformed officers.

"Attention!" someone called, and they all stood when a tall man with a perfect profile and crisp uniform leaned against the podium: Lieutenant Gunderson.

"At ease," Gunderson said, and they sat. "Officer Gentri, your prisoner has escaped."

An officer chuckled and turned to her. "Where are you hiding him, Gentri?"

"He escaped on your watch, not mine," she replied.

With a tap on the podium, the active wall came to life with a vid showing Nick dazed and fumbling about on a gurney before a cloud of dust filled the room. Before the dust cleared, the vid filled with static and faded to black. As the vid looped behind him, Gunderson spoke.

"Our target is Nick Zanek. Whoever helped him are professionals with access to tech gear. They may be preparing for another attack, so we need to find them and stop them."

"Current location?" her sergeant asked.

"He and his accomplices are off the grid, but they can't avoid the biotag readers forever, and we'll nail them when they surface again."

"Force level, sir?"

"Armed and dangerous. Shoot first."

Gentri leaned over to her sergeant, "A kill order? What's with him?"

Her sergeant sneered and lowered his voice. "He's politicking for assignment to Admiral Morrell's Security staff," he said and popped up a vid of Gunderson and Rivan Tellar.

She shook her head. "He's kissing the right asses."

"And he'll ride your glory all the way there if you let him."

"If they kill him during an escape," she said. "That'll effectively confirm his guilt."

"That'll save a lot of money on a trial."

"But if he's not one of the terrorists, the killers are free, and more innocent children could die."

Gunderson slammed his hand on the podium. "You still with us, hero?"

"Yes sir. Sorry sir."

"Our job is to filter the false positives," Gunderson continued. "Squads A and D are in the field, rapid deployment. Squads B and C here with me watching the screens. Profiles are on your links. Dismissed."

Gentri's squad followed their sergeant into the surveillance hall and manned the consoles. In front, Lieutenant Gunderson stood at the main active wall that writhed with a shimmering sea of colored dots tracking every biotag on the station.

With the wave of a finger, she hid the non-threatening green dots and only red and yellow dots remained. The few reds were wants and warrants targeted for immediate arrest. But Nick's red dot would flash if his biotags appeared, and the display showed only steady red.

It was the myriad yellows where they focused their attention. These were the anomalies where a biotag had not matched to the hundred-odd bio markers in the database. The yellows implied a clever criminal was trying to scam the readers, and the squad's job was to screen them. Each console managed nine displays that cycled every ten seconds. Any positives flashed yellow and would be detained by a security spider and visited by a live police officer.

She keyed her console to display the blue dots of security spiders and droids scurrying to check each of the yellow dots. The automated systems were too fast to track as they zipped through troubling profiles and scrolled through facial and morphology recognition, so Gentri focused on the manual checks.

"No one can evade our systems," Gunderson said from over her shoulder. "It's only a matter of time before we get them."

***

With Socket in the lead, Cookie pushed Nick's chair through the passages between structure and machinery. The foldable wheelchair was nothing like Nick's old chair: just bare wheels and a seat with a seatbelt and maglocks. But pushing him in the chair was easier than carrying him.

On a turn from the passage to a flume damp with organics, Nick spoke up. "We're heading for hydroponics?"

Cookie nodded. "They'll expect us to take the fastest path to the docks. This ain't it."

"They'll still be waiting for us."

"We won't be there."

"You gonna tell me the plan?" Nick said.

"No."

At the end of the flume was another large, grated vent that opened to a room so long the arc of the torus appeared in the deck's contour. Perpendicular to the wall stretched hundreds of ten-foot diameter translucent tubes packed like straws in a box. This was hydroponics, running just below white-zone.

Cookie frowned and pulled up the schematic.

"What's wrong?" Socket asked.

He pointed to their location. "The grate is supposed to be behind the tubes."

"Hydroponics is a critical system," Nick said. "Security has cameras and motion detectors there. We won't have cover."

"We can't stay here," Socket said.

Cookie poked a small mirror through the vent. "The camera is above in the corner and unlikely to spot us if we hug the wall."

"Where's the motion detector?"

Cookie shrugged. "Not in view. Let's go."

Socket opened the grate, stepped out, and edged her way to the hydroponics tubes, careful to stay against the wall.

Cookie lifted Nick and his chair into the room, stepped inside, and replaced the grate.

When the frame blinked yellow once, Nick stopped and tapped the link.

"I think we're in trouble."

***

One of Gentri's displays flashed yellow with an anomaly needing a manual check: something had triggered a motion detector in the secure hydroponics deck between security sweeps.

Out of her sight, Lieutenant Gunderson walked towards her. "What is it, Gentri?" he said from behind her.

She jumped at his voice. "Bogie in Hydro F73, sir."

Gunderson raised his link and turned away. "Corporal Rayan, take your squad to F73."

"On our way," squawked Rayan from the link.

Gentri tapped into the security camera and a tiny pixel near the edge of the display rippled.

She zoomed in and the tiny squares divided and resolved into the shape of a wheelchair. After tightening the focus, she gasped at Nick Zanek's face.

***

Nick flipped the link to show Socket the group of blue dots converging on the hatch to the adjacent compartment.

"Shit," she said and waved to her partner. "Sergeant, you need to see this."

Nick drummed his fingers on the chair. "If you won't share your plan, perhaps you might rethink it."

Cookie joined them, frowned at the link, and nodded. "So, where to?"

Nick tapped the link a few more times and led them to the service hatch of a hydroponics tank. "Inside."

Socket opened the hatch, and a blast of fetid air forced her back. "Phew."

"We'll need those," Nick said and pointed to bags hanging outside the hatch.

Cookie rifled through a bag and removed waders, goggles, and a small tube with a mouthpiece and nose clip. "What's this?"

"An oxygen scrubber," Nick said. "It's a high-CO_2 environment inside, and we'll need them to breathe."

After dressing, Cookie picked Nick up in a firefighter's carry and stepped into a slurry of recycled nutrients and a jungle of genetically modified soybean plants. Socket stowed the folded wheelchair under the surface and closed the door just as Corporal Rayan opened the hatch to Hydro F73.as Gentri watched??

***

After seeing Nick's face, Gentri swapped out the screen to keep it from Gunderson's view.

"Rayan is converging," Gunderson said from behind her. "Do we have confirmation, Gentri?"

She jumped again at her lieutenant's voice. "No sir. Negative bogie at Hydro F73. Spurious signal."

He studied her and waved a finger over the screen where Nick had appeared, but Nick, the wheelchair, and the little squares had disappeared.

She frowned. "And do you mind not breathing down my neck? Sir."

He raised his link. "Sweep the area, Rayan," Gunderson said and examined her as he lowered the link. "It's important this guy never sees the light of day, Gentri. Understood?"

"Yes sir," she said.

He walked away, and she cued up her message detailing Nick's attempts to alert security before the explosion. After removing Gunderson from the routing, she hesitated.

Was he innocent or one of the bad guys? He saved my life, so I owe him something. But if they find out what I'm doing, it will end my career with a one-way ticket to vacuum.

For a moment, she let her hand linger on the monitor where Nick had last appeared. "Good luck," she said and sent the message to Admiral Morrell.

***

"What's the plan?" Nick asked as he squinted through the translucent shell of the tank.

Cookie pushed through another tangle of intertwined stalks. "We make our way to the maintenance dock on W45 and commandeer a barge."

"What about the USF and Troopers along the way?"

"Elizabeth told us you'd help us improvise."

"Uh-huh," Nick said and spit out a leaf. "Then what?"

"They'll pick us up after we clear the station."

"And how is a ship gonna do that? Traffic control vectors all shipping to the docks."

"They have a maintenance ID," Socket said.

"Support barges are built for only a pilot and copilot," Nick said. "Will we have enough air?"

They did not respond.

"Right. Then we'll be OK if they pick us up right away." A blue dot appeared on the link, and he tapped Cookie on the shoulder. "Stop. Move into the middle."

The team squirmed into the snarl of vines as the shadows of police moved past the translucent shell.

Once the shadows passed, Cookie turned to Nick, "Where to now, genius?"

"There's a hatch at the other end leading to an elevator and the agricultural deck."

When the exit appeared, Cookie and Socket were sweating. But the level of the soupy liquid rose to their calves, and a loud whining filled the tube.

Socket stopped. "What's that?"

Nick's eyes opened wide. "Crap. They're harvesting."

"What do we do?" Cookie asked.

"Run!"

From a rail hanging below the top of the tank, eight rows of whirring blades descended and sheared the plants an inch above each of the trays. One headed their way.

They scrambled for the hatch, but the door was stuck. Nick tapped on the link again as the surging liquid carried the harvested soybeans and leaves past their legs, through the grates, and into the food processors.

Cookie ripped a tray from its rack, spilled the plants into the soup, and headed for the harvesters.

"Stop, Cookie," Nick said. "You can't—"

"It's gonna slice us up, kid."

"You can't break anything, or the techs will come to investigate."

Socket put a hand on his shoulder. "Tell me you know how to get us out of here."

The blades screamed closer.

"I know how to get us out of here."

"You're lying," Cookie said.

"Hold your breath and dive!" he said as the shears reached them.

USF Detention

Through the corridors of the detention facility, the *boom* echoed of Meriel's impact on the padded ceramic door.

"Let me out! They've got her. That bastard Khanag should burn in hell for this! Let me out!" She ran into the door again but lost her balance and fell.

Outside, Jennifer stood with a USF guard at a monitor.

The guard shook his head. "I've never seen anything like this."

Jennifer's eyes glistened. "I have."

"Get Kostanza!" Meriel shouted. "I need to talk to Kostanza."

Jennifer nodded to the guard who clicked the intercom.

"He's gone, Meriel. Left on a private yacht a half-hour ago."

"No," Meriel mumbled as her eyes darted to each corner of her cell. "No. No."

```
"SECCON One. All security personnel
report."
```

"Time to leave," the guard said and took Jennifer's arm. "Station security is locking us down."

While he led Jennifer to the exit, a tiny object fell from the air vent into Meriel's cell.

***

A click brought Meriel's eye to the floor by her side. To hide it from the surveillance camera, she slid in front of it and inspected it with her hands.

An inch long, it was flexible and thin and vibrated at her touch. Guessing it was an audio device, she turned her head from the camera, and fixed the device against the temporal bone behind her ear.

A generic electronic voice spoke. "Don't talk. This unit can't broadcast. Please wait until it verifies your identity." One second and a click later, Jerri's voice came on. "Hey, girl. This is a recording. When we're nearby, we'll interrupt with live instructions. Now, here's the plan . . ."

Elizabeth's voice cut off the recording. "Hey, M. Do as you're told and don't out-think this. We can't hack into the corner camera, so we're going to fool it with a false image. The holo will be for those looking from the door. When the lights blink out, stand under the camera. Until then, pace in the middle of your cell."

Meriel paced the cell as instructed but peeked up as a tiny hole appeared in the ceiling near the camera and from it poked a tube. The lights winked off, and she scurried into the corner below the camera.

The lights came on again, and the tube unfolded a display in front of the camera. In the middle of the cell appeared the hologram of her pacing the cell.

The odor of caramel tweaked Meriel's nose, and she glanced down at a yellow circle on the floor the diameter of her shoulders.

"The yellow circle is decuring plastisteel," Elizabeth said. "Put your arms to your chest and don't move."

Beneath Meriel, the floor trembled and descended like a cargo elevator into the superstructure below her cell. Waiting for her in the tiny space were a sausage-shaped droid and three small construction bots.

She touched down on the new deck, and the bots rushed to repair the damage they had created. But the tubular droid moved through a hole in the plastisteel bulkhead, turned to her, and stopped. She followed, and he led her through a ragged tunnel of plastisteel, bucky-sheet partitions, and metamaterials. It was carved out to just her size and led to a service hatch where John and her sister waited.

"Sandy?" Meriel asked as she hugged them.

John shook his head as he handed her a green Tech service jumpsuit to match his. At his side, Elizabeth disconnected a tap she had placed on the monitor to Meriel's cell.

"I told Jeremy not to let you do something stupid like this," Meriel said as she dressed.

"We're adults and can decide for ourselves," her sister said. "But hey, we can put you back if you like. I mean, if you're too much of a wimp and prefer to die. Straight back, no problem."

Meriel smiled and pushed her forward.

"No?" Elizabeth pointed to the duct in front of them. "Then time to go, kids."

The droid cut through the partition and led the bots through it, and Meriel took a step to follow.

Elizabeth grabbed her arm. "Other way."

"Where are they going?"

"To be recycled. Eddie will meet us back at the *Amelia*."

"Eddie?"

"The hot dog."

"Is this your plan?"

Elizabeth pointed a thumb at the retreating droid. "His."

The passageways led Meriel, John, and Elizabeth through an Escher of gravities that serviced the shops to a maintenance yard. Beneath them, the damp floor shook.

"Where are we?" John asked over the rumble.

"Dunno," Elizabeth said.

Behind a pressure door in the shadows lay an ellipsoidal inspection pod with the green and silver markings of the Techs on the bottom half, and clear plastaglass on top. It was smaller than a transport pod with a bigger propulsion system but only a single seat.

"We need to hurry," Meriel said. "Are you sure this will work?"

"This is the fastest way, and no one gets hurt." Elizabeth said on her back from beneath the dashboard as she ripped out the transponder. She surfaced again and raised an eyebrow. "No one gets hurt, right?"

Elizabeth glared as John slid into the pilot's chair and engaged the restraint system. From a hook on the wall, she took three vacuum-rated warm-suits, threw them in the back of the pod, and entered.

"What are those for?" Meriel asked as she climbed in and decoupled the pod from the dock.

"Just in case," Elizabeth replied as John energized the pod.

Meriel took her arm. "In case of what?"

A door opened to the thunder and the splash of water that drowned out Elizabeth's response.

The pod was not designed for passengers, so Elizabeth wedged herself in and sat on the inspection equipment behind the single seat. Meriel had no place left to sit and bent over next to John at the helm. She had nothing to hold on to, and when their pod jerked forward, she fell to her knees and stayed there.

Their pod jostled to the back of a line of larger excursion pods, each equipped with clear cockpits, roll cages, and harnesses.

The thunder got louder as one by one the excursion pods disappeared out of sight into the dark.

"Hold on," John said.

Meriel gripped the seat, but that was not enough to keep her knees on the deck. And when they were thrown into the cascade of water, the falls roared and rattled them within the cockpit like marbles in a cup.

***

In the same arc of the torus as Meriel, Stark parried flirts from the ambassador's wife at the Ostara party. Beatrice finished another scolding of the citizens as the canopies constraining the aeration falls and river rotated away. Behind him crowded the partiers in La Mère Catherine.

"Here they go," Beatrice said with a misty gaze and a soft voice. "Yosemite Valley is like this in spring."

"You've been to Earth?" Kostanza asked, as if admiring a treasure he could never possess.

"Yes, many times," she said, her chin held high. "We have a summer home in the Tahoe Arcology and it's a short shuttle ride from our home in Moon-1 . . ."

Stark imagined spring on Earth with the snowmelt swelling the rivers and waterfalls. But he frowned as a line of a dozen pods shot through the falls, dropped to the surface of the river, and followed its course.

Beatrice put her hand to her mouth. "More sacrilege."

A green and silver pod careening behind the others caught Stark's eye. Moments later, two pods with security markings raced past the window.

He tapped his ear. "Comm, any alerts?"

"Two, sir," the *Intrepid's* comm officer said. "A status change on Miss Smith."

"Proceed."

"Station security reports she's been kidnapped."

Stark stood. "And the other?"

"Station Master Sikibo has died."

"Call General Quarters," he ordered. "Cancel shore leave. Coming aboard." He turned to Bakshi. "Excuse me, Mister Ambassador."

Beatrice stood and waved as he rushed out the door, while Bakshi glared at her and then at Stark.

***

Just above the river, the maintenance pod halted its drop. The sudden stop slammed Elizabeth and Meriel back on the pod deck, and then to the back of the cockpit as it shot out from the waterfall.

The water slid off the cockpit, and the falls appeared behind them, the source so close to the transparent torus shell that the water appeared to pour from the stars. For a moment, Meriel forgot her troubles until two red security pods appeared.

"Trouble, John."

He nodded. "We'll stay with the crowd until we can edge up to the top and follow the torus."

Before the river ended, with a third of their journey left, the chain of pods reversed course.

"We're not going back," John said and jerked the joystick.

The pod plunged into the river but recovered and separated from the others. Moments later, a loudspeaker blared behind them.

"Tech pod, your transponder is malfunctioning. What's your ID number?"

John let the pursuing pod pull up to their right, then jammed the stick hard right, ramming its engine. The security pod spun, pinning the officer to the side of the cockpit like a centrifuge.

"Time to go," he said, but three more security pods surrounded them to the sides and above. To limit their advantage, John dove into the air gap between the river and a section of the canopy that had yet to open.

Under the canopy, John skipped off the swells of the rapids, knocking three of their pursuers into the canyon walls. While he concentrated on evading security, the Hope sisters clattered within the cockpit unable to find handholds.

On one bounce, Meriel accidentally grabbed the joystick and dropped their pod onto the last pursuer who had slipped beneath them, knocking it into the whitewater. The red pod bobbed and bumped against the bottom of Meriel's pod until the cockpit of the security pod popped off and the police officer jumped into the river.

"Up to the shell," John said as he regained control and raced their pod past the canopy and the river. "The gravity is lower." He jerked the stick back and raced up, leaving their pursuers in the river.

Without visible exhaust and camouflaged against the trees and brush, they climbed upward, leaving security behind.

"We've got another tail," John said as the pod rushed toward one of eight major spokes of the station.

"How the hell could they know?" Meriel said but glimpsed a flash of the pod's silver on the terminal lake. "Damn."

"They'll catch up soon," he said.

Meriel shook her head. "The slugs will arrive first."

"Tech pod," they heard through the shell. "Stop or we'll open fire."

Elizabeth smiled and leaned over John and tapped the console. "I have an idea. Move over, John."

John rose, and Elizabeth took the helm. She pulled up a holo of the tram routes and steered toward the maintenance airlock at the circumference of the torus. A lock recognized their pod, and she pulled into it. But the other pods did not enter the adjoining locks.

"We're trapped, Liz," John said. "How does this help?"

"Wait," Liz said.

The cockpit groaned as the pressure dropped inside, and they yawned to clear their ears.

"What are the others waiting for?" he asked. "Whoa! Is this pod vacuum rated?"

"Sure," Liz said, and opened the outer door of the airlock to space but remained in the lock.

A tram approached and Meriel shook her sister's arm. "Liz?"

"Wait, wait," Elizabeth said.

The tram raced past, and she maneuvered outside the lock. Out into vacuum, without resistance, the compressed air pushed the pod faster and kept accelerating as they chased the tram.

The pod's speaker alarmed. "This is your final warning. Stop or we'll shoot."

Meriel glanced back at the flock of security drones chasing them. "That didn't take long."

"Almost there," her sister said as they neared the rear car. She raised her wrist. "Eddie, we need you near . . ." A sign rushed past. "Near tram stop W2-38—"

Banging drowned out her voice and they turned as slugs chipped the cockpit sending cracks through the shell like lightning between dust clouds.

Meriel gripped her sister's shoulder. "Liz?"

"Almost . . ."

Elizabeth reached behind her and held out the warm-suits she had taken from the pod bay. "Our stop."

The tram slowed as it neared the station, but the pod did not, and slammed into the coupling at the back of the tram. As they fumbled with the warm suits, air whistled through the growing cracks in the cockpit.

***

At tram station W2-38, Eddie fussed with a utility panel while a sensor stalk monitored the squads of police and security running past.

One police officer raised his wrist. "This is Schmidt at—"

His sergeant covered his mic with her hand. "Don't call it in, for God's sake. The USF is monitoring. Stay on your inter-squad link."

"Yes, ma'am."

"The UNE blew it. She's ours now and we won't let her go."

"How about we arrange an accident?"

She grinned. "As soon as we catch her."

When the officers followed their squad, Eddie raised his EM sensor waiting for an update from Elizabeth.

Outside the window, a Tech pod smacked against the approaching tram, the same pod he and Elizabeth had targeted for Meriel's escape. The cockpit shattered, the pod drifted away, and three lifeless warm-suits floated free with security drones in pursuit.

Inside the station, Eddie trembled and curled up in a ball with his sharpest probes poking out, giving him the appearance of a security spider.

***

Inside the tram's coupling bellows, Elizabeth pushed Meriel and John into the tram and released the pod. Outside, the security pods followed their Tech pod and the three warm suits that floated away from the torus.

When the doors to the station opened, they ducked within the crowd of debarking passengers and slipped into the nearest service hatch.

***

Minutes later, Eddie stopped shaking, and a sensor array rose from within the urchin he had become. On the twenty-first scan cycle, he stopped as Elizabeth waved through an HVAC hatch in the ceiling.

One by one, he returned each of his probes to the designated slot in his body and resumed his sausage shape. After the next wave of officers passed, he backed into a maintenance corridor where the team waited.

Inside, Eddie handed them security uniforms and stunners.

"I told you," Elizabeth said and patted Eddie on his top. "Tech is transparent. No one notices the droids, or maintenance, or any of the tech that keeps them alive."

Eddie waved a probe, and they followed him through the service infrastructure.

***

Outside customs and the biotag readers, the Enterprise docks bustled with grav sleds and cargo handlers. At the berths, the *Amelia's* silhouette appeared with a blank marquee.

Elizabeth patted Eddie's dome. "Tell Teddy we're here."

A light blinked on Eddie's antenna, and the airlock opened. After the biotag reader blinked with the glitch, John, Elizabeth, and Meriel lowered their heads, hustled across the docks, and entered. Inside the lock, Meriel hit the close-lock pad.

John sighed. "Safe."

"Not until we've jumped," Meriel said and tapped the inter-ship link from the doorframe. "Get us out of here, Teddy."

She followed John and Liz to the lounge where John flopped on the couch.

"Three whiskies," Elizabeth said, and Eddie busied himself at the replicator.

Meriel put her fingers to the back of her ear. "Why aren't the umbilicals decoupling," she said, drew her stunner, and headed for the bridge.

Teddy appeared at the bulkhead door. But behind her stood a tall woman with a spacer's ponytail and the stars of a Trooper admiral on her collar.

Meriel raised her stunner, and Admiral Morrell narrowed her eyes with a tolerant frown she might give a three-year-old child.

Meriel spun to police aiming stunners at John and Elizabeth.

"You want to put that down?" Morrell said. "Then we can talk."

"I'm the one you want," Meriel said. "I'll surrender, but only if you let them go."

John took a step toward her, but an officer gripped his shoulder. "Meriel, this isn't—"

"You two gotta get Sandy, John," she said and turned back to Morrell. "This is how it's gonna go. I lead you out to the docks. After they undock, I surrender. Nobody gets hurt, right?"

"Pull that trigger and your life is over," Morrell said.

"Meriel, don't!" Jennifer said as she pushed her way past the police and into the lounge.

"Officers, stand down," Morrell said. "You too, Ms. Hope."

"Please," Jennifer said. "Listen to what she has to say."

Meriel lowered her stunner, and an officer held her wrist.

"Ms. Hope, I am Admiral Morrell, the Security Tech Master. The Council of Masters under Chairman Belson has received fresh evidence relevant to your murder and terrorism charges. Because Enterprise is your legal guardian, they have agreed to review your appeal. Do you wish to surrender to Enterprise custody?"

Meriel pursed her lips, but Jennifer nodded emphatically.

"The alternative is we turn you back over to the USF." Morrell said. "Do you wish to surrender to Enterprise custody?"

"Ah, yes?" Meriel said, and Jennifer sighed as the officer took Meriel's stunner.

"Since your re-arrest by Enterprise did not violate the terms of the Aldebaran Accord, you are ordered . . . what's the name of this ship?"

"*Amelia*, ma'am," Teddy said.

"You are ordered to house arrest on the *Amelia*, Light Speed Yacht... whatever. Do you swear to appear for hearings and testimony if called by the Council?"

"Yes," Meriel said.

"Here's your proximity tracker."

An officer held up the anklet.

"They're expensive, so it'll stay here with us for safe keeping." Morrell nodded to the police, who holstered their weapons and filed out the airlock.

"That's it?" Meriel asked.

"Just leave before the USF finds you," Morrell said and followed the police out to the dock.

"Thank you, Jen," Meriel said and hugged Jennifer.

"Thank me after you've gone. The UNE doesn't know yet. Go. Now."

"Do you know where Kostanza went?" Meriel asked.

Jennifer frowned. "No. Why?"

"Come with us."

"You need representation here to pursue the appeal."

"What did this cost you?"

"My integrity is intact," Jennifer said with a smile and hugged her again. "Now, get out of here and go get Sandy. Hurry."

The airlock door closed, and Meriel hurried to the *Amelia's* dockside window.

"Teddy, where is everyone?" Meriel asked as the police cordon circled Jennifer.

"*Tiger* is waiting to pick up Nick. The Vingels are there with Jerri. Elizabeth, come forward and sit comm for me."

"Socket and Cookie?"

"They're Nick's extraction team," Teddy said and left for the bridge with Elizabeth.

"So where are they" Meriel asked over the inter-ship link.

"Don't know. I'm busy undocking. Leave me alone."

"The *Tiger* should've picked them up by now." Elizabeth said from the bridge. "Jerri says UNE Marines are deploying near the infirmary. She thinks the escape went bad."

Meriel waved to Jennifer as the umbilicals disconnected, and the *Amelia* pulled away from Enterprise.

Jennifer returned the wave from the dock window and tapped on it using the Bon Voyage messaging system. As her departure message emerged on the *Amelia's* window, an officer turned and stood behind her.

```
Fiat justitia ruat caelom.
```

"What does it mean?" Meriel asked.

John touched the window frame and the Galactish translation displayed below the Latin.

```
Let justice be done though the heav-
  ens fall.
```

Meriel tapped the inter-ship link. "Liz, I think Jennifer is in trouble. Can you hail the Troopers to help her?"

"I'll try, M."

Another phrase appeared.

```
Etsi autem ceciderit super te.
```

The dock seemed safe with Jennifer inside the police cordon, but something flashed in the officer's hand behind her. The window translated.

```
And though they fall on thee.
```

"No!" She slammed her fists on the window. "Help her! Teddy, call the Troopers. Where are the Troopers?"

"They're trying," Elizabeth said.

Jennifer glanced at her link, nodded, and held Meriel's book up with a smile. But her expression faded as she dropped the book and collapsed. The assailant slipped the weapon back into his uniform and slunk back into formation.

"No. No. No!" Meriel banged on the window as the Troopers took the assassin into custody and others treated the fallen Jennifer.

As the *Amelia* sped away from the station, Meriel slumped to the deck.

John kneeled and held her shoulders. "M, honey."

Her head raced at light speed over the things she should have done but didn't do. About whom she trusted but should not have, and the steps she took without double-checking how safe it was.

If I had stayed away from John, Sandy would never have been in danger. And if I had accepted Kostanza's offer, Sandy might be with John by now and Jennifer would be unharmed.

"People who help me keep getting hurt," she said with her head on her fists. "And Sandy . . ."

***

The report of Sandy's kidnapping flashed on Captain Stark's screen.

"Damn. We brought her here, and now she's in danger."

"We were under orders, Captain," the XO said.

"But we did it. Get us out of here."

On the tactical holo, an unfamiliar ID followed a trajectory to a jump point at 2-g.

"What ship is that?"

"Merchant, sir. ID's corrupted."

"Merchants don't run a 2-g. Follow that ship. Comm, send a message probe to fleet. Begin . . ."

"Enterprise won't permit undock, sir," the pilot said.

"Open a line, Comm."

"This is the Enterprise Pilot Master. How can we assist, Captain?"

"Clear my path," Stark ordered as the unidentified ship accelerated to the jump point.

"I'm sorry, Captain. Your nav should have cleared *Intrepid's* departure with traffic control—"

"This is a military mission!"

"Sorry, sir. Repairs are—"

Stark pounded the arm of his chair and stood. "Clear my path, or *I* will clear it!" He turned to his weapons officer. "Deploy the disruptor cannon."

Ambassador Bakshi's voice came over the comm. "Desist, Captain. Any military action taken against the station rather than in defense of it will violate the Aldebaran Accord."

"Where are you, sir?"

"At the airlock."

Stark signaled the comm officer, and a holo appeared of Bakshi with a squad of USF.

"Leave them and come aboard," Stark said.

"They come with me, Captain. Our mission is to retrieve the terrorist escaping on that ship."

"What business is that of the navy? She was in USF custody."

"We are deputized officers of the court," Bakshi said. "And she escaped USF detention awaiting sentencing. The UNE has an interest that justice is served."

Stark did not reply.

"And you remain under my command, Captain."

"Yes, sir."

He signaled to cut the communication, and the holo vanished. "Let them board but keep them bottled up. Pilot, find a hole in this chum. XO to my ready room."

The doors slid shut behind them, and Stark tapped a button to shield their conversation.

The XO handed him a q-chip. "Ms. Hope's lawyer copied us on her appeal to the Enterprise Council of Masters."

He inspected the chip between his fingers and gave it back to her. "Have the JAG Officer review it and report to me."

"Aye, sir. Enterprise security said Ms. Hope is in their custody."

"Apparently not according to Bakshi. Is Miss Smith on that ship?"

"Unknown, sir."

Stark leaned back and frowned. "Bakshi's put a thumb on the scale of justice." He tapped his console. "Pilot, follow that ship. Major Glinnik, report to me with a squad and keep Bakshi's USF team off my bridge."

Enterprise Station—Outbound

Jerri read the barge's ID numbers from the *Tiger's* comm console. "Yes, that's them. 9A8."

"They're late," Captain Vingel said. "Set an intercept vector to—"

An officious voice blared from comm. "Garbage scow H445. Please keep your distance. We have a security breach and traffic is restricted.

"We have a barge to pick up, sir," Jerri said. "It's off course and heading for a shipping lane."

"This is the USF. Repeat, stay outside the security zone or you will be fired upon."

"Hey, garbage waits for no man. This has toxics. We don't want a nasty spill on our hands, now do we?"

A laser flashed past their bow, and their consoles blinked.

"Repeat, keep your distance or we won't miss next time."

Captain Vingel frowned but nodded.

"We will comply," Jerri said. "Out."

Molly stared at the image of the barge. "Well, let's hope they figured out how to make their air last."

"Support Barge 9A8," Jerri called. "This is Garbage Scow H445. We're running late. Cookie? Socket?"

But there was no one conscious to reply.

***

"Finish up, kids," Teddy said over Amelia's PA. "We'll jump early. And check Liz's update for LeHavre before we sync."

Elizabeth's message appeared on the active wall in the lounge.

"What's it say?" John asked while working on a link.

"It's a heads-up for LeHavre about the politics on Enterprise," Meriel said. "Teddy says the UNE is behind the instabilities. What are you working on?"

"It's for Becky," he said. "How's this: 'Papa and M will be home soon—'"

"No, no. You can't say that."

"We're encrypted, M. Secure."

"I'm a UNE fugitive, John. Nothing is that secure."

"How about 'Papa will be home soon with your sister—'"

"Can't say that either. They might think you're the one who kidnapped her."

"I don't want Becky to worry."

She shook her head.

"You're paranoid," he said, but she rolled her eyes at him. "Right, time to be paranoid."

Meriel typed a quick text.

```
Miss you. Be home soon. Love you
forever.
Papa.
PS: Merry L sends kisses and hugs.
```

John hit the send button. "Ready to sync, Liz."

"Done," Elizabeth said. "M, incoming encrypted text for you."

Out of John's sight, Meriel decrypted a private message from prosecutor Kostanza.

We have her. Are you ready to listen now?

Here's what you must do . . .

Chapter 19
Free Space

LSY Amelia

Meriel viewed the constellations from the window of the *Amelia* after the short twenty-AU jump to the Kuiper Belt of the Procyon system—far enough to be impossible to find.

These same stars had enthralled her since childhood, only in different positions viewed from Procyon. Here, Cetus had a bright extra star with Sol added, and Canis Minor missed the Little Dog Star. She had told Sandy it was a spacer habit to check the stars to orient yourself, like checking for the Southern Cross on Earth or DX Cancri on Haven.

Sandy.

John stood next to her and put his arm around her. "We'll get her back, sweetheart. We have to."

"Any word from Nick or the *Tiger*?" Meriel asked when Teddy joined them. "We can't lose him."

"I know," Teddy said. "He's family. We'll meet the *Tiger* here. We have thirty minutes before our EM reaches the beacon and UNE eyes. Then we head for Lander."

Meriel chugged a glass of juice. "Why wait for the *Tiger*? And why Lander?"

"That's my home base. I have legal and financial resources there."

Eddie took Meriel's empty glass and handed her a refill from the replicator.

"Lander is in the wrong direction," Meriel said. "We need to find Sandy."

"The UNE won't take kindly to my disappearing with a fugitive. They'll figure out you're not on Enterprise and we're friends and come looking for us, M."

"And they'll start with your home base," Meriel said. "Are you listening, Liz?"

"Yes," Elizabeth said from the bridge. "Teddy, do you really think Lander is going to face down the UNE Navy's missiles for you?"

Teddy frowned. "But we need to regroup."

"It's too late for that. We need to rescue her now before she disappears into the Archtrope's labyrinth."

John paced. "I want to get her too, M. But we don't even know where she is."

"Yes, we do. Etna."

Elizabeth entered and scowled. "God, I hate that place."

"You're guessing," Teddy said.

"Why not take her to Calliope? Or Chosho?" John asked.

"Or Seiyei," Elizabeth added. "They might have another Hydra there."

"Calliope is too far," Teddy said.

"Seiyei is in the same star system."

"But the Troopers are limiting travel to Seiyei."

Elizabeth nodded. "The Troopers don't control Etna."

"Neither does the UNE," Meriel said. "Etna's corrupt. The Archtrope does whatever he wants there and has for decades. Teddy, about the help you have on Lander. You don't need to be there physically, do you?"

Teddy shook her head.

"What can we do there we can't do on Etna?"

Teddy blushed. "We can hide you until we're sure where Sandy is."

"I won't hide from this," Meriel said.

Teddy went to the replicator and ordered snacks. "They used a small vessel to escape on the outbound. They'll need a larger one for the jump to Calliope."

"We'll never get her if she's transferred to a bigger vessel," John said.

"Where would they find a bigger ship?"

The sisters answered at the same time. "Etna."

"And it could be Khanag's," Meriel added.

"I think Meriel's right," Elizabeth said. "*Amelia* is fast. We can catch up to them at Etna and retrieve Sandy before she's transferred. If she's not there, we've only lost a few hours."

John leaned against the bulkhead and folded his arms. "I'm in."

"So, we head for Etna," Meriel said.

Teddy raised her voice. "Excuse me. This is my ship."

"But we—"

"*Ma'am* is how to address your captain," Teddy said. "Liz, your bridge rated Exec-2?"

Elizabeth smiled and nodded.

"Take the XO chair."

"Aye, ma'am."

"John, you want to sit nav?"

He nodded. "What's our course?"

"Work up jumps for Lander, Etna, and Wolf. I'll join you in a moment and advise you."

Eddie rose to follow John to the bridge, but Teddy stopped it. "John will sit nav for jump, Eddie."

The droid found a corner and slumped as if someone had taken his favorite toy.

"He seems dejected," Meriel said.

"Ignore the drama. He watches a lot of soap operas." She patted the cushion beside her, and Meriel sat. "You and I are on opposite ends of the caution scale, girl. So, you think Khanag is behind this. What makes you so sure?"

"I got a message on Haven. After the invasion, after the shooting was over, he threatened me. It's personal. I'm sure he's involved. He aims to hurt me, hurt us."

"Kind of self-centered, no? He's got a fleet and you're, well, you're just . . . you."

"He promised to kill John and the girls in front of me."

"Yeah, that's personal. But it doesn't have to be Khanag who wants Sandy on Etna. There're other parties to the Treaty of Haven. Every one of them wants to discredit it and harm you."

"He's the muscle for them all."

Teddy nodded. "Looks like they've added the UNE Navy now too. If they're using her to get to you, they won't kill her."

"Maybe not, but . . ." Meriel stared at her hands. "She's only twelve, Teddy. They'll . . . hurt her. Because I love her."

"You searching for an excuse to not care about anybody? To push them away? Actually, it's a good one. Join me, dear."

On the bridge, Teddy took the captain's chair. "Liz, drop a message beacon for the *Tiger,* and route a single jump to Etna, John," Teddy said.

Elizabeth groaned. "We'll be vegetables."

"The jump disorientation and fatigue aren't as severe on the *Amelia*. Juice up though. ETA to jump?"

"Five minutes," John said. "We might beat the kidnappers inbound."

Elizabeth frowned. "So, what're we gonna do when we arrive?"

They turned to Meriel, but she avoided their eyes and strapped herself in for jump.

Tai-Pan

On the *Tai-Pan's* bridge, General Khanag tapped his command console.

"Is the cargo secured, Captain?"

"Yes, sir."

Khanag scanned the Cephus League manifest and glanced up. The usual parade of penitents from the captured ship was missing.

"And the crew?"

"Sir, the ship was lightly crewed and they ... did not survive interrogation."

"I see. Sync with their comm for messages."

"Aye sir. Incoming, General. Urgent. Your eyes only."

Khanag tapped the arm of his chair and a hologram popped up.

```
Kidney of UOD match to DNA of Marge
Tsoget. Organ sourced from the Society
of Pious Sisters (SPS) with clinic on
Etna. SPS group has Archtrope legal
counsel on the board of direc-
tors . . .
```

"Comm, who is this from?"

"Unknown, sir. But the packet header notes a reply from an anonymous GRL you used to contact Ms. Hope."

Khanag flipped through the file of documents accusing the Archtrope of corruption in the organ trade.

He shook his head. *Rumors that GNN debunked years ago,* he thought and moved a finger to the delete icon.

But the morgue stills flashed, and he winced.

His son's face appeared, peaceful as if he were sleeping.

Touching the face, the vestige of something kinder washed over him, something gentler than the brutal mining camps and drug dens of his youth. He rubbed his forearm where the snake and blade tattoo covered the scars from injected euphorics used to recall the memories of kindness buried deep since his childhood. And between the highs, an echo returned each time he touched the silver elephant charm that hung from his neck.

The drugs had nearly ended his life many times before the Archtrope found him and gave him a purpose. In the years since, he had averted his eyes from the inconsistencies in his missions and closed his ears to the cries of his victims. It was in the name of the greater good: building a world where lost souls such as his had value. If he did not probe too deep, his purpose remained intact. And the more devoted he became to this larger purpose, this better world, the more the echoes weakened.

And then his son was born, and the echo came in a child's voice.

A woman's hand touched his shoulder. "He was beautiful," his XO said from behind him.

"Yes. And taken from us too early, Isolde."

"Who sent this?"

"Scurrilous rumors sent by the Hope woman to test our faith in the Archtrope."

Stills of the other dead corsairs followed, and then pictures of the dead and injured passengers and crew from the *Tiger*. When Meriel Hope's bruised and bloodied face appeared, he scowled.

"Where is she now?"

Isolde checked her link and raised an eyebrow. "Escaped from custody on Enterprise."

He sneered and jabbed his finger on the delete icon, and Meriel's dossier disappeared.

"Set course for Etna."

Calliope Orbit, Tau Ceti System

The Archtrope took the hookah mouthpiece from his lips, blew a cloud of honey-yellow smoke, and laid his head back on the thigh of a naked concubine. Outside the window of his yacht, the domes over the Calliope colony gleamed in the light of Tau Ceti.

Seide entered. "Insomnia again, sir?"

"Yes. My mind is buzzing with opportunities and alternatives. How do you do it, Edward? Sleep soundly?"

"It brings some peace to think of seeing my family again."

"Soon." The Archtrope rose, drank from an open whiskey bottle, and waved. "Bring her."

A concubine entered dragging a drugged Charlene Samuelson behind on a torment chain. "The novice is ready, your Eminence."

"Prepare her."

Samuelson staggered to Seide and threw herself at his feet. "Please, sir. I beg you—" she began, but the concubine triggered the torment chain, and Samuelson writhed in pain.

Seide frowned and closed his eyes but offered no help as other concubines joined to drag Samuelson away. "Your holiness, there's really no reason to—"

"Must I constantly remind you of your children, Ed? And why do you bother me during my . . . meditations?"

Seide's hand shook, and his voice tightened. "We found the destination address for the dossier."

The Archtrope took a Soberal pill from the table and washed it down with a soda. "And?"

"It was sent as a reply to a link requisitioned by General Khanag."

The Archtrope curled his lips and narrowed his eyes. "Bitch!"

"And the mission to incinerate the corsair bodies failed."

He jumped to his feet and kicked the hookah which crashed against the wall and spilled water and coals over the floor. "How? I had good people on that job."

Seide focused on his shoes. "Apparently there was unexpected resistance."

The Archtrope shook his head. "Where is Khanag now?"

"Unknown, sir."

"Don't just sit there," the Archtrope said to the lounging concubine. "Clean it up." He turned to Seide "Send a message to all our agents. See to it Khanag never meets Hope."

"And if he does?"

"That he doesn't leave alive."

Chapter 20
Etna Station, Etna 320 System

Etna Station—Inbound

Meriel stood at the window in one of *Amelia's* staterooms and stared out at the depressing black of the Etna system, as John snored in their bed. This was the Ciberitus Sink, the darkest dust cloud next to the Coalsack Nebula. Deep within, the solar system was still congealing into planets from asteroids rich in resources.

Inside the Etna system, planetesimals swept lanes of dust and resource rich asteroids into what would become the orbit of planets in a billion years.

Only the dim, hazy light of Etna 320 broke the gloom, amplifying the lifelessness. Hedonism, religion, and suicide in entertaining forms were the dominant pastimes.

Lives are short here, including ours now.

Ever since Khanag had murdered her parents, Meriel had worked ceaselessly to fill the hole in her life by bringing those she cared for together, to be with her. Her need for them was selfish, and her longing to fill that hole put them all in danger.

Her search for a home only made things worse. Those she loved most were scattered across the galaxy at more risk than ever, and those nearby might die here with her.

Because I love them.

"Love isn't without risk," pastor Lee had said. *But I didn't mean to put* them *at risk.*

"New messages," she said to trigger her comm feed.

"White, Erik. UNE arrest warrant, urgent. News alert, LeHavre Medical School," the console recited.

"UNE warrant, delete. White, go."

Erik's face appeared in a vid with the refugee camp in the background. The camp and people were all coated in the familiar brownish-gray dust of Haven, and a familiar dry tickle rose in Meriel's throat.

"Hey, M. Just an update so you don't worry. Anita and I are taking up the slack on distributing rations. The camp is getting crowded, and resources are getting scarce, so we're making the ration kits smaller." He panned his link to an APC. "Captain Abrams is here full time now with a company to patrol the camp and keep things from getting out of hand.

"The Grange is working up training programs and model farms with refugee teams." The vid swapped to an animated map of the area. "They've cleared out a few acres nearby and are building a soil processing facility next to it."

The vid switched back to Erik before panning over to Anita in front of a score of refugees digging a shallow ditch. "Anita is running classes on how to lay subsurface drip irrigation once the soil is ready."

Beside Anita, Becky sat with Dumpy. But when Erik passed, she waved and ran to him.

"Is that for Papa?" Becky said. "Can I leave a message too?"

At the sound of his daughter's voice, John sat up.

"Sure, Princess," Erik said.

Becky took the link and held it close to her face so only her mouth was visible.

"Hi, Papa," Becky said. "How's Merry? We haven't heard anything. Tell Sandy that Jimmie's dad got their tractor—"

The picture zoomed back, and Becky's smiling face appeared with Erik by her side holding the link farther away.

"Jimmie's dad got a tractor and he let me ride their horse. They wouldn't let me go fast though, so we gotta wait until you get our tractor. Erik and Anita are fun, but it's lonely without everyone here."

The girl frowned and her voice softened.

"You're late, Papa, and I miss you. Did you get Sandy? Tell Merry I'm OK, and I know you'll come after me too."

Becky pursed her lips, glanced away, and gave the link back to Erik.

"Well, that's it for now, M," Erik said. "Oh, we haven't heard from Penny or Sam and there's some trouble in the med school up on LeHavre. I'll keep you up to date. Out."

"God, I miss her," John said.

Meriel nodded. "What was that about Penny and Sam? Cue news feed, LeHavre medical school. Go."

```
"IGB News of the Galaxy Tonight with
Frank Masure: An explosion at the Le-
Havre Medical School. The cause has
not been determined. The explosion co-
incided with the arrest of Meriel Hope
for the terrorist attack on Enterprise
that killed hundreds. Station security
has not concluded the two events are
connected. However, station residents
are nervous about possible terrorism
such as occurred on Enterprise . . ."
```

"Damn, they want to blame me for that too."

The replicator chimed and two juice packs and safety cups of coffee appeared.

"Morning, hon," she said, took the coffee and juice, and sat next to John. With a finger, she brushed a stray lock of hair from his forehead.

He took a sip of juice. "Damn, they say a jump field is just EM. Then why do I always feel like crap."

"That was a long jump," Meriel said and massaged his neck.

"You're worried about Penny and Sam?"

"Yes. The corsair bodies are nearby in the morgue. I wonder if the explosion was intentional."

"The bodies have been there since the *Tiger* attack. Why destroy the evidence now?"

She shook her head and sighed. "I'm sorry."

"For what?"

"For dragging you and Sandy into this mess."

He turned and held her close. "Regret is another enemy now."

With her head on John's chest, she stared out the window at the Etna star within the sea of black.

"Etna was Marge Tsoget's last stop," she said. "Maybe her ghost still haunts it."

"Rise and shine, swabbies," Teddy called over the PA. "You're needed forward. We have news."

Meriel and John met Elizabeth entering *Amelia's* small bridge.

Teddy nodded and flipped a virtual toggle above her command console. The image of a small vessel with big jump fans appeared.

"Is that Sandy's ship?" Meriel asked.

"I think so. A packet boat winked-in before us, inbound from Enterprise. The ID is different, but the jump-field spectra match."

Meriel gripped John's hand. "We have a chance."

"They'll dock in a half hour," Teddy said. "Status, Liz?"

Elizabeth scanned her console. "Inside the Etna system. One-g decelerating. Three hours ETA."

"We'd arrive sooner with more deceleration closer to the station," he said.

"Panic stop?" Teddy said, and he nodded. "This system is too dirty, John, and the two-sigma safety envelope is one chance in twenty of dying. That's too dangerous."

"Security might take us out first if we come in hot," Elizabeth said. With a swipe of her hand, she projected a newsfeed on the head-up display. "You should see this."

```
"This is Lance Freiden of GNN. Just
in, UNE courts dropped all charges
against President Biadez in the so-
called Haven affair. Meriel Hope, the
lead witness against the former presi-
dent was convicted of the brutal sabo-
tage of Enterprise Station. Thousands
were killed and thousands more injured
by the drug-addled terrorist . . ."
```

Meriel lowered her gaze and bit her lip. "That'll bury our evidence of the Treaty of Haven and the *Tiger* attack."

"They're gonna shout that news so loud and so often no one will hear what Haven has to say," Elizabeth said.

"They have different ears out here in the far stars," John said.

"But fewer guns."

```
"This just in, former UNE President,
Alan Biadez, has recovered from his
life-threatening illness."
```

"Right on cue," Meriel said and shook her head.

In the vid, Biadez stood with a generous smile in front of the ornate edifice of the Archtrope's cathedral on Calliope amid a crowd of reporters. The grey at his temples added a touch of wisdom rather than age.

"Bastard," Elizabeth said.

A beep distracted Teddy, and she left for the bridge.

> "My friends have told me I should stop the rumors, so I thought it a good time to meet you. Yes, the remission was complete, and I am ready to return to public life."

Meriel took a swig of coffee. "What BS. He faked the illness and resigned to head off impeachment."

A reporter off-camera called a question.

> "Is this a miracle cure?"
> "You could say that, yes. My recovery was due to a combination of medical miracles from BioLuna and spiritual guidance. The Archtrope of Calliope gave me the strength to weather this rough time. My wife, Ellen, and our children are thankful for his support and your many good wishes."

Another reporter raised his hand, and Biadez nodded.

> "Sir, will you be running for reelection?"

Biadez tossed his head back and laughed.

> "Certainly not. President Toyama has done an excellent job. I hope he continues his role throughout his term.
> "Does this mean you are retiring from public life?"
> "Retirement sounds so boring. What will I do out here, fish?"

The reporters laughed along with Biadez.

> "Actually, I've not had much time to consider my future. I've never felt

```
better and have always been an active
man. There are many roles where my ex-
perience and knowledge might help the
people of the galaxy. Thank you for
coming and I invite you all to my re-
ception tonight."
```

Biadez stepped away from the podium, followed by a half-dozen burly men in sunglasses.

Elizabeth scoffed. "Got that, 'people of the galaxy'? He's eyeing something bigger than the UNE."

"What the hell is bigger than the UNE?" John said.

Meriel stared into the blackness of the Etna system. "None of this helps Sandy."

As they decelerated on approach to Etna Station, the *Amelia's* crew ate breakfast in the lounge. Teddy transferred the virtual consoles to the active wall and leaned back with her arms crossed.

"Something wrong?" Meriel said.

"There's a halo of ships around the station, but they're not docking. Half of those docked are hiding their IDs. Only a few cruise liners are docked."

"Why?"

Teddy shrugged. "Can't tell. No comm chatter."

"You have a logistics module on *Amelia's* nav system?" Meriel asked.

"Just like the *Tiger* upgrade."

Elizabeth blushed. "We skipped the training."

"I can figure it out," Meriel said. "Buyer. Etna. Real time."

The nav console displayed the star sector.

```
"Route?"
```

"Etna local."

The display zoomed in to the Etna system and the nearby colonies. Beneath an icon for the station appeared a list of numbers, each followed by an arrow pointing down.

```
0.08 Titanium (machined, kg)
0.07 Bucky tubes (spool)
0.07 Lithium (solid, mg)
 . . .
```

Meriel frowned. "No one is selling anything."

"How do you know?" Elizabeth said.

"The prices are low and declining."

"What are they expecting?"

"These aren't futures," Meriel said. "These are spot prices, real time. This is happening now."

Elizabeth pointed to the list of numbers. "What does '0.08' mean?"

"Normalized sales price. The actual price changes. This allows a buyer to distribute his budget." Meriel raised an eyebrow. "So, if they're not selling, what are they buying? Seller. Etna. Real time."

A second list appeared with arrows pointing up.

```
 0.99 Fare to Lander (all classes
one way)
 0.99  Fare  to  Enterprise  (all
classes one way)
 0.99 Fare to Wolf (all classes
one way)
 0.98 H&K 3445 Tase pistol
    . . .
```

"Damn. They're trying to get off. That's why the ships are holding. The people who want to leave are bidding up the tickets. These vessels are waiting for the bids to rise."

"How humane," Elizabeth said and rolled her eyes.

"Why do they want to leave?" John asked. "What are we heading into?"

"They need Troopers here to stabilize this," Teddy said. "It'll be dangerous to dock."

"We can't wait," Meriel said.

John grabbed another sandwich from the replicator. "You said most of the docked ships aren't broadcasting their IDs. Isn't that illegal?"

"This is Etna, dear."

Between swigs of juice, Elizabeth stabbed her fingers through a holo of the station. "Maintenance docks?"

"Full," Teddy replied.

"Ambulance?"

Teddy tapped her link. "I changed our registration ID to an NGO ambulance to help with humanitarian aid: medical staff only, no room for passengers."

"How do we find out where they're taking Sandy?" John asked. "Track her biotag?"

"They've removed it by now," Meriel said.

He nodded. "We expect them to transfer to a bigger ship on the way to Calliope, right? What ship might that be?"

Teddy's fingers flew above on the virtual console. "With the ships masking their IDs, I can't tell."

Meriel took John's hand. "Then we have to free her first."

"We have eyes on the station," Teddy said and turned to Elizabeth. "Liz, you remember Chen's Apothecary?"

"Sure."

A confirmation message from Blue Dragon appeared above Teddy's display. "They're expecting you."

John nodded. "So, the three of us will go, and Teddy will stay on board ready to run?"

"You need to stay here," Meriel said to him.

"I won't let you two go alone."

Elizabeth frowned. "How chivalrous."

Meriel shook her head. "No, John. If something happens to me, Becky can't lose you."

"What will she think of me if I come home without her sister?" he said.

"She'd think you're alive, John," Elizabeth said with her arms crossed. "And she'll be grateful every morning when you wake her and every evening when you tuck her in."

John shook his head. "But during the day, she'll feel guilty I chose her over Sandy. I'm going."

Meriel turned to Teddy. "Teddy, we can't just waltz onto the station. I'll set off all the alarms, and Elizabeth may have an arrest warrant waiting for her too."

"Brian Chen can change the biotag database," Teddy said.

"Even Nick couldn't do that," Meriel said.

"Brian's an IT Tech Master. He *owns* the database." Teddy glanced at the status dashboard on the active wall. "OK, get ready. It'll be about a half hour to dock."

Elizabeth inspected the hidden cabinets in the lounge.

"What are you hunting for, Liz?" Teddy asked.

"Weapons. We don't know what's out there."

Etna Station—On Station

Teddy docked the *Amelia* at an emergency clinic empty of patients. A single nurse met them at the airlock.

"Your clinic is small for a space station," Meriel said as they checked in.

"It's not meant for citizens," the nurse replied. "It's for the injured from the mining colonies and asteroids.

"Don't the miners have more accidents than citizens?"

The nurse tapped her console. "Certainly, but few are worth the trip here."

Meriel nodded. *Is this hospital part of the Archer organ-trading pipeline?*

"Can you clear us through customs?"

The nurse shook her head and pointed to the door. "Across the docks."

Outside the clinic, Meriel sprinted past the blue-zone bars and duty-free shops. Behind her, Elizabeth and John lifted a teenager-sized cooler covered with biohazard labels onto a grav sled, their means to disguise Sandy's escape.

The docks were quiet, with closed security screens protecting the retailers. And the few open taverns were empty of patrons.

"Looks like the plague hit them," Elizabeth said.

Under a marquee reading, 'Port of Entry. Welcome to Etna Station,' Meriel opened a door to a cavernous space where silhouettes of a riot played on a translucent panel. It might hold thousands of people, but now was empty except for a line of poles, beyond which shimmered a red-light curtain.

Elizabeth stopped and shook her head. "Did I tell you I hate this place?"

Glowing green tiles led to the single pole that blinked green: the proximity scanner and biotag reader. Behind them, the one-way doors closed.

"If Brian's ID database swap doesn't work, we'll never leave," John said.

Meriel stepped forward to the green pole which read her biotag. A holo surrounded the pole, and within the holo, a customs officer appeared, yawned, and inspected her.

"Did you take your meds, Mrs. Helgar?"

"Ah, what?" Meriel said.

Her documents popped up in front of her, and he pointed to a medication schedule. "See here."

```
Rayna Helgar: Ctzn. Wolf Station.
Certifications: MedTech 3, EMT 2.
Medications: Chlirocipanex (generic), daily (alarm).
   . . .
```

"Says here you've got a medication flag on your ID."

"OK then, yes," Meriel said and tipped her head to the translucent window. "That's a lot of protection to keep people out."

"It's keeping them in."

"What's on the other side?"

"People waiting to leave. And they're impatient. Those your spouses behind you?"

John and Elizabeth's passport data displayed alongside hers. They were posing as a communal family: same last name, same address, and same routes.

She blushed and turned to John who blushed too, but her sister grinned.

"Uh, we're . . ." Meriel stammered.

The officer shook his head. "This is Etna, Mrs. Helgar. Nobody cares." He peered past her to the cooler. "Anything to declare?"

"No. Say, are you following the terrorism trial on Enterprise?"

"No." He squinted at her. "You sure you want to do this?"

Meriel blanched. "What?"

With a thumb, he pointed to the shadow play of chaos. "You really want to go on station?"

"Yeah. Humanitarian assistance. Emergency pickup. Why?"

"Well don't go through that door." He tipped his head toward the main exit. "You're not from here and they'll kill you for your ID. Grab some maintenance blues from the closet over there. Use those and leave through the security exit. And on the outbound, avoid the crowds. Go to security and tell them you're lost."

"And calm down, for God's sake," the customs officer said to Meriel as he passed them through. "You're jumpy as fugitives."

The odor of disinfectant and cleansers filling the maintenance closet almost masked the reek of sweat and sewage, but not quite. She wrinkled her nose at the blue coveralls and considered foregoing the disguise. But after glancing back at the chaos outside, she changed her mind.

They could not take a chance. She put the suit on and sealed it to her neck, holding her breath and cringing when the filthy fabric touched her skin.

Meriel dragged a wet-vac for extra camouflage as they left through the double security doors at the customs exit. The inner door slammed shut, the outer door opened, and the crowd pushed past Meriel and her team to assail the inner door. As they elbowed their way through the crowd into the corridor, the portal filled with a noxious gas. The crowd rushed to leave and swept Meriel and her team along with them into the corridor as the outer door closed behind them.

Odors of fear and sweat from the crush of people filled the corridor. But the stench from their maintenance blues kept the crowd from pressing too close. As they hurried away, a blue flash distracted her, and Meriel turned as an electric arc discouraged the rioters . . . by killing them.

Meet the Chen's

The Chen's tiny shop stood at the intersection of pink-zone, for those who danced at the edge of perdition, and black-zone, for those who had already fallen off. The laser burns and slug holes on the front of the shop were new since their last visit but only added to its charm.

Inside, small bins lined the walls, each with medicinal herbs and potions for clientele unimpressed by traditional doctors. One drawer bore the same poppy symbol used by the Archers, once to imply opium, and now heroin.

From behind the counter, Mrs. Chen greeted Meriel and Elizabeth but gave John the side-eye. "Come," she said, and led them through the light curtain.

Meriel stopped at the entrance to the secret room where months ago she had met her sister, beat up and running from the law. But the old woman shook her head and waved them through a small kitchen and into the bathroom. Instead of pushing the flush handle, she lifted it, and the wall slid back to expose another hidden room the size of a large cargo hold.

To one side of the door stood a row of bunks, a kitchenette, and racks of clothing. And from a grav sled, a crew of men in Tech green and silver unloaded a score of crates.

In one corner of the room, Mrs. Chen's son, Brian, chatted on a headset with his hands behind his back. Two dozen holographic images hovered around him of the shop, the docks, and a dozen other places Meriel did not recognize.

"I see the *Amelia* at the clinic dock, Teddy," Brian said. "No, I don't need another droid. And the Enterprise comm sync? Acknowledged. I'll forward your report to my Domain Master."

"Brian," Mrs. Chen said, but he ignored her.

"No, Teddy, that won't work. The Archers have upgraded to RT encryption. Yeah, I know. The organ trade can afford better tech than Lander. Jeez, Teddy, don't gush. It's only a job."

"Brian!" Mrs. Chen said.

Brian lowered his legs from the console, spun his chair around, and smiled. "Oh. Hi, Liz," he said, and then with less enthusiasm, "And you, M. You know about this gift Teddy is sending?"

"No," Meriel said. "What was she 'gushing' about?"

"I made Tech Master, and she's all congratulations and stuff."

"Did the comm sync have updates about the explosion on LeHavre?"

"No," he said. "Why?"

Elizabeth glanced at Meriel. "Our friends are there, and we haven't heard from them."

"Sorry," Brian said and turned to John with no joy at all. "And who are you?"

"He's a friend," Elizabeth said.

Brian studied him. "The conflict here is covert."

"For now," his mother said.

Meriel put a hand on John's shoulder. "He's a farmer, not a soldier."

"Sure," Brian said.

"And he's Sandy's father."

"Sorry, man."

Elizabeth took Brian's hand. "We need your help. Did Teddy tell you what we're up to?"

He nodded. "We tracked the ship as it docked and followed them inside. No biotag for her, but we found the others." He zoomed into an image of a girl being dragged across the dock. "Is that her?"

Meriel pursed her lips and took John's hand. He put his arm around her and nodded.

"Recognize anyone else in that group?" Meriel asked.

"No," Brian replied.

"Zoom. Pan faces," she said, and the vid focused on each face. Kostanza was not among them. *Where is he?*

Brian gave her a sideways look. "Who are you expecting?"

"Nobody. What else do you have for us?"

"Next," Brian commanded, and the console swapped a schematic for the vid. He pointed to a grid of rooms. "We think she's here in HB334h."

Meriel used hand motions to rotate and zoom further into the region. "H deck, black-zone."

"Deep in the lab space of Kelton Bioinformics. Archer space. The Archtrope uses the labs for organ laundering."

"What's that?" John asked.

"Bioengineering the DNA markers so the Troopers can't trace the organs to the original owners."

"How's that even possible?" Elizabeth asked.

Meriel scrolled through the schematics. "Where's Khanag?"

Brian shrugged. "Don't know. But he's not here."

"You're sure?"

"I'm sure."

Meriel bit her lip. Until that moment, Meriel thought Khanag had teamed with Biadez to kidnap Sandy, and that Kostanza was their mouthpiece. *Is Kostanza's offer still valid?*

"What is it, M?" John said, but she shook her head. He turned to Brian. "So, how are we going to get Sandy out?"

"I need to work with my people on that," Brian said. "Your raid has to be quiet, or it will end up in open warfare."

Elizabeth scowled. "And that's a bad thing?"

"We live here, Liz. Yes, that's a bad thing."

"Archers are evil, Brian."

Brian swapped a display to Etna's political divisions. "But they control almost thirty percent of the station. Even the Masters couldn't contain it if it becomes a shooting war. Lots of innocents will get spaced, and the Archers don't care. Etna will be uninhabitable."

She pointed to the bright red icon on his console. "Hmm. And what about that one? The one that says, 'Vent to Space.'"

"That will open a section of the torus to space to damp an uncontrollable fire or riot."

"I didn't know they even considered that," John said.

"Every station can do that. Better to lose a few than everyone. And we might need it now."

"How so?"

Brian frowned. "The Archers snuck a sympathizer onto the Council of Masters, and he's been bringing his own people in. Not sure who we can trust."

"Is your cold war the reason people are in a hurry to leave?" Meriel asked.

"That, and an entire daycare center of kids went missing. Everyone knows the Archers are behind it, but the Techs haven't been able to prove it. Their plant on the Council is slow-walking the indictments."

Elizabeth nodded. "Like I said. Archers are evil."

"Come," Mrs. Chen said, took Meriel's arm, and led her to a vault door across the room.

"Why all the space?" John asked as he followed.

"Side business." She stopped and turned to them. "This is the hard part. Waiting. Stay alert. But—"

A crate fell from a stack and interrupted.

"Hey, Godzilla, back the hell away," Mrs. Chen said to the Tech crew in perfect Galactic. "Brian, get the hell over here and supervise your people."

"Whose idea was the communal family?" Meriel asked.

"Your sister thought that would be fun. The techs were thinking of killing you and starting fresh."

"Ah, how would that—"

Mrs. Chen smiled. "I'm joking."

"Right," John said.

"Come," the old woman said and took their arms.

Past the crates from which stunners and small blasters had spilled, Mrs. Chen waved her hand at a button on the wall. The vault door slid open to reveal a room filled with Archer weaponry.

"You'll need some of these," Mrs. Chen said.

Anti-personnel weapons hung on hooks near the door: stunners with fanny packs for recharge, a point-EMP to stop a heart or reboot a brain, flechette pistols that sprayed a pattern of needles to incapacitate but not kill.

In rows stood pulse rifles with the power of blasters but no recoil—the same weapon the corsairs used during the *Tiger* attack. These could disable an opponent but do minimal damage to the station.

There were enough weapons here to arm a revolution or prevent one.

And the Etna Techs had them.

***

When Meriel and John left with Mrs. Chen, Elizabeth put a hand on Brian's shoulder.

"I missed you," Brian said.

"I've been busy with a hijacking and invasion, Brian. And my asshole ship won't pick me up."

"Can you stay after we get Sandy?"

"Ask me after," Elizabeth said. "But I doubt the Archers will let us hang around after we steal their prize."

He tipped his head toward Meriel. "You two enjoy this combat stuff?"

She rolled her eyes. "It's better than waiting to die. You don't approve of my sister."

"She's disruptive. Things break near her. Like bad karma, Liz."

"That's pretty Zen for a Tech."

"Life's more than tech. It's risky being around her."

Elizabeth frowned. "That's what she thinks, too. But she doesn't cause it."

"Causation is science, correlation is risk, and risk is what the Techs minimize."

"But you're helping her."

"Because she's right. And her heart is in the same place as yours."

Over Brian's head, a monitor cycled the news feeders.

```
"IGB Newsflash. Stegman Tamari was
found paralyzed and near death after a
severe stroke. Mr. Tamari served as
the special assistant to Hideo Asurini
and chief negotiator to the Inter-
Station Subcommittee, forging closer
ties with Sol. Chairman Asurini had
these words . . ."
```

"Bad news," Brian said.

"Why?" Elizabeth asked.

"Tamari is a friend. Not a Gaia fanatic like his boss, Asurini."

From between them a probe at the end of a rod snaked toward the display. They followed the limb to Eddie, who hovered behind them with another probe.

"Damn that's creepy," Brian said. "Is it yours?"

"I'll bet he's the gift Teddy promised," Elizabeth said.

"Hey, tin man, wait over there in the corner."

Eddie's lid turned a grayish blue, and he complied.

"Teddy calls him Eddie," Elizabeth said with a grin.

"Him?"

"Long story."

"So, what the hell am I gonna do with him . . . it? It's a maintenance droid."

"He was more once."

"Sure," he said and slipped his hand into hers. "How about a bite to eat?"

The sound of a door opening brought Elizabeth's head around and she smiled. "Maybe later," she said, and joined her sister and John.

"Now this is more like it," Elizabeth said when she entered the vault and ran her hands along the weapons, grinning like a child at a toy catalogue.

On the wall with the side arms, she found a flechette pistol like Abrams's but larger. She took it from the wall.

"I had to leave one like this behind," Elizabeth said as she felt the balance.

"Assassins," Ms. Chen said. "For a big man."

Elizabeth sighted the weapon. "Maybe."

Mrs. Chen pointed to a full-size armored dummy at the end of the room and then waved to clear the area. "Go ahead."

With two hands, Liz found the target with the laser sights. She fired, and the dummy exploded with limbs in every direction and the chest pinned to the wall six feet off the deck.

Elizabeth nodded. "Yeah, that's what I'm talking about," she said, took the holster, and continued her tour.

She stopped next at a metal cage holding heavy weapons. Behind a plastisteel screen hung blasters and laser gattlers, incendiaries whose toxic fumes could never be eliminated from the station's air supply, ancient rockets, and plastic explosives powerful enough to rip Etna's hull apart.

"Shame we can't take some of this with us," Elizabeth said with a hand on her hip.

"They'd crack the torus like an egg," Meriel said.

Elizabeth scowled. "That'd be a good thing."

Incursion

"Brian, what's taking so long?" John asked with a cup of noodles in his hand.

"The Techs haven't found a fool-proof way to get you in and out, John. Be patient."

"It won't matter soon. They're going to transfer Sandy and we won't have another shot to save her. We need to act now?" he said and waved to Elizabeth and Meriel.

"I don't think—"

Meriel walked up to them. "Now, Brian,"

"Ok," Brian said and pulled up a schematic holo.

"How accurate is this?" Meriel said.

"Good for the bulkheads, pressure integrity, maintenance access, HVAC, and utilities. Interior walls change all the time."

"What else do you have?" Elizabeth asked.

"You've seen the weapons. Gramma's got uniforms, warm-suits, hard-suits—"

"Grav sleds?"

"Yes," Mrs. Chen said and pointed to vehicles parked by the wall. "And utility carts."

"Anything discrete for tracking?" Elizabeth asked.

Mrs. Chen took a small link from the cage and peeled a transparent dot from a sheet. "Here," she said, pressed the dot to Meriel's little finger, and gave her the link. "This will work anywhere on the station and out to ten clicks."

"You can't go straight at them with force," Brian said and zoomed into a secure pressure barrier to Archer territory. "They'll swarm and close the blast doors, which we can't break without explosives."

"Then we must be within the Archer perimeter before they suspect what we're doing?" John asked.

"Right. The Helgars, you three, have the IDs of Archers we've detained. The Archer database downloads from ours, so you're good."

"So, we take a cart and a grav sled to Archer space and the ID's get us past the blast doors."

"Ok, we're in and we find Sandy." Meriel said. "How do we get out?"

"Walk out with your Archer IDs." Brian said and pointed to a box on the schematic. "We'll have *Amelia* meet you at the airlock here."

"And if there's a problem?"

"If there's a problem, signal us and we'll extract you."

"How?" Meriel said.

Brian handed her a tiny device the size of a bent pin. "Attach this Utility FM transmitter to any service line, electrical, cable, appliance, whatever. Tap code-V. Three short and one long."

"No one's gonna figure that out?"

"They don't monitor the utilities as far as we can tell. They're blind and won't know. If they try to use it and make a mistake, it dies."

"Signal isolation?"

"We supply their power. They can't silence a UFM and still breathe."

"Emergency power?" John asked.

"Anything is possible. But their current plan is to take the station from the top down, not fight for it from the bottom up."

"For now," Mrs. Chen said.

Meriel paced. *What would Cookie think?* "Nothing is this easy, Brian. What's wrong with the plan?"

Brian narrowed his eyes. "Kelton Bioinformics absorbed and expanded the immense compute farm of the Genomic Research Center. The Helgars, the real ones, imply it holds a massive DNA database for the Archtrope."

Meriel nodded. "If they have a database, Elizabeth and I are probably in it. Biadez has been tracking us for a decade, and the Archers are on the same team. Brian, can you be sure?"

"No. We can't hack it," Brian said. "And if they check your IDs against that, it'll alert security."

"Maybe they already have," Elizabeth said.

"You'll know the first time they check your biotags."

Meriel nodded. "So, if they let us pass once, we're good?"

"You're good unless security queries the Kelton database. But that's unlikely."

John raised his hand. "Unlikely, but not impossible? What might cause that?"

Brian shrugged. "Unusual behavior. A security question the real Helgars know the answer to, but you don't."

"Then what?"

"You have only thirty seconds before security will shut the blast doors. No more. You're locked out and need to return here."

"Thirty seconds?" Elizabeth said. "That's not very long."

How do I save my friends in those thirty seconds? Meriel thought.

"Where's our ride?" Elizabeth asked as Brian downloaded the rescue plan to burner links. Mrs. Chen opened the compartment doors where Meriel was mounting the open cart.

"And where do you think you're going?" Elizabeth said.

Meriel bit her cheek. "It's better if I go alone, Liz. They'll not be expecting just—"

"Yeah, yeah. You trying to take care of us again?"

"It'll be easier to infiltrate if—"

"Shut up. We're coming with."

Meriel drove the cart down the corridor with John in the middle and Elizabeth to his right. As they rounded the corner to the first security checkpoint, Meriel slowed.

"It's too close," Meriel said. "The blast door is another fifty yards."

The Archer raised his hand as they pulled up and stopped. After the reader checked their biotags, his wrist-link flashed green. Meriel relaxed and pulled away, but the security guard raised his hand again.

"Reyna," the guard asked. "How's your brother?"

A security question. Crap! "He's fine."

The archer narrowed his eyes, glanced at his link, and raised a finger to tap it.

Elizabeth reached out and grabbed the meat of his hand, twisting it into a wrist lock and driving him to the ground. John leapt out of the cart to subdue him.

"That could start our thirty seconds," Meriel said and ran to the blast doors. "Sorry."

"Meriel, wait!" John called.

Twenty seconds later, Meriel was inside the Archer perimeter expecting the blast doors to close.

To her left, Elizabeth and John ran toward her. But down the corridor next to the blast door, out of sight of her team, an Archer security team turned the corner.

Thirty seconds had elapsed since the security check, but the blast doors had not closed. The three of them could take the Archers, she was sure.

But that wasn't Meriel's plan.

She kneeled with her right hand behind her head to warn her team. Then with her left hand she hit the close button next to the door.

"I'm Meriel Hope. Take me to Kostanza, and—" she said, but before she finished, a rifle butt cracked her forehead.

***

"No!" Elizabeth shouted and dropped two of the Archers with a round of flechettes.

John slipped his pulse-rifle under the door to jam it, but the rifle snapped in half as the door seated itself into the slot in the deck.

With a guess at the door's thickness, Elizabeth applied a shaped charge to a seam.

"You're not supposed to have that," he said.

She set the detonator. "Uh-huh."

When the smoke cleared from the explosion, a person-sized hole appeared, and John ran toward it. But through the haze came a grenade.

"Down!" Elizabeth yelled and tackled him, and they rolled behind the grav sled. "God, I *really* hate this place."

Shrapnel from the explosion scored their body armor and penetrated the hard plastic wall behind them.

And a broken panel from the grav sled sheared off John's leg at the knee.

Double Eclipse

"Merry L," a voice called.

Meriel woke in the hold of the *Princess* while the other children around her slept. Her mother had stopped snoring, and Meriel reached out to her, but a sharp pain shot through her left hand.

"Wake up, Merry L."

She fought through the headache to open her eyes but squinted in the bright haze. "Sandy? Is that you?"

"Yes."

"Oh, thank God," Meriel said and turned her head to the voice. Sandy stood next to her with a smile and the traces of tears on an unwashed face.

"How are you, hon?"

"I'm fine, M." She raised her arm to show the brown stain of dried blood on her sleeve. "They removed my bio-thingy."

"I'm sorry. Did it hurt?"

"A little," she said, and put a hand on Meriel's. "I tried to remove the straps, but they're locked."

Still in her Archer jumpsuit, Meriel's ankles and right arm were strapped to a chair. A transparent case enclosed her left hand, and through it an IV flowed into her basilic vein. She struggled but could not free herself from the straps or the rigid case.

"What are we gonna do?" Sandy asked.

"We're gonna leave, is what we're gonna do. Did you check my pockets?"

The girl nodded. "Nothing."

Damn. The UFM's gone and the link. Nothing to signal Brian with.

On a placard by the door was stenciled HB334h, and above that, "Intake Processing."

"Processing for what?" Meriel asked and tested her restraints again. "Did you try to leave?"

"The door is locked," Sandy said and frowned.

"Why the long face, kid? We've been in tough spots before."

"Last time it didn't work out so good."

"Better for us than them."

"They destroyed our entire farm, Merry."

"But we walked away, and they didn't. Don't worry. We'll get outta this."

"How?"

"We've got friends, hon. Never forget," Meriel said and scanned the room. "Come closer," she whispered. "They're listening and watching, and I want to talk to you in private. Can you see a camera?"

"No."

"Anything in the corner of the ceiling, anything blinking?"

Sandy shook her head. "There's a tiny dot in the corner."

"Can you reach it?"

"If I stand on the counter."

"Is there a pen nearby?" Meriel asked.

"There's a stylus."

"Jam it into that dot and break it or drive it into the wall."

When Sandy completed her task, Meriel stopped whispering.

"OK, now we can talk. Did they take the necklace?"

"No," Sandy said and lowered her sock.

"Great. Take the q-chip from your necklace and put it in the pocket of my coveralls. Now, see the tape on my little finger? Remove it and put it on the back of your cross."

"What is it?"

"It's a tracker. Your body heat will power it."

"You can find me with this?"

"Our friends can," Meriel said as Sandy returned the cross to her ankle. "Now listen up. There are times you can't wait for things, and you need to help yourself. I don't know how much time we have, so you need to remember."

"OK, shoot."

"First, don't let them give you anything, pills, liquids, or poke you with needles. Tell them you have allergies or anything. That'll stall them until they can test you."

"Sure."

"Second, don't let them restrain you, but they might try. If they do, before they tighten them, slip your hand in it, and tighten your fist. You can slip your hand out easier."

"Ok, what next?"

"Third, find a way out of the room," Meriel said, and they brainstormed about means to escape: doors, vents, utility access. But none seemed possible from where they were.

"If you escape before I do, head for the infirmary at the docks, It's on the map. You remember where those are?"

Sandy nodded but frowned. "Sure. At the corners where the corridors cross."

"On the way, never hide in a recycling chute or enter a room you can't get out of . . . What is it, hon?"

Sandy peered at her and gripped her hand. "Merry L, I don't want to grow up this fast."

Meriel opened her mouth to reply, but the world fogged again. "Have faith, honey. Our Songline doesn't end here."

"I know," Sandy said as Meriel's world went dark.

***

Meriel drifted in the blackness of space with only the dim glow of Etna to orient her. Her entire body burned from the inside and vaporized the last of her tears. She opened her arms to let the pieces fall away and dissolve. It was the open space she loved, even if it hurt.

"Leave me here," she said and closed her eyes.

"Come back, Merry," Becky's voice drifted past.

"Where are you?" Meriel mumbled, not knowing if she were awake or dreaming.

"Here, Merry."

An image came of the two girls hiding in the shelter under their farmhouse kitchen as laser sights dotted their chests. But before Meriel reached them, General Khanag approached with his blaster drawn, and he fired.

Meriel screamed.

She blinked and squinted into the bright overhead lights, struggling against the restraints to defend the girls from Khanag, but they were not there. Instead, she was in a stark white room, shivering with a cold sweat and stinking of fear. Her head, and every muscle in her body, ached.

She had lost track of the times they had cycled her through the roller coaster ride of drugs that dragged her from the ecstasy of her family on Haven to the horror of Khanag murdering each one in front of her. And at the end of each ride, a shot of Soberal made sure she was acutely aware of the hell they were putting her through.

"HB334h, HB334h . . ." she muttered, blinked to focus, and slowed her breathing.

"What's she babbling about?" a woman said.

To Meriel's side, a fat, unshaven man in a stained white lab smock removed the syringe from the IV connected to her left wrist. She turned her head checking for Sandy, but found only a splitting headache, and she squinted at a stab of pain.

"We'll begin in another minute or two, Ms. Hope," the man said.

A woman, pretty except for a scar crossing her cheek, took him by the arm. "Better make it longer. She almost didn't make it the last time."

"Whatever."

The woman frowned. "They need her to walk in front of the camera and deny her charges."

Meriel's half-open eyes caught the fat man's attention. "Ah, there you are."

Meriel blinked to clear her head and winced at the throbbing pain.

"Headache? We can fix that." He shook a vial and held it near her eyes.

The label said Aristopine, the addictive medication they used to silence her when she was twelve. It would not end the pain, just her concern for it.

Her right shoulder hurt where blood stained the sleeve and trailed down her forearm to her palm. There, a fresh tattoo burned, an inventory control tattoo like on the dead bodies on Haven.

"What's this for?" she asked.

"Don't worry. It's not for you."

"Indulge me."

"Blood type. DNA phenotype. HLA sensitivity," he said as he inspected amber vials and put some on a tray by her side.

"And my ID?"

"They won't care who you are."

She glared at him. "A brand. Like meat."

"And a reminder that we own you now. We have a mortgage on your body, and you pay with the parts. One more time, Ms. Hope. Let's begin with confessing that you invented the Treaty of Haven."

She scowled. "Not for nothing. Let the girl go, and I'll give you what you want."

"I can't do that."

"Kostanza promised if I surrender to you and admit to the Enterprise damage, he'd let her go."

The dirty smock grinned. "Who's Kostanza?"

"You lying sack of—" she yelled and battled her restraints until the headache stopped her.

"You've created quite a stir," the lab coat said as he mixed a new cocktail of drugs from the vials on the tray. "Your avatar can't walk into a courtroom or stand in front of news cameras and confirm your statement. We need your continued cooperation, and the girl guarantees it. You're rather resilient, and we've held off, but we'll start this regimen on her the next round."

"Why? She has nothing to offer."

He smirked. "Your pain is only to demonstrate what we'll do to her while you watch." He leaned in closer. "The girl is much smaller than you, and resuscitation could be... problematic."

The ache returned to her stomach. *No one could be so cruel.*

"We have alternatives, though. What shall it be?" He held up a jar. "A tiny mushroom to ruin her liver?" He swapped the jar with a vial. "Maybe a genetically matched virus to slowly destroy her brain."

"You wouldn't. She's a child."

"You're not, and you're the point."

"If you hurt her, I'll never help you. Please, if I know she is safely with her father, I will do what you want."

He grinned in her face, and his breath sickened her. "But then we lose our leverage, and you'll kill yourself."

He's right.

"A stalemate then. We don't trust each other." He completed his mixture and filled a syringe. "And so, it's my turn. You will confess, and you will both remain captive. That is my solution. So, let's begin—"

Her jaw tightened. *No time to be timid.*

"If you want us to cooperate, you gotta try harder. She can do this in her sleep." *C'mon John, you know where she is. I'll stall as long as I can.*

He gave her a side-eye. "It's more than enough for a child."

"You know nothing of what we live with every day on Haven."

He stopped. "It's paradise."

She scoffed. "It's a desert with six trillion predators. One bite or sting is worse than anything you have here. So, prove it to me. Prove to me you can hurt her. Give me all you got and maybe I'll believe you." *Hurry, John. I didn't mean it to go this way. But we need you now. Come get her.*

The lab coat increased the dose and injected it into the IV.

But from behind her came the voice of the only person who could make things worse.

"Give us a moment," General Khanag said.

The Right Hand of Death

Meriel shuddered, and the hair on the back of her neck tingled as she fought against her restraints. The assistant rushed out of the room while the stained smock stared. "Ah . . . You shouldn't be here."

"I can be where I choose. Leave. Now."

"Yes . . . sir," the dirty smock said. With a glare, he set the timer on the IV and backed out the door.

Meriel stopped fighting, slowed her breathing, and faced the general.

"Your circumstances cheer me, Ms. Hope."

"You've been quiet since Haven."

"After your lies, I have time on my hands," he said as he examined the instruments of torment on the tray.

"Did Kostanza send you to make the trade?"

"Who's Kostanza? And why should I care?"

Crap! "He promised to free the girl if I surrendered."

"Seems he lied."

"You didn't kidnap Sandy?

"This is His Eminence's doing, not mine."

"Free the girl. I'll say whatever you want if you free her."

"Not now."

Meriel closed her eyes and bit her cheek. "Then why are you here?"

He glared at her. "I came to watch you die."

She looked into eyes cold as a hiranth who's only purpose in life was death.

"Not to kill me yourself?"

"Unfortunately, I can't," he said and raised his arm to show an amputation cuff. "Our chat is on the condition I don't interfere. But it won't matter. There won't be much left of you when they finish. Oh, they will reanimate you. You have made yourself too important in their schemes to deserve a quick death. But there will be nothing left worth killing."

"Does the cuff protect the girl?"

"Yes," he said.

"Then let her go. She's innocent."

"His Eminence says no one is innocent."

"You know better. Please, Khanag. She's a child."

"Others have died for you. Why not her?"

She winced at the sting of truth, and despair crept into her voice. "Why do you even care? Why did you come after me on Haven? Surely my death means nothing after you murdered everyone on my ship."

Khanag leaned over and glared. "Because you murdered my son," he said through exposed teeth. "And every day you live, you remind me he does not."

"What?"

"He was one of your prisoners on the *Tiger,* executed without tribunal, without honor."

She nodded. "The captain was your son."

Khanag turned away.

"We didn't kill any of the corsairs," she said. "Who told you that?"

"I have it on good authority."

"Well, your authority is wrong. They committed suicide."

He stared at her. "That's an honorable death for a corsair. What new deception is this?"

"I have no reason to lie. The medical examiner's report has the proof you need in the files."

"I destroyed your slanders."

"There's another copy in my breast pocket. Read it for yourself."

She followed his eyes to her pocket and upward to the tip of the scar that crossed her body. With a finger, he traced the scar from her ear to her collarbone. As he did, his sleeve rode up to expose the snake and dagger tattoo along his cephalic vein.

"Some wounds are too deep to hide," he said, but he did not seem to refer to her.

"It is sad that your son died," she said flatly. "But we didn't kill him."

After another quick glance, he removed the q-chip from her pocket, tapped it on his link to copy it, and scanned the coroner's report.

"If what this says is true, my son died a martyr's death."

"Better he not die at all," she said.

"We all die. Better to die in the service of a cause larger than yourself."

"And you think the Archtrope is that cause?"

"He saved me from the drug dens as he has saved tens of millions of others."

"He runs those dens."

"Only to embrace those who suffer. His outreach has salvaged millions on Calliope and the thousands in my fleet. You say you aren't a terrorist. Tell me you won't destroy his good works if they free you."

"It's not his 'good works' that bother me."

"And now you would have me believe a dossier meant solely to poison my relationship with the Archtrope? The media and the UNE debunked those rumors years ago."

"The dossier evidence is new and wasn't meant for the media. You're smarter than all of them. They were meant for you."

He frowned and slipped the q-chip back into her pocket. "There's no direct involvement with His Holiness."

"Everyone involved connects to him or his proxies. You know how extensive his reach is. And how deep. You're part of it."

With narrowed eyes, he said, "Even if the rumors are true, it does not outweigh the good he has done."

"We have a different perspective."

"There are degrees to corruption, Ms. Hope, and I don't need your forgiveness."

"I don't offer it. A man once told me it's not my forgiveness you need, but God's."

"I don't need your god either. The Archtrope is my savior. Before him I sought death."

"He *is* death, Khanag, and you're his right hand."

He scoffed. "And still you expect me to believe your myth?"

"Rather than his? Yes," she said. "Please, I will admit to anything, if you let the girl go."

"Why? She will only end up like you, a terrorist, spawn of terrorists." He turned away. "She won't last here. They might make an example of her to show you how sincere they are."

"No, no . . ." she pleaded.

He paced again and scanned the room before putting his hand on the plastaglass case that trapped her left hand. After a click, the pressure on her hand eased.

"But if you die before her, I will see to it she arrives to her father unharmed."

She tilted her head, and a crease appeared in her brow. "On Haven, you promised I would watch her die."

"That was a moment of rage."

"Then kill me now and free her."

Khanag raised the amputation cuff again. "Perhaps we will meet in different circumstances, Ms. Hope." He leaned over, exposing a necklace with two charms: a silver elephant and a poppy. "And then I will kill you," he said and left the room.

"Khanag! You bastard," she called after him until the drugs dragged her back into the world of pain.

***

A woman with a scar across her cheek entered Sandy's new private room. Without glancing at the girl, she reached up to adjust a camera. And when she did, her sleeve slid back to expose the snake and blade tattoo on her forearm.

She checked the restraints holding Sandy's legs and clenched fists, opened a drawer, uncovered a tray with sharp instruments, and stood quietly by the door.

A chubby man in a dirty smock entered, dragging an octopus-like device with multicolored tentacles snaking along the sides.

"What a wonderful day for a chat."

"If you hurt me, she'll find you, you know," Sandy said.

"Who are you talking about?"

"Merry L. She'll find you, and you won't like what happens."

Standing by the door, a glimmer of a smile flashed across the assistant's face but just as quickly disappeared.

"Don't be silly, child. Your friend is in no shape to help anyone. Please, dear. It'll be so much more pleasant if you cooperate with us. See, I'm a nice man: I said 'please.'"

"No."

"Well then, you're just another nerve on her body we want to . . . tweak." He grinned, exposing bad teeth. "And a nerve more sensitive than others. Let's see now where to begin." He inspected her as if she were one of the surgical tools on the tray.

"May I see?" he asked and tapped her forehead above her eye patch.

"No."

He ignored her and lifted the edge of the patch, but she jerked her head away.

"Ah, sensitive about that."

Sandy pursed her lips and fought back tears, unwilling to reveal how much it hurt to be different to avoid them hurting her more.

His assistant frowned and took a step forward, but she stopped and bit her lip.

His voice turned to honey. "We don't want to hurt you. We only want Ms. Hope to cooperate. And you can help."

"No."

"You know, we have excellent facilities here. We can get you a new eye."

"I'll get one at home in a year."

"Oh, my. You may not be going home for a while." The wicked smile returned. "You won't have to wait here. We have exactly your color."

"I'm your prisoner. You can do what you want."

"We'll give you a new one, same as the other, right away. And you'll be free to return home. But you must help us with Ms. Hope."

"What about depth perception?"

"Sure. Just like new."

He's lying. Would they kill someone just to match my eye color?

Of course she wanted a new eye, but not this way, and she could never be sure.

"No."

"Imagine it, dear. You'll be normal again and the other kids won't stare at you. You'll be pretty again."

"Papa says I'm pretty now," she said through the tears.

"But you know bet—"

"Stop," the assistant said, grabbed his arm, and pulled him away.

He slapped her so hard she fell. "While you're here," he said between clenched teeth, "you f'ing stay the hell out of my way!"

The woman ran from the room, and he turned back to the tray of instruments, prepared a syringe, and held it close to Sandy's face.

"Let's give Ms. Hope one more chance before we start on you," he said and laid the syringe back on the tray.

The door shut behind him with a metallic click and the bio-ID pad on the door blinked red, leaving her no escape.

Sandy had spent her entire life on a farm in the open with people who cared for her. The most vicious animals on

Haven, even those that might kill her, were understandable. Until the accident with her eye, she had never seen a doctor. And except for a few hours during the invasion, she had never been afraid.

But this world—space stations, faster-than-light ships, soldiers, and mean people—was foreign to her.

Merry L promised to get us out of this, but she's not here, and that means she's in trouble.

This room was not where she and Meriel had worked out escape plans, and Sandy had to start from scratch. A quick survey of her room exposed only heavy equipment, the instruments on the tray, and cabinets. The lock on the door blinked red, as did every drawer and cabinet.

Only one ceiling vent fed air into the room, and it was wide enough to fit her. *But there's nothing here that can get me inside that vent.*

Meriel's whispers came to her. "Focus on the problem right in front of you. Once you begin you will only have a few seconds."

Sandy unclenched her fists, pulled her hands from the restraints, and freed her feet. From the instrument tray, she grabbed a scalpel and stood on the counter to break the surveillance camera. Jumping off, she hurried to the door but did not touch it, fearing it might set off an alarm.

After a brief inspection, she found a seam and used the scalpel to pry off the cover. Behind the fingerprint scanner was a tangle of tiny wires and boards.

No way am I going to figure that out.

Next to the sink was a dumbwaiter which Sandy inspected. *To freedom or the recycler?*

Under the sink, she found a utility panel and popped it out with the scalpel. Inside was enough room to fit her, but the pipe chase was too narrow for her to escape.

Hearing footsteps in the corridor, she hurried back to the chair and slid her hands back into the restraints but kept the blade in her palm.

No one came, and as she waited, she made her plans.

Pulling her hands from the restraints again, she climbed onto the cabinet, and with the scalpel, unscrewed the ceiling vent cover, and held onto it.

From the instrument tray, she took the surgical tape and went to the door. On the bottom of the door jamb below the lock, she taped the blade of the scalpel. To the door itself, she loosely taped the handle of the scalpel so the instrument would fall when the door opened. If it fell, it might stop the door from closing again.

If. Might.

Then she threw the vent cover against the door.

***

Outside Sandy's room, the bang on the door brought a guard to investigate. Once inside, he found the chair empty and glanced up to an open vent.

He raised his link. "This is Cooper in interrogation. Prisoner Smith has escaped. Alert Dean Yutousov and bring droids to search the ducts."

As he left the room, the aide who had assisted in Sandy's torment walked over to the door. There, a glint of steel caught her eye from a scalpel that had, for some unknown reason, fallen from the tray and blocked the door open.

***

When the room was quiet again, Sandy left her hiding place behind the utility panel. The scalpel still blocked the door open, and she peeked through the crack where a woman in white shoes stood.

The woman dropped her link and bent over to pick it up, and Sandy scuttled backward. Through the crack in the door, the woman faced her with a finger to her lips, the assistant with the scar on her cheek and a swollen eye.

"Your friend is near," the assistant whispered. "Down the corridor to your left, turn right and second door on the left." She pointed to the scalpel on the deck near the door. "And don't forget that."

The aide stood again with her back to the door, and Sandy snuck out behind her.

Outside Meriel's door, the man in the dirty lab coat stood checking a link. He raised his head and walked toward her, but she backed into the adjacent corridor before he spotted her.

Voices came from the opposite hall, and she ran through another corridor. That became a dead end, and as the voices approached, she backed into a door.

Inside was a large room where people lay strapped on gurneys; some appeared sick and others lay still, and each had a tattoo on their palm. Breathless and panicked, she ran between the gurneys, searching for an escape.

On the opposite side of the room was a stack of crates and boxes marked "Biohazard" and "Biowaste" where she might hide. Before she reached it, a moan distracted her.

"Help me, please," a bald man croaked as he struggled with his restraints. "They'll kill me."

She eyed her hidey-hole again, bit her lip, and approached him.

With the scalpel, she cut the strap that bound his hand, but as she slit the second, the door beeped. She put the blade within his reach and turned to run, but he grabbed her wrist.

"Follow me out," he said. From his sock, he removed something tiny. "In case I don't make it, take this." Into her palm, he pressed a biotag like the one they had removed from her hours earlier.

The voices from the hall entered, and she ducked as the captive freed his ankles. The chatter stopped when he rose from the gurney, and they chased him as he ran out the door.

Instead of following, she scrambled into her hiding place and wedged herself behind the boxes. There she sat with pounding heart and hugged her knees.

Moments later, the boxes shifted.

Did he tell them about me? If he didn't, then no one knows I'm here, and no one will come for me.

But at the inlet to her shelter, a tube like a security spider arm snaked around the corner, and she scuttled backward. Tiny motors whirred and metal scraped against metal as a circle of light grew and brightened.

The probe reached her refuge, snaked toward her, and blinked.

***

In the ready room of Khanag's corvette, a monitor played scenes of Meriel's agony. He frowned and switched to the holovid of the ceremony where he pinned the captain's bars on his son's collar.

"She won't last much longer," his XO said over comm. "And this will be over. Any change of mission, sir?"

"Negative."

"Pilot, initiate undock sequence."

Unsettled, Khanag paced, sat, and then rose again.

"Exec, my ready room."

"Aye, sir," she said and joined him.

He waved his link near the console and dossier pages scrolled past. "Did you review these?"

Her eyes darted back and forth between Khanag and the files. "Rumors of children turned into addicts and sold into slavery. Organs belonging to missing persons. Complaints from competitors of the Society of Pious Sisters. Yes. Old allegations."

"Your assessment?" he said but raised his hand for silence until an officer with a red collar passed.

"Yes, it's possible," Isolde replied. "A few rare mistakes can be expected in the billions of transactions."

"And the Tsogets?"

"That's new. They challenged the Prophet's descendance from the Imperials. Maybe a zealot recycled them to protect his Eminence. A trivial thing, beneath the concern of such a great man." A hard edge tinged her voice. "Or you."

"I care nothing for his pedigree. I only care for the lost souls he has saved."

She touched his hand. "Like us."

He nodded. "The Hope woman told me our son died with honor."

Isolde's face softened. "She can prove it?"

He scrolled to a new file. "The toxicology report identifies our standard prisoner defense. They wouldn't know to fake that. I confirmed our son's DNA with the Kelton database." He tapped his desk.

```
Identity Nurendra Khanag 8776488.
Captain Soldiers of Providence. DNA
relationship Subedei Khanag and Isolde
Vanor.
```

"I will tell the fleet," Isolde said and laid her hand on his shoulder.

"Not yet."

"Why not?"

"His Eminence told me they were all executed."

She scowled. "He lied?"

Khanag did not respond, and she scanned the records. "We might reconsider the inevitability of those transaction mistakes."

Isolde turned to leave but stopped at the report from the console.

```
"Additional relationship match found
in database. Inquiry?"
```

Isolde spun around. "There's a DNA match to someone else."

"Who?" he asked.

"Confirm inquiry," she said to the console.

When the response appeared in the holo, Khanag jumped to his feet. "Exec, abort the undock. And have the ship's doctor accompany me ashore to the genetics lab."

"Aye, sir."

***

Meriel woke nauseous from the drugs in an empty room and struggled in her bindings. But unlike her prior efforts, the case that trapped her left hand rattled. Her hand moved within the case, but the IV needle running through the case and into her vein still pinned the case to the back of her hand.

This will hurt, but screams are nothing new here. She drew her hand back, and it stung, but she kept on pulling until the needle rotated and tore her skin. The tip struck a bone, and she screamed and yanked. The IV joint snapped, and her hand slipped out.

With her teeth, she tore out the needle and then used her free hand to release the other restraints. She stood, the nausea increased, and the room spun. Dizzy, she stumbled and hit her head on a cabinet as she fell to her knees and threw up.

On her hands and knees, she waited until the spinning stopped, and she rose. First, she broke the surveillance camera mount and then searched the drawers for bandages.

As she wrapped a plastapatch on her wrist, a deathly pale woman with ragged hair startled her. She jumped back, but then recognized her own reflection in a metal tray. She rubbed her cheeks to bring some color back and then tied her hair in a ponytail.

A twinge in her right shoulder brought her gaze to a fresh wound, and she pulled up her sleeve. There she found a small puncture surrounded by a purple bruise. With her injured left hand, she pinched the skin where something hard was buried. Ignoring the pain, she squeezed until a tiny disk popped out: a material tracker. Like the cargo she had wrangled for a decade, they had tagged and tracked her.

She put the tracker in the tray and combed the room for a link. In one drawer, she discovered pre-made syringes of Psychogel-H: Aristopine. Her hands shook. *All this will go away, all my problems. And Sandy . . .*

As she closed the drawer, the door lock clicked, and she slipped behind the door. It opened, and the man in the stained smock stepped through.

"We seem to have a little camera trouble, Ms. Hope," he said as he entered the room but stopped at the empty chair. Before he said more, she slammed the edge of the instrument tray into his neck.

With both hands on his throat, he stumbled backward and slipped on Meriel's vomit. As he fell on his back, his head hit the deck with a crack, and he lay wheezing.

Meriel searched him for weapons, then took his link and a penlight from his breast pocket. Using his thumb, she accessed his link to scan for his prior locations and found four room numbers. None of them were her goal at HB334h.

They moved her.

As she removed his dirty smock, he grabbed her wrist and coughed blood, adding new stains. But she pried his fingers from her wrist, removed the smock and shoes, and put them on.

She could still save him—a quick puncture below the swelling and a straw inserted into his trachea would do it.

No.

Instead, she took his outstretched hand and dragged him to the door. She placed his palm on the ID pad and opened it before his biotag could register his death.

"There's a special hell for people who torture children," she said and shut the door behind her.

Outside on the corridor wall, she found a chart and matched the link's room numbers to their locations.

The roar of grinding gears and conveyors met her in the first room. From one end flowed small bags with red and orange labels. On the way to the other end, machines sorted the bags into refrigerated containers labeled "SPS."

The Society of Pious Sisters. These must be transplant organs.

The next two rooms were empty, but when she neared the fourth room, she spotted the back of an armed Archer talking with two women, and Meriel slowed.

Next to the guard, a beautiful woman with striking violet eyes yelled at the aide with the facial scar. As Meriel approached, the aide's eyes opened wide, but instead of sounding an alarm, she turned away. Meriel strolled by and peered inside the room, but it too was empty.

"She's just a kid," violet eyes said to the aide. "How could she figure it out?"

"I don't know. She—"

The guard slapped the aide in the face and raised his hand to slap her again. But at that moment, a bald patient ran past, slashed the guard's upraised arm with a scalpel, and continued running. The guard grabbed his bleeding arm and yelled into his link as he raced after his attacker. And the woman with violet eyes tugged the aide back the way Meriel had come.

Around the corner, Meriel ducked into a utility room and messaged Blue Dragon.

```
Brian. I'm free. Can't find Sandy.
```

Brian responded by voice. "It's about time. Liz and John are panicky."

"Where are they?"

"They're holding a position near the clinic, waiting for word from you. I'll patch them in. How did you end up so deep into Archer space?"

"No clue," Meriel said. "They put us together but then separated us. Where is she now?"

"Ah . . . she's been moving. She's not far, but you can't get to her from where you are."

"If you know where she is, aim me there."

"It's complex, Meriel. You'd never remember it all. Use the UFM, and we'll come get you."

"Archers took it. If it's complex, guide me or download it to this link."

"Ah, where'd you get the link?" Brian said as if a lit fuse burned its way past him.

"From an Archer who won't need it anymore."

"They can track it, and you need to get rid of it. We know where you are now. I'll send help to your position, and we'll extract you."

"Who?"

"The *Tiger* just docked with Cookie and Socket."

She closed her eyes and hugged herself. "And Nick?"

"He's here too."

Meriel could not speak. *Thank you*, she prayed.

"Meriel?"

"Give me a second, Brian." *They're in danger again, because of me.* "If I leave Archer territory, I'll need to fight my way back in again. But I'm already inside now."

John's voice broke in over the crack of blaster fire. "Come back, M. I can't lose you both."

"We're not losing anyone, John," Meriel said and glanced at the tattoo on her palm. "Brian, can you perform any ID or security magic from there?"

"No, M. It's Archer territory. Wait there. Help is almost to you."

Tapping her foot, she inspected her bloody smock and ill-fitting shoes. But thoughts of shoes were crowded out by all the horrors that might befall a child alone on Etna, how to prevent them, and which were fatal.

Instead of blaster fire or explosions announcing help had arrived, the walls vibrated softly, and a tap came from a locker.

Meriel tapped back. "Hello?"

The hinges glowed red, dripped off, and the door swung open. Inside stood Eddie, and behind him was a hole her size.

"Hi, Eddie," Meriel said, and he tipped his lid in a nod.

With a probe, he gently took the link from Meriel's hand, crushed it, and dropped the pieces on the floor. With another probe, he fused the bits to the deck with a laser.

After inspecting her head to foot with a sensor stalk, he moved to another locker and cut the lock with a torch. Inside were fresh blue coveralls, a tinted visor with a splash guard, and shoes.

She dressed and stepped toward the locker, expecting Eddie to lead her out through the hole. Instead, he handed her a multi-mop backpack and shocked Meriel by opening the door to the corridor. After lowering the splash guard, she followed him through the corridors, ignored by everyone, including security.

Elizabeth was right: Nobody notices a droid. And nobody notices the janitors either.

Down passageways, past bulkheads and blast doors, Eddie led her through laboratories of white-robed technicians, clanking machinery, and conveyors. At the end of a corridor, Eddie stopped at a door with a bio-ID keypad, played with it, and entered.

Inside, uniformed guards searched a room filled with a score of bodies on gurneys. The guards scanned the palm tattoos of the patients, and Meriel closed her fist.

Eddie breezed past them to a far corner of the room and examined it while Meriel feigned a biohazard cleanup with the multi-mop.

When the others left the room, Eddie glided to a stack of boxes and probed the gaps with his sensors. Then he slid away and wiggled his top.

Meriel removed her visor. "Sandy?"

The girl scurried out from her hiding place and jumped into Meriel's arms.

LOX

"You OK, sprite?" Meriel said and hugged her tight.

The girl nodded and smiled, but tears filled her eyes. "You're not."

Meriel's hand shook as she brought her fingers to the cut on her forehead.

"Not your head either, M." She put her palm on Meriel's cheek and gazed into her eyes with a frown.

No tattoos, Meriel thought and kissed Sandy's palms, "I'll be OK. But we need to get out of here."

"How did you find me?"

Meriel tapped on Sandy's sock that hid the necklace and cross.

"It's the tracker, hon," Meriel said as she scouted outside the passage. "They know we've escaped. We gotta move."

"Where to?"

The droid displayed a holo of the station with icons for their location and their rescuers. The clinic where her friends waited was on a different arc of the torus, past blast doors and security checkpoints. And Meriel could not just walk out with Sandy at her side.

"How can we get there without getting caught?"

Eddie displayed a path through Archer controlled territory and a spoke to the core, and a tram that would take them down another spoke. He tipped his top as if asking for approval.

"Ready for another adventure, sprite?" Meriel said to Sandy.

The girl glanced away for a moment and then turned back to Meriel with a timid smile and a nod.

"Let's go."

The droid led them through the station infrastructure, service corridors, and maintenance rooms smelling of stale oil and ozone. Where the path was too narrow to pass, Eddie cut them a wider hole. When there was a gap too wide to jump, he transformed himself into a bridge. At each dead end, he carved a new door. When they passed through a confined space without breathable air, he provided rebreathers. And each time Meriel asked how far, he pointed forward.

Artificial gravity varied on the sides to match the orientation of activities along their path. Alerted to the change, they held onto the walls and rotated to the new orientation, and if not warned, they fell. But as they got closer to the core, their step was lighter, and they could jump farther. Their speed increased until Eddie stopped at a sealed blast door.

"You didn't expect this?" Meriel said, and he moved his top from side to side. "I guess that's a no."

The droid projected a hologram showing their current location on the schematic. On the opposite side of the door was the station core and tram yard.

With a dashed line, he highlighted the path of a tram that followed the transport tube around the circumference of the core and down the adjacent spoke to the emergency clinic where her friends waited. But the door above them was not on the plans.

"What are we gonna do?"

After inspecting the seal and the panel next to it, he removed a pry bar from his body. He jimmied the panel without success and then cut it open with his torch attachment. Once inside the box, he played with the wiring, but the door did not move. After connecting his power probes to various wires, he still could not energize the door.

Meriel leaned against the bulkhead, and Sandy took her hand.

Eddie stopped and studied the door again and used the cutting torch on it. But he made only a deep groove: the door was too thick and dissipated the heat before he could cut all the way through.

If the door was impenetrable, the frame was not, so he jammed the pry bar into a corner between the door and the wall to lever it open. The bar bent, but the door did not budge.

Each time he failed, he pulled out another tool—grinders, drills, hydraulic jacks—and tried again. Then he stopped and stared at the door.

"Do you—" Meriel said, but Eddie lifted a red disk antenna like a stop sign.

"But—" she asked, but he raised the disk again, and she sat.

A few minutes later, the droid lowered himself to the deck beside them.

"Can't figure it out?"

He rotated his lid from side to side.

"Is there another path?" Sandy asked.

He shook his lid again, leaned forward, and stared at the deck.

Meriel patted his shell. "Did they take your eidetic cognition core?"

He tilted his top as a child might who did not understand an instruction.

"Did they take your smarts?"

He tipped his top up and down.

"I think we should backtrack and—"

He turned to the blast door, back to her, and nodded again. On the door, he projected the schematic, but Meriel rose to leave.

With a blunt appendage, Eddie tapped her on the shoulder and pointed to the hologram's dashed line tracing the path to safety, beginning at the tram yard on the opposite side of the core.

"Not unless we get through that door," Meriel said and led Sandy back along their path and rounded a corner into an adjacent passage. There, Eddie stopped her with another tap on her shoulder, raised the red disk, and glided back toward the door.

"What's he doing?" Sandy asked, but Meriel shrugged, unable to observe him around the corner.

A minute later, a distinctive sweet-sour smell reached her, and she peered back into the passageway. There was the droid with his shell open and tubes spraying frost on the door.

Damn! "Hey Eddie, what are you doing?"

He spun his top and extended his limbs to their full length, which Meriel understood as panic. As second later, a door slammed shut to isolate Eddie. A flash blinded her, and she jumped back into the passage, grabbed Sandy, and held her close.

Behind her, the door failed, and a blast of hot gas and shrapnel shot past them, blowing Meriel and Sandy deeper into the side passage.

When the fog and dust cleared, Meriel peeked around the corner. The door was gone. And so was Eddie.

"Did he touch the wrong thing?" Sandy asked.

There were no signs of typical explosives: lingering smoke, cordite smell, or ozone tang. But the bulkheads were damp.

They did not find him as they approached the door. But beside the wreckage of the doorframe, twisted out of shape, was the control panel. Inside it was a q-chip embossed with the letters EDy.

"He did it intentionally," Meriel said. "Eddie's power came from oxygen and hydrogen. His little body had the explosive power of a rocket engine if he released it all at once."

"He blew himself up for us?"

Meriel nodded. "To open the door."

"Shouldn't we say thanks and say some words like Pastor Lee?"

Meriel held up the q-chip and smiled. "He's still with us," she said, put the chip in her pocket, and climbed the ruined ladder into the core.

Their duct paralleled one of the station's spokes. Within them ran bucky-tube cables moored to the central axis, and out to the opposing spoke. Pods and trams traveled through them, turned, and disappeared into other spokes. Around the axis, utility conduits ran to the hemispheres that sealed the core at both ends.

Machinery crowded the core, but no people. Instead of their voices, it echoed with the songs of vibrating cables and the whoosh of trams and pods. But the stale air smelled of age.

Meriel helped Sandy climb out into the core, glad to be in the open, and smiled at the sight of the tram yard that would carry them to safety.

But above them, a passing tram slowed for a turn, and from inside the car, an Archer poked his companion, pointed to them, and raised his link.

"We need to move, sprite," Meriel said.

"Where to?"

Meriel pointed to the other side of the core cylinder, past tram tubes, rushing pods, and conduits. "See those windows? That's a tram yard. We're going to jump for the service entrance beyond it, there."

"I can't jump that far."

"Close your eyes and visualize it. Big push. Tuck and flip, three-point crouch . . ."

"But M, I can't do this. I'm not like you."

"You don't have to be me. Just be you, and you can do this."

The girl gripped Meriel's arm. "Jump with me."

"Too many degrees of freedom, hon, and we'll spin. I'll go first. When I wave, you jump. OK?"

"No," Sandy said and hugged her.

"Remember, courage is doing what you need to do even when you're afraid."

"I'm not afraid!" Sandy said and dropped her gaze. "It's my eye, Merry. I can't tell distances with just one. I can't . . ."

"OK. Here's what I'm going to do, and you follow. The core is about three-hundred feet in diameter. From where we are, the station is rotating counterclockwise. I'm going to aim about forty feet ahead of our target. Got it?"

"Give me something relative."

"The same length as the tram yard window."

Sandy closed her eye and imagined the rotation. She opened it again and nodded.

"Remember, big push," Meriel said. "There's air here, and it'll slow you down. Ready? Just follow my smile." She jumped and half a minute later, flipped, landed, and waited on the opposite side.

After crossing herself, Sandy crouched and jumped. At first, she smiled with the sense of flying. But her trajectory was off. She twisted with body English to change path, which threw off her landing. Instead of a crouch, she caromed off Meriel, belly flopped, and skidded on the hard cylinder wall.

"Forgot to tuck?" Meriel asked with a smile and offered her hand.

"Sorry, Merry."

"You did fine, hon. Just a minor course correction."

Their destination was a short distance away, and they got on their knees. The centripetal acceleration allowed them to stand, but the slow rotation at the core gave them no traction to walk.

"We need something to push against. See those rungs? I'll boost you and you grab one. OK?"

She nodded, and Meriel meshed her fingers together to create a foothold. The girl kicked up and grabbed the rung, and the reaction sent Meriel backward until she found another rung. From it, she pushed off to meet Sandy.

"Is it always this hard?" Sandy said.

Meriel pushed off another rung. "It is if you don't have mag boots, or suction cups or compressed air."

The last rung was on the service entrance of a tram maintenance depot, and inside, normal gravity returned orienting 'up' to the torus axis.

Dim lights came on and followed them along the tubes to the platform. Parked there was a line of five old tram cars, each of which might hold sixty passengers. Three rails ran along the length of each tram and disappeared into the transport tube at the dark end of the yard.

Inside the tram, the floor lights led them to the cab where a wave of Meriel's hand brought up virtual controls.

"Where are we going?" Sandy asked.

"To the docks and our ship," Meriel said as she traced a route with her finger on the schematic. "Eddie showed me."

Meriel touched the icon for their destination, and the cars lifted slightly and lurched backwards: they were in the last car and not the lead car. They left the cab and took a seat, gazing out the window as the tram clattered out of the depot into the dark.

The transport tube guided the tram around the core and into a spoke of the torus, rotating the cars with the bank of the rails to maintain 'down' with the centripetal acceleration.

The wheels squeaked and squealed along the curve, and Sandy leaned into Meriel, but the car held together.

"I'm hungry," Sandy said. "Can we stop for something to eat?"

"Not yet, hon. We'll meet our friends soon. Then we can eat."

The windows flickered as advertising came alive on the windows, and Meriel relaxed, but Sandy remained tense and stared at nothing. Then she turned Meriel's hand over to expose the tattoo.

"I saw things, M."

"Tell me," Meriel said and held her tight as Sandy spoke of the victims on the gurneys.

"They all had marks like yours, M. Why?"

"Some evil people put them there."

"Our teacher told us there are no evil people, only the sick or misguided."

"Your teacher is being charitable," Meriel said. She had her own history with these butchers, and misguided could not explain their actions. "I'm sorry you had to see that."

"One of them gave me this." The girl held out the tiny biotag the man on the gurney had given her in trade for the scalpel.

Meriel took the biotag and followed Sandy's arm until her eyes reached the child's sweet face. *She's here because of me. Because she loves me.* Meriel's eyes narrowed. *And because of a lot of evil bastards.*

"This will help, hon. If he's a missing person, they might know he's here."

On the windows, holovids advertised android escort services, casinos, exciting memory implants, wireheading, and drugs illegal on any other station.

"They can do that?" Sandy said, staring wide eyed at an ad for physical reconstruction into animals. The vid showed before and after stills of people whose faces had been converted into cats and dogs.

"Can doesn't mean should," Meriel said and turned Sandy's head away.

At the turn from the spoke into the torus, the tram reached a residential neighborhood and slowed for a station.

"Come, hon," Meriel said and stood.

"Is this our stop?"

"Not yet, but we need to be ready."

The doors opened, and people crowded past, each with bundles and suitcases.

A woman pushed them aside as she elbowed her way aboard. "Oh my God, I thought a tram would never come!" she complained to her companion as the tram filled with people.

"What happened here?" Meriel asked.

"They vac'd the apartments to extinguish the fires, and there's not much left," the woman said, her finger twitching from Rejuve.

The doors closed, and the tram jerked into motion.

"Where is this going?" the woman asked.

"The emergency clinic docks and immigration," Meriel replied.

"That's the wrong way, dear. The refugee ships are on the other side of the station."

"I can't reprogram it." Meriel said and wondered if the *Amelia* could hold a tram full of people.

The tram made another stop, and more people crowded on. But Archers boarded the tram two cars forward, and Meriel froze. One glanced in her direction, checked his wrist, and marched toward them.

"We're getting off," Meriel said and grabbed Sandy's hand. With the girl close behind, Meriel elbowed her way to the doors, but the doors shut before they reached them.

Flashes lit the car, and the tram shook and creaked.

Sandy smiled. "Fireworks!"

After another silent flash, the vibration bucked the tram and threw the passengers off their feet. A hundred yards past the front car, a tear opened in the hull and people flew into space through the breach followed by hydroponics factories. The tear did not stop and ripped along the bucky-sheet seams and down the spoke toward them.

Breach

Slugs whistled over the makeshift barrier near the emergency clinic where Elizabeth, Socket, and a squad of Tech Security maintained suppression fire. Behind them, John sat with a splint that tied his thigh to his prosthetic lower leg and surveilled the Archer barricade forty yards away.

Next to John, Cookie pinged Brian on his wrist-link. A holovid appeared of Brian in front of a series of displays with Tech Masters dressed in green and silver.

One Tech waved his hands. "The Archer uprising has trapped thousands in B deck. We need to focus on getting them out."

"They need an intact hull first," Brian said. "That should be our priority."

A pulse rifle popped, and Brian ducked as his camera panned to steel shutters closing off the hold from the corridor.

"You can't sacrifice the people to save a pile of bucky-sheets," someone said off screen. "Green-zone sectors three and eighteen are already at vacuum."

"The station is the people's best shelter," Brian replied as the whomp of an explosion came from the corridor outside. "And I won't sacrifice their protection."

"We don't have time for arguments, Brian. The Archers are right outside your door."

"No one gets through those doors," Mrs. Chen said from out of Cookie's view.

"The Archers killed the Station Master, Brian," said another. "We don't have a coordinated response."

Brian closed his eyes. "Then *we're* the response. Evacuate black-zone sectors five and six. Those are on opposite sides of the station. Warn people to get to safety and we'll depressurize it. That will save the civilians."

"But—"

"Do it or resign," Brian said and returned to his link. "Cookie? Status."

"They have us pinned down near the clinic," Cookie said. "They're using frag grenades and incendiaries. Are they legal?"

"In black-zone, legal is what the Archers say it is. Try again. You only have a hundred feet to the clinic. Meriel's tram will stop in blue-zone just in-station from customs. So, make sure you're on the blue side of the blast doors."

Cookie checked the section designators. "Yup. Why?"

"We're gonna vac black-zone next door."

"Finally," Elizabeth said. "Ahh . . . where's Meriel?"

"On the way," Brian said. "We've still got a blip from the tracker Meriel gave to Sandy."

John piloted the drone beyond the opposing barricade and frowned at an image of Archers carrying long crates.

"Where in hell did they get those?" Cookie said.

"What?" John said.

"Old school. RPGs. Those can pierce the torus."

"Maybe that's what they want," Elizabeth said as the drone took a fatal hit and crashed between the barricades.

Cookie shook his head. "They're not suicidal." He scanned the docks. A blast door separated the two barricades between blue-zone and black-zone. "Damn, they want to space *our* side."

Through the barricade, Cookie spotted an Archer unpacking grenades from the crate and another loading a launcher. "Suzy, see that guy preparing to launch? Can you make the shot?"

Socket eyeballed her target and nodded. Narrowing the choke on her pulse rifle, she dialed in the range.

"Clock is ticking, dear," Cookie said.

Her shot punched the Archer back into the crate of grenades, and his live grenade exploded, detonating the other grenades and showering them with debris.

The explosion ripped the hull open like paper, and the Archers and their barricade disappeared through the breach.

And Cookie and his team would soon follow.

***

A second explosion shattered the transport tube carrying Meriel and Sandy's tram. Safety interlocks engaged the emergency brakes, which knocked the passengers down and Sandy and Meriel against the window. With the tube broken, the front cars whipped like a serpent's tail and banged against the broken tube as the helpless passengers clattered within.

Two lead cars were thrown free. One hit the spoke and cracked open, ejecting passengers like peas from a pod. Another car with the Archers flew through the tear and tumbled into space. The inter-car door closed to maintain pressure but bowed outward.

"Out, everyone. Out!" Meriel shouted and shoved Sandy ahead of her.

At the station door, Meriel helped others pry the door open and held it as the passengers from the last two cars rushed to safety, the first of which being Sandy.

Pressure integrity failed in the adjoining car, the inter-car door slammed shut, and the stragglers joined the debris that now orbited the station. Meriel's ears popped as the door buckled outward, and air whistled through it: the car could not save them if that last door failed.

The tube lurched again, and the car shook.

A passenger brought a breaker bar from the station to jam the door and relieve her. After the last survivor exited the car, the inter-car door tore free and the station door slammed shut, flinging the bar through the car window.

"Where are you going?" Meriel called as she and Sandy followed the crowd hurrying out of the station into a passageway. But before anyone answered, Etna shimmied, and the station ceiling collapsed.

***

The blast doors rammed closed to protect Cookie's team, but debris blocked the seal and air screeched through the cracks. The dropping pressure caused the door behind them to slam shut, trapping them in an area that would be at vacuum within a minute.

Cookie opened the emergency cabinet, grabbed the sealant hose, and sprayed it into the gap. But the crack was too big and sucked the expanding foam through before it could harden. He threw debris to fill the leaks, and his team copied him. The next time he sprayed the goop like a fire hose, the foam hardened, the seals held, and the screeching stopped.

"How long will it hold?" John asked.

A pop and whistle of a leaking seal told them not long.

Cookie tapped his wrist. "Brian, tell Meriel not to come here. And find us a place to redeploy. In a hurry."

"Sergeant," Socket said and pointed to an armed drone crawling along the seam of the breach.

"Down!" he called, but not before the flechette pierced her leg armor and sliced through her femoral artery.

Ghost

When the dust cleared, Meriel and Sandy inspected each of the exits and found them filled with debris. Over shattered plastaglass, Meriel led them through the window to the control panel. It did not respond, and Sandy showed her the broken cables.

With the tram gone, there was no safe path to the emergency docks. There were thousands of miles of passages and ducts, and without a schematic, they would starve before reaching safety.

Her hand shook again, and she tightened it into a fist.

"What are we gonna do, M?"

"I've never solved a problem by quitting. Come on."

At the end of the broken cables was an access hatch blocked by rubble. Together, they moved debris and wrestled with bucky-tube reinforcing to expose a panel controlling a dogged and locked access hatch. A green light on the panel showed it was live, but it did not respond, and Meriel stared at it.

"What are you thinking, Merry?"

"I'm thinking they can't get too us. You have the tracker, so they know where you are, but they don't know how to help us."

Meriel pried open the cover of the panel to expose two simple power leads to a board.

"Give me your necklace hon," Meriel said, took it and used it to short the power leads. Each time she touched the wires, the power light blinked off and on.

Meriel frowned and closed her eyes. "Ok, what was the UFM signal? Code-V, code-V. Three dots and a dash."

She shorted the power leads in the code sequence and the light blinked. A second later, she tried again and repeated the sequence for another minute.

Nothing.

Sandy took Meriel's hand. "What do we do now?"

"We find another way," Meriel said and turned back to the station.

A click sounded behind her.

"M, what's this?" Sandy said.

Meriel returned to the control panel and gasped. There, a blinking arrow appeared, like those once used to guide her through the simulators.

"What is it?" Sandy asked as she returned the necklace and cross to her neck.

Meriel grinned. "My friend."

The hatch led Meriel and Sandy from panel to panel to an electronics service cabinet that opened to black-zone. They were out of the maze of infrastructure but not safe yet.

Past shuttered shops and sealed blast doors, they followed the empty corridor until shots rang out and they ducked into the ruined doorway of a looted pharmacy.

"Look for a link or a means to communicate," Meriel said.

As they searched the store, the blaster fire got louder, and the ozone smell grew stronger. When laser beams flashed past the end of the passage, they slipped out the back into a service alley where a fallen Archer lay.

Meriel relieved him of his link and stunner and with Sandy, hurried into a café. Through the broken window, she checked for sentries and the source of the fire.

After a sentry passed, she glanced around the corner. Twenty yards away, Archers defended a makeshift roadblock. Another twenty yards farther, shielded by buildings and burned-out vehicles, Cookie fought alongside a squad of Chen's people. But Meriel and Sandy would not survive a run past the Archers and no-man's-land to meet them.

"We need to revise our plan again," Meriel said and tapped a code into the link.

"About time," Nick said. "What took you so long?"

She smiled but could not speak and bit her lip.

"M? We're not encrypted."

"Is that your friend?" Sandy asked.

Meriel nodded. "It's good to hear your voice, Nick."

"You too, M. Now to—"

"You got us here," Meriel said. "But I don't see the infirmary."

"It doesn't exist anymore, and we've had to move our rendezvous. Cookie redeployed and should be near your position."

She held up the link's camera to show him the barricade. "The Archers are holding them back, and we can't get to them."

When boots on debris announced the sentry's return, Meriel cut the audio and tucked herself and Sandy under a table. The footsteps passed, and she stood, scanned outside the window, and switched on the sound again.

"Nick, we can't wait. They're blocking us on both sides, so we can't get out through the docks. We need to get back into the station."

"Wait there. Cookie will circle around to get you. Say, Elizabeth is fuming that you ditched them at the blast door. That was stupid."

Out of sight from the door, Meriel paced over shattered plastaglass that crackled under her feet. "It saved her life," she said, avoiding mention of her deal with Kostanza. "Nick, I heard about the med school explosion on LeHavre. That's where Penny works."

"Aunt Penny?" Sandy said.

"Yes, hon. Nick, did you hear any more?"

"We just got a news update. Archer agents tried to incinerate the morgue."

"Is Penny OK?"

"Cops reported she got trapped with Sam. But they're both fine, M. Being rescued now."

"Thank God," Meriel said and peeked around the doorway.

"IGB says the entire research section was hanging like a balloon on a string."

"Did they say anything about the corsairs in the morgue?"

"No."

"So why try to incinerate them?"

"Maybe there's a connection we haven't made yet."

The sentry neared, and Meriel and Sandy ducked under the table again.

"Nick, this is important," Meriel whispered. "Tell Teddy and the Vingels the corsair captain who suicided on the *Tiger* was Khanag's son."

"No kidding?"

"Nope. He admitted it. And we already have vids of the two of them with the Archtrope. That implicates the Archtrope. We're one step closer to nailing him. The bodies are much more important now. Ask Jerri to get the news to Jeremy and Penny as soon as they can."

Sandy frowned. "M, if you have vids, why do the bodies matter."

"Source DNA," Nick said. "And data in a file are no substitute for the body. Did anyone try to match their DNA? Criminal records? Relatives?"

"That's what Penny was working on." From her pocket, she retrieved the q-chip holding the dossier and tapped it on the link to copy it. "DNA match, corsairs to all databases."

"That'll take forever," Nick said.

```
"Insufficient resources to fulfill
request."
```

"Your link isn't smart enough, M," Sandy said.

"And there's not enough compute power nearby for it to steal," Nick added.

"Brian mentioned a DNA database run by Kelton something. Can you find out where that is?"

"Kelton Bioinformics. It's close. Just through the convention—"

An explosion outside brought Meriel's gaze to the window. When the smoke cleared, Cookie returned fire from the rubble of a shop.

"What was that, M?"

"A failed rescue." She took Sandy's hands and faced her. "I'm gonna do things that may upset you."

"Like?"

"Ah, violent things."

Sandy raised an eyebrow with a lopsided smile. "I saw what you did at the farm, Merry L. I know you can do that stuff."

"OK, then. Let's go," she said, but boots scuffed nearby. Pulling the stunner from her belt, she crawled to the door, and stood.

The Archer entered the café and Meriel fired. But the armor mitigated the stun, and the Archer groaned. She went to him and lifted the visor to find the Archer was a woman, which made no difference to Meriel's stunner, and the Archer fell.

Taking the Archer's belt with a blaster and a grenade, Meriel slung it over her shoulder and crawled back to Sandy.

"We need to go, hon." As soon as she stood, another Archer appeared outside the window and raised his weapon.

Meriel fired first, and he froze in mid-step. When he collapsed, more Archers from the barricade turned to her, and one aimed an RPG at the café.

"Cover your ears!" Meriel shouted and ducked to shield Sandy, but the explosion knocked her off her feet and onto the deck.

The ringing in Meriel's ears muffled Sandy's shouts. Suppressing the dizziness, she rose, found the link under the debris, took Sandy's hand, and ran to the back of the café.

"We're leaving, Nick," she said into the link. "I can't hear anything, so I'm giving the link to Sandy. Tell her where to go."

Sandy took the link, listened, and nodded. Then she dropped the link and tugged on Meriel's hand.

But Meriel picked up the link again. "We need it for a while longer," she said and followed Sandy.

With the explosion still ringing in her ears, Meriel followed Sandy through an office to an IT room with a thick bulkhead door. A biotag reader blinked yellow on the doorframe, and from it glowed a holo of a keypad. In the middle of the door, a snowflake glittered inside a yellow triangle. Below that in stenciled text read:

```
Kelton Bioinformics.
Restricted access. Hazard warning.
Please see Dean J. Yutousov
```

Sandy stopped and struggled with the hand wheel, but it did not budge. After Meriel failed to open it, she took Sandy's hand to drag her away.

"They're coming for us," Meriel said, but though Sandy's mouth moved, Meriel could only make out 'Nick.' She shrugged and shattered the biotag reader with her blaster, and the hand wheel spun free. Together they entered a dark hall and closed the thick door behind them.

As Meriel jammed the wheel with the blaster, steam condensed from her breath, and she shivered at the sudden chill

She turned to floor lights, and a hall filled with a matrix of plastaglass cubes that extended from floor to ceiling. Within each, quantum computers lit up as Meriel's link stole the power needed to complete her DNA search request. And around each computer, cryogenic coolant boiled, and the floor rumbled.

Sandy smiled as the pools bubbled like champagne and said something drowned out by the ringing in Meriel's ears. But before Sandy touched the plastaglass, Meriel pulled her hand away.

"Don't touch anything," Meriel said, her breath frosting the walls. "It's cold as space in there and your hands will stick."

Eighty feet away at the far corner of the hall, moisture that escaped the dehumidifiers had frozen the hand wheel on the exit door. As Meriel kicked the wheel, her hearing returned.

"I'm cold, M."

"Tuck your arms in," Meriel said. *That won't be enough. We gotta leave or we'll freeze to death.* She glanced back, but a banging from the entry door told her there was no retreat.

On the wall, she spotted a fire alarm, but before she pulled it, the link flashed and announced the results from the quantum computers.

```
"Priority search complete. Four DNA
matches found for Tiger Corsair-8, Le-
Havre Station Medical School Laborato-
ry."
```

Meriel stopped. "Corsair-8. That's the captain."

"Merry?"

"Just a second, hon," Meriel said and lifted the link. "Match with whom?"

```
"Isaak Tsoget, Seiyei Station.
Marge Ito-Tsoget, Seiyei Station.
Isolde Va—"
```

"Pause. So, the corsair captain is related to the Tsogets, that means . . . Damn! Nick, are you there? I know why the Archtrope tried to destroy the corsair bodies. This will blow the lid off his operation. We've got to tell Khanag."

"M?" Nick said. "What are you still doing with that link? Drop it and find Medusa's. I told Sandy how to get there."

"On our way," she said and ground the link under her heel.

When she pulled the fire alarm, the computers tripped off, and the room filled with a fire-retardant fog and the red glow of emergency lighting. With the room warmed, her next kicks freed the wheel.

"Come on, Merry," Sandy said as she pushed the door open, but the banging on the entry door became louder.

"We need to lose our tail, hon. Hold the door open for me."

Taking the grenade from the belt over her shoulder, Meriel spat on it repeatedly and pressed it against the frigid plastaglass where it froze instantly. After checking that Sandy held the door open, she set the timer for ten seconds.

A crash came from the corner of the hall and a shout, "Stop where you are!" But the fog hid her and scattered their lasers.

The echoes of running boots and vortex rings of pulse rifles followed Meriel as she ran out the exit door. Once outside, she slammed the door shut, grabbed Sandy's hand, and ran.

At the whomp of the detonating grenade, Meriel turned as a freezing mist seeped under the warped doorframe and frost spread around it in a growing circle.

No one will follow through that.

"Where to?" Meriel asked.

Sandy pointed ahead to fallen gates of chipped gold and a worn staircase that long ago might have been white. Smoke crawled out of the dark, onto the ceiling above them and over the gates like the entrance to hell.

"We're heading into that?" Meriel asked.

Sandy nodded, took Meriel's hand, and led her forward below a decrepit marquee that blinked *King Xerces Palace.*

Chapter 21
Echoes ET 2142

Etna Station, On Station ET 2142

The gleaming gold gates and pristine marble steps of King Xerces Palace stood within walking distance, but the limo-pod would not let them exit. Within, Marge Tsoget sighed and returned her attention to a holo of a book projected from her link.

"Did you read this line, dear?" she asked her husband. "'When our gods go to war, it is we mortals who suffer.'"

Isaak drummed his fingers on his knee. "de Merlner? I skimmed it, dear."

She tapped her link again, and the text vanished. "Which war do you think he was talking about?"

"All of them," he said as a holo appeared with scenes of Etna's luxury hotels and white-zone parks.

> "Welcome to Etna, the newest of the York class stations. Why deal with low-g asteroids, high-g planets, and the uncertainty of domes when you can choose a station with a comfortable and reliable gravity and atmosphere."

The holo split into scenes of bulky grav-suits and overcrowded domed arcologies.

> "Join us here on Etna, where opportunities abound for all. Etna Station

```
is the entertainment destination of
the Ciberitus Sector with the latest
in amusements for families."
```

Vids of schools with attractive children appeared followed by families at play at a white-zone beach.

```
"Just say 'yes!' to a wonderful new
chapter in your life."
```

The kiosk had targeted the vids for them, but when Isaak smiled for the first time since they left Seiyei Station, she did not care. She leaned into him and dreamed of the future: guaranteed citizenship, a safe place to raise their children, and tenured chairs where they were free to conduct research at the limits of their imagination. She smiled. And Etna allowed the rarest of opportunities: a fourth child. Even without the luxurious white-zone apartment, the offer was so compelling they left their positions on Seiyei without notice.

But making the dream come true still required a successful interview with Dean Yutousov.

With a tap on her bracelet came a projection of two boys jumping on the couch in their suite.

"Sansin, pick up the link," she said.

The largest boy tapped his forehead, and the image switched to soldiers in hard-suits fighting outside a spaceship. "What Mom."

"Just thinking about you. How's it going?"

"Ulie is being a butt, and Timojen won't stop crying."

"Show me," she said, and the scene changed to a toddler scampering across the room. "What's he chewing on?"

"I don't know, but he screams when we try to take it from him."

With a wave of her fingers, the security camera zoomed in on the toddler with a silver elephant charm in his mouth.

She glanced at the bracelet on her wrist and smiled at the gap where the charm had once hung.

"Are you safe?" Isaak said.

The image swapped back to the space battle. "Sure, Pop. Say, we wanna get—"

"We'll be home in just a few hours."

Sansin stopped. "With your new jobs?"

"Yup. We'll take a tour of the station then. But first we need to close the deal. Order whatever you want from room service. And order up some swimsuits. White zone has a beach."

Ulie tapped out of the game and came to Sansin. "Really?"

"Will do," Sansin said, "But hurry." The image flashed on the space Marine game momentarily and blinked off.

Isaak gazed out the window as the limo inched through the white-zone agricultural deck. But his smile drifted into a frown as if the expansive gardens had no effect on him.

"I should've stopped us from taking that research fellowship," Isaak said. "I never guessed genetic anthropology was such a political quagmire. This is our last chance before—"

"Don't say that, darling. You're resourceful and brilliant. It's just that your research is . . . controversial. The Archtrope is influential on Calliope." She patted his arm. "But out here they're free and respect your scientific rigor. Did they describe your new project?"

"No. The dean implied he would announce it after the party."

"Whatever it is, the stipend and salary are phenomenal."

"It's for both of us, Marge. Just think. We'll be able to send the boys to university on Sirius."

The limo stopped under the marquee for Xerces Palace, the sparkling white-zone convention center. At the top of the stairs, a costumed concubine met them, scanned their biotags, and led them through a gate of golden filigree.

Inside, Marge's attention flowed up beyond the top of a double column of broad-leafed catalpas to the wide expanse of the white-zone arboretum. Above them, the agricultural deck glowed green through the plastaglass roof on the opposing arc of the station's torus. Beyond, a single hazy star glittered in the empty blackness of the Etna 320 System. The view enchanted Marge, so new and shiny compared to Seiyei Station's pragmatic gray.

Past a small stage where three women in blousy silks sat cross-legged on cushions, playing pan flutes and tabla, their guide stopped and knelt.

A beautiful woman with violet eyes approached, and Marge caught Isaak focusing on the leg that escaped the floor-length gown split to the hip. Only after Marge's elbow met his ribs did he look up.

"Mr. and Mrs. Tsoget," the woman said with a stunning smile. "My name is Ms. Blanchette. Dean Yutousov asked me to greet you and invite you to a private discussion before you get lost among your guests. Are you ready now?"

"Of course," Isaak said.

Blanchette led them between the catalpas into a suite with a view of the white-zone park, stopped, and touched the wall.

A door slid away. Inside, a man wearing a tailored dinner jacket stood beside a clear desktop where a small lamp hovered. On the desk in front of two chairs lay buttons that might be lapel pins.

Around the room on the active walls, vids of attractive researchers using intricate equipment alternated with stills of a quantum computer facility and breathtaking views of the campus of Etna University.

"Mr. and Mrs. Tsoget," Blanchette said, "let me introduce you to Dean Julian Yutousov."

"Julian, please," the dean said and reached out his hand. "No need for formality among friends. I hope your reception is to your liking?"

Isaak shook the offered hand. "It's marvelous" he said and ran a finger under his collar.

"Sit please. Wine? Etna produces an excellent Merlot."

They shook their heads.

"Water perhaps?"

The Tsogets nodded, and from a crystal pitcher on the bar, Blanchette poured two glasses of ice water, added a slice of lemon and sprig of mint, and set them in front of the couple. With a nod to Yutousov, she left and closed the door behind her.

"Isaak, and Marge, thank you for coming so far to join us. You're about to embark on a grand journey here at the Genomics Research Center. We have the largest genetics database and computing facility outside Sol system, everything you will need to continue your genographics research."

Marge smiled and took Isaak's hand. This was the culmination of their dreams, of their years of study and research.

"Your stipend and budgets are quite generous, but we think suitable for how much we respect your work."

Marge blushed.

Yutousov took the pin in front of Isaak and tapped it on the desk. "But first, bring me up to speed on your latest research."

"You've read my recent article?" Isaak said.

"Of course, but walk me through it."

Isaak leaned forward in the chair and tapped his wristband to engage his link with the local compute resources. "It began as an academic question into how much we could deduce from the mitochondrial DNA signature within a population."

With a few motions, a 3-D graph appeared on the active wall, crowded with lines of different colors, each highlighting a genome sequence. He zoomed into an area to highlight just three.

"It was simply an experiment to establish baselines and topology thresholds for bloodlines. Here you can see—"

As Isaak spoke, the dean zoomed to a footnote.

"And this note regarding the Archtrope?" Yutousov said. Next to the paper, a vid appeared of a large, fit man in the white robes of a priest, his dark hair in a top knot.

Marge's eyes darted between her husband and their host.

"Well, one of our base samples was from Genghis Khan," Isaak continued. "An anomaly in the data set found less of the Khan's DNA in our sample from the Archtrope than the background population. It's so sparse he might have been raised on Sirius, rather than Earth." His eyes widened. "You can imagine our surprise at—"

Yutousov spun the pin. "Interesting. Where did the genetic material come from?"

"Birth records," Isaak said. "The Archers sainted his mother, and it became part of the library at her shrine."

The pin slowed its spin and stopped, and Marge's heart jumped at the etched symbol of a four-leafed poppy. She glanced at Yutousov's expressionless face and back on the desk where a similar pin lay in front of her.

"The DNA could miss the paternal genome," the dean said.

Isaak smiled with an excited glint in his eyes. "No. We took the sample from the footprint on the birth record."

"Ingenious," Yutousov said. "In essence, your research proves His Eminence is *not* descended from the Great Khan and the Imperials."

"Well, that's one way to interpret it, but it's an academic study, and only an example of the methodology."

Yutousov nodded but waved a hand. "I'm sure, Isaak, but before we proceed with your appointment, you must disavow your conclusions. It's quite a bit too controversial, even for us here at the institute."

"It's a method, not a—"

"Someone might use your method to reproduce your results," the dean said.

"The validity is—"

"That's not the point. Surely, you didn't think His Eminence would let this go. His descendance from the great prophets and warlords is a pillar of his moral authority."

Isaak stared at his hands, and Yutousov lost his charm.

"I believe you've had this discussion before, yes?"

Isaak nodded. "Many times. Using the ... His Eminence's genetic material was a prank by my graduate students."

"But you submitted the paper."

"I had to, or they would have cut my research grant."

"Well, Isaak. Your work is truly brilliant, and we want your formidable talents here with us. Unfortunately, for a family man, controversy can be worse than failure. But you can easily remedy this. You only need to disavow the inferences of your research."

"That was the best work of my life," Isaak said. "The best years of our lives—"

Marge turned to Yutousov. "Wait. This is an academic issue. The invitation assured us our tenured positions were confirmed."

"My request is straightforward," Yutousov said as he examined his fingernails. Behind him, the Tsogets' children appeared on the active wall surrounded by strange men in black uniforms.

"You can't," Marge said and waved, but the children did not react.

"Of course we can. And if you comply, we'll put your income in escrow, guaranteed."

Marge gazed at her husband as the elation and confidence drained from his face, and his eyes jumped from object to object.

"We have only a minute for your decision."

She squeezed her husband's hand and nodded.

"As soon as you sign, Ms. Blanchette will escort you to your reception to begin a wonderful evening and a lucrative new career."

Marge cringed at the frightened expressions on her children's faces, but Yutousov remained passionless.

"I assure you that you will return to your children tonight."

Isaak nodded, and an affidavit appeared stipulating the DNA sample came from a lab assistant and not the cult leader.

Isaak's shoulders slumped as he scrolled it. "This will end our careers"

"But you have a home with us here, now," Yutousov replied.

Marge had stopped listening, and her hand went to her mouth. Without drawing attention, she took Isaak's hand and pointed to the medical consent and directives attached to the affidavit that surrendered any rights to their children and their own bodies.

Isaak stood up straight, and when the dean glanced away, Isaak grabbed the lamp and struck him on the side of the head, knocking him off his chair. Marge jumped to her feet and Isaak rushed her to the door. But Blanchette appeared in the portal flanked by two burly men.

Before they could react, Blanchette touched Marge and Isaak on the neck. They twitched for a moment before stiffening, their shock and panic left with no means of expression except their darting eyes. As they fell, the guards caught them and returned them to their chairs.

Yutousov stood and pressed a handkerchief to the gash on his temple. "Your lack of cooperation is unfortunate, and changes nothing."

Blanchette took Isaak's hand and with it made his mark in the signature block. Marge groaned when Blanchette took her hand.

"Don't struggle, now," Yutousov said. "The catatonic affects the large muscle groups and is only painful if you resist. I'm sorry I misled you, but you must stay with us for a while. The addiction is rapid and the withdrawal agonizing. You understand, this is just business."

Marge's eyes went to the display where the black uniforms hustled her children from the room, and she grimaced but could not scream.

"Don't worry. They will live. The Archtrope needs brilliant young men, as I am sure your boys will grow to be." He sat on the edge of the desk and Blanchette tended his wound. "Now, back to business. The Archtrope of Calliope invites you to accept his teachings and submit to his mercy." Julian checked his cuticles. "His Archers are humanitarians and respect the lives of all those who labor for the greater good." His hand covered a yawn. "Join the true believers in rebuilding humanity. If you submit, your places in his kingdom and in paradise are assured. Marge, Isaak, blink if you agree."

Leaning over, Blanchette checked their eyes. "The paralytic has taken over."

"Silence is consent," Yutousov said, shook his head and turned to Blanchette. "Seems the archivists were sloppy and left some genetic material on the birth records. We need to remove it so Isaak's results can't be duplicated."

She nodded. "I'll book transport to Seiyei."

Yutousov swapped the display to a list of names. "And we'll need a more tractable genius to develop the DNA cloaking to expand our organ business."

Blanchette scrolled through the list. "The next candidate is a Professor Kelton from Lockyear. He's more of a chemist than a big data whiz."

"Arrange an interview. Meanwhile, let's try to salvage another use for our guests and recoup their transportation costs." The holo beeped, and he scrolled through the data with a wave of his fingers. "Ah, here we are. I don't think we can wait on this. Calliope is short on kidneys and pituitaries with her tissue match. Bon Voyage, Marge," he said and waved without glancing toward her. "It was good to meet you."

Paralyzed by the catatonic that protected her organs, Marge's gaze jumped between the medics who carried her to a gurney and wheeled her down a service corridor. Her heart raced as the instrument arms of the surgical robot cut open her abdomen, and delirium swept her into the arms of a feeding mantis. When the robot arms came away with her bloody kidney, her eyes widened, and her mouth locked in a scream without voice.

Chapter 22
Etna 320 System, ET 2188

Etna Station Proximity, ET 2188

Four decades later, and a hundred-thousand miles from Etna station, General Khanag studied Meriel's dossier and a holovid of Marge Tsoget taken at her graduation on Seiyei Station, years before he was born. And in his hand, he held his necklace with the elephant charm and Archer poppy.

On another monitor, Khanag observed his XO interrogate Julian Yutousov. He struggled no longer and stopped threatening the Archtrope's retaliation, resigned by drugs and pain to his plight.

"I was under orders," Yutousov croaked from his ruined mouth.

"I understand you had discretion in how you execute those orders," the XO said.

"It was forty-six years ago, Isolde. Surely time has—"

"To summarize," Isolde said, "His Eminence contracted you to engage the Tsogets' genius at recoding the genetic markers to make it impossible to track transplant organs. But your enticements were insufficient, and the Tsogets proved . . . uncooperative. You recycled them. Is that it?"

With his chin on his chest, Yutousov nodded meekly, and the XO faced the camera.

"Your verdict, sir?"

"Begin the contest," Khanag said and turned away as his crew cheered.

He toggled the comm and returned his attention to the Tsoget vid. At the cuff of Marge's sleeve, a bracelet adorned her wrist, and from it hung an elephant charm. He opened his hand to examine the identical charm on his necklace.

He did not want to believe Hope's evidence of corruption or the implication his fleet protected the Archtrope's illicit enterprises. Even the DNA records and the coroner's reports could have been faked.

He doubted Hope's dossier until the vid of Marge Tsoget and the elephant charm.

The charm was with him before the drugs, before the labor camps, before the dealers named him Mouse, and before his many overdose deaths and resurrections by the EMTs. He kept it even after his savior, the Archtrope, gave him purpose. The charm was a ghost haunting him: it *was* "him" rather than what he *believed*.

And now it lay in his palm alongside the poppy charm given to him by the Archtrope himself.

"They're ready, sir," Isolde said as she joined him.

"Such a small thing to make a mockery of my life,"

She turned off the vid. "The DNA test was a match?"

He nodded.

"And you trust the source?"

"It's a third-party database." He slammed his fist on the arm of his chair, adrift in the world he had helped to create.

"Timojen is a worthy name."

"I don't know myself by that name," Khanag said, and removed the poppy charm from the necklace. "His Emin . . . our leader said my parents sold me for drugs."

She put a hand on his shoulder. "If he did that to you, he likely did that to more of us."

He tapped the poppy charm on his desk and frowned. "Ms. Hope has f'd up my life again."

"Our lives," Isolde said, returned the elephant charm to his necklace, and clasped it behind his neck. "If the Hopes are not the drug smuggling terrorists he said, then our son died for nothing."

Khanag could forgive everything but that. He loved the Archtrope for saving his life and for giving him a mission larger than himself. He could forgive the deaths by his hands and accept the stains on his soul for the pain he caused. Everything. Even lying about it. But he would not forgive the lie that led to the death of his son.

"Perhaps he died to open our eyes," he said.

"This changes everything."

"Are you with me?"

"Forever."

From his desk, he took the precious golden box the Archtrope had given him and put the poppy charm in it. After tossing it into the recycler with the fabricated evidence against the Hope family, he swapped the display to a view outside the ship.

There Yutousov and Blanchette struggled in their warmsuits against the chain tethering them to an escape pod.

He tapped his console. "Ms. Blanchette. Mr. Yutousov. Pay attention."

They waved their arms and pleaded, but Khanag had cut their audio feeds.

"Your situation is perilous. Each of you has air for an hour. The ePod has an oxy-regen that can support you for another three hours, which might allow a rescue. However, the pod will not open for two hours. You can wait and savor your last moments with each other. Or you might offer your tank to your partner and extend their life."

The ePod could not save them. With the chaos on Etna, no one would respond to the EM screamer. What was left inside would be ugly if anyone ever found the pod.

Through the PA, his crew called out bets, the odds now three-to-two, for Blanchette to steal her partner's tank and let him die.

"How you spend the rest of your lives is up to you now."

A moment later, the crew cheered as Blanchette locked her legs around Yutousov, trying to crack his helmet with a wrench.

"Round up the Archtrope's priests onboard and have them join Yutousov," Khanag said.

"Aye sir," the XO said. "Course?"

He switched his console to monitor Meriel's interrogation room on Etna Station, but only white noise appeared along with a blinking "Status: Missing."

He smirked. "We have an appointment with Ms. Hope."

The XO raised a brow. "And you know where she is now?"

"I know where she *will* be. Threaten her friends, and she'll come to us."

"And then?"

"If she's the terrorist we are led to believe, she cannot control her passions, and she should die like the insects under our heels."

Etna Station—On Station

Sandy's nose wrinkled at the tart smell of ozone and burning organics as she led Meriel through a smoky hall tinted red by emergency lights. Under their feet, shattered plastaglass crunched over blast scars that marred the floors. Limbs from a massive tree littered the deck and under them lay bodies. And past them, a double row of fallen trees led to a way out.

"Which way now?" Meriel asked.

Sandy closed her eyes. "After the IT room, he said to cross the convention hall and take the stairs to the right. Then down the avenue leading to Medusa's Garden, which faces the docks. The *Tiger* will pick us up there in thirty minutes. Oh, and Nick said to call Brian 'cause he's switching from the *Tiger* to the *Amelia*."

"Good girl."

"What happened here, M?"

"Antipersonnel. Sonic. Hard to tell. Maybe both."

"Eek!" Sandy yelled, jumped to the other side of Meriel, and pointed to a body that stirred and crawled toward them. "What's wrong with him, M?"

Meriel kneeled. He was old with stringy white hair and hollow eyes. His fingers twitched as he reached out to her, and she stood and backed away.

Another man stumbled past as if blind, and Sandy shrieked as he brushed past her.

"Can we help them?" Sandy said.

"No. This is Rejuve poisoning. They're gone and not coming back."

Blaster fire met them near Medusa's, and they hurried inside to hide. When the clamor ebbed to sporadic fire, Meriel peered out the ragged door.

Bodies of civilians in street clothing littered the deck with a few black-suited Archers strewn between them.

"The fighting here is over," she said. *And the bad guys won.*

Marquees that usually announced ship, next stop, and departure time were blank.

And the *Tiger* was not there.

She let her breath out slow as the dock lighting flickered, and bucky-sheets rumbled and moaned.

"What's that, Merry?"

Meriel rubbed her hand along the bulkhead that tingled with vibration. *A vessel can only take so much.* "The station is dying." *It won't be long until we run out of air . . . if the hull remains intact. But help isn't here.*

A claxon blared, and she returned to the door. Across the dock, thirty corsairs marched toward a berth with a ship bristling with weapons.

That could be Khanag's ship!

The corsairs formed ranks and quick-marched down the docks, posting a sentry at each of the berths. Those not posted split into teams, switched on shoulder lights, and entered the stores heading for Meriel.

"We have to move again," she said.

A single guard in body armor stood at the airlock of the menacing ship with his helmet by his side. A plan took shape, and she crawled back.

"Want to play a game?"

Sandy nodded. "Can we get something to eat?"

"Later, hon. Wait here."

Meriel crept over to a dead corsair, put on his uniform and cap, and holstered his stunner. Searching the other bodies, she found the next-most important item for her disguise—a pair of wrist restraints with a torment chain.

"Hon, these are training cuffs," Meriel said as she clamped the cuffs around Sandy's wrists. "When I wink at you, act like you're in pain."

"Like how?"

"Kinda go weak and groan and squint and stuff. Like you do at home when you don't want to eat your vegetables."

Sandy frowned at her. "What are we going to do?"

"You're going to be my prisoner and we're getting on that ship."

"But it's full of bad guys."

Meriel smiled and shook her head. "Not enough."

In the black corsair uniform, Meriel crossed the dock, dragging Sandy by the torment chain.

The guard came to attention. "What's your business?"

"I'm bringing the prisoner to General Khanag," she said. "She's going to His Holiness. She's a real pain in the ass and the sooner I can offload her, the better."

"He undocked an hour ago.

Crap! "Your captain told me he's gonna escort the general out," she said and scanned the area.

He raised his forearm. "I didn't receive orders—"

Before he engaged his comm-link, she jabbed the wedge of her hand into his throat. He gasped and put his hands to his neck which gave her time to draw her stunner and shoot him in the face. As he fell to the deck, she took his arm.

"Help me, hon," Meriel said.

Sandy grabbed his other arm and helped her hide the man around the side of the airlock. "Can you teach me to do that?"

Am I stealing her innocence like Khanag stole mine? "Cookie's a better teacher. If you really want to learn."

Sandy pursed her lips.

"Sure, hon," Meriel said and hugged her. "Soon as we get home."

Meriel took the man's stunner and locked the hatch from the inside. Then they searched for any crew who might still be aboard and object to being hijacked.

The ship was all structure with few bulkheads and no creature comforts. Gangways and ladders led to platforms oriented in every direction. Handholds and gimballed jump chairs were located everywhere. *They must be zero-g most of the time.*

Each jump chair had a weapons rack and nutrition tubes on its side, primed for long jumps and extended battles.

Of the entire ship, only the bridge was enclosed with blast walls that might survive a hull breach and depressurization. Within it, they found two officers, who Meriel marched out onto the dock and stunned.

Returning to the bridge, she found the stations organized by function like the *Tiger*: The comm and maneuvering controls were familiar, but she did not recognize navigation. After strapping Sandy into the pilot's chair, she sat next to her in the command chair.

Once buckled in, head-up displays popped up at each console and a larger one in the middle of the bridge.

"That's new," Meriel said. "One common view."

Below the display and along both of her armrests, controls with unusual icons emerged. Not knowing which buttons might blow them up or alert the Archers, she left them alone.

One icon appeared familiar, and she tapped in the emergency number for Brian.

"Sorry we couldn't get to you, M. Where are you now?"

"A corsair ship. Can you tie Nick in?"

"I'm here, M," Nick said.

"Comm and propulsion look similar. Nav is Martian, as far as I can tell. And an entire section is unfamiliar." She raised the link and sent him a vid.

"Those are weapons. Ordnance," he said. "Damn. You're on a Razor-class warship. It's a big gun with a bigger engine."

"I don't know how to use it."

"Grant me remote access."

"How do I do that?" Meriel asked.

"Request automatic docking instructions through comm. I'll answer with a Trojan horse."

"The same virus they used to zombie the *Princess*?" she asked and sent the docking request.

"Similar. Here we are. Your official name is *Boomslang*."

"That's a killer snake," Sandy said.

"Well, that fits," Meriel added. "It's part of Khanag's fleet."

Sandy grinned at her. "I think we should change it to—"

"That's about all I can do for now," Nick said. "Give me a few minutes."

"What about Liz and—"

"They're here and we're busy. Now leave us alone."

She cut the connection and pouted without enough information to worry properly.

"Merry. What's Rejuve?"

"You concerned for the people we saw on Etna?"

The girl nodded. "How many more are there?"

"I don't know, hon."

"You said we can't help them. Why not?"

It was a child's guilt, the desire to save everyone, to never allow suffering. *God knows I've felt enough of it.*

"Rejuve is a drug that makes people live longer and still look young."

"Isn't that good?"

"For a while. But it steals from your DNA to feed your telomeres."

"Telo . . ."

"Did they teach you about chromosomes in school?

Sandy frowned. "No."

"That's OK. A few decades after starting on Rejuve, it poisons your system. It fries your organs, nervous system first."

"Shouldn't that be illegal?"

"It is. Everywhere but Etna."

Two lights beeped on her console, and she pressed the first button. Nick appeared in a holo, with Teddy behind him, and Meriel and Sandy both grinned and waved.

"It's good to see you, Meriel, Sandy," Teddy said.

"Thanks for being here for me," Meriel replied softly.

Teddy bit her lip. "We all missed . . . you."

"Clock's ticking, M," Nick said. "Your ship has a new ID, and you should have command control soon. You'll have Teddy's visualizations, but navigation will seem like a Nav-1 trainer. That's the closest I can get from here."

Meriel examined the instrumentation. *Six-axis control for translation and rotation as expected.*

"Traffic Control is focused on evacuation," Nick continued. "So, you'll need to pilot it manually until you jump."

"I haven't had to do that since my solo," she said. "Comm says this is a tug. Anyone who sees our silhouette will know better."

"Best I can do now. Molly says the *Tiger* is leaving. The *Amelia* and I will stay close until you're safely away from the station. And Jerri says to be alert for special navigation and maneuvering options."

"Like what?"

"Like better algorithms for classical mechanics and—"

Teddy interrupted. "Mine has better relativistic dynamics. The guy who integrates near-field Nakamura into nav will make a fortune."

"But the jump drives won't work without understanding Nakamura's gravity field equations," Nick said

"Nobody understands Nakamura."

"How can we jump if we don't grok the math?"

"Napoleon didn't need to understand Newton's calculus to bombard Vienna and—"

"Whoa guys, focus," Meriel said. "I don't see the weapons icons."

"Not yet," Nick said. "Let the translator work. The AI will figure it out, eventually."

"How long is 'eventually'?" Meriel said and swiped a screen over to Sandy. "Can you read the outbound commodities for me?"

"Right," the girl said.

Meriel scrolled to the next comm message. It was from the airlock where corsairs had gathered.

"Open the lock, sailor," an officer said. "You're under arrest."

"Fuel green," Sandy said. "Air and water, green. Batteries, yellow—"

"You're mistaken, sir," Meriel said. "I brought a prisoner on board to ferry to His Holiness."

"You're on the wrong ship. Let us board and we'll sort this out."

With fuel and air green, Meriel began the departure sequence, and the umbilicals detached.

"M, there's the whole undock checklist here," Sandy said.

"Later, hon," Meriel said and returned to comm. "I'm attempting to comply, sir. I'm in over my head here."

"Don't undock or we'll shoot you down."

"You can't do that, sir. The prisoner is aboard. His Eminence will be righteously pissed if you harm her." She panned the camera to wide-eyed Sandy who held the chains in front of her. "See? You know she's escaped. I'm only trying to return her to the Archtrope's custody and finish our mission."

The officer checked his link and shook his head. "Acknowledged, sailor. Just stop and open the airlock. We'll straighten this out."

The final docking clamp released, and her ship drifted free.

"Sorry, sir. I must have hit the wrong switch, I—" She switched off comm and turned to Sandy. "Cross your fingers, hon."

Etna Station—Outbound

Slowly, Meriel backed the vessel out with the translation joystick. The mass was not evenly distributed along the axis, so the ship wobbled. Six axes were too much for her to think about, so she brushed a few controls on the virtual console over to Sandy.

"Hon, you have attitude control now," Meriel said.

"You mean like angry or stubborn? How can I do that, Merry? The ship doesn't feel."

"Attitude is the orientation of our ship to the dock. Try to keep the red dots inside the circles. The trigger is the thrust."

"Like a gas jet?"

"Right."

"When you release the trigger, the RCS will neutralize the rotation.

"What's the 'RCS?'"

"Reaction Control System. Just keep the dot within the circles."

Continuing to back out, Meriel lost her vector. With the aft thrusters, Sandy overcompensated the yaw, and they banged into a docked ship.

"Sorry, M."

"It's fine, sprite." Another crunch vibrated through the hull, and an outside camera went dark.

"Oops." Sandy twisted her legs as if her body English might reorient the vessel.

Without traffic control, the Archers could not track her, but she could not track the trajectories of other vehicles either. Smaller vessels clanged against the hull, and tiny maintenance pods and personnel in jetpacks caromed off. Their ship's jump fans were stowed or would have sheared off.

The girl grinned. "Wow. A spaceship is easier to fly than I thought." A damaged scaffold banged on the hull and flung dock workers from it, and she cringed as it screeched against the hull.

"Oops," Sandy said. "Merry, I'm really hungry. Can we—"

"We're almost clear, hon. Just a few minutes."

Meriel busied herself rotating the ship and engaging the main engine to leave. The acceleration pulled her into her chair, and she relaxed for the first time in hours. "Lean back. We're in a hurry."

Sandy did not respond, and Meriel turned to her, but the girl was not there. Meriel jumped from her chair and ran through the gangways. *What if someone was still aboard?*

As she searched the communal head, a woman's voice called from behind her.

"Stop where you are! Hands up."

Slowly reaching for her stunner, Meriel tensed to spin.

"You don't want to do that."

Bong!

Meriel spun to a wobbly corsair holding her head and Sandy behind her with a fire extinguisher. With a kick, Meriel knocked the blaster from her hand, and the sailor ran into the airlock and slammed the door closed.

"No, wait!" Meriel shouted, but the woman hit the open button and the lock shot her into space like a cannon.

Sandy cocked her head and spoke with her mouth full. "That was stupid. She didn't check the warning lights," she said and took a bite from one of the tubes of food concentrates that filled her pockets.

"I guess she thought we were still docked," Meriel said as she stared at the food and licked her lips.

Sandy finished her tube and handed one to Meriel. "Merry, I think we should rename our ship."

Meriel hesitated. *How far is cannibalism from stripping people of their organs while they still live?*

The girl stopped chewing. "What's wrong?"

Too late. "Nothing, hon. Thanks," she said and took Sandy's hand. "So, what name do you like for the ship?"

"Pandora."

Meriel bit her lip. "Who released evil into the world," she said, and Sandy nodded.

How many innocents died because of this ship? But I'm the one who brought all the chaos to Etna in search of her. Will I cause even more suffering with a warship?

Back in the bridge, they strapped themselves in their chairs, and Meriel increased the acceleration. "Relax, it'll be awhile."

Sandy took a bite of food and pulled up the undock checklist again. "M, it says here that the undock maneuvering can be set to autopilot."

"Sure. Got another food pack?"

"Here," Sandy said and threw Meriel a tube, but it fell short.

"We're at one-point-five g, hon."

Sandy tried harder but missed again, fighting to hold her arm up until Meriel took the tube.

With the food in one hand, Meriel cycled through the views to a panorama near the station, hoping to spot pursuers. Rather than the familiar wash of stars, the bridge turned black.

Sandy gasped and gripped the armrest. She had not seen the Etna solar system on the inbound, and growing up on Haven, she had never viewed the heavens devoid of stars. She reached for Meriel's hand.

"Yeah, it does that."

In the blackness, only Etna Station's shrinking image was visible, as their last handhold to safety disappeared behind them. Meriel changed the view to forward, which was absent any light at all, and used nav to add the major constellations and waypoints.

Next to her, Sandy absorbed everything, having the time of her life, but Meriel's tension returned.

"Nick, where are you?"

"Where to, captain?" he said over the comm.

"I'm not a captain. I'm a thief."

"Then where to, thief?"

"Nick, has everyone reported in? Are they ok?"

"Cookie and Socket are outbound on the *Tiger*, a little banged up. Liz and John are with them, but I don't have detailed status."

Meriel closed her eyes and placed her hand where the cross once hung.

"M, you all right?"

"We're fine. A few bruises." She turned to Sandy. "Tell him what you saw."

"You tell him."

"Tell me what, M?" Nick said.

"They're not just smuggling organs, Nick. They—"

"Of course they are. Penny's dossier on the—"

"No, Nick. They're taking organs from living people, maybe using captives."

"Right. Conflict organs from—"

"No, Nick. *Here*. Here on *Etna*. This isn't some forgotten mining colony everyone knows is a shithole. Everyone thinks they're safe here on a station. And the Archers are running it."

Nick paused. "You saw this?"

"Yes. A warehouse full. And I'll bet there're more. We thought Etna was one stop on the way to the bottom. Maybe this *is* the bottom."

"Damn. We have to tell Brian and the Troopers what's going on."

"It's worse. The Archers have access to the secure DNA databases. The Archtrope can find the tissue types of powerful people and their families and then supply them with replacement organs. One of the ... Archers told me they have a mushroom or a virus to damage any organ they want. That means they can create the demand. There should still be evidence if Brian can get a team into Archer territory."

"I'll let him know. Say, Teddy's found us a safe place to meet up. We're on the way there."

A pock-marked rock appeared on Meriel's display with the callout *A-NEM-S443*.

"But I don't know how to jump this bird," she said.

"Neither do I yet, but you shouldn't anyway. The Etna system is too dirty, and you'll only have two-sigma safety."

"I'm not doing that, ever."

She programmed the coordinates into Nav, and a holo filled the bridge with a globe of the Etna solar system. At the edge of the globe, was a flag with their destination, and on the periphery, arrows blinked with annotations for the nearest stars and distances. At the center, a flag appeared with a call out *Boomslang*.

"It's local," she said.

"An hour away at 2g. But you won't be able to see it until you're on top of it. Liz says to call it NEM-Sx. We'll meet you there."

"Corsairs could be right behind me, Nick. I might have to take an odd route to lose them."

"Just be there, M."

But Meriel had a mission. "I need to dock with the *Tiger* first, Nick."

"Why?"

"Liz will know why. Did you tell them the corsair captain from the *Tiger* attack is Khanag's son?"

"Not yet, we've—"

"Then match the DNA profiles within the dossier."

"Why?"

"You won't believe me unless you find out for yourself."

"Try me."

"The corsair captain's DNA is a match to the Tsogets."

"What does that—"

"And forward my texts to Elizabeth. Privately."

"No need, M. I'll patch her in live."

"Private. Just do it."

```
Liz, I need your help to get Khanag
off our backs. He was here. I saw him
debark from the docks. Check the vids
and DNA profiles in the dossier. I
plan a flyby to drop off Sandy and
then confront him. I need your help
with this. M

No way, no how. Liz

I'm not asking for permission. I'm
asking for help. We can end this if I
talk to him. M

NO

Help me. Khanag's son is . . .
```

Elizabeth's voice cut through the comm. "M, I won't help you do—"

"Liz, the corsair captain is Khanag's son. And his DNA matches the Tsogets—"

"This is crazy. Don't—" Elizabeth said, but her voice disappeared into a buzz of static.

Meriel toggled virtual comm buttons without reconnecting. "Liz?"

"Was that Elizabeth?" Sandy asked.

"Yes, hon."

"What's crazy?"

"Nothing," Meriel said but caught the girl's frown.

Sandy turned away, but her expression changed from suspicion to worry.

Meriel drummed her fingers on the armrest. "So, what happened to my sister?"

As with a Nav-1 trainer, Meriel zoomed the logistics display with her fingers. A tiny ring marked Etna Station next to her ship at the center of the globe. One by one, more ships blinked in a halo around the station as their positions resolved. She waved a finger, and the trajectories showed them en route to the major gravity anomalies for jump.

Three vessels broke the pattern, heading for NEM-Sx with two blue icons and a single green. Meriel touched the blue icons and callouts identified them as an ambulance and a garbage scow.

"I think that's the *Amelia* and *Tiger*."

Above the weapons panel and to the right, a holo of a translucent blue hand appeared, and the console spoke.

```
"Confirm target acquisition."
```

"Negative!" Meriel said. "Not targets."

"Who's the third?" Sandy asked.

Meriel touched the icon and a blank ID popped up: a ship invisible except for the ionization trail of a high-g burn. And its course would intercept her friends.

"What's that?" Sandy said.

"Dunno."

Meriel tapped on the icon and a vector arrow for trajectory and acceleration: three-g's.

```
"Friendly. Count one."
```

"'Friendly.' Is that Papa?"

"I think it means friendly to this ship, not to us." *And they'll kill us if they can.* "Nick, Liz. A ship is heading for you," she said over comm, but received only static.

Curious about its purpose, Meriel put her hand inside the blue-glove holo. The annotations changed, and as she moved her hand back, the holo zoomed out to expose an array of green dots approaching from the edge.

```
"Friendlies. Count fourteen. Rela-
tive plus one-g. Intercept in six
minutes."
```

"Intercept. That means they'll catch up," Sandy said.

"Right. We're not fast enough. Get ready for acceleration, hon. Take a breath and let it out slow."

At 2.5-g, they sank deeper into their jump chairs, and the green dots at the edge of the globe stopped getting closer.

"Agh," Sandy groaned as her weight doubled and pressed on her chest. "How long . . . are we going to . . . do this?"

"Not long." *I hope.* "Keep your arms in."

```
"Friendlies on approach, our vector.
Relative plus one-g. Will intercept
in . . . five point eight minutes."
```

"Can we go faster, Merry L?"

Adults could survive five-g without acceleration drugs, but Sandy could not take that.

"Let's see if they know this trick."

Meriel dialed up the acceleration another g and compensated with negative g from the artificial gravity like a grav sled. The display showed them pulling away, but only for a moment.

```
"Friendlies on approach, our vector.
Relative plus one-g. Will intercept
in . . . five point five minutes."
```

"It's not working," Sandy said.

"They're soldiers. They can always pull more g's than we can. If we stay on this course, I'll lead them right to the *Amelia*." *And I still can't figure out how to shoot back.*

She struggled with the commands and instructions, some of which referred to Archer terminology she did not understand.

Frustrated, she waved her hands. "Tactical?"

The display sliced in two like a half-orange with diameter lines every thirty degrees. Her ship was at the center and the approaching ships on the peel.

"Defensive?"

The display filled with lines in different colors, some facing the approaching corsairs, others leading away.

"What do the lines mean, Merry?"

Meriel shook her head. "They might be ship headings or escape routes." *Or missile trajectories.* "Teddy should see this."

"Arm weapons?" Meriel guessed, but nothing changed. "Damn!" she said and hit the console.

Sandy waved. "M, the checklist says something here about an . . . in-dock interlock—"

Meriel's console flashed red. "Just a second, hon."

A red dot blinked within the spherical display near the center where their ship should be. The green dots disappeared, replaced by a foggy blur.

"What the hell? Where did they go?"

> "Critical warning. Bogie targeting ping. Weapons lock imminent. Range window fifteen seconds relative. Suggest jump or evasive. Recommend cloak."

"Cloak?" she mumbled. "How the hell do I do that? Cloak." she commanded, but nothing happened. The comm light blinked, and she tapped it.

"This is UNE Destroyer *Intrepid* hailing gunship," a man said. "Declare or be judged hostile."

Meriel's scopes lit up with the weapons lock, and she slammed the comm button. "Negative, negative, *Intrepid*. We're refugees from Etna and a humanitarian crisis. This ship is disguised."

"Identify yourself."

Meriel broadcast the bridge cameras, and Captain Stark appeared within a holo of the *Intrepid's* bridge.

"Ms. Hope?"

"Captain, Sir, I can explain—"

"Is that Miss Smith with you?"

Meriel nodded.

"Well, I'll be," Stark said with a smile, but quickly regained his dour expression. "Enterprise informed me you are under house arrest on the *Amelia*. That isn't the *Amelia*."

"So, you're a Trooper now?" She pushed buttons and icons on the head-up display, searching for defensive weapons, none of which worked.

The green dots reappeared on the tactical display, and a voice came from Stark's bridge. "Captain, a fleet is approaching. They're not broadcasting their IDs."

"Are they your allies?" Stark asked.

"No. They're Archer corsairs and aim to kill me, just like you do."

"I have no such intention."

"Maybe not you personally, but—"

"Come about, Ms. Hope. We can protect you and escort Miss Smith to her father."

"Which is where I'm headed."

Possibilities raced through Meriel's head. *Enemies ahead and behind. Which would win in a fight: a single destroyer or a fleet? How could I know?*

Then who is likely to kill us first?

"We're between them, closer to *Intrepid* than the Archers," she mumbled. *The Archers have no limits on their behavior, but Stark might . . . maybe. And his first concern was Sandy. Then can I use the Intrepid?*

She grinned and maneuvered the Boomslang to intersect *Intrepid*. "Coming about, Captain."

From behind Stark came a shout. "Disable that ship, Captain!"

"Excuse me for a moment," Stark said and turned as Ambassador Bakshi stormed onto *Intrepid's* bridge followed by a squad of USF uniforms, their hands on holsters. A UNE officer with a major's oak leaf surrounded them with an equal number of Marines but let Bakshi through.

"Disable it now!" Bakshi shouted.

"Like I said, Captain, not you personally," Meriel said as the Boomslang headed for *Intrepid* at full speed

"There's a child on board, Sir," Stark said. "And that ship can fight back."

"Arrest them, Captain!"

"They are approaching voluntarily, Ambassador, and I won't endanger you or this ship with a confrontation."

A warning sounded on the *Boomslang,*

```
Warning. Friendlies. Targeting
ping."
```

… and another on the Intrepid.

```
"Threat warning. Pinged by targeting
computer. Yellow alert. ESM scanning."
```

"General Quarters," Stark ordered. A claxon blared in the holo, and the destroyer's bridge glowed red behind the captain's image.

"Does ESM ID Ms. Hope's ship as hostile?"

"Negative, Sir."

"Identify the threat," Stark said as the USF and Marines stood toe to toe at the edge of the holo.

"Arrest them now," Bakshi said. "Or I will relieve you of command."

"Mr. Ambassador, we are preparing for battle, and your safety is my primary concern—"

"Fire on that ship," Bakshi shouted.

"Belay that order," Stark said. "Major Glinnik please escort our guest to my ready room."

When two Marines took Bakshi's arms, the ambassador nodded, and his USF escort drew weapons. The Marines engaged them hand to hand, and the buzz of stunners and the bang of a blaster echoed in both bridges.

On the *Boomslang*, Meriel and Sandy ducked as laser sights flashed from the chaos on the *Intrepid*'s bridge, though only the image reached them.

"Merry, do we have to stay here?" Sandy said.

"Nope."

As the marines subdued the USF, Meriel's console flashed again, and claxons sounded on the *Boomslang* and *Intrepid*.

```
"Warning. Weapons lock. Friendlies."

"Weapons lock. Fire control en-
gaged."
```

"Unidentified vessels," Stark said. "This is UNE Destroyer *Intrepid*. Stand down or expect a fight."

"Welcome *Intrepid*. This is Etna Security, Captain," said a voice over Stark's PA. "We are pursuing an escaped prisoner. Please withdraw in the spirit of cooperation."

"They're lying, Captain," Meriel said. "That's a corsair fleet, fourteen strong, and they're not your friends."

On Meriel's tactical display, the trajectories of both enemies converged on her position, but she would reach the *Intrepid* first.

"The UNE has jurisdiction here," Stark said as his image wavered. "Stand down."

"They're attempting to jam our EM, sir," came the voice from Stark's holo.

Meriel interrupted. "I think they're arranging an 'accident' for you, Captain."

"Hope's ship is not decelerating," Stark's comm said.

"Decelerate and prepare to be boarded, Ms. Hope," Stark said. "That's an order."

"Sorry, Captain. I'll take my chances on the run."

```
"Launch alarm. Impact fifteen seconds."
```

"Who's firing!" Meriel yelled and pounded her armrest.

"Targets, Sir?" the watch officer reported behind Stark.

"Anything that shoots at us," Stark commanded without emotion. "Ms. Hope, I'll be in touch. Out."

Laser pulses from the *Intrepid* shined past the Boomslang and shielded them from most of the corsairs' missiles. Her plan was working.

Almost there.

On the tactical display, the remaining missiles chased her as she raced toward the destroyer.

"How the f . . ." Meriel smashed her fist on the console again.

"M, the checklist here says there's an in-dock interlock that secures the weapons and jump drive," Sandy said and swiped the checklist back to Meriel.

"Where?"

"There on the last line. It's the padlock icon on your chair."

Meriel tapped the icon, and the weapons console came alive.

```
"Dock safety interlock disengaged.
Weapons, live."
```

But nothing happened.

"How in the hell am I supposed to figure this out in real time?" Meriel said and scowled at the screens. "Defensive." A list appeared, and she scanned it but recognized nothing.

She was out of time, and the Archer missiles sped closer.

"Automatic," she said.

Her weapons spun to face the incoming missiles, and the tactical display rotated with it. Her ship's defensive systems discharged starbursts to confuse infrared guidance and screamers and chaff for EM targeting that filled the display with a cloud of tiny objects.

"Offense, live," she said.

Almost, almost . . .

```
"Charging. Live in ten minutes."
```

"Minutes? For god's sake, this is a firefight!"

A loud bang interrupted. The ship lurched, and only the harness kept her in her seat. Interior structures broke free and slammed to the deck at 2.5-g's, with one piece hammering her shoulder.

The *Boomslang* passed the *Intrepid* in a blink and then jigged into the shadow of the destroyer. The larger warship shielded them like a bow shock as they sped away, its silhouette disappearing in the glow of exploding missiles.

Meriel let out her breath and leaned back in the chair.

"Who won, Merry L?" Sandy asked.

"I hope they both lost."

"Is this the plan?"

"Kinda," Meriel said and dialed down the g's.

"Are we safe now?"

Meriel glanced at the battery icon. "If we don't have more visitors for seven minutes," she said and changed course to intercept the *Tiger* and the *Amelia*. She smiled and pointed to the two blue objects on the display.

"That's Teddy and your dad, hon. It won't be long now." She tapped the comm. "Nick, do you read?"

"M don't come any closer. Khanag's locked mines on our—" Nick said, but the transmission returned to static.

On the tactical display, the third ship heading for NEM-Sx uncloaked and resolved into a green dot. With the blue-hand holo, Meriel zoomed into a warship almost as large as the *Intrepid*.

"Damn, give us a break," Meriel said.

```
"Critical warning, weapons locking.
Range window one thousand miles. Sug-
gest jump or evasive. Recommend
cloak."
```

"Tell me how, damn it!" she shouted and checked the charging timer: five minutes.

```
"Missile lock. Flagship. Friendly."
```

"Flagship? Whose flagship?" *Friendly . . . Oh crap!*

Her comm blinked.

"Announce, *Boomslang*," said an unfamiliar voice. "Your ID is corrupted. What's your mission?"

She zipped the front of her jumpsuit and pulled the cap over her brow. After Sandy returned the cuffs to her wrists, Meriel opened a comm channel.

"Prisoner delivery for His Eminence," she said.

"Show me."

She panned the bridge camera to show Sandy in restraints, and a holo of a ship's bridge appeared. Slapping a riding crop on his boots, General Khanag stepped into view, and Meriel shuddered.

The Black Swan

Meriel pushed back in her chair as if to escape. *It's too soon! Sandy's still with me.* The blood pounded in her ears and her eyes darted between the weapons icons, all of which were still charging and would be for another four minutes.

He's here to kill me. My friends are the bait to trap me, and I have no choice but to shoot. But I can't.

"Ah, Ms. Hope," Khanag said. "I counted on your resourcefulness. Who else is on board?"

"Only the two of us."

A red curtain of light scanned the bridge and continued into the rest of the ship.

"Destroy them and her friends, sir?" someone said behind him.

Khanag raised his hand. "Wait."

"Is that the guy?" Sandy whispered, and Meriel nodded. With eyes wide, she reached out to hold Meriel's hand and let the torment chains fall to the deck. "Was this the plan?"

"Not exactly. Not with you here." *I screwed up again and dove into a black hole. If I'd taken Stark's offer, we might've stayed alive, at least for a while longer.*

Another weapons alarm beeped, and the score of green dots returned to the tactical display. The lead vessel had the same call-out flag as the corsair who fired on the *Intrepid. Or were they only firing on me, and Intrepid was in the way?*

Comm interrupted with another fresh voice. "*Tai-Pan*, this is Admiral Goff of the Soldiers of Providence. You have detained our prisoner. Please release her."

"God, will this never end?" *Think, girl.* It would be impossible to escape them both without a fight. *Like a melee, take them out one at a time. Who will be within striking distance first?*

The display reported three minutes for her weapons to charge. *Damn. There must be a way to speed this up. Or slow them down. Stall?*

"This is General Khanag. Stand down."

"We have orders, General, and you have no authority here."

"Noted. But my fleet does, and they will arrive in moments. Stand down."

"My fleet will be in range in five minutes," Goff said. "You have until then."

While her enemies argued over who would kill her and Sandy first, she glared at her console: two more minutes to charge.

"God, this is an emergency!" Meriel said. "Charge faster. We're going into battle."

```
"Confirm. Battle Stations?"
```

"Yes!"

A claxon sounded throughout her ship.

```
"All hands. Battle Stations.
Weapons charging from main reactor."
```

The lights dimmed, and weapons consoles on the bridge stations came alive. The bank of lights on her command chair flashed, and her virtual glove now glowed red.

```
"Lasers charging. Missiles arming.
Guns live."
```

She slipped her hand into the red glove. A small hologram appeared with icons: missiles, EMP, laser cannons, railguns, and other weapons Meriel did not recognize. She switched them all live and held her finger over the launch button.

Only the rail gun icon turned from yellow to green and flashed a silhouette of a guided slug shooter. *One at a time, before the others are in range.*

She locked on *Tai-Pan*. "This'll have to do," she said and opened fire.

"She's fired, sir," the woman's voice said.

"Evasive," sounded from the *Tai-pan*. "Disarm the threat but keep them alive. And cut the comm," Khanag said and his holo flickered out.

Meriel leaned back. "Disarm me, how? I'm a thousand miles away."

Light beams lit up space outside her ship. "Oh, Crap!" *But lasers travel at light speed.*

"What, Merry?"

The *Tai-Pan's* lasers warped the *Boomslang's* frame and fused the railguns to the hull. Ceiling panels fell and sparks sprayed in every direction from frayed cables. The bridge filled with a fire suppression fog that sparkled like a nebula in the light of broken optical fibers.

A falling cable tray struck Meriel's ear and pinned Sandy to her seat. Immediately, Meriel shut off the engines to zero the acceleration and let the ship glide. After snapping out of her restraints, she reached for the girl, pushing away the weightless structures floating past. But Meriel found Sandy unconscious with a wound on her forehead.

"Sandy, honey," Meriel said. "Wake up. Please." From the first-aid pack on her suit, she took a plastapatch spray and covered the wound.

"Honey, can you hear me?" Meriel asked, but Sandy sat strapped into her chair, her arms floating free.

Meriel examined the girl's skin for bruises and her arms and chest for broken bones or swelling but found none. She bit her lip. *What about internal injuries that could kill her before I can help?*

She pressed Sandy's cheek to hers and closed her eyes. *She'll die here. Because of me.*

"Please, God. Help her. I'll never ask for anything again. But this one time, please."

Sandy did not wake, and Meriel held her tight.

Without her, nothing matters anymore. The muscles on Meriel's jaw tightened. *He killed them, my parents, my friends, and now her.* With a scowl, she gritted her teeth and reached for the targeting glove for whatever weapons she could use against him.

"Merry, why are you crying?"

Meriel gasped. "How do you feel, hon?"

"My head hurts," Sandy said. She put a finger to Meriel's ear and from it carried away a bead of blood. "You're hurt too." She shook her finger and the red drop floated free.

Meriel held up three fingers. "How many?"

"Ten," Sandy said and smiled at Meriel's frown. "Ten, if you include the ones you're hiding. Cut it out. I'm fine."

Meriel's blood wicked into her hair as she regained her chair and reengaged the main engines. The guided slugs from her railguns found the *Tai-Pan*, and a call-out appeared on the tactical display.

Moments later, a holo of Khanag reappeared on her bridge, his uniform torn at the shoulder. A yellow light flashed around him, and his bridge showed the same sparks and lights as in hers, and the comm chair was vacant.

"Well, did you get that out of your system?" Khanag said.

"We're not dead," she said, her eyes wide.

The translucent glove glowed red, and she slipped her hand into it again. Near it, the remaining icons switched from yellow to red.

A woman's voice spoke from Khanag's bridge. "Sir, her weapons are live and locked."

Khanag's voice was firm. "Wait."

Meriel stared at the launch button. *I'm fully armed now. And the man who killed my parents is in my gun sights.*

A vision came of her mother's death in the freezing cargo hold, and Meriel blinked to suppress the flashbacks.

God, not now! she thought and blinked rapidly.

His holo flickered again. "We could destroy each other, if you knew how to use the weapons you command."

Meriel's hands trembled as she recalled her years on meds when she had forgotten the people she loved most. *And it started with him.* Her finger neared the launch button. *If I kill him now, the orphans won't have to worry about him coming after them. But if I shoot, Sandy will die.*

His voice broke through her thoughts and dispelled the vision. "Do you still aim to destroy His Eminence?"

"Who says I want to destroy him? I just want you and him and all your goons to go back to your cesspools and leave us alone."

"Those who threaten you now aren't in my fleet and don't answer to me. But if you're interested, I can save the girl."

Meriel's heart jumped. "You once tried to kill her."

"I could save her now and deliver her safely to her father."

"How can I trust you?"

"Because we've never lied to each other," he said.

He was right . . . Wait. "You said I've never lied to you. Then you read the dossier?"

Khanag nodded. "It is . . . intriguing."

"And what is the price for her life?"

"Your promise to relent in your mission against the prophet."

Meriel furrowed her brow. "Why would you take my word when I want you dead?"

"I am grateful you have restored my son's honor. Your evidence proves he died by his own hand to avoid interrogation. His corsairs will honor his sacrifice."

Khanag leaned over, and the necklace with the silver elephant charm swung free, but the poppy charm was gone. He tapped Sandy's pendant where the cross hung, and she covered it with her hand.

She was about my age when he killed my parents. And she looks like me: dark hair and eyes.

"Is she a believer?" he said.

"Faith is stronger than belief."

"In what does she place her faith?"

He's going to kill us. "Her father. The goodness of people."

"And?"

Meriel closed her eyes and smiled gently. "Me."

Khanag nodded. "I withdraw my promise that you will watch her die."

Meriel flinched, recognizing his threat but not his mercy.

I might shoot, but he would annihilate us, along with the Tiger *and* Amelia. *I've trapped Liz and my friends in a killing field. Again.* She took her finger from the button and removed her hand from the red glove.

"The Archtrope murdered your parents, Timojen," she said softly. "Why do you still protect him?"

Khanag studied her in silence. "Do you promise to stop your campaign against His Eminence?"

"I agree, but only him. Not Biadez or Rhodes." She crossed her fingers.

He nodded. "I will extend the same promise to your friends if you swear to forging the Treaty of Haven and deny your allegations."

She shook her head. *All this time, that's what this was about.* "The treaty is in the public record now. I can't change that. And you already have my avatar to lie for you."

"If your allegations are factual, they must stand on additional evidence."

"If I disclaim the treaty, will you publish it?"

"I have my own uses."

"Why would you not just kill us after I've given you what you want?"

"I can kill you whenever I wish, Ms. Hope. But I told you, we've never lied to each other."

Our only defense against them, my only weapon to hurt them for my parent's murder, I will now give him in trade for my friends. And I will deliver the fate of Sandy and Haven into his hands.

"Merry L?" Sandy said.

Meriel pursed her lips. *He didn't promise not to kill me. Why would he not lie about that if he planned to kill us?*

"The fleet draws near, Ms. Hope," Khanag said.

She took Sandy's hand. "And you promise Sandy's safe delivery to her father?"

"Yes. By the safest means I know."

"Then yes, I will deny the treaty," Meriel said, "if you will leave them alone." She dictated a brief statement disclaiming the Treaty and her charges against the Archtrope.

A long silence followed before Khanag spoke. "I may have misjudged you, Ms. Hope."

The corsair fleet came in range and the commander interrupted. "This is Admiral Goff, General. Time's up. We're taking custody."

"We have everything we need from her," Khanag said. "Our mission is complete."

"Our orders are to detain her, Sir. Hope, come about and prepare to be boarded."

"No," Meriel said.

Khanag smiled. "That's a Razor, captain. You'll never take her alive."

"Alive was optional," Goff said. "All ships, fire at will."

The lights flickered red again on Meriel's bridge.

```
"Missile launch. Impact fifty-eight
seconds. Recommend cloak and evasive."
```

She banged on the chair. "Damn you! You still didn't tell me how!" Scrambling to realign her weapons to the Archers, the panel went dark, and the glove returned to an innocent blue.

```
"Weapons inactive."
```

She glared at Khanag. "You did this?"

"The *Boomslang* is part of *my* fleet, Ms. Hope, not Goff's. I can freeze your ship whenever I want."

"You bastard! You promised to keep her safe."

He could have killed us at any time. And chose now, after he got what he came for. She banged on the launch button over and over and pounded the panel.

Another squawk of alarms announced the *Tai-Pan's* missiles racing toward them. On the tactical display, missiles from both fleets converged on her ship, but none aimed at her friends. There were only seconds left.

"You met me here just for this?" she said.

His expression hardened. "As you said, I am the hand of death." He fired another flight of missiles and disappeared into hyperspace.

Meriel ignored the audacity of a two-sigma jump and squeezed Sandy's hand. "I'm sorry hon. I didn't mean this to happen."

"It's not your fault, Merry L," Sandy said as the missiles sped toward them.

"No, but I'm responsible." *She is going to die because of me. If I'd never met John, had never been to Haven to meet her, had never publicized that damn Treaty, she'd be alive tomorrow.*

An incoming message from Khanag blinked on her console, but at the same time, the weapons panel woke, and the blue glove glowed red again. Meriel jerked upright, and with a determined grin, slipped her hand into the glove. "We're not done yet."

She spun the turrets to target the missiles from the *Tai-Pan,* but before she could figure out which of her weapons would stop them, Khanag's missiles raced past her.

The briefest flashes marked their impact on Goff's missiles, but her display showed more Archer missiles cutting through the debris. And from Khanag's direction, the final flight of the *Tai-Pan's* missiles rushed toward her. She could not defend against both and made a calculation.

Khanag waited for Goff to fire first: he didn't want this outcome.

This was an armored warship, and she guessed it might survive everything but a direct hit. So, toward Khanag, she discharged defensive flares and EM screamers. But to Goff's missiles, she aimed her guns and opened fire.

The hull of the *Boomslang* vibrated with the hum of laser fire, and the lighting flickered as the ship rerouted the energy to the weapons. With missiles, she took out the next flight from the corsairs, but more followed. Groff's fleet was too large and too well armed.

After two minutes of continuous fire, the lasers overheated and shut down, and she was down to small-caliber slugs.

Now's the time to jump out of here, but I don't know how!

"Is this part of the plan, M?" Sandy said.

Meriel gritted her teeth as Goff's fleet approached unopposed. Without lasers or missiles to defend themselves, they would destroy her gunship and her friends.

Another missile raced past from the *Tai-Pan*. Meriel read the radiation spectra on the threat warning flag and her mouth fell open.

It was a nuke.

The damage radius appeared on the display and the *Boomslang* was within it. The ship banged and vibrated as radiation shielding slammed into place and lurched as it rotated to put the heaviest shields—the engines—toward the missile.

She grabbed for Sandy's hand and held her breath as the missile sped through the debris. Moments later, a bright flash overloaded her display, and they covered their eyes from the glare.

***

On the *Tiger,* the bridge crew sat glued to their displays as swarms of missiles headed for Meriel's ship, unable to contact her or the *Amelia*. At the comm console, Captain Vingel leaned over Socket's empty chair and tapped the comm-link. In the middle of the bridge, a holo of the infirmary appeared with Elizabeth and Cookie.

"Sergeant, are you seeing this?"

"Yes, sir," Cookie said.

"Assessment?"

Cookie frowned. "Fog of war, sir. Not enough tactical information."

"Can we EVA and defuse the mines, sergeant?"

"No, sir. Not with Khanag in signal range. And the Archer fleet is approaching."

On the display, missiles from both enemy fleets raced toward the *Boomslang*.

But Khanag's ID changed to white and blinked LKP: Last Known Position.

"Damn," Elizabeth said. "He jumped."

"Khanag's gone," Captain Vingel said. "He can't activate the mines. Buckle up and prepare to get underway."

"If Meriel knew what she was doing, I'd expect chaff and defensive flares about now," Cookie said and raised an eyebrow. "And there they are."

As they watched, Khanag's missiles flew past Meriel.

"He wasn't targeting her."

"I don't get it," Elizabeth said when the last missile from Khanag's LKP passed Meriel's ship.

Even at three thousand miles, their holograms sparkled with EM noise from the flare of the exploding missile. A white ball emerged on the display and encompassed the combatants. As the ball dissolved, the ship IDs reappeared. Khanag's was gone, and the corsair fleet's IDs blinked yellow with distress messages.

"No," John said and collapsed into a chair. "Sergeant, you know what that was?"

"Yes, John," Cookie said softly.

"M, Sandy, where are you?" Elizabeth said.

***

In the pitch-black of the *Boomslang's* bridge, Meriel caught the blink of a single icon reflected in Sandy's eye.

"Are you ok, hon?"

"Sure, Merry," Sandy said.

One after another, the systems refreshed, and the tactical display appeared with the ships, but no missiles, and no Khanag.

"Health status, *Boomslang*," Meriel said and the data for her and Sandy appeared above the tactical display, all nominal.

The comm panel blinked with Khanag's voice message, and she tapped it.

```
"I've never lied to you, Ms. Hope.
You are the means for Miss Smith's
safe return.
   "Tell them my son died with honor."
```

"What happened, M?" Sandy asked.

"Khanag never aimed for us and froze my weapons so I couldn't stop him. He judged me too squeamish."

And he's right. Untold thousands in Goff's fleet are dead or dying. I'm not meant for death on this scale, horror of this magnitude. But his people are. Those who executed the invasions of Haven and decades of organ smuggling aren't afraid of killing thousands of people, or a million . . . or a station.

"Health status, ships in range," she ordered, and callouts appeared above the markers for the *Tiger* and the *Amelia*, both showing doses no higher than a long jump. But the callouts for Goff's fleet were off-scale high.

Zooming the tactical display, Goff's vessels drifted within a nebula of ionized debris as if the life had been sucked from them.

"What did all that?" Sandy asked.

"An EMP," Meriel replied but left out the details.

Khanag had exploded a tactical nuke. In a vacuum, it could not deliver a concussive punch, only energy: EM to fry their electronics and gamma rays and ionizing neutrons to poison them and make the rest of their brief lives a living hell. The effects were so cruel the civilized worlds had banned them two centuries ago.

Of course Khanag had one. And he used it knowing her Razor was shielded.

EPod screamers from the blast zone echoed on the *Boomslang's* bridge, and Meriel toggled comm off to silence them. It was unlikely anyone would be alive by the time rescue came.

If Khanag was trying to scrub his trail, this would do it.

"And they'll all blame me."

Chapter 23
Asteroid NEM-Sx, Etna 320 System

The *Boomslang* hid behind the asteroid and waited to dock with the *Tiger*. All three ships remained dark, not wanting to leave a trail of EM traffic.

At the *Boomslang's* airlock, Meriel held Sandy's hand as their ship lurched and the *Tiger's* docking clamps whirred into place.

"I want to stay here with you," Sandy said, her face somber.

Meriel kneeled by her side. "Your papa needs you, hon."

"He can come with us."

The airlock door slid away and there stood John, leaning on a cane with a splint on his artificial leg.

"Sandy!" John called.

Sandy glanced back to Meriel and then ran to him. "Papa!"

"Permission to come aboard," Meriel said.

"Granted," came Molly's voice over the PA, and Meriel rushed to embraced them both.

"Khanag locked mines onto our ships and we couldn't—" John said.

Meriel pulled away. "They're not still—"

"No, Captain Vingel and Cookie are EVA defusing them." He closed his eyes. "I was afraid I'd . . ."

"Hush," Meriel said and pointed to his leg. "You hurt yourself, old man?"

He whacked the splint with the cane. "Cookie's field dressing. The *Amelia's* replicator is working on a patch." He touched her ear and Meriel winced. "We need to get something for that."

"How is everyone?"

"They're safe. Liz and Socket are wounded but stable."

Meriel kissed him and took off through the familiar passageways to the *Tiger's* infirmary. There she found her sister conscious with a wide smile and bandages on her shoulder. Next to her, Socket slept with her leg in the Med-Tech.

"Hi, M," Elizabeth said and accepted her hug. "We need to get Socket to LeHavre for surgery."

"How is she?"

"Stable. Cookie says she'll be good as new after we get her to a doc."

"And how about you?"

Elizabeth tipped her head to her bandaged shoulder. "Laser. Cauterized and all but hurts like hell."

Sandy entered with two cups of stir fry and John close behind. She kissed Socket in her sleep, handed one cup to Meriel, and then hugged Elizabeth. John sat next to her and fussed with a medicated bandage for Meriel's ear.

"How are you, kid?" Elizabeth asked.

"I'm fine," Sandy said and wedged herself between John and Meriel. Then she took Meriel's hand and turned her palm over to show the tattoo.

Elizabeth frowned. "They can remove that on Lander. Lord knows I've gotten rid of worse. You remember the one—"

"I'll keep it to remind me who and what we're fighting," Meriel said.

"So, what happened on Etna?" Elizabeth asked, and Meriel described her confrontations with Khanag.

"And you think Khanag is one of the Tsoget boys?"

"Yes. If Khanag's son is related to the Tsogets, so is Khanag."

"We can't prove that," John said as Sandy crawled into his lap.

Meriel nodded. "We can't, but *he* could. He could check his DNA with the Tsoget DNA sequence in Penny's dossier to confirm he was one of their sons."

"Wow. Then the Archtrope killed his parents, and maybe his brothers too, and has been lying to him for years. Khanag must be really pissed." She shook her head. "But I don't get it, M. He had your promises, and your false confession and didn't need you anymore. Why didn't he kill you?"

Meriel tapped her link to recall Khanag's last message before he jumped.

```
"Tell them my son died with honor."
```

"He wants me to tell his son's story."

"Khanag doesn't care about the people he killed or the hijackings?"

Meriel nodded. "He only cared about his son's honor."

Elizabeth frowned and shook her head. "He didn't need you to tell his story. The dossier had evidence of his son's suicide. His son died here on the *Tiger,* and he only needed to push a button to destroy it and kill us all. What stopped him?"

"He said he may have misjudged me."

"When?"

"Right after I completed my end of the bargain."

Elizabeth nodded. "You're famous now, and—"

"Notorious," Meriel said.

"Even better. People will hear you now. You're useful to him."

John raised his eyes from his link. "The news feeds have nothing about your denial of the Treaty of Haven. If he meant to discredit you, now's the time to release it."

Elizabeth nodded. "He can stick it to the Archtrope just by holding on to it."

John stood and picked up Sandy, who put her arm around his neck without waking. With his other hand, he reached out to Meriel. "I have a cabin, M. Come."

As Meriel stood, Molly's voice came over the PA. "The *Amelia* is docking port-side."

Meriel kissed John, Sandy, and Elizabeth and hurried to the airlock.

A minute later, Nick rolled up in a mess chair strapped to a dolly. "Say, look what Brian and I cooked up. It's even got maglocks."

Meriel kissed him on the cheek and squeezed his hands.

"So, I guess we're both convicted terrorists," he said.

"Yeah, don't forget escaped convicts."

She handed him the biotag Sandy had given her. "This is from . . . a captive they were processing. See if Brian can track whose it is and alert the Troopers."

Nick nodded.

Teddy entered the lock with a big smile and hugged Meriel. "Where's Eddie?"

Meriel handed her the EDy q-chip. "Sorry, he didn't make it."

The *Tiger's* security alert flashed the cabin lights and switched them to red.

"Not again."

Molly's voice came over the PA. "Hope, report to the bridge."

"Aye, ma'am," Meriel said and ran down the passageway. At the bulkhead door, she stopped and saluted. "Hope on deck, ma'am."

In front of them, Captain Stark appeared in a holo.

"Stand down, *Intrepid*," Molly said. "*Tiger's* weapons are stowed. So are *Amelia's*." She waved Meriel inside. "Join us, Chief Hope."

As Meriel walked to the center, she traded nods and smiles with Jerri.

"How did you find me?" Meriel said as she stepped into view of the camera.

"Your gunship left a wake of debris," Stark replied. "I see you have returned to house arrest."

"There may be survivors on . . ."

Stark shook his head. "No, ma'am. Is Miss Smith with you?"

Meriel bit her lip. "Yes, sir. With her father."

"I'm hoping to speak with you."

"What are you waiting for?" Ambassador Bakshi said from behind Stark. "They're helping a fugitive!"

"We have no warrants for any of them and no authority to detain them," Stark said.

"The Aldebaran Accord requires you to—"

"I received a dispatch from Enterprise that they rescinded invocation of the Accord. That ends UNE jurisdiction. It also means I no longer report to you, and this conversation is a courtesy."

"But I . . . she's sentenced to death!"

"Ms. Hope's sentence is pending an appeal to the UNE Supreme Court."

"Wait, Captain," Bakshi said. "There has been no appeal."

"I filed it," Stark replied.

"You don't have the authority! Destroy them, I said."

"No one uses my ship as a personal bludgeon, *sir*. Major Glinnik, please remove the Ambassador from my bridge. With all due decorum."

"You can't do this! I'll have your career—" Bakshi sputtered over his shoulder as Glinnik and a squad of Marines pushed the ambassador out and closed the bulkhead door.

Stark turned back to Meriel. "You're invited aboard for a chat, Ms. Hope."

"Thank you, Captain. Another time, perhaps."

"Then, if you would please accompany me."

"You told me I wasn't under arrest."

"As you said, there's a humanitarian crisis on Etna, and we request your help."

"The *Tiger* must decline, Captain," Molly said. "We have a mission home."

"The *Amelia* is too small," Meriel said

"You have another ship," Stark replied.

Meriel glanced at Molly. "Captain Stark, are we in immediate danger?"

"No ma'am."

"Then I'll get back to you, Captain. Out."

On the way back to the infirmary, Meriel met Cookie as he exited the airlock.

"There you are, kid," he said. "What took you so long?"

"I love you too," she said and hugged him.

Cookie turned to Captain Vingel as he entered. "Damn, Captain. We got a big new gun and couldn't use it."

Meriel saluted, but the captain opened his arms for a hug.

"You're not crew this tour. You're the mission," he said and tapped his collar pin. "We cleared the mines, XO, *Tiger* and *Amelia* both. Nav work us up a route to LeHavre."

"Aye sir," Jerri replied as Captain Vingel strode to the bridge.

Back in the infirmary, Meriel told the team her plans to help Stark on Etna.

"You're not going alone," Elizabeth said.

Teddy stood behind Elizabeth. "And you need a pilot who can jump your Razor."

"Who's gonna fly the *Amelia*?" Meriel asked.

Teddy held up the q-chip. "Eddie."

Nick wheeled up next to them. "And you'll need a tech to decode your systems."

Cookie stood with Elizabeth. "No one goes back to Etna without security. Right, dear?" he said, and Socket gave him a thumbs up from the MedTech.

Meriel smiled and faced Elizabeth. "Exec, how long to prep the *Boomslang* for departure?"

Elizabeth glanced at Teddy. "A few hours."

"Three max," Teddy said.

"Ping me when we're ready to get underway," Meriel said and left to join Sandy and John.

In the *Tiger's* largest stateroom, Meriel laid snacks next to the bed where John lay Sandy. After tucking her into the sleep net, he sat on the edge and fussed with the splint on his leg, while she told him of her plans.

"I want you home with us, M," John said. "We need you."

"I can do more on Etna."

"You've done enough."

"They need our help, John. The Chen's are still there, and we can't desert them.

John shook his head. "You haven't told me everything that happened."

"Maybe later, John," she said and unzipped his pant leg to expose the splint taped to his thigh. When she removed the pressure bindings on his thigh, the lower half of his artificial lower leg fell off and blood seeped from the crack in the cybernetic knee joint.

"That's gonna take more than a tune-up," he said.

Meriel made a quick stop at the replicator and returned with the patch. After welding the sections of his artificial leg together, she pushed him back on the bed and lay with Sandy between them.

"Sandy was very brave and went through a lot," Meriel said and brushed a lock of hair from the girl's forehead. "It may take awhile for it to sink in. She's gonna have to talk it out, and—"

Sandy yawned and hugged her father's arm. "When will we be home?"

"A little more than a day, sprite. But you'll be sleeping most of the time."

"He told me they'd get me a new eye," Sandy said.

"Who?" John asked.

"A guy in a dirty white coat."

Meriel flinched at the memory of the torturer twitching and dying at her feet.

"He said I'd be pretty and normal."

John hugged her. "You can't get prettier than you are."

"And who wants to be normal, anyway?" Meriel said. "You're exceptional like the rest of us."

Sandy beamed at her.

"People can be really mean when you don't give them what they want," Meriel said. "The people who love you don't care about your eye patch. Just like your hair color—not good or bad. Look." She opened the neck of her coveralls and traced the beginnings of the long scar etched into her body from the *Princess* attack.

Sandy frowned and nodded.

"This screwed up my friendships when I was your age . . . until your father. So, do you love me less because of this?"

"Don't be dumb," Sandy said, rolled over, and closed her eyes.

Meriel bit her lip and John took her hand. "We'll take care of her, M."

John followed Sandy to sleep, and Meriel rolled out of bed. Out of sight, she tapped the q-chip on the nightstand and cued the dossier with the evidence of organ smuggling. The first to pop up was the holovid of Marge Tsoget's graduation.

"Sorry to wake you, Marge," Meriel said. "Other people need to know about what happened to you. Then you can rest in peace."

A tap sent copies of the dossier to Frank Masure at Intergalactic Broadcasting and Uriah Limets at Interstellar News Service. Then she scheduled a delayed drop of the dossier to arrive at the other independent news wires two days later to give IGB and INS the scoop.

When done, Meriel lay down with Sandy tucked between her and John. But she could not shut out the scenes of the dead on Etna or Goff's fleet.

Sandy opened her eyes and smiled with half opened lids. "Are you going to rename our ship?"

Meriel nodded. "*Pandora*. For all the trouble we brought here."

Sandy shook her head. "That's not the reason."

"Then why?"

Sandy closed her eyes again and snuggled in. "Because hope was the last thing left inside."

***

Holding Sandy and Becky's hands in hers, Meriel walked through a field of wheat stretching to the horizon. John and Elizabeth were with her and the orphans from the *Princess*.

Somewhere brave people fought for their lives, but not here.

Somewhere good people spiraled down into the mining colonies, but not here.

And as the clouds drifted past, they spoke to her. "Captain."

Meriel opened her eyes.

"Captain, the *Boomslang's* ready."

"Be there presently."

She rose, and careful not to wake them, kissed John and Sandy and secured them in the sleep net.

When Meriel stepped through the bulkhead door, Elizabeth piped her aboard.

"Captain on the bridge," Elizabeth declared from the *Boomslang's* comm console.

"As you were," Meriel said. "Engineer."

Nick saluted. "Aye, ma'am."

"Begin official ship's name change to *Pandora*. Comm update."

"Comm-sync complete, ma'am," Elizabeth said.

> IGB News tonight, Enterprise courts have refused to confirm the conviction of Meriel Hope for the deadly terrorist attack. Citing conflicting evidence and mitigating circumstances, the Masters' Court will rule shortly . . .
>
> From her bedside, Jennifer Churchill, the lead defense counsel for Hope in the UNE terrorism trial, had this to say.

"Oh, thank God," Meriel said and put a hand on Cookie's shoulder.

The vid showed Jennifer sitting up in a hospital bed with cords and tubes snaking past the edge of the image to the curved plastaglass of a MedTech. At her side was Meriel's blood-stained book.

> "Ms. Hope was framed for the attack on the Enterprise. The perpetrators destroyed her ship and ruined her reputation. These ruthless murderers are part of the same group who tried to silence me when I presented exculpatory evidence to the Masters—"

In the vid, Jennifer winced, and another voice took over.

> "Jennifer, enough. No more questions, please."

Jeremy's face appeared in the view.

```
"I'm sorry, that's all for today.
Ms. Churchill is recovering from a
life-threatening wound. Please be pa-
tient while the Masters review the ev-
idence. This is their station, and
they have the greatest interest in
sifting through the truth and the
lies . . ."
```

Truth. Lies. Khanag said we've never lied to each other. Why did he believe me?

"Captain," Cookie said to Meriel, "We're light on crew. I took the liberty to draft a recruiting flyer."

```
Spacers wanted.
Hazardous duty, small wages, life-
threatening conditions, long months in
the black, and constant danger.
Honor and glory await if mission
successful. Combat experience strongly
desired.
Safe return doubtful.
```

"I like it," she said and turned to Teddy. "Pilot, plot a route to Etna."

"Aye, aye, Captain." Teddy saluted, leaned over to Nick, and pointed to an icon on her nav console. "Did you figure out what this means yet?"

Meriel patted the *Boomslang's* armrest. "Comm, contact the Chens."

"Yes, ma'am. But why?" Elizabeth asked.

Meriel smiled. "This is a gunship. We need to reload."

Chapter 24
Free Space

Tau Ceti System

Edward Seide studied his link as he paced the Archtrope's yacht and stepped through the Go display.

"Have a drink, Ed," the Archtrope said as he studied the stones. "You distract me."

Seide waved to a concubine who delivered a whiskey with a bowed head. But he did not raise his eyes from the link.

"Is there a problem with our upcoming tour to bless the holy sites?"

"The arrangements are complete, your eminence. We only await Admiral Goff's escort."

"So, who authorized Khanag's visit with Ms. Hope and made this trip inevitable?"

Ed ran a finger around his collar. "Uh, Admiral Goff. But he assured Ms. Hope's safety with amputation cuffs.

"Unwise still."

Seide's face lit up with a flash from his link and his jaw fell open. "Goff's not coming," he said and swiped the vid to the room's holo projector.

In the middle of the room appeared a split screen with a tactical display of Goff's fleet on one side, and Khanag's nuke eliminating them. At the end of the vid appeared a scene of two warm suits fighting outside an ePod. As the image zoomed in, one figure smashed a wrench on the visor of the other. The image swapped to the helmet cams and a closeup of Blanchette's feral scowl as she cracked Yutousov's visor.

The Archtrope's scowl matched Blanchette's. "We will need to begin our tour without the escort," he said and stared at the loop of Yutousov's dying spasms.

Sethemba Nebula

Meriel woke from jump in the command chair with the image of the dying Archer in the dirty lab coat reaching out for help with one hand and spitting up blood. She sat up and shook her head.

On the tactical display, the Ciberitus Sink had receded into the field of stars.

"Status," she said.

"All stations green, Captain," Elizabeth replied.

"And the fleet?"

"On our heels," Cookie said.

"Pilot, how long to jump?"

"An hour, ma'am," Teddy said.

The dream continued to rattle around in Meriel's head as she downed a juice pack. She did not regret his death, only her part in it. She had killed him to protect herself and others, but she had done it in an icy rage and left him to suffer his last moments alone.

"Proceed," she said and rose. "I'm going EVA."

At the airlock, she dressed in a hard-suit and clipped a tether to it. When she connected the helmet, the audio clicked on.

```
"And in News of the galaxy tonight,
former UNE President Allan Biadez has
announced his wife Ellen and children
will join him with the UNE fleet near
Alpha Centauri A. After his miraculous
recovery on Calliope, President Biadez
```

```
is negotiating a trade arrangement
with Alpha Station . . ."
```

When the air pressure equalized, Meriel switched off the news feed and jumped out of the airlock.

People find meaning in the drift of flower petals in a stream and clouds in the sky, and Meriel found them in the stars. Space was where she made sense of her life, where between absolute zero and a supernova, only one thing mattered: the heart.

She was alone but not lonely, adrift within the constellations: a star added here, another missing there, but still intimately familiar.

The Sethemba Nebula lay a light-year away: a spectacular display of hydrogen-alpha reds and oxygen III greens blazing through pillars of nebulosity. Seen from Earth, it was just one of the Milky Way's myriad dust clouds. But close-up, it was so vast, it brought the eyes up the same way as the vaulted ceilings of the ancient cathedrals once did to evoke the wonder of heaven.

She smiled as she had when she was nine years old.

"Mom brought me near here for my first EVA," Elizabeth said.

Meriel turned to her sister floating nearby in a hard-suit framed by the *Boomslang*.

"Me too."

The Razor-class gunship did not share the same sleek river-pebble shape of their *Princess,* instead gangly and foreign, dark with EM absorbing coatings even in the nebula's glow. It was a warship with huge jump-fans and massive power-to-mass ratio for high-g burns to avoid detection and capture: the perfect pirate ship.

"Well, you're not our *Princess,* but I suppose you're home."

"For now." Elizabeth put her helmet against Meriel's like their mother once did to communicate without the comm system. "You may have been right about Khanag."

"And wrong about everything else."

"I think I know why he let you go."

Meriel scowled. "To tell the galaxy his son died with honor."

"You hate him," Elizabeth said and blinked away a tear that couldn't fall in 0-g. "More than anyone or anything."

Meriel narrowed her eyes and nodded.

"And he hates you just as much. But he loved his son more, and he wants you to understand. You know what it feels like to lose the ones you love most in the world."

Elizabeth smiled gently. "You're both alive because you remembered what you love rather than what you hate."

Meriel took her sister's arm and together they gazed at the nebula. A ship winked-in nearby, and another, and another until a warship appeared that could destroy them all.

"Time to go." Meriel tapped her wrist to engage the ship's comm. "Cookie, Teddy, prepare to jump."

"Aye, Captain."

Chapter 25
Jira-1 System

Haven—Johnston Rift

Children played in the streets of the Johnston Rift refugee camp and interrupted Erik White's lecture. In a wide-brimmed hat and cargo shorts, he demonstrated how to use the mapping app to layout the trenches and pipes for drip irrigation. Lars and Yuri Yuan were in the audience with shovels in hand. Across the street, Marta and Julia manned the ration kit packout lines alongside Anita and the farm families.

Since Meriel's last visit, the camp had doubled in size. The leaders had formed a police force who patrolled during the day, while the Haven Marines patrolled at night. Any Archers they discovered were moved miles away to their own camp.

As Erik spoke, his audience's attention turned to the packout teams who deserted their stations and gathered to one side of the tent. His link buzzed with a call from Penny, and he waved for Anita's attention.

"Hey kid. Turn on the LeHavre government channel," Penny said.

Erick tapped his link and the demonstration program switched to a live-feed from LeHavre. To the right of the podium sat Masters Jerrett and Lukas and to the left, Admiral Morrell. The chyron at the bottom read:

```
Joint Emergency Session, LeHavre
Council of Masters and Assembly of
Citizens.
```

Behind the podium stood John, and at his side stood wide-eyed Sandy with an eye patch matching her navy-blue formal dress.

LeHavre Station—On Station

"Station Master Lightfeather on Enterprise has offered LeHavre a place in the Far Star Alliance," John said from Masters' Hall on LeHavre Station. "That agreement will initially join us with Lander, Wolf, and Dexter in a mutual defense and immigration pact. As a first step, they provided replicator code to build out Haven's food and mining industries to support our growing population. Also, refugee ships will not be refueled for the flight to Haven unless the passengers complete a month-long training program." John waved his hand to his right. "And Troopers under Admiral Morrell here will enforce that order. This—"

Applause drowned him out, and he waited for quiet before continuing.

"Thank you. But this is only the beginning of negotiations that aim to reduce the load on Haven's fragile ecosystem and secure a successful future. Thank you. Chairwoman Lukas will answer questions."

Lukas shook John's hand and put her other hand on his shoulder. After she replaced him at the podium, John took Sandy's hand and left the stage where Colonel Lee stood with Becky in tow. On seeing her father, she scrunched her face, broke Lee's grip, and ran to them.

"Did you miss me, Princess?" he asked when she jumped into his arms.

Becky nodded, and with her face nuzzled into his neck, turned to Sandy "Did you get a new biotag-thingy?"

Sandy nodded and took her hand. "And this one says we're sisters," she said, and Becky grinned.

Lee leaned over to John. "Two months won't be soon enough. We're getting a thousand refugees a week now."

"And Archers?"

"We're weeding them out. They have their own camp and we're watching them. Any word from Meriel?"

John frowned and shook his head.

The lights flashed red in the auditorium and a holo of near space appeared on stage. At the center, an icon denoted LeHavre in orbit near Haven. A planet's diameter away, a flag blinked.

The PA system blared.

```
"Station alert. Unregistered vessel
 ID inside security perimeter."
```

The flag blinked red with the details of a warship bristling with weapons that could turn LeHavre to dust. The audience gasped.

John ran back on stage. "Master Jerrett, that may be Meriel."

```
"Incoming comm request for Colonel
 Lee."
```

On the stage in the middle of the holo, Jerrett raised his hand. "Hail them, comm. Unknown ship, identify yourself."

A window opened in the holo to display the bridge of a gunship obscured by sparks and the fog of fire suppression. An image emerged of Meriel sitting in the captain's chair with Elizabeth, Teddy, Nick and Cookie at their consoles.

"LeHavre Station, this is Meriel Hope on the *Pandora*. Let me introduce you to the representative from the Etna Tech Masters."

The camera zoomed out to show Brian Chen and his mother.

"Who generously brought us sixty industrial aeroponics factories and replicators to produce more—"

An image of missile tubes and weapons replaced them and zoomed out to show a much larger warship, with the ID *Intrepid*.

"And the first ships in the Haven Navy."

Appendix:

Excerpts from Meditations: The Diary of Neuchar de Merlner, Europa, 2112

Neuchar de Merlner (ref. Galactipedia) taught philosophy at the University of Europa, Martinsburg, during the twenty-second century. His early treatises on epistemology and hermeneutics focused on observation and validation. Though well-regarded, his brethren considered him too grounded in science for their lofty speculations. De Merlner is much better known for his less rigorous works such as the aphorisms, some of which are published in his diary.

Only a few of de Merlner's writings escaped the UNE's "Uni-formation" Laws that standardized knowledge and opinion in Sol system. Those remnants were smuggled off-planet to the far stars before the UNE took control of Europa's communication grid.

Considered a post-modern ecstatic philosopher, de Merlner incorporated the Greek "anima" and the spiritual into his writings to comment upon the existential human experience. As such, he was deeply loved or hated depending upon the convictions of the reader.

Life as we know it
Verse 42: Nova Conta, Section 3–*Spiritus* (Spirit)
La Vie comme elle est (Life as we know it.)

Behind the murmurs of revolution and immigration, flickers appear of the first skirmishes of an existential battle between gods. Humans are the weapons with which this fight is waged, because these are not the ethereal gods of myth, but *our* gods.

It is the human experience to worship gods: gods of the sky, or the earth, or the microscope. They reflect our orientation to life: aggressive or fearful, loving or domineering, prescriptive or absent; but worship we do. They become our template with which to order a reality we *can* not, or *will* not, comprehend.

The gods we worship need not be defined within a religious tradition, but it matters not: we drape our belief systems over the same structures and react as if we lived in ancient Athens, Jerusalem, Medina, or Uppsala. And belief powers our passions.

We atheists say we worship no god, as if to burnish our ignorance, while draping our science and logic with the same cloak of myopia, groupthink, and illusion as the most fervent believers, and cowering in terror from anomalous data as if we were primitive shrews.

Like Descartes' God, many of us know She exists because there is an absent place in our psyche filled only by Her. And we fill that hole in various ways, by religion (God, Allah, Jupiter, Zeus, Odin . . .), selfish pleasure (Dionysus, Bacchus, Hedone), science (Thoth, Athena), or ourselves (Narcissus).

Within that structure of belief, there has always been a conflict between the gods within us. In ancient Rome it was Bacchus vs. Jupiter (pleasure vs. order), in 20th Century Europe it was Zarathustra vs. God (fact vs. faith), and now it is Gaia vs. Prometheus (safety vs. progress).

Gaia is the goddess of the Earth and stays there for she *is* there. Those who worship her orbit Earth and Earth society, needing nothing but a healthy Earth. And as they worship the Earth, they worship themselves. She looks inward to find beauty and security.

Prometheus brought humans fire and was eternally punished for it. Because with fire, man rose above the beasts and challenged the gods themselves. With fire, humans had power and progress and could forget the gods and imagine themselves with the same power. He looks outward toward opportunity.

The conflict now is between those who perceive Earth as the center of the universe and those who perceive a universe with no center at all, or rather a center that moves with the human heart. This idea turns its back on Earth and threatens it only because it does not care. Above all things, gods want devotion, and so this threat is existential.

Must those who choose the stars worship a god who does not care for them?

Must Prometheus bow to Gaia?

Why not leave Earth to Gaia, and the stars to us?

Because when our gods go to war, it is we mortals who suffer.

Grace
Verse 26: Nova Conta, Section 3 – *Spiritus* (Spirit)
La grâce (Grace)

God offers us all redemption without condition and the peace that comes from it. But we have no proof of this peace if it is offered only in heaven after we die. If we have no proof of an afterlife, then why bother with God?

We bother because the peace offered is the peace *during* our life, not peace in *heaven*. Redemption occurs here while you breathe, and forgiveness comes from God.

It is beyond mere mortals made of heart and flesh to forgive the callous murder of the innocent. And it is beyond us to forgive ourselves for those deepest of sins, those acts of knowing cruelty that warp the skeletons of our adulthood with guilt. But God can forgive and will if you ask. That is why it is called *God's* grace, and why it is a miracle.

And granted that miracle, we may live full lives again and benefit others, not to seek forgiveness, but because we've been blessed.

Tyranny
Verse 87: Nova Conta, Section 4 – *Rei Publicae* (Politics)
Tyrannie (Tyranny)

Can a people tranquilized by centuries of liberty and freedom, resist the cancer of tyranny in the guise of dictator or administrative state? Moreover, can a people, blessed by freedom and knowing no other, sense tyranny's iron grip before it closes?

The historian cannot answer, but we, the people, can: because it is in our bones to resist *the tyrant*.

We know in our hearts that Boudicca and Joan are not legends but history. That despite the faithless Caesars and faceless bureaucrats, resistance to tyranny is necessary even when we fail. For if we do not resist, what we lose is not some abstract concept like "freedom" which we value only when it is gone; we lose the living presence of love, as tyranny squeezes it from all we care about—our community, our family, and eventually ourselves.

We resist now before we have nothing left to fight for, to avoid the tragic choice between our lives and our souls.

As if by God's Hand
Verse 34: Nova Conta, Section 3 – *Spiritus* (Spirit)
Comme Si Dans les Mains de Dieu (As if by God's Hand)

Once in an age, the forces of darkness align to bend the arc of history.

And once in an age, the arc of history bends around the wheel of one committed person who, acting from his or her own virtuous interests, changes the course of humanity: the child who raises the flag above the barricades; the mother who thrusts the picture of her murdered child before the soulless eyes of the tyrant; the girl who refuses to deny her love for God even as her flesh burns at the stake—an individual who grips their shred of civilization with both hands and will not give it up.

Through the fidelity of that individual, the complex interrelationships constructed by the powerful to order society to their personal ideologies and selfish interests collapse under the weight of justice and moral right.

The light of their virtues burns throughout history, despite the fog of interpretation. When this light is observed, it needs no explanation. It is remembered though demagogues, and armies strive to erase it from our hearts. Volumes are written to describe these single acts of faithfulness, but words are never enough. It is proof humans are more than animals and God lives in each of us.

That person acts not from selfishness or the lust for fame but instead from love and commitment. "Hero" is a label bestowed by those of us who benefit from their virtues, not a crown they reach for. For that person, there is no other way. He or she can live no other life and be fully human.

As if by God's hand, through that individual the forces of darkness are dispelled, and humanity is saved from the abyss.

I assign to you the mission to be that person every day of your life in small ways with every breath you take, and someday you too may be the wheel around which history bends.

I assign this to you because civilization and freedom are not inevitable. Sometimes that person does not appear, and the forces of darkness consume everything, and civilization is lost for centuries.

Glossary for Earthers

The authors have done their best to use Earther vernacular in the event unredacted editions of this work will be smuggled past the UNE censors. However, some distinctions common to spacers may be unfamiliar and we thus offer this brief glossary.

Arcology

A densely populated structure or hyperstructure common on Earth and its moon. Popularized by twentieth-century Earth visionary Paolo Soleri, who coined the term.

AU

Astronomical Unit. One AU is the distance from the Earth to Sol, or about 149 million kilometers. The speed of light is about 0.3 million kilometers per second, so it takes an electromagnetic (EM) signal about eight minutes to travel one AU.

Bon Voyage System

Only bridge traffic control is allowed during dock and undock. To accommodate well-wishers, dock windows and some ship windows are equipped with message systems for a parallel means to send greetings.

Communications beacon

Physicists have not figured out how to send radio and other electromagnetic (EM) signals faster than the speed of light (FTL), so FTL ships consistently outrun their messages. Since information is often more valuable than mass, ships carry messages and news-storage systems that synchronize with beacons near stations. Ships resync on-board memory with

Cruiser

Mark IX Сила Грузчик, or Power Loader designed on a Russian colony near Bernard's Star. They are nicknamed "Cruisers" because to English speakers, the name sounds like "silly cruise-chick." Cargo handlers sometimes refer to themselves as Cruisers, but the term is considered an insult if used by anyone else, especially when referring to a woman.

EM

Electromagnetic waves, like radio, TV, light, infrared, ultraviolet, gamma, and X-rays, which travel at the speed of light.

EMP

Electromagnetic pulse. A strong EM wave that zaps all nearby electronics.

ESM

EM Support Measures. . Though technology has advanced significantly since the age of surface ships, the conceptual steps for warship defense: threat detection/¬identification, tracking, and engagement, have not changed. ESM is the technology behind that, providing threat solutions to the fire control computers.

ET

Earth Time. A useful baseline for coordination in time. Loosely based on Earth Standard Time and the convenient assumption there is one single time for everything in the universe. ET is useful in all astrophysical calculations and has nothing whatsoever to do with the timekeeping devices on each ship, station, or asteroid. An exact correlation is exceedingly difficult over light-years because everything of interest moves at fractions of the speed of light. Navigation computers only have a useful approximation.

Floor and deck

Floor typically refers to the horizontal platform under your feet on a colony, moon, or planet with a stable gravity. Deck refers to the similar structure of a vessel. However, stationers think of their stations as stable and permanent and use "floor." Spacers often use "deck" on a station, which identifies them to stationers.

Grange

Voluntary organization of Earth farmers first organized in the United States in the nineteenth century. Earth agriculture became socialized by 2040 under UN regulations, and land productivity has declined ever since.

Gravity well

A large mass that distorts space-time like a bowling ball on a trampoline.

Hydra

Global Communications Executive or GCE. Miltech R&D. When wars are lightning fast, communications are the deciding factor. A GCE can commandeer communications, blind an enemy, and control all their weapons systems. They are decisive in high-tech habitats like colonies or stations. Their major purpose is to cut off life support.

ISA

Interstellar Sports Association. Galaxy wide group of sports teams that adhere to the ISA's rules for acceptable pharmacological and biological enhancements to human performance to assure fair competition in sports.

JCS

Church of Jesus Christ Spaceman. Loosely parallels twentieth century Judeo-Christianity.

Jump

Hyperspace jump.

Laws of Navigation

In common language these can be stated as (1) all positions are relative (there are no fixed reference points, only conventions); (2) everything is moving all the time; and (3) you can only know for sure where things were, not where they are. (0) Law 0 was included later to keep the math honest. Law 0: the arrow of time is unidirectional.

Light curtain

Archaic technology from the early twenty-first century where an array of low-power lasers separated adjoining rooms with a translucent curtain of light. It replaced the modestly priced hanging beads found more commonly in environments with steady gravity. Light curtains were also less likely to become a safety hazard if gravity shifted or was lost.

Link / LINC

Logical INterfaCe. I/O device connecting humans to raw IT/compute resources, communications, and peripherals. They appear in the form of implants, jewelry, headgear, rings, and almost any portable device. Links steal whatever external devices they can access to respond to the user's requests. Often keyed to a biotag for ID tracking and security.

LSM
  Light Speed Merchant.

LSY
  Light Speed Yacht.

Mess hall or mess
  On ships, the dining area is called the mess, and the kitchen is called the galley.

Nambli-Khoza scale
  Ranks habitats by human livability based on a ratio of infrastructure needed to support life there. Earth is the baseline at 1.0. Haven is 0.6. Most colonies are no higher than 0.06, and stations average 0.13.

Nav-4
  Navigator, rating-4. This designation refers to the skill level of a navigator as assessed by an independent agency. For example, John's post is chief warrant officer of navigation. A nav-5 rating qualifies one for posting to pilot and senior navigator for a mid-size merchant ship like the *Tiger*. Post differs from rank, such as captain, commander, pilot, chief warrant officer, petty officer, or seaman. Rank and post are also different from skill level.

OOD
  Officer On Deck or Officer of the Deck. The OOD is the ship's officer in charge of the bridge during a shift and serves as the direct representative of the captain.

Sphere of uncertainty
  Sometimes just known as the 'sphere.' When you jump, there is uncertainty in time and space about where you will end up. This is because of your lack of certainty of the positions and masses of everything along your path. This uncertainty is shown by

drawing a sphere around a calculated destination. The second law of nav says, "Everything is moving all the time," so it is difficult to calculate precisely where you will end up, unless you know every mass and where it's all going. That's impossible to do without infinite compute resources. So there is always an uncertainty of where you'll end up, and that uncertainty can be shown as a sphere. It's actually more like a sphere with a hollow center because there is a vanishingly small chance you will hit what you aimed at. The sphere grows exponentially with distance, so shorter jumps have smaller spheres.

Ten stages of a spacers' party

(1) uncomfortably shy and distant; (2) polite or coy; (3) friendly and engaging conversation; (4) double entendre, puns, and sexual innuendo; (5) loud and bawdy; (6) out of control, partial undress, drinking with your worst enemy; (7) looking for trouble; (8) finding trouble, confrontation/altercation; for large parties, rioting; (9) nursing wounds; and (10) Soberal (TM), sleep, or rehab.

Tranq boost

Tranquilizers, called "tranq," are needed to overcome the long periods of disorientation during jumps. Tranq-boost is a stronger tranq that suppresses the imagination and memories, which can overwhelm some people during jumps.

UNE

United Nations of Earth. Intergovernmental organization of 804 nations, states, planets, colonies, and moons within the Sol star system dominated by planet Earth.

UNEN
UNE Navy.

Warm-suit
Emergency gear for an air leak. Warm-suits have a carbon mesh and an inflatable, clear hood to allow the wearer to survive in a vacuum for a few hours. A rebreather and temperature control are built in. It has no protection against hard radiation or weapons.

Wink-in
When an FTL object comes into your view, you have no sense of it before it physically arrives. That's because it is moving faster than the photons or EM radiation that would tell you it's coming. When the FTL object arrives, it appears followed by its EM and looks like a weak flash, or a wink.

XO
The executive officer, or first officer, who is next in command to the captain.

Zone, (e.g., White-Zone)
Sections of a space station are segregated by purpose: Blue for spaceship docks, Red for security, Green for industry and shady business, and White for government, finance, and wealthy residences. Some stations have other colors to warn non-residents of danger, like Etna's black-zone.

Haven's indigenous species
Culpa: Meat eater the size of a cat. Cannot digest human proteins. Primary prey are larger herbivores like Dumpy. Lifespan of 10 years.

Gorpa: A prolific squid-like bottom feeder of the inland seas of Haven. Lifespan of 2-8 years and mates bi-monthly.

Gril: Tiny herbivore the size of a termite. Communal in large colonies led by a group of queens. Collects water in underground hives. Lifespan of 3-5 years.

Hiranth: Meat eater the size of a small wolf. Cannot digest human proteins. Primary prey are culpas. Packs can take down a small orbanth. Lifespan 8-20 years.

Kintil: Herbivore about the size of a cicada. Dies every year. Lays eggs dormant during the droughts.

Lermel: Armored herbivore the size of a beaver. Lifespan is 18-20 years if it can escape the culpa. Becky's pet Dumpy is a lermel.

Orbanth: Armored herbivore the size of a buffalo. Has a crest that runs from nose to back of head for individual defense. Travels in herds and uses defensive circles of males to protect young and sick. Lifespan of 60 years.

Tark: Amphibian at the top of the food chain in Haven's inland seas. Main diet is Gorpa. Lives for 40 years.

Cast of Characters

Major Characters

Meriel Hope

    AKA M, Merry L. Chief Petty Officer Logistics on LSM *Tiger*. Exposed the Treaty of Haven and the Haven embargo that implicated BioLuna, Allan Biadez, and the Archtrope of Calliope in the illegal takeover of the Haven colony. Partner of John Smith.

Elizabeth Hope

    AKA Liz, Littlebit. Bridge officer, LSM William S. Thompson. Sister to Meriel, survivor of *Princess* massacre, and accomplice in exposing galaxy-wide corruption.

John Smith

    Farmer on Haven and partner of Meriel Hope. Pilot and Navigation officer, LSM *Tiger*. Sergeant in Haven Militia.

Alessandra Smith

    AKA Sandy. Twelve-year-old daughter of John Smith.

Rebecca Smith

    AKA Becky. Eleven-year-old daughter of John Smith.

Charles Cook

    AKA Cookie. Sergeant of Marines, UNE Marine Corps Expeditionary. Retired. Chief Petty Officer Security, LSM *Tiger*.

Jeremy Bell

    Lawyer. Now under retainer of Pacific League representing Meriel Hope and LSM *Tiger*.

Kim Mahn
Detective, Europa Police. Retired.

Suzanne Soquette
Chief Petty Officer Communications, LSM *Tiger*.

Warrin Lee
Ordained Minister. Colonel in the Haven Militia.

Benjamin Abrams
Captain in Haven Marines

Molly Vingel
Executive Officer, LSM *Tiger*

Richard Vingel
Captain of LSM *Tiger*

Jennifer Churchill
Lawyer and advocate. Associate Partner at Hansen and Brimmek

Theodora Duncan
AKA Teddy. Founder of Galactic Navigation. Influential inventor of the Nav-RR9x generation of navigation programs and the popular game "Where's Teddy." Captain LSY *Amelia*.

Archtrope of Calliope
Spiritual leader of the Archer Cult. Mastermind of a crime, drug, and organ laundering empire controlling a quarter of human space.

Subedei Khanag
General of the Draconian Shipping League, rebranded to Soldiers of Providence. Captain, *Tai-Pan*.

Ellen Biadez
> Wife of Allan C. Biadez. Heir to the Serrofa fortune, and Chair of the Serrofa Foundation.

Other Characters
Nurendra Khanag
> Captain in the Draconian League. Son of Subedei. Killed in the attempted hijacking of LSM *Tiger*.

Edward Seide
> Editor-in-Chief of the Galactic News Network and media syndicate

Allan C. Biadez
> Former President of the United Nations of Earth. Head of the Biadez Charitable Foundation.

Cecil Rhodes
> President and CEO of BioLuna Corporation, the largest supplier of medical equipment, biologics, and bioinformics corporation in the galaxy.

LeHavre Station
Herold Jerrett
> LeHavre Station Master

Svetla Lukas
> Chairwoman, LeHavre Council of Master

Sven Tervain
> Security Tech Master and assistant to Herold Jerrett

Enterprise Station
Kofi Sikibo
>Enterprise Station Master

Rivan Tellar
>Communications Tech Master and Assistant to Kofi Sikibo

Jergen Belson
>President of the Enterprise Assembly of Citizens

Hana Belson
>Wife to Jergen. Heir to Abramowitz estate

Nickolai Zanek
>Owner/Operator of Enterprise Cyber Security (ECS). Friend of Meriel Hope

Stenopolis
>AI assistant to Nickolai Zanek at Enterprise Cyber Security

Betty Oliver
>Security Master. Former Station Trooper Commando

Mrs. Stropchik
>Social Services clerk

Rosalita Gentri
>Patrol Officer, Enterprise Police

Bon-Hwa Gunderson
>Lieutenant, Enterprise Police

LSM Tiger Crew
Richard Vingel
>Captain

Molly Vingel
> Executive Officer

Jerri Vonnegut
> Pilot and Chief Navigator

John Smith
> Pilot and Navigator

Suzanne Soquette
> Chief Petty Officer Communications

Meriel Hope
> Chief Petty Officer Logistics

Benjamin Cook
> Chief Petty Officer Security

Etna

Julian Yutousov
> Dean/President of Genomic Research Center, Etna University

Miss Blanchette
> Administrator/Dean, Genomic Research Center, Etna University

Brian Chen
> IT Tech Master, Etna Station

UNE

Darius Stark
> Captain, UNEN *Intrepid*

Stephanie Bologova
> Executive Officer, UNEN *Intrepid*

Yegor Bakshi
Ambassador Extraordinaire

Beatrice Bakshi
Heir to Cupola estate and CEO of Cupola Foundation.

Nobuku Sobrietz
Judge, UNE High Court

Kamal Kostanza
UNE Prosecuting Investigator

Tai-Pan
Subedei Khanag
Captain

Isolde Vanor
Executive Officer. Mistress of Subedei Khanag.

Orphan Children from LSM Princess
Meriel and Elizabeth Hope
Penny Hubbard
Anita and Harry Fisher
Tommy and Sam Spurrell
Erik White

About the Author

Ray Strong is an award-winning author who lives in the San Francisco Bay Area with his wife and three kids. A geek by nature, Ray learned how to build spaceships in college and is saving up for a trip to outer space.

Ray's passion for sci-fi began the moment he picked up his first books by Andre Norton and Robert Heinlein. He bought back issues of Heavy Metal just for "Starstruck" and still hopes for the next episode in the Chanur saga.

Personal Note:

Thanks for reading my book. If you enjoyed it, please take a moment to write a review at your favorite retailer.

Friend me on Facebook at:
> https://www.facebook.com/ray.strong.399

Follow me on Twitter:
> http://twitter.com/RayStrong8

Subscribe to my blog:
> http://impulsefiction1.blogspot.com/

Ray Strong

Made in the USA
Middletown, DE
23 March 2023